Also by THOMAS TRUMP

Crime Fiction

I dedicate this book
to my beloved parents,
Olive May Trump and Thomas Trump

I also dedicate this book
to my wife SEVIL TRUMP,
the love of my life.

Not bad stories but
this book is riddled
with spelling and
grammatical errors.,
Such a shame.

Introduction

During the early 1900s, Detective Inspector Chris Hardie and his trusted Detective Sergeant George House of Winchester Criminal Investigation Department (CID), investigated the murders, which seem to have no motives or reasons. The cases were complicated, but after many twists and turns, they were able to solve the cases.

Winchester, Ancient Capital of England is a city and the county town of Hampshire, lies in the valley of the River Itchen, surrounded by magnificent green countryside.

The early 1900s, Winchester was a small compact city of about twenty thousand people, dominated by the Cathedral with many communal packed streets, all within easy reach of the main high street. The high street was long, and upwards, but most of the shops with their bow fronted windows or open fronted was situated at the bottom end, around the Guildhall,the street lights ran on gas and were lit by teams of lamplighters.Roads leading both ways from the high street, was also full of shops, pubs, barbers, rag and bone merchants, butchers and even a stable for horses all made up the bustle of the Winchester High Street.

It was a friendly town, in which most everybody knew each other. Murders and violent crimes were relatively rare, however murders, rapes, violent crimes occurred, most of the crimes were young lads scrumping apples, children on their way to school trying to pinch a sweet from the many sweet shops in the town, very few crimes were committed that warranted the birch, or imprisonment.

Detective Inspector Chris Hardie and Detective Sergeant George House, investigated the murders, investigations were not always straightforward, range from the very simple straightforward to the very complex and complicated, the detectives were taking a meticulous approach to gathering the information needed.

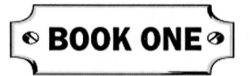

BOOK ONE

INSPECTOR
CHRIS HARDIE

THE POSTMAN
CALLED

Chapter One

Ohe winter night was cold and dark, the midnight hour had already passed. Two shadowy figures stood at the entrance of a short lane leading to a cottage.

"You keep watch, I shall not be long," one of the figures said to the other.

The one who had spoken, pulled the collar of his overcoat up, and adjusted his trilby before moving into the lane. The lane was uneven, with patches of grass and turf, and bare ground, the shadowy figure walked carefully, his feet performing as though he was marching the slow march, half inch below the rim of his trilby, his eyes stared straight ahead of him, never leaving the dimly flickering light of the cottage ahead of him he made his way up the stone path as he peered at the cottage.

He took his hands from his overcoat pockets, and stretched them forward, knowing that bearing his way to the short flagstone path leading to the front door of the cottage, it was a small wooden gate. Vaguely he saw the gate, but his eyes never strayed from looking straight ahead as his hands fumble along the top of the gate for the rope loop that kept the gate together with the gate post. He lifted the loop and stepped onto the flagstone path, he sighed, and only then did his eyes stray from the lighted window, as he turned and replaced the loop closing the gate.

A shadow light playing on the path from the window, enabled the figure to walk to the front door with more confidence, where he stopped a moment, and allowed himself to breath deeply. The low sound of the gramophone playing a record drifted to him, he smiled. He put his hand into his overcoat pocket, took a deep breath, then took hold of the brass knob of the front door with his free hand. The front door opened to the turn of the knob, the music became louder, as he slipped inside, and quietly closed the front door behind him.

The sound of a shot shattered the silence of the night, then vaporised into the same silence within a moment, and all was as silent as it was moments ago.

Chapter Two

Detective Inspector Chris Hardie, leaned back in his chair, staring at his hands that was resting in his lap twisting a pencil, he was deep in thought. He heard Detective Sergeant George House, so deep in thought, it took Chris several seconds to realise that he had been spoken to, he lifted his head as he threw the pencil on his desk, and with a slight grin on his face turned to George.

"Sorry George, deep in thought, what did you say?"

"Has a date been made for Mrs Paris case?" George asked

"I haven't heard anything yet," Chris replied. "We should know very soon."

"It will be another conviction for you," George said with a grin. "It will look good on your record."

"And your record George, we are a team, but my mind was on Christmas, only a couple weeks away."

"Is that a problem?" George asked.

"No, not really, I have to make my mind up who I shall have Christmas dinner with, that's all," Chris leaned forward twisting a pencil between his fingers. "At least Elizabeth is alright and she got over her flue."

Chris reached for the phone receiver as the phone rang.

"Oh Sergeant Williams," Chris spoke into the receiver. "Good news I hope?"

A couple moments later George watched Chris replace the receiver.

"Not good news," Chris said to George as he replaced the receiver. "A body has been found out at Littleton, the body of a man was found in a small cottage that laid back from the road, it seems that the postman found him."

"Motorbike?" George asked with a slight grin.

"Good job you have one," Chris replied. "Otherwise it would mean a lot of pedalling the heavy old bicycle."

"I'll be off and get it then," George said getting up and taking his overcoat. "One thing it's not raining, I should not be longer than ten minutes."

"I have to get more information from Sergeant Williams," Chris answered following George by taking his overcoat and trilby from the hat stand. "I'll see you outside the Police Station."

Chris was buttoning up his overcoat as he approached the sergeant's desk.

"What is the address of the cottage Sergeant?" Chris asked.

"Fir Cottage," the sergeant Williams answered.

"Any idea where that is Sergeant?" Chris asked.

"On your left as you go through the village," sergeant Williams replied. "Constable King will be waiting for you."

"Oh," Chris replied. "Don't recall the name, is he new?"

"Took over just as Inspector Noal left," the sergeant replied. "He is keeping the postman with him who found the body, and before you ask, I have informed Mr Bob Harvey the Police Surgeon, we uniforms are always on top of everything," he added with a smirk on his face.

"Good man," Chris replied with a smile being familiar with the attitude of sergeant Williams.

"Well here is my lift," he said hearing the spluttering of a motorbike outside. "You know where I am," he remarked about to leave the police station.

"Constable King thinks the man had been shot," sergeant Williams added.

"Thank you," Chris replied as he left the station and crossed the pavement to where George was waiting on his motorbike.

George entered the village of Littleton from the Stockbridge Road, Chris sitting behind George, had one hand around his waist and another holding on his trilby, he saw a policeman standing on the side of the road, George had also seen him and started to pull over stopping in front of him.

As soon as George stopped, Chris got off and shivered and pulled his overcoat closer around himself before speaking to the constable. "I am Detective Inspector Hardie, and this is Detective Sergeant House."

"Morning Sir" the constable replied respectfully, touching the brim of his helmet.

"You are new Constable?" Chris asked.

"Yes, took over a few months ago, the last constable was promoted and moved on."

Chris nodded his head. "Have you been inside the cottage Constable?" he asked.

"I have Sir," replied the constable taking out his black notebook, and thumbing throughout the pages.

"Put that away Constable," Chris said. "Use it in court when you have to, have you touched anything?" he asked in a serious manner.

"No Sir, just took a look at the body, scanned the room, then secured it," replied the constable, replacing his black notebook into his top tunic pocket.

"Good man," Chris praised him. "Now where is the postman who found the body?"

The constable cleared his throat. "Not knowing when you would arrive Sir, he asked if he could continue with his round, residences here do not like to be kept waiting, so I allowed him to carry on, with the understanding that he would return as soon as he had finished."

George who had parked his motorbike and began walking over to them, stood by Chris.

"Do you know this postman Constable?" Chris asked showing a little annoyance in his voice.

"Yes Sir, he has delivered my mail since I have been in the village," he answered.

"Do you know his name?" Chris asked.

"Peter Wright," the constable answered.

"You saw the body, do you know who the dead person is?" Chris asked.

The constable put his hand to his tunic pocket and felt his black notebook, then decided against taking it out. "His name is Mr Len Hogan, a freelance reporter, I have met him a few times in the White Horse pub along the road."

Chris looked at George, who had remained silence, then turned again to the constable.

"The police surgeon, a Mr Bob Harvey will be arriving, please wait here until he arrives, and bring him in," Chris said.

Followed by George, Chris made his way down the lane. "Constable King is as tall and thin as a lamp post," Chris remarked as he took care where to step. "I had to look up to him," he commented.

George grinned. "Can't have a constable looking down at his Inspector," he laughed loudly.

"He looked down on you as well," Chris replied with a grin. "This damn lane needs seeing to," he added as he almost twisted his ankle.

"Postmen don't usually go into the house, do they George?" Chris asked as he opened the front door of the cottage.

"I wouldn't think it's normal," George replied. "But then this is just a small village, who knows what the custom is here?"

Chris stopped in his tracks. "Careful George, it seems a milk bottle has been smashed here," Chris remarked, looking at the smashed bottle right in front of the front room door that was wide open.

Chris stepped over the broken glass, but was unable to clear the milk that spilt over the floor lino, Chris stopped, he saw the body of a man about five feet from of him, sitting on a sofa, as though he was looking at the gramophone a few feet in front of him.

"Anything wrong?" George asked Chris as he waited outside the door ready to enter.

"Just wondering George," Chris replied. "Was this bottle smashed after the body was found or before, because if it was before then footprints of milk would be seen going to the body, we know the constable saw the body and the postman."

"The postman might have seen the body but did not enter," George offered.

"How would he have known the man was dead then," Chris pondered. "Anyway the constable did, he said the man had been shot, you can't tell that from here," Chris argued.

George took a stride into the room, and stood by Chris looking at their feet, they were standing in a very thin layer of milk.

"Watch me as I go over," George said.

George walked normal to the sofa, then looked at the floor behind him, he saw his first two steps made an impression on the lino, but the third and forth had faded.

"We'll have to wait until we have questioned the postman and the constable again," Chris remarked going to the body.

Both Chris and George looked down on the body of a man, who was sitting up straight on the sofa, his dead eyes looking towards the gramophone. Chris looked at the gramophone, one had to wind it up to make the turntable turn, he crossed to it, and saw a record was still on the turntable, the needle arm resting on the centre display of the record. "The record played itself out," he remarked returning to where George was standing.

"He looks in his fifties," George remarked. "Shot at close range into the forehead."

George searched the immediate area for the gun but no sign of a gun.

"Better search his pockets George," Chris suggested. "I'll take a look around the house."

It was a two bedroom cottage, one large master room, and one small room, no larger than a broom cupboard. A bathroom and a outside toilet, a kitchen that furnished a sink, table, chairs and a dresser. The small bedroom was made into an office, it contained a desk, filing cabinet, it was untidy, newspapers everywhere, and partly written story scripts covered the desk.

Chris looked in the pockets of his clothes hanging in the wardrobe, he searched in each drawer, read a couple of the correspondence that he found in the drawers, then replaced them. He checked the bathroom, then the kitchen, he was satisfied. By the time he entered the front room, he found Bob Harvey, the Police Surgeon there.

"Hello Bob," he said as he entered. "A long way to come, sorry about that."

"Not your fault," Bob replied with a smile. "Anyway, it looks like straightforward killing, the shooter must have known the victim, he was shot with the gun almost touching the forehead, do you know his name?"

"Yes," replied Chris. "Seems he is a reporter, name of Len Hogan."

"According to what I found in his wallet, he is a freelance reporter, sends stories to three or four national newspapers," George butted in.

"Well I found his bank book, he was wealthy, he earned good money," Chris remarked. "Still the money won't do him any good now, he has a fine wardrobe of clothes, and he certainly liked his Scottish camp coffee, you can take the body Bob whenever."

"Wagon is on it's way I hope, I shall take him to the hospital to make an autopsy, what about relatives?" Bob asked.

"Not a clue at the moment," Chris replied. "Unless George found anything in his wallet."

"Not a thing," George replied. "At least not anything about relatives."

Chris shrugged his shoulders. "Could be a difficult one this," Chris said with a slight smile. "Still something may turn up, has that postman turned up?" he asked looking at George.

"Yes he is outside with the constable," George answered.

"Well let's see what he has to say, we'll talk to him in the kitchen George," Chris said.

As George left the room, Chris turned to Bob. "How you're getting back Bob?" he asked.

"I have my motorbike," Bob replied. "I've told your constable what to do when the wagon arrives, is that OK, only the wagon won't be able to get down the lane."

"Sure Bob," Chris agreed. "You'll be gone by the time I have finished with the postman, I'll look forward to your report, however any idea how long he's been dead?"

"I feel that this one is straightforward, he's been dead give or take an hour about twelve hours," Bob replied.

Chris took out his pocket watch. "Well it's almost twelve, midday now, that means he died around midnight last night," he said.

"Pretty much so," Bob agreed. "I'm not a detective, but navigating this pathway in the dark hours, I wouldn't bet on it being a stranger in the dark."

Chris smiled leaving the room. "Nor would I Bob," he agreed.

Chris entered the kitchen and found George and the postman already seated, Chris took a chair, sat opposite the postman.

The postman looked about thirty, he was clean shaven, passable in looks, with dark hair and average height. Chris introduced himself and George.

"Thank you for informing us when you found the body," Chris said.

The postman shrugged his shoulders, but did not speak.

"I have to ask you routine questions for the report, can you tell me your name and address please?" Chris asked noticing that George already had his notebook open.

"My name is Peter Wright, and I live at 19, Clifton Terrace, Winchester," he answered.

"Thank you Mr Wright, are you married?" Chris asked.

"No I'm single, I lived with my mother until she passed away," Peter replied.

"Sorry about that Sir," Chris remarked. "At least you do have a job, how long have you been a postman?"

"Just over a year, but this round about four months," Peter replied a nervous grin on his face.

"Oh, you don't keep one round all the time then?" George queried.

"No we change over every so often, it allows all the postmen to know each round, in case of an emergency I suppose," Peter replied.

Chris watched as George was writing his shorthand, then turned and looked straight at Peter's face.

"Take us through your finding of the body Sir," Chris spoke.

Peter shifted in his chair, then cleared his throat. "Hardly a day go by, when I don't have a letter for Len, I mean Mr Hogan. After a while he started to offer me a cup of tea, we became very friendly, so much so, that now when I have a letter I just walk in, the door is always open, I had a letter for him this morning, and as usual I opened the door and walked in, I saw him sitting on the sofa, but he did not answer my hello, so I went over to him and saw the hole in his forehead, I knew he had been shot, I then contacted the village constable," Peter explained in a serious voice.

"You had a letter to deliver for Mr Hogan this morning then?" Chris said.

Peter nodded and took a letter from his pocket which he handed over to Chris.

"Thank you," Chris said taking the letter. "This will be detained by us for a while."

Peter nodded his head again.

"When did you drop the milk bottle?" Chris asked not knowing whether or not it was him.

"Oh, yes," Peter sat up in his chair. "I had forgotten, when I deliver here the milk is not usually outside, Len takes it in, seeing the milk still on the door step without thinking I picked up the bottle and carried it inside. I dropped it on my way out of the room where Len was, my mind was in sort of a panic, it slipped from my hands without me realising it, I just ran from the house to the Littleton Police House."

The sound of footsteps and muttering outside the kitchen made them all look up.

"Don't worry, it's the body being collected," Chris said.

"The milk from the broken bottle, must have spilt on you?" George asked ignoring the interruption.

"It did," Peter answered. "But it was only after I had spoken to the constable, and cooled down, that I saw spots on my shoes and trousers, I wiped it off."

"Being single, what do you do with yourself a nights?" Chris asked with a slight grin on his face. "With the town full of soldiers."

Peter shook his head. "It don't worry me, I don't drink, even if I did I could not go out until the late hours, I have to be up very early in the morning around five thirty."

"As early as that?" George enquired.

"Well I have to cycle to the General Sorting Post Office, when I get my round, I have to cycle over here to Littleton to start my round, people here expect their mail at a regular time."

"So you must be use a bike riding from Winchester to here in the dark."

"It's not a problem to me," Peter replied with a grin.

"So last night you were at home and in bed around midnight?" Chris asked.

"Fast asleep as well," Peter replied shifting in his chair.

"I take it during the time you and Mr Hogan were having a cup of tea together you chatted about this and that, did Mr Hogan ever mention to you about any relatives he might have?" Chris asked.

Peter thought for a while. "He told me his wife divorced him several years ago, he said when he was a young reporter, group of reporters to stay up all night drinking and smoking, it seems that police stations and courts had special reporters room where they all gathered awaiting a result of some kind, anyway, his wife got fed up with it, and eventually left him, and ended up with a divorce, I don't think he had any children."

"Anyone else, a brother, sister, uncle or what have you?" Chris asked.

"Not that he talked about," Peter answered.

"I'm sorry we have to ask all these questions Mr Wright, it is routine," Chris assured him. "Will you call in the police station during the next few days, and sign a statement of what you have just told us?"

"I will," Peter nodded.

"Well if Sergeant House have no further questions, I think you can go, I'm sorry to have made you late," Chris looked at George who shook his head.

Chris held out his hand which Peter took. "Thank you Mr Wright for your cooperation."

"No problem," Peter replied with a smile.

"Mind that lane, I almost twisted my ankle coming down it," Chris remarked.

"Don't worry," Peter replied as he left. "I can do it in the dark."

Chris saw the postman out, then came back to rejoin George at the table.

15

"Well George, what do you think?" Chris asked.

George smiled. "I was thinking, solving this case can't be that easy."

Chris returned the smile. "I see what you mean, Bob said the murder took place around midnight last night, now if the murderer came from outside the area, it's as well to assume that he cycled, our postman is used to that, navigating that lane in the dark would be tricky, our postman has just told us he can do it in the dark, as far as I can see, there is only one thing missing."

"What's that," George asked.

"The motive," Chris answered. "What possible motive would a postman have for murdering one of his deliveries who he is friendly with?"

George shrugged. "At the moment I have no idea."

Chapter Three

"Call the constable King in, there is a phone in the room, I'm phoning the police station," Chris said to George leaving the room.

Chris entered the small office room and phoned the police station, Sergeant Williams answered.

"Inspector Hardie here Sergeant," Chris spoke onto the receiver.

"Nice to hear your voice Inspector," came the reply.

Chris smiled to himself. "I need a bit of help, would Sergeant Bloom be available?" Chris asked.

"Sergeant Bloom is on a walk around, spying on the Beat Bobbies," Sergeant Williams replied grinning to himself.

"Well I need him," Chris said. "I don't want you in trouble."

"We uniforms are trained to use our own initiative," sergeant Williams replied. "I'll see if I can contact him, you want him at Littleton I take it."

"Good man," Chris replied. "I would appreciate it sooner than later, everything quiet back there?"

"Of course," sergeant Williams replied. "Why would it not be?"

"Just asking Sergeant," Chris answered with a smile on his face as he replaced the receiver, he knew that sergeant Bloom would arrive very soon.

Chris returned to the kitchen, George and constable King was seated there talking.

"I have just phoned the police station," he spoke to both of them. "Sergeant Bloom is on his way, should be here within the hour.

"Now Constable," Chris said turning to him meaning to ask him something then for the moment changed his mind. "I know one can't join the force under five foot, ten inches, but I know of no limit after that, just how tall are you?"

"Six foot, six inches," replied the constable with a smile.

"How tall is your wife?" George asked.

"Five foot, one inch," replied the constable.

"She looks up at you then," George continued.

"That's how it should be," replied the constable feeling at ease. "All people should look up to the law," he smiled.

"Even Inspectors?" George muttered grinning.

"I heard that George," Chris replied with a smile. "Now let's get on, it's now coming to one o'clock," Chris said as he took out his pocket watch. "Do you have anything urgent to do, I mean like dinner time or appointments?" Chris asked the constable.

"My wife expects me when she sees me," constable King replied. "I have nothing on."

"Good man," Chris replied. "Is this your first murder case?"

"Yes it is," replied the constable.

"This is your area constable," Chris began. "You are responsible for the law in this area, and we like to work with the village constable, but this is your first murder, so please don't be offended with me bringing over another sergeant, Sergeant Bloom you'll find has a wealth of experience, when he comes, he will probably want you to accompany him knocking a few doors, the victim was shot about midnight last night, someone might have heard something, but be sure we will include you on our investigation when we are in your area."

"Thank you Sir," replied the constable. "I take no offence, it will be an experience for me."

"When you get that experience constable," Chris remarked. "You will never let a person out of your sight that found the body before that person has been questioned."

"I shall remember," constable King replied. "I had a feeling that you were not happy about it," constable King gave him an embarrassed smile.

"Where is your house constable?" Chris asked.

"Two minutes from here," came the reply.

We will be here for some time yet, why not pop home and tell your wife you might be late, she might be cooking your dinner," Chris offered.

"I'll do that Sir, would you like me to bring back a flask and sandwiches?" the constable asked getting up.

"No thank you constable, before this case is over, we will probably call in for a cuppa," Chris replied. "But when you get back, George and I will have to question the local landlord," Chris added.

"The White Horse," remarked the constable standing up and looking down at them. "Top of the hill, five minutes walk, landlord name is Jason Morrison, seems a decent person, well liked," the constable said as he ducked under the door to leave.

George smiled as he looked at Chris. "Liquid lunch?" he asked.

"Yes," Chris replied. "Would you sit indoors all night fully dressed, even with your shoes on?" Chris asked. "You see the victim had shirt, tie, pullover, jacket, trousers and shoes on, his slippers was beside the sofa, it seem to me that he had been out."

"I see what you mean," George replied. "While you were searching the house, I searched the room, apart from the sideboard, a couple of chairs and the sofa, the room was empty, what you might call a proper bachelor room. I did check the gramophone, wound right down it was, the two paraffin lamps were empty, and there was plenty of ashes in the hearth, I doubt if it was cold in here."

"Exactly," Chris replied. "It was not cold, so he must have been out."

"Do you think he was shot outside, then brought here?" George asked.

"Two things leads me against that happening," Chris answered. "First I wouldn't like to carry a body down that lane in the dark, secondly I don't think the murderer would put on a gramophone record. If he had been out, and I am sure he had, the local pub was perhaps the only place he could go, unless he went outside the village, the landlord will tell us."

"I took a walk around the cottage," George spoke. "There is a lean to at the back, with a bicycle in it, it had a paraffin lamp on the front, it was empty."

Half an hour later constable King entered the room ducking under the doorway.

"The wife said you are very welcome any time," he was standing and looking down on them.

"Give our thanks to your wife constable," Chris said standing up followed by George. "But now we are going to the pub, will you wait for Sergeant Bloom, wait in here, he will find you, tell him where we are."

Chris and George entered the public bar door, and felt the instant heat of the large open fire that was burning, two locals was sitting by it talking, they glanced as the visitors entered then carried on with their talking. The bar itself was quite large, and had a counter that stretched the entire length the whole room. The landlord was reading a newspaper, he looked up and smiled. He was a well built man with a handlebar moustache which he twisted it as he welcomed them. Chris instantly thought of Inspector Noal who had a similar moustache.

"Two pints of your best bitter landlord," Chris said with a smile. "And I wonder can we get a sandwich?"

The landlord smiled. "Beef, egg, sausages, bacon, cheese, with or with out tomato or ham?" he asked.

"Well that's a selection," Chris smiled. "What do you fancy George?"

"I'll have a bacon sandwich," George replied.

"And I'll have sausage sandwich," Chris said.

"I'll get your drinks first, then I'll bring the sandwiches," the landlord said taking a pint glasses, he turned away to the row of barrels on a stand behind him.

Slightly bending, he turned on the brass tap of one of the barrels, and waited until the glass was full before turning the tap off, after repeating the action, the landlord placed the two pints before them.

"With the sandwiches, that will be ten pence," the landlord smiled.

Chris put a shilling on the counter, the landlord pulled out a wooden drawer from under the counter, put the shilling in, and took out twopence change. "Thank you gentlemen," he said. "Now I'll see your sandwiches."

Chris and George chose a small table away from the fire, it was not long before the landlord came back with the sandwiches.

"Before you go landlord," Chris said as the landlord placed a plate in front of each of them. "I am Detective Inspector Hardie of Winchester CID, and my colleague is Detective Sergeant House, if after we have eaten our food, would you spare a moment I need to ask you a couple of questions?"

"Of course," replied the landlord, he looked around the bar. "I don't expect anyone else to come in, the time is approaching when I turn them out, give me a nod," he smiled as he departed.

"You know," remarked George. "This village is a quite lazy village, it's hard to realise that we are at war, and over in France men are dying and living in trenches."

Chris took a drink to wash down some food. "You had a rough time," Chris said as Inspector Noal flashing through his mind.

"It's a place I don't want to see again," George remarked chewing his food. "But I think constantly of the men especially my mates that I left behind."

"I expect you do," Chris remarked. "We British are lucky in a way, we are an island people, if it was not for the waters that surrounds us, the fighting could be on our soil."

"You're right there, the French and Belgium people suffer as well, their villages just like this one, destroyed let alone acres and acres of land and forest blown up." George took a drink. "Those waters are the value of several battalions to us."

Chris pushed away his plate, and took another drink. "Well that went down good," he said looking at George, who seemed a little depressed.

"George, you done your bit, you got wounded and could have lost your life, be proud," Chris tried to cheer him up.

"I guess you're right," George responded. "Can't help thinking about it though."

Chris caught the eye of the landlord, and lifted his empty glass, the landlord nodded.

With two fresh pints in front of them, Chris invited the landlord to stay. "Your wife makes a fine sandwich," Chris remarked.

The landlord smiled taking an empty chair. "She do, but I made them, my wife is shopping in Winchester anyway whatever it is, I'm not guilty," the landlord tried to joke.

"I'm sorry landlord, I believe you are Jason Morrison?" Chris asked.

"That's right Inspector, what is the problem?" the landlord asked.

"You know a Mr Len Hogan?" Chris asked.

The landlord smiled. "Old Len, of course I do, he comes in most nights."

"I'm afraid he has been found dead," Chris said taking a sip of his drink.

"Oh my God," the landlord said seriously. "Was it his heart?"

"Well," Chris replied. "In one way I suppose, but I'm afraid he was murdered."

"How, why, not in Littleton," the landlord said in a fluster. "He was in here last night."

"I'm afraid he was found dead in his cottage this morning," Chris informed him.

It was moments before the landlord spoke, his face serious.

"I wish you hadn't told me Inspector, that was a nasty shock," he said in a serious voice.

"Sometimes my job is nasty landlord," Chris remarked. "We are also affected by what we have to do, but it has to be done, now you saw Mr Hogan last night, how did he seem?"

The landlord seemed a little more relaxed, he rested his arms on the table. "I was a little busy last night, but when I spoke to him, he seemed alright, nothing out of the usual. Len is a reporter you know, and a story teller, he can keep you interested for some time telling the stories he had reported during his time, it was a closing time when he left with the others," the landlord looked towards the fire.

"Those two were with him," the landlord indicated with his head, the two men sitting by the fire.

"After they left, I cleaned the glasses and bar, and swept up, it must have been after ten then I turned off the paraffin lamps, I checked the door, and looking out, I saw Len still talking with a few people, after I turned the lights out, they must have moved on, I went upstairs."

"Thank you landlord," Chris said. "Did he ever talk to you about any relatives he might have?"

"If he did I must have forgotten," the landlord said after a moment thought.

"With his reporting he must have been away from the village a lot?" George asked.

The landlord smiled. "No, very little as a matter of fact, he did most of his stories from home."

"Really," Chris remarked.

"Yes," carried on the landlord. "What I can make of it, he did travel the country in his younger days, made a lot of contacts, he made contacts in hospitals, prisons, and police stations, factories, and what have you. When a story breaks in any of these places, his contact phones him with the details. Len being a freelance, sells the story to the paper who specialise in a particular kind of story, if the paper prints the story, then Len would get paid for it from the paper."

"Really," was all Chris could think of replying.

"It must pay well, he never seem short of a bob or two," concluded the landlord.

"Do you happen to know how long he has been in the village?" George asked.

"Well let's see," answered the landlord. "I have been here five years almost, he was here when I arrived, I may be wrong, but I am sure he told me he had moved in about a year before, of course at that time, he was younger and away from the village a lot, but I would say about six years."

"Anything else you can tell us about him?" Chris asked.

"We were friends, landlord and customer friendship if you get my meaning, but in a small village like this, everyone knows each other."

"Thank you landlord, you have been very helpful, I feel however I should speak to those two men by the fire," Chris said taking a drink.

"They won't mind," the landlord said getting up. "I fetch them over for you."

The two men it seemed were brothers, both retired, neither of them had married, and had worked a small holding all of their working life. The landlord introduced them as Bill and Tom Witcher. Chris introduced George and himself getting a surprise look from them both.

"I need to ask you both some questions concerning Mr Len Hogan, who I believe you both knew him, but first would you both have a drink with us?"

"We don't like to offend," Tom grinned. "We are drinking boilers."

Chris saw the landlord watching, and indicated with his hand for drinks for the brothers as the brother pulled up a chair each.

"I believe that you both were friends of Mr Hogan?" Chris asked.

"Yes," the brothers said together. "He's a laugh that one," Tom remarked.

"I'm afraid I have bad news for you," Chris said sombrely. "Your friend Mr Hogan was found dead this morning."

The brothers looked at each other, it was clear by their faces that the news had shocked them.

Bill gave a weak smile. "You got to be mistaken, he was alright last night, we were with him, having a laugh."

"I'm sorry," Chris replied. "There is no mistake, Mr Hogan was shot around midnight last night."

"There you are then," Bill smiled. "You must be mistaken, it must have been near midnight when we left him at the lane, it was pitch black, only those who knows the village would walk in safety down that path in the dark, we were talking outside until the landlord put out his lights, then we walked with Len to his place, ours is a bit farther on, shot you said, did you hear a shot Tom?" Bill asked his brother, who was shaking his head.

"Well it happened around midnight, perhaps you were out of earshot when it happened," George said, as the landlord brought the brothers their drinks. "Can you tell us what you were talking about?"

"Just the normal, stories of his reporting," replied Bill. "We had to laugh, he was telling us about a case he reported, then he accused himself of libel."

"Really," Chris said. "What was that about?"

The brothers looked at each other. "You tell Bill," Tom said to his brother. "You tell better than I."

"Well it seemed that this young lady, was suing a man who had promised to marry her, then with the date already set, he backed off, anyway, Len reported the case, and as he told us, dug up some dirt on the woman, she had been having other affairs, Len was telling us about this big court case."

"Did he mention any names?" Chris asked.

"No, Len would never gave names, he was always wary of doing so, I think it's wrong, a man asked a woman to marry him, she accepts, but along the way he finds out that they are not suited, when he breaks it off he is sued for money," Bill shook his head.

"It's protection for the woman, Breach of Promise to Marry," Chris answered. "Men will sometime propose to a woman, just to get her in bed, the old testament tells you that if you propose marriage to a woman and takes her virginity, then do not marry her, the man must pay the going rate for her virginity," Chris explained.

George looked at Chris with a little surprise, the brothers just stared at him. "I never heard or thought of it that way," Bill said looking at his brother. "I suppose it's only right," he said wondering what the going rate was of a virginity.

"How long have you lived in the village?" George asked.

"All our lives," replied Bill. "We been farmers, had a small holding all our lives, now we are having it easy, lay in bed until eight in the morning, don't we Tom?"

"We certainly do," Tom agreed.

"Do you know if Mr Hogan had any relatives?" Chris asked.

"He had a wife once," Bill said.

"Do you know if he had any enemies, I mean anyone you know who did not like him?" Chris asked.

"Not ones that we know," Tom answered.

"How do you mean?" Chris asked.

"Well, this case he told us about," Tom answered. "Len moved here to hide in a way, he felt someone was trying to get revenge on him for his reporting of the case, we told him he was dreaming, he was perfectly safe in Littleton."

"Did he listen to you?" George asked.

"I'm sure he did," Tom replied. "Although he was very careful when he left the village."

"Was this case he was on about local then?" George asked.

"I'm sure it must have been, but he never said," Tom answered.

Knowing that they would be getting no more information from the brothers, Chris and George finished their drinks, they thanked the brothers, and Chris went over to the bar and settled for the drinks with the landlord, they shook hands as Chris thanked him for his cooperation.

"Should you think of anything that might help us, please let constable King know, I also need to know anyone who might have a revolver in the village?" Chris requested.

"I will do my best Inspector, I am really shocked about old Len," the landlord promised.

"I should have paid Chris, you paid last time," George said as they made their way back to the cottage.

Chris gave a laugh. "It was a working lunch wasn't it, we were investigating the crime, it will go on expenses."

"There's Sergeant Bloom," George said as they came in sight of the lane.

Sergeant Bloom smiled as they approached.

"Glad to see you Sergeant," Chris said with a smile. "Have you met constable King?"

"I have, tall chap I must say," sergeant Bloom replied.

"I'm leaving things with you sergeant, we must get back to the police station, you know the drill, secure the place, tell constable King to keep an eye on it, and tell him to write out his report while it's still fresh in his mind, it's best for him to keep the key of the cottage," Chris remarked.

"What are you going to do now Sergeant?" George asked as he got his motorbike ready.

"Real old detective work," sergeant Bloom smiled. "Knock some doors."

"Good man," Chris praised. "By the way, if you are agree I am going to ask Chief Inspector Mullard if I can keep you for a week?"

"Great by me Sir," sergeant Bloom replied.

"Good man, then I'll see you back at the station," Chris said getting on the motorbike behind George.

Jason Morrison the landlord had watched the detectives as they left, he crossed the bar and bolted the door, there was still forty minutes before closing time. Back behind his bar, he drew up two boilers placing them on the counter.

"Have these on me," he said to the brothers who was again sitting beside the open fire. "I have to go upstairs to make a phone call."

The brothers got up going to the counter. "We don't want to offend the landlord do we Tom?" Bill said with a wink.

"No, it's a sin to offend," Tom replied as they took the drinks and returned to their table in front of the fire.

Chapter Four

*I*t was well after three in the afternoon, when Chris and George finely entered their office.

"I'll need your report George," Chris said as he followed George taking off his overcoat. "I will need to study it."

"I'll get straight on to it," George said with a smile. "Hope you can read my own shorthand writing."

Chris smiled to himself as he took off his trilby and hung it. "I'm popping up to talk to the Chief Inspector Mullard," said as he left the office.

It was passed four when he returned, he found George still typing his report.

"That man must be lonely," Chris said sitting behind his desk. "He wants to know the inside of a cat's behind, still," Chris continued as he opened a desk drawer and took out a new folder. "He did agree that Sergeant Bloom can work with us a week," Chris said writing the name Mr Len Hogan, Littleton on the folder cover.

The Police Surgeon Bob Harvey knocked the office door and entered.

"Hello Bob," Chris said looking at him. "Never expected to see you, come and have a seat," he offered.

"Had to pop in and pick something up," Bob replied as he took the interview chair. "How did you leave the Littleton case?" Bob asked.

Chris smiled. "It seems a strange case, I spoke to the landlord of the local pub, also I spoke to two brothers, who walked with him last night to the top of his lane, they said they left him about midnight, but heard no shot."

"You have to allow a little time either side of the time I thought it happened," Bob replied. "You can't judge the dead moment just looking at a body."

"I realise that Bob, the postman at the moment seems to be the main suspect, but I have a lot of checking to do, I could do without this one."

"Well," Bob said getting up. "I have things to do, I'll get in touch."

"Your autopsy report may give me a lead, once I have the bullet," Chris smiled.

"It's in his brain, I will have to dig it out, I shall be doing the autopsy in the morning," Bob said getting up from his chair.

As Bob left, Sergeant Bloom entered.

"Come and sit down Sergeant," Chris offered. "How did you get back?"

"I had my bike Sir," sergeant Bloom smiled as he took the interview chair.

"Coming back was a bit easier for me on the backside of a motorbike than going," Chris smiled. "All up hill going from here," Chris remarked.

"Anyway good news, you have permission to work with us during the next week," Chris told him. "From now on cut the Sir out, we are working as a team in the office, I'm Chris and that's George," Chris said indicating George with his head.

"How did you leave it over there?" Chris asked.

"I locked the cottage, and roped the gate, but it would be easy for anyone to get in, it's a secluded cottage, I told constable King to check it regularly, gave him the key, and told him he was responsible for it, regarding letting anyone without signing. No joy with the house knocking I'm afraid, they must sleep deeply out there, no one heard a sound," sergeant Bloom replied. "But the houses are well spread out."

"Mainly farm workers, or retired people, early to bed, early to rise," Chris replied.

Sergeant Bloom smiled.

"It will mean a lot of work for you," Chris commented.

"I'm ready Sir, sorry, Chris" sergeant Bloom replied with a slight blush on his face calling his superior officer by his Christian name.

"Get your notebook out then," Chris smiled. "Tomorrow I want you to get information as much as you can about a postman, a Mr Peter Wright, 19, Clifton Terrace in Winchester, and also find out as much as you can about the landlord of the White Horse in Littleton, his name Jason Morrison, use your authority if you have to, I'll back you, and use this phone here whenever you want," Chris continued as he tapped the office phone.

Sergeant Bloom smiled as he closed his notebook. "Got all that," he said. "I'll be on it at first light tomorrow morning," he said putting his notebook in his top tunic pocket.

"Good man," Chris replied. "Get along home to the little lady, tell her you will be very busy for the next week."

After Sergeant Bloom had left Chris rubbed his hands together to get his circulation moving. "He did well on our last case," he remarked.

"I agree," remarked George. "Pity we can't have him."

"We could as a matter of fact, but he's only two years away from retirement on a sergeant pension, if he came over to us, he would lose his rank, and start as a detective constable," Chris stated.

George nodded his head understandingly. "These are the contents of Mr Hogan's pocket," George said, emptying a bag on the desk. "A few notes, but mainly letters from sundry people."

Chris started moving items across his desk with a pencil. "Everyone seem to carry a penknife," Chris muttered moving one across his desk, together with a hanky, a couple of pencils, and some loose change.

"Not much there George," Chris remarked as he opened the wallet.

"What have we here," he murmured, the wallet was full of letters, a press card, and some money. "Two weeks wages of mine in here," he remarked counting the money.

He scanned through the letters, seemed to be from newspapers. "I'll have to study them later," Chris sighed, and collected the items, replacing them in the evidence bag.

Chris took from his pocket the letter the postman had given him, he looked at the envelope, which told him nothing, then decided he would deal with the lot later, he placed the bag in the drawer of his desk.

Chapter Five

Chris met Elizabeth as usual on her way home from work.

"Darling," she said reaching up and kissing him on the cheek. "When you were not in front of the bank, I thought you were not seeing me tonight."

"It could have been that way," Chris replied as they started to walk home.

Elizabeth grabbed his arm as usual snuggling up to him.

"I have another case this morning, been on it all day, however at the moment there is not a lot I can do, but you never know what's around the corner, so should you not see me any night, you will understand."

"Of course I will silly," Elizabeth replied. "Is it a serious case?"

"Suspicious, so yes it is," Chris answered.

"Oh dear darling," Elizabeth replied. "I never realised there were so many murders going on until I met you, it frightens me the way you talk."

"It's a part of life unfortunately," Chris replied. "If there were no murders I would be out of a job."

"Why," Elizabeth said. "There are always robberies, vandalism, that sort of things, I can't imagine society without a police force."

"I was speaking about the detective branch of the police force, the uniform branch deals with much of the petty crimes, however I don't think I would be happy wearing a uniform, and walking a beat," Chris remarked as they started to walk up Alresford Road.

Olive opened the front door with a smile, as Elizabeth followed by Chris.

"Just in time," she said. "The dinner is ready to serve, how are you Chris?" she smiled as Elizabeth and Chris were hanging their outdoor clothes.

"I am well thank you Olive," Chris replied. "It do not get much warmer."

"Both of you go into the dining room, it's warmer in there, your father never leaves his armchair."

"I heard that," Ron shouted as he smiled at Elizabeth and Chris entering. "I'm just having a break from all the chores my good wife gives me."

"I heard that as well," Olive replied from the kitchen. "What have you done all day, oh I am sorry, you washed and shaved, dressed and had breakfast and lunch, and oh yes, you cleaned your shoes."

"I need a break after all that," Ron smiled. "Anyway Chris how are you?"

The meal of pork chops with potatoes and vegetables filled Chris up, but he could not resist the apple pie and custard that followed.

Chris leaned back and put his hand over his stomach. "I am absolutely full Olive, couldn't get any more down, I really enjoyed the meal," he said as he pushed his dessert plate away. "Ron is very lucky to have such a cook," he flattered her.

Olive smiled. "At least you enjoy a good meal, meals don't just appear, takes a lot of preparation, a little appreciation now and again helps," she remarked looking at Ron.

"I always enjoy your cooking," Ron replied understanding that her remarks were thrown at him.

"I know that," Olive replied. "But you could say now and again how much you enjoyed them."

"But you know I do sweetie, otherwise I would not eat them, they say the proof is in the eating," Ron remarked with a smile.

Olive looked at her husband, and shook her head. "Come along Elizabeth let's clear this table, allow Chris to sit back and have a pipe who have worked hard all day," she emphasised looking at Ron.

Elizabeth looked at Chris as she got up to help her mother, they smiled at each other knowing that the banter between Olive and Ron was good nature.

For Chris the evening passed in a relaxing atmosphere, in which he sat on the sofa with Elizabeth close to his side, with the radio playing dance tunes, Elizabeth had fallen asleep at times, and Chris himself had felt very sleepy. It was gone ten when Chris kissed Elizabeth goodnight at the front door before making his way to his lodgings.

Chris hurried with his morning chores, he shaved, dressed and ate the breakfast that his landlady Mrs Dobson had prepared for him, he was hoping to see Elizabeth. He was in good time as he strolled down the high street. He looked at the bank as he passed, and wondered if he was too early. Chris caught sight of Elizabeth approaching as he reached Dolcis the shoe shop, he quickly stepped into the entrance and waited for Elizabeth to pass.

"Good morning Elizabeth," Chris said causing her to sidestep with alarm.

"Oh Chris, you fool, you gave me a heart attack, I was in deep thought," Elizabeth said reaching up and kissing his cheek.

"What about?" Chris asked leaving the shop entrance and making his way to the kerb, so that he could walk with Elizabeth to work, while protecting her on the inside.

"I don't know about you, it was a lovely lazy night last night, I just miss you when you are not around, I was so sorry you had to leave me last night," Elizabeth grinned as she grabbed his arm. "I just missed you."

"Sorry about that I must apologise to Olive and Ron falling asleep like that," Chris replied.

"I understood darling," Elizabeth said. "So do mum and dad, so no need to apologise."

They walked a few paces in silence. "This new case of yours darling, anything like the last case?" Elizabeth asked

Chris took time to answer. "Well if you really want to know," he said squeezing her arm with his free hand. "No women are involved at the moment, it was a reporter who was shot and killed."

"You will catch the person responsible darling, I'm sure of that," Elizabeth said quietly as they stopped at the bank entrance. "Will I be seeing you tonight?"

"Can we play it by ear Elizabeth, I was unable to do a lot yesterday, but I must start inquiries in urgency today, so I don't know where or what I will be doing."

Elizabeth let go of his arm, and pulled up his overcoat collar. "Forget me darling, just catch whoever is responsible, I love you," she said planting another kiss on his cheek before walking into the bank.

Chris walked back to the Police Station, he knew one thing for sure, he could never forget Elizabeth. He entered the station, and went to the desk, where Sergeant Dawkins was greeting him with a smile. "Morning Sir," he said.

"Morning Sergeant, although too cold to be a good one," Chris smiled undoing his overcoat buttons. "Sergeant Williams off duty?"

"His days off," sergeant Dawkins replied.

Chris entered his office, taking off his trilby and overcoat, he was just seating himself behind his desk when Sergeant Dawkins entered with a steaming hot cup of tea.

"That was quick Sergeant," Chris praised. "I can do with that, it was cold walking to work."

Sergeant Dawkins made no comment, he smiled and left the office. Chris took up the cup and drank, it was hot, and Chris felt the warmth as it went down.

George walked into the office, he took off his overcoat, and hung it on the hat stand, then blew his lips while rubbing his hands.

"Blasted cold outside," he murmured as he made for his desk. "What do we do today?" George rubbed his hands again as he sat at his desk.

Chris smiled. "Wait I suppose," he replied. "Can't really make any move until we get Bob's autopsy report, and then perhaps Sergeant Bloom might turn up with something."

"So an easy morning then," George smiled. "I can get on with the shop break in, I shall be out for a couple hours."

"If you are back early enough we will have a liquid lunch," Chris suggested.

"I will do my best," George replied as he got up from his desk. "Almost a waste of time coming in here," he smiled as he left.

The morning went quick, and when George entered the office again it was almost one in the afternoon.

"Any luck?" Chris asked as George hung his overcoat.

"I'm getting there, I have a report to do, but I can leave it until after lunch, it will take some time."

"If you are sure, I could do with a break, and by the time we get back Sergeant Bloom might have some information for us," Chris replied.

It was after two when Chris followed by George returned to the Police Station, Sergeant Bloom was talking to the desk sergeant as they entered the station.

"Come along in Sergeant," Chris invited.

"Well Sergeant," Chris said.

Sergeant Bloom cleared his throat, as he looked at the sheet of paper in front of him.

"I did several telephone calls," he started.

"Mr Peter Wright seems came from Yeovil in Somerset with his mother about five years ago, his mother bought a house in Clifton Terrace, number 19 in Winchester. His father was already dead. He had a sister who committed suicide about six or seven years ago. Now the story goes that his sister was engaged to a rich farmer, he was the Lord of the Manor, who proposed marriage, then after sleeping with her, went back on his proposal. However Jessie, that was her name, took him to court, and was awarded £2000 for breach of promise to marry," sergeant Bloom swallowed before carrying on.

"After the case it seems a lot of stories appeared in the local newspaper about her, and alleged carrying on with other men, it was thought that the rich farmer whose name I haven't got yet was behind it, to cut a long story short, Jessie committed suicide, and the family moved to Winchester."

"You have done well, good man," Chris praised him.

"That's not all," sergeant Bloom carried on. "Doing some checking on Mr Jason Morrison of the White Horse Littleton, it seems he is Mr Wright's uncle on his mother's side. He served in the Boer War, came out, and eventually took over the pub," sergeant Bloom concluded. "Is as far as I've got."

Chris looked at George, who was looking at the sergeant amazed. "You have done really well sergeant, how the hell did you get all that information?"

"Last night I went out and saw a mate of mine who works at the post office, it seems that Mr Wright do not mind telling of his family's history, I phoned a couple newspapers in Yeovil this morning, and eventually struck lucky with the Yeovil Globe a local newspaper, it was them that print the story which was sent to them by a freelance journalist."

"Well I must give you full marks," Chris replied. "Have you had a meal yet?" he asked.

"No, I didn't have time, surprising how the time goes when you're investigating," sergeant Bloom replied.

"Well get off home now and have a meal, report back in the morning, I'll have another job for you to do by then," Chris replied.

"Thank you Chris, I do feel a little peckish," sergeant Bloom replied getting up and leaving.

"Sergeant Bloom's story has a familiar ring to it, a bit like the Witcher brothers told us of the story Len Hogan told them," George remarked.

"Chris smiled, picked up a larger envelope that had been placed on his desk, he is a good man, and I agree about the story," he said to George as he looked at the envelope.

"This must be the autopsy report," Chris remarked as he started to open it.

Chris read the report concerning Mr Hogan of Fir Cottage Littleton, all the usual information was there, he had been shot through the head at close range, the shot had killed him, Mr Hogan was quite healthy, apart from a cyst on his liver, not thought to be serious, and a stone in his kidney that was dormant. Chris looked inside the envelope and saw a small package, he shook the envelope and the package fell out, it was the bullet that Bob Harvey had taken out of Mr Hogan's brain.

"This looks familiar," Chris remarked passing the bullet to George.

"The bullets once fired look all the same to me Chris," George commented. "However this bullet is heavy and slightly bigger than the one in our last case the murder of Mr John Paris," he added.

"Larger calibre," Chris replied. "Remember in Mr Paris's case the guns were women's handguns, so small that it could be carried in the pocket without being noticed."

George passed the bullet back to Chris. "We will know once we find the gun, if we ever do," Chris remarked. "If we find that Mr Hogan has no relatives living, who will claim the body I wonder?" Chris added.

"If it is not been claimed, he will be taken to Magdalene Mortuary for the time being, perhaps if he has left a Will, whoever benefits will see to it," George replied.

Chris read Bob's autopsy report again, then passed it to George, who after reading it twice passed the report back to Chris. "Do it help us?" he asked.

Chris shook his head. "This morning I read all the letters that we found at Fir Cottage, nothing that could gives us a clue, the letter that the postman was delivering to Mr Hogan needs some thought however."

George looked up. "Why is that?" he asked interested.

"It only had blank sheets of paper in the envelope," Chris replied.

"There has to be a reason," George murmured.

"I agree, I did fingerprint the sheets, and found only my own on them where I took the sheets out of the envelope, that's a lesson learnt for the future," Chris thought for a while.

"It means another trip for you out at Littleton, have another search of the cottage, then see the landlord Mr Morrison, you know what to ask, why he didn't tell us he was the uncle of Mr Wright, ask him his opinion of Jessie Wright's death, and whether he knew Mr Hogan was the reporter responsible for her death. You know what to ask, and make constable King a part of it, it might help him in the future," Chris commented.

"That will take almost a day," George replied with a smile.

"Well you do have your motorbike, for that reason I shall interview the postman again tomorrow, first I shall find out what time he finish work," Chris answered.

Chapter Six

Chris met Elizabeth by the Butter Cross situated in the high street.

"You managed to see me then," Elizabeth smiled giving Chris his usual kiss on the cheek. "I am so pleased," she said grabbing his arm as they started to walk downtown.

"I may not be able to make it tomorrow night, I have a late appointment, but have no idea of the time as yet," Chris answered.

"Still I have you tonight," Elizabeth giggled. "Mother will be pleased, how did your day go darling?" she asked.

"All new cases are a puzzle for the first few days, that is until you get a few facts that can be pieced together, I never seem to get an open and shut case," Chris replied.

"The trouble with this case, it is outside Winchester, and I have a feeling it will go much wider."

"I have faith in my soon to be husband, I am sure you will solve it," Elizabeth replied squeezing his arm and giggling.

Chris remained silent, he was not so sure.

Olive was at the door waiting to welcome them home, with a quick cheek kiss for both of them, Olive helped them with their top coats, then almost pushed them into the warm dining room, where they found Ron already at the table, and the food laid.

"I saw you coming," Olive said as she sat. "Now eat while it is nice and hot."

Chris enjoyed the meal, after which he followed Ron and sat in the armchair that face each other. Chris took out his pipe and lit it, and puffed on it contentedly. While the women cleared the tea things away and washed them up, Chris and Ron exchanged a few words about the ongoing war, until the women made their appearances.

The rest of the evening was spent listening to the radio, as they all played board games, and it was gone ten when Chris kissed Elizabeth goodnight at the front door.

"You have been very quiet tonight Chris," Elizabeth said. "Is everything all right darling?"

"I'm sorry," Chris replied a little embarrassed. "I did not intend to be, but my mind kept focusing on this case of mine."

"I guessed as much," Elizabeth replied pretending to sulk. "I thought I was a distraction for you?"

"You are," Chris replied. "But sometimes the mind controls you regardless of any distraction, please give my apologises to Olive and Ron, I did not intend to be a sour grape."

"You are silly Chris, Mum and dad understand that at times you are under strain, so do I, so go home and get a good night sleep, I will see you when you are able," Elizabeth smiled offering Chris her lips.

Chapter Seven

George did not go to the Police Station the next morning, he gave a quick check to his motorbike, and wrapping himself up as warm as he could started off towards Littleton, he had already phoned constable King of Littleton, to meet him at Fir Cottage.

Just after nine that morning George brought his motorbike to a halt, at the top of the lane, constable King was already there waiting for him.

"Morning Sergeant," constable King greeted him. "Find it nippy riding that thing?" he asked as George dismounted and wheeled the bike to a safe parking place.

"It's a bit," George replied rubbing his hands together, and stamping his feet. "Anyway constable, let's have another look over the cottage, we are trying to find a letter or such that will lead us to Mr Hogan's relatives."

"I did make a few enquiries," constable King remarked as they both walked the lane. "No one seem to know of any."

"There must be someone," George replied. "Perhaps we can find a letter from his solicitor or bank that might help us."

Constable King unlocked the cottage door, and allowed George to enter.

"Not much warmer in here," George remarked, as he started to rub his hands again. "Now I am going into his office, you can start with this room," George said indicating the room where Mr Hogan was found. "Look everywhere, keep any letters that you feel will help."

The constable smiled, and entered the room, while George made his way to the small bedroom, used as an office.

It was some time later, George and the constable met in the kitchen. "I've found a few letters and his bank book that might help," George remarked pointing to a large envelope he had placed on the table. "Did you find anything?"

"Just these two letters, they seem to be from friends, and this envelope was under the mattress," replied the constable.

George took the envelope and opened it, it contained money. "Must have been for emergencies," he remarked taking the money out and counting it. "There is seventy pounds here," George said passing the envelope and money over to the constable.

"Count it and seal the envelope and sign your name, just to be on the safe side," George smiled.

"Right," remarked George taking the sealed envelope from the constable and putting it in the large one that he had taken from the office. "It is just opening time, I have to go to the White Horse now, there are questions I need to ask the landlord, if you are free I would like you to come with me."

"I'll be glad to," replied the constable with a smile. "It will be a first for me," he said eagerly.

The bar of the White Horse was empty, but very warm, Jason Morrison was behind the bar, he looked up as they entered.

"Well Sergeant House, and Constable King, unexpected customers at this time," he smiled. "Business or pleasure?" he asked.

"A bit of both," George smiled back. "We are allowed a break, what do you drink constable?" George asked.

"Black and Tan beer please," replied the constable.

Then that will be a bitter and a Black and Tan please landlord," George said. "And while we are drinking if you can spare the time, I have a few questions for you if you don't mind."

"Not at all," replied the landlord. "Take your drinks over to the table near the fire, I'll join you, I don't expect any customers in this early," he said putting the two pints on the counter. "That will be five pence please," he said.

George gave him sixpence, and pocketing the penny change nodding to the constable to follow him over to the fire.

Once seated they both took a drink. "It's cold outside, yet we still come in to buy cold beer," George remarked placing his glass on the table. "And that bitter is cold."

"There are pokers there," the constable replied looking at several pokers standing in a frame by the fire side. "I have often seen locals put a poker in the fire for a while, then taking it out and putting the poker in their drink to warm it."

"I don't like hot beer," George replied with a smile as the landlord joined them.

"Right gentlemen, I'm all yours for a while, how can I help you?" the landlord asked with a smile.

"We are stumped at the moment Mr Morrison, there seem to be no one to claim Mr Hogan's body, would you know if he had any relatives?" George asked.

Mr Morrison thought for a while. "Has I told you before, I don't think he have ever mentioned his family," he replied. "I could ask around, it seems he has lived at a lot of places, his job I suppose, you mention a place and he will straight away say that he knows it."

"You said he came here before you Mr Morrison?" George asked.

"That's right, I have been here five years almost, he was here when I arrived, I may be wrong, but I am sure he told me he had moved in about a year before."

"So you have never met him before, or even heard of him?" George asked.

"I came from a small village in Somerset, Crewkerne, I had a pub there, the White Horse," he said with a smile. "I had not met him before I'm sure, but being a reporter, I might have read his stories, even seen his name."

George took a drink, he could not argue with what was said.

"The postman Mr Morrison, how well do you know him?" George asked as he placed his glass on the table.

"I am impressed Sergeant, you obviously know that Peter is a nephew of mine," Mr Morrison replied. "Is that a problem?"

George shook his head. "It would have been better had you told us before," George remarked.

"I was as shocked as everyone else about the death of Mr Hogan, it didn't enter my head to mention about my nephew, of course had I been asked, I would have said," Mr Morrison replied.

"Of course, you knew about Mr Wright's sister committing suicide," George asked.

"That was very sad," Mr Morrison replied the smile gone from his face. "Jessie was my niece, she was a lovely girl, stories in the newspaper drove her to it."

"You did not know who wrote those stories?" George asked.

"I read the stories printed, they were disgusting, but I did not see the name of the reporter, why are you telling me that, was it Len Hogan who wrote them?" he asked.

"I'm afraid so Mr Morrison," George replied.

Mr Morrison stood up, anger showed on his face. "I wish I had known, then I might have killed him, no collection for him will take place in my pub," he said storming off from the table.

George looked at constable King who seem a bit bewildered as to what had gone on.

"What do you make of that constable?" George asked.

"He seems angry," the constable replied.

"Take note Constable," George said. "Is it a true anger or false, I gave him the perfect excuse to show anger, he don't want to answer any more questions, showing anger was one way that he could storm off trying to avoid answering the questions."

"I say," replied the constable. "I would never have thought of that, do you think he is involved?"

"Only more time and investigation will tell us that," George answered finishing his drink. "Anyway, I have to get back," George said standing up.

"I'll go over and calm him down then if you are ready we will leave," George went up to the counter, where Mr Morrison was polishing a glass.

"I'm sorry you are upset Mr Morrison," George said placing his glass on the bar. "But you asked me a question and I told you the truth."

"It's me who should apologise Sergeant," Mr Morrison replied. "I just lost it, I'm sorry, allow me to buy you a drink on the house."

"Thank you, but I have to get back, we may meet again, by the way, I have to see your nephew again, would you know if he is on the phone?" George asked.

The smile appeared on the landlord's face. "Not Peter, when he is at home, he is in another world, he wouldn't like intrusions such as a telephone."

The Constable and George walked back to the lane. "Don't worry about the landlord, I know you drink in there, but the local pub landlord has to keep friendly with the local policeman, he will probably buy you drink when you next enter."

George sat on his motorbike, and started the engine. "Keep the cottage secure constable," he raised his voice a little over the clanking of the engine. "We will meet again."

Chris made is way back to the station, the old town clock in the high street above the Butter Cross said almost three pm. He had been to court giving evidence regarding a sheep rustling case. He pulled up his collar, and pulled the brim of his trilby, the traffic was quite heavy not only with horse drawn vehicles but with handcarts. Many people seem to be out, and Chris thought that they must be making Christmas shopping.

Sergeant Dawkins greeted him. "Getting colder," he smiled. "Snow by Christmas."

"Hope not," Chris answered as he took off his overcoat. "However you could be right, is Sergeant House back?"

"He's in the office Sir," sergeant Dawkins replied.

Chris entered the office. "Afternoon George," he said making for the hat stand and hanging his coat and trilby. "Cold enough to freeze the brass."

"Yes I agree," George nodded with a smile. "How did the court case go?"

"Got a conviction," Chris replied. "But it was an open and shut case, caught in the act, he will get a couple of years I expect."

Chris crossed to his desk. "How did it go at Littleton?" he asked as he sat.

George got up and placed a large envelope in front of Chris, then re seated himself. "I took constable King with me as you suggested, we spent some time going through the cottage, in that envelope, he pointed with his finger at the envelope he had put in front of Chris, are several letters in it," he said. "And his bank book with some cash that constable King found under the mattress."

Chris nodded his head, feeling the envelope but not opening it.

"Then we went and saw the landlord of the White Horse," George continued as he related what had taken place.

"You think the landlord knows something?" Chris asked.

"I'm sure of it," George replied.

"Well let's examine what we have about the case," Chris suggested. "At Littleton we have a freelance reporter has been shot dead by a revolver, gun not yet found, we know his reporting was mixed up in a suicide of a young woman that happened in another County, in Somerset, and we know that the young woman's family moved from Somerset and now living local, I have an idea that we will soon know the motive, even if we don't find the killer."

Chris saw George nodded.

"Everything is conquered by perseverance," George said.

"I sincerely hope so," Chris smiled as he took out his pocket watch and checked the time, well I am off to see the postman," he remarked. "I saw Elizabeth last night, and told her I had an appointment for tonight, what about you, want to come with me?" Chris asked.

"I have today's report to write, I could do with the time, who knows what tomorrow will bring," George replied.

"OK, George," Chris replied, picking up the envelope that George had given him. "I'll read these at home tonight," Chris said as he put on his overcoat and took his trilby.

"Don't lose it, there is money in there," George remarked as Chris was about to leave the office.

"Really," replied Chris. "I'll take out the price for a cab," he joked.

It was a up hill walk to Clifton Terrace from the police station, and by the time he was knocking on number 19, he felt a little breathless, but felt a little warmer.

Peter Wright opened the door, and a look of surprise was clear on his face.

"Inspector," he said, his face changing to a smile. "You are the last person I expected to call, come on in, you must be freezing," he offered.

Chris smiled as he took off his trilby and entered. "Not really the walk up here warmed me a bit."

Peter closed the front door behind him, and ushered Chris into a front room, that was warm with a open fire burning. "Oh, I'm sorry," Chris said seeing a man sitting at a table. "Have I come at a bad time?"

"Take a chair Inspector," Peter smiled. "This is my life-time best friend Reggie Shepherd."

Reggie Shepherd stood up and offered his hand, Chris noticed he was sturdy build, around six foot tall, with a pleasant face and a mass of black hair well combed. He was wearing a single breasted brown suit, which was undone.

"I am Detective Inspector Hardie," Chris introduced himself as he shook the offered hand. "I did not mean to interrupt, but I have a few questions to ask."

"I can guess what they are about," Reggie replied. "Peter has told me the story."

"You can ask me what you like Inspector," Peter said as he watched Chris seat himself. "Reggie knows more about me than I know myself."

Chris undid his overcoat buttons, and allowed the warmth of the room penetrate his body. "Well Mr Wright, I need to clear up a few points, but first of all, you did tell me you had tea with Mr Hogan whenever you delivered him a letter."

"That's correct Inspector," Peter answered.

"So you would be on a sort of friendly terms?" Chris asked.

"I suppose I could say yes to that question," Peter replied.

"While you were talking did he ever mention family, you see I have no one I can contact regarding his death, and it follows no one to claim his body," Chris said.

Peter thought for a while, shaking his head. "No, I don't think he ever mentioned any family."

"Pity," Chris replied. "He don't seem to have any relatives."

"Had you known Mr Hogan or heard of him before you met him at Littleton?" Chris asked.

"Postmen change their rounds, as people change their homes," Peter replied. "I could have met him on another round, I don't know everyone I deliver to, hardly see most of them, I just put their letters through their letter box, and I'm gone, why is it important?"

"It might have been," Chris answered. "You see Mr Wright, we dig into everyone connect with the case, you finding the body naturally we had to find out about you, while we accept everyone's word is truth what they tell us, we still have to confirm what they tell us is the truth?"

Peter looked at the Inspector, the smile gone from his face. "So Inspector, what have you found out about me?" he asked.

"Very little about you Mr Wright, we know you came here after the death of your sister, you came here with your mother who also died a while back. We also know about the suicide of your sister," Chris replied.

"What has my sister to do with Mr Hogan's death?" Peter asked getting annoyed.

"That's what I'm trying to find out, should there be a connection," Chris answered. "Would you tell me about your sister?" he asked.

"I can tell you that," Reggie interrupted. "I was once engaged to her, Jessie was a beautiful young woman, in looks and build, she had long flaming red hair. We all went to the same school, and our families were close friends, when the Boer War started I joined up, and was sent to south Africa with the regiment, came back in 1902, and started to see Jessie, and we eventually became engaged that was in 1904, I was still in the army, I was doing my twelve, I actually left the Army in 1908. The trouble was, I was often away, during which time it seems that Jessie met this Lord of the Manor, he was handsome, single, rich and powerful, he was also a magistrate. Although I hated, I did not blame Jessie, she would have had a good life with him, far better than I could give her. Anyway, she broke off our engagement, and the Lord of the Manor proposed marriage to her, as soon as he had got her into to bed, he called the wedding off," Reggie looked at his hands that were resting on the table.

"To cut a long story short, the families all chipped in, and he was taken to court for breach of proposal to marry, and he lost, and had to pay handsomely," Reggie gave a weak smile.

"Afterwards, Jessie and myself got engaged again, we thought everything was finished with regarding this Lord of the Manor, but we were wrong, he wanted revenge, then stories began to appear in the local newspapers, suggesting that, Jessie was known as a loose woman, and that the Lord of the Manor had been betrayed by the justice system and he had been disgraced by the court case, he was gentry, and we were commoners. We all chipped in again and took the newspaper to court for libel, but the paper had top lawyers, and went on about the freedom of speech for the press, and we lost that case, Jessie fell into a depression, and as you know committed suicide."

"Thank you Mr Shepherd," Chris replied. "I'm sure you covered the story, now I must tell you that Mr Hogan was the reporter who might have written those stories in your local newspaper."

"Now I can understand why you're asking me if I had known Mr Hogan before, the truth is I didn't," Peter said looking at Reggie.

"Inspector, do you suspect Peter of killing Mr Hogan?" Reggie asked with a straight face.

"We suspect everyone Mr Shepherd," Chris replied. "But information we have Mr Wright is certainly not a suspect."

"However I did meet your uncle," Chris added, looking at Peter.

"You mean uncle Jason, he has the White Horse," Peter replied.

"You should have told me," Chris said.

"Well at the time, it never crossed my mind, we were dealing with Mr Hogan," he replied sincerely.

"What was the reason you moved from Somerset to Winchester Mr Wright?" Chris asked.

"Mother became depressed, with the lost of the case against the newspaper and Jessie's suicide, she thought everyone was talking behind her back, she wanted to move and decided to come to Winchester, she wanted to be near her brother who had the pub at Littleton, uncle Jason was the only family she had left," Peter replied.

Chris rose from his chair, and buttoned up his overcoat.

"Well I must be on my way," he held his hand out to Reggie. "Thank you for the information," he said shaking his hand. "You don't live here do you?"

"No, I came down last weekend, I still live at Crewkerne," Reggie replied.

"The same place as Mr Morrison came from," Chris remarked. "Where are you staying here?" Chris asked.

"I have B&B at the Queens in Upper Brook Street, I shall be gone in a couple of days."

"Have you been to Winchester before?" Chris asked making his way out of the room.

"Passed it in the train," Reggie answered with a smile. "But this is my first stay."

"Well enjoy your stay," Chris remarked as Peter showed him the front door.

Chapter Eight

The morning was cold and brisk, Chris turned up his collar as he made his way down the high street. He was late, he had not managed to see Elizabeth the night before, he passed well dressed women in their heavy top coats, and with their fancy hats displaying piles of feathers and birds, artificial flowers and even fruit. Chris looked at the bank where Elizabeth works as he passed, he would have loved to have seen her.

He was smiling as he entered the police station.

"Morning Sergeant," Chris said to sergeant Williams at the desk.

"I'm not a lover of this cold weather," he said unbuttoning his overcoat. "Where is Sergeant Dawkins, I thought he was on duty?"

Sergeant Williams looked at the large brown colour clock on the wall behind him. "I thought it might have warmed up by this time," he replied without a smile. "Day off for Sergeant Dawkins."

Chris ignored the remark. "So everything alright?" he asked making his way to his office.

"No trouble, all quiet," replied the sergeant.

"Morning George," Chris greeted as he hung up his overcoat and trilby.

Sergeant Williams knocked and came in with two hot cups of tea. "I thought you would like a warm up," he said placing a cup before the two of them.

"Very thoughtful of you Sergeant," Chris praised him as the sergeant with a smile left the office.

Chris turned to George. "Now let me tell you how I got on with the postman."

Chris related what had taken place at Clifton Terrace, without interruption from George, who sat silently listening to every word.

"What is this Reggie Shepherd like?" George asked as Chris finished.

"Pleasant enough," Chris replied. "The trouble is he is going home this weekend, at the moment he is staying at the Queens, in Upper Brook street."

"Is it a problem for you?" George asked.

"I don't know," Chris answered. "He told me he was in the Boer War and had done his twelve before he came out, to my mind as he is deeply involved with the Wright family, he could own the gun we are trying to find, he also lives at Crewkerne in Somerset, the same town or village that Mr Morrison came from, in fact both of them were in the Boer War, both could have a revolver?"

"I see," George remarked, seeing the implication. "He must have been in love with this Jessie, he got engaged to her twice, it could be he took his revenge out on Mr Hogan for her suicide."

"I was in a difficult position George," Chris continued. "I can't go around making every Tom Dick and Harry a suspect, he was in Winchester on the night that Mr Hogan was killed, but would he have known his way to Littleton at that time of night, and don't forget, anyone going down that lane at midnight would have needed a torch, which in itself would have been risky, but being an army man he might have got hold of a gun, we must not forget that Mr Hogan was killed by a revolver, it's a pity we do not know the make."

"No way of getting him to stay longer I suppose," George replied.

"Already in my mind George," Chris answered. "Anyway, I did read those letters you brought back from Littleton, I must phone his bank, the other letters are from reporter friends of his, none of them mentioned any family."

"Let's hope the bank can throw some light on it, I haven't opened this money envelope, I see it was signed by constable King, so I will keep it unopened for now," Chris said putting the envelope in a drawer of his desk.

"I'll ring the bank while it's on my mind," Chris said reaching for the phone.

"Ah, Sergeant Williams," he spoke into the receiver. "Would you get me the Barclay Bank please, you will have to look the number up," Chris replaced the receiver before sergeant Williams could think of a reply.

Chris drummed his fingers on his desk, few moments later the phone rang, Chris lifted the receiver.

"Barclay Bank," said a voice.

"Good morning," Chris answered. "I would like to speak to the manager please."

"You are speaking," came the reply. "How can I help you?"

"I am Detective Inspector Hardie of Winchester CID, I am making enquiries regarding a Mr Len Hogan who has an account with your bank."

"Bear with me a moment Inspector," the voice said before the line went dead.

"He's checking I think," Chris said to George while covering the mouthpiece with his hand.

"Sorry about that," came the voice. "We have several Hogan with us Inspector."

"The one I'm interested in lives at Littleton," Chris stated.

After a moment silence, the voice came back. "Yes Inspector he has an account with us."

"Mr Hogan was found dead last Monday, I have his bank book here with me," Chris replied. "But I cannot find anything about his relatives, I wonder, would you know if he had any relatives?"

"Well I am shocked with your news Inspector," the voice said sounding sad. "He was a pleasant man, in answer to your question, he did not have any relatives, his wife divorced him, and his parents and the rest of his relatives I believe are dead, or have lost contact."

"Well thank you Sir," Chris answered. "At least we do not need to keep looking."

"I do have his Will, Inspector," the voice said, making Chris sit up.

"You do, don't one usually leave Will with a solicitor?" Chris asked wanting to get his hands on it.

"Usually," came the voice. "But our Mr Hogan hated solicitors for reasons of his own."

"What were your instructions regarding the Will?" Chris asked.

"I was to send it to an address in Somerset, should anything happen to him," the voice said.

"I'm afraid I need that Will Sir," Chris said.

"Not possible Inspector, as the banks manager I must obey instructions."

"Yes, yes," Chris replied. "I respect that, but I am afraid this is a murder inquiry, Mr Hogan was murdered."

"Oh dear," answered the voice. "This is tricky, can I suggest that you call in bank sometime later today, that will give me time to contact the head office for instructions, I am sorry to hesitate but it involves banks confidentiality."

"Well I do have things to do this morning Sir," Chris replied allowing his excitement to cool. "I'll see you this afternoon then."

"I'll expect you," the voice answered, and the line went dead.

Chris looked at George. "Mr Hogan left a Will with the bank, the manager was asked to send it to an address in Somerset if anything should happen to him."

"We can guess this address," George replied. "Strange though, it means that Mr Hogan did not know they were in Winchester, otherwise he would have altered the address where to send the Will?"

"That is a thought George," Chris replied. "Another question did he know that the postman was the brother of this Jessie who committed suicide."

Chapter Nine

Sergeant Williams poked his head around the door without knocking, making both Chris and George to look at him. "Sorry," Sergeant Williams apologised. "But you are needed, it seems a postman living at 19 Clifton Terrace has been found dead."

Chris looked at George, and both had the same thought. "His name is Peter Wright?" Chris asked.

"Correct," sergeant Williams replied. "I have already phoned Mr Harvey, and sent a constable there."

"Good man," Chris praised as he rose to get his coat and trilby followed by George.

Slightly out of breath, from the police station to Clifton Terrace was all up hill, Chris and George was let into the house by a constable who was guard. Chris knowing the way, made for the room he was in the night before, and found Bob Harvey was examining the body. He stood as Chris and George entered the room.

"Chris, George," he greeted with a weak smile. "You give me no piece do you."

Chris shook his head. "I can tell you this is a big surprise to us," he murmured.

"Well he has been strangled," Bob replied. "He is a strong young man, so whoever did this must have had strength, I doubt that it could have been a woman."

Chris looked down at the body. "Must have happened between four and five this morning," he remarked.

Bob looked at Chris astounded. "You are almost right as far as I can judge, is that a guess or do you know something I don't?" he asked.

"I was with him last night," Chris confessed. "Last night he was dressed in slacks and shirt, then I know he goes for work at five am, and now he has his uniform trousers on, I just assumed that he was up getting dressed for work."

"Thank you Chris, you have just confirmed my own opinion, you know him then?" Bob asked.

"He is the postman who found Mr Hogan at Littleton, the morning he was found shot," Chris informed Bob.

"Was he really," Bob replied in a surprised tone. "You are thinking that the two are connected?"

"At the moment I don't know what to think, but it do seem likely," Chris replied looking around the room. "Don't look as though there was a struggle, nothing seems to be out of place," he added.

"I hope this one has relatives," Bob remarked. "I already have Mr Hogan at the morgue."

"He has an uncle who keeps the White Horse at Littleton," George replied. "He will take over I would think."

Bob looked down at the body. "Well, all I can say at the moment, he was strangled with a thin rope, not thin enough to cut however, so there is no blood, he was killed around four or five this morning, the rope or whatever is not here."

"Thank you Bob," Chris replied as he watched George searched the body. "I can't do much with the body, so take it when you are ready."

"The wagon should be here any time now, no need for me to wait, I let you have the autopsy report as soon as I'm able," Bob spoke as he packed his doctor bag ready to leave.

"I'm going to speak to the constable, George," Chris said as he walked with Bob. "Better search the house," he advised.

Chris walked to the door with Bob. "At least he was not shot," Bob remarked as he opened the front door to leave.

"Perhaps whoever did it, realised the noise would be a bit risky," Chris ventured his opinion. "How did you get here?"

"I walked," Bob smiled. "It's only a few minutes from the hospital."

Chris watched as Bob walked away, then turned to the constable who was on guard. "You are constable Stabford aren't you?" Chris asked with a smile.

"I am Sir," replied the constable, happy that Chris remembered his name.

"Who found the body constable?" Chris asked.

"No idea Sir," replied the constable. "I was phoning in the station as usual, and was told by sergeant Williams to get up here, make sure the house is secured and let no one in apart from the police surgeon who was on his way."

"I see," Chris remarked. "How did you get in?"

"The door was open Sir," replied the constable.

"Did you enter?" Chris asked.

"Just to see the body Sir," replied the constable. "Then I came out here and waited for the police surgeon or yourself to arrive."

"Good man," Chris replied. "I want you to stay for a while."

Chris entered the house, he looked around the room, as his mind went over the reason for Mr Wright's murder, at the moment he saw no reason for it. He heard the noise of the morgue wagon arriving, Chris remembered the two men who entered the room with a stretcher and a red blanket, he had met them once while on a case at Lower Brook Street.

"Come to take the body, Inspector," spoke one of the men.

Chris nodded his head, as he watched the men put the stretcher on the floor, lift the body onto it, and cover the body with the red blanket. Without another word, with one man in front of the stretcher and the other at the back they carried the body from the house, Chris felt a little sadness, he had liked Peter Wright.

Chris looked at the photos on the sideboard, they were photos of his family Chris thought. He pulled open the drawers of the sideboard, which as full of odds and ends, none of which was of any interest to Chris. He opened the sideboard cupboard which full of books and Chris moved the articles around, found nothing that he was interested in, and closed the cupboards, not really disappointed, he had not expected to find anything.

George entered the room. "I have searched the bedrooms, there are three, one room obviously belonged to his mother, never been touched, still full of her clothes and bits and pieces. The other room is almost bare with just empty furniture in it, Peter's room was a clutter, bed unmade, clothes all over the place, proper bachelor room," George informed. "Found nothing of interest."

"Never expected to George," Chris replied. "I told him last night, that I did not suspect him as the murderer of Mr Hogan, and it seems I was right, but why was he murdered, what did he have to do with Mr Hogan apart from being Jessie's brother, and if someone is getting revenge for Jesse's suicide, why murder her brother?"

George shrugged his shoulders. "There is a question," he replied.

Chris took out his pocket watch. "It's now just half past one, we better get to the bank, it's on our way back lucky enough, did we find any keys on him?"

"That's all he had on him," George replied taking a bunch of keys from his pocket and handing them to Chris. "There is his wallet and some loose change with a wrist watch on his dressing table upstairs, perhaps a knock on his door interrupted his dressing."

"That could be an explanation," Chris agreed. "Let's talk to the constable about locking up, and get to the bank, I shall be very interested in what the manager has to tell us."

Chris gave the keys to the constable after first making sure that one fitted the front door. "Lock all doors and windows constable," Chris told him. "Make sure all is secure before you leave, then report back to the station tell sergeant Williams that I will expect whoever found the body in my office by the time I get back, which will be I expect about four pm."

"Very good Sir," replied the constable taking the keys that Chris handed to him.

It was well past two when Chris and George entered the bank. Once having introduced themselves, they were ushered into the manager's office without delay. Chris saw that the manager was a well built man, his head was partly bald apart from hair that grew around the side of his head. He had a round face, wore glasses, and had a moustache that covered his upper lip. He looked smart, wearing a collar and tie, and a dark pin stripe three piece suit. He stood up as the detectives entered and offered his hand.

"I am the manager," he said. "Mr Albert Dawse."

"I am Detective Inspector Hardie, and my colleague is Detective Sergeant House," Chris introduced themselves.

"Please, seat yourselves," Mr Dawse offered.

Chris and George sat in the two chairs in front of manager's desk.

"I am sorry to have to ask you, but you do have identification, you see this is about bank confidentiality," Mr Dawse said apologetically.

"Don't apologise Mr Dawse," Chris said taking his warrant card from his pocket, followed by George. "We should have shown it to you straight away, it is us that should apologise," Chris remarked allowing Mr Dawse to examine the cards.

"Well they seem to be in order," Mr Dawse replied giving the warrant cards back.

"Now gentlemen since your telephone call, I have been on to the head office for advice, since you said that Mr Len Hogan is deceased, head office see no reason why you cannot read his Will, I am told to keep the original, but give you a copy, which I have already had duplicated for your personal police file."

"That's very thoughtful of you Mr Dawse, please thank your head office for their cooperation."

Mr Dawse gave a weak smile, as he handed Chris an envelope. "This is the original," he said.

Chris took the document from the envelope and for a while studied it. "This Will was made 11th November, 1911, four years ago, are you sure there are no other Wills?" Chris asked as he handed the Will to George.

"There I can't help you Inspector, I saw him myself about two weeks ago, he made no mention of it then, I would doubt it," Mr Dawse explained.

"Who do you have to send it to?" George asked placing the Will on the desk in front of Chris.

"The address is on the envelope," Mr Dawse replied. "A Mrs Wright, lives in Somerset."

"I'm afraid it won't get there," George replied.

"Oh," Mr Dawse replied. "Why is that?"

"Since this Will was drawn up Mr Dawse," Chris interrupted. "The family have moved to Winchester, I'm afraid Mrs Wright has died, only her son was left, and he lived at number 19, Clifton Terrace."

Mr Dawse scribbled the address down. "You have been a great service to me Inspector, thank you, I will forward it then to her son."

Chris looked at George a faint smile on his face.

"I am afraid Mr Dawse, since I spoke to you this morning, a dramatic change has altered things, Mrs Wright's son Peter was found dead this morning."

Mr Dawse looked at Chris dumbfounded. "What are you saying Inspector?" he asked.

"As far as we know at the moment Mr Dawse, all the Wrights concerning this Will are now no longer with us," Chris replied, feeling a little sorry for Mr Dawse who seemed to be flabbergasted.

"Oh dear oh dear," Mr Dawse muttered. "Now what am I supposed to do?" he asked as though expecting Chris to tell him.

"Mrs Wright do have a brother, a Mr Jason Morrison who keeps the White Horse public house at Littleton," George offered.

Mr Dawse quickly wrote the address down. "I have no idea how this will work, after all Mr Len Hogan's estate was left to Mrs Wright, this Mr Morrison had no part of it."

Chris looked again at George, unsure what to say.

"You will have to take advice from your head office," George said with a smile.

"Yes, yes," replied Mr Dawse quickly. "It's tricky to be sure."

"Are we talking a lot of money here?" Chris asked.

"You say you have his bank book Inspector, quite a bit there, he also owns his cottage at Littleton, and have quite a sum invested, I have all his documents in the vault, which again makes me feel sure that there is no other Will, off hand I would say he is worth altogether close on sixty thousand."

"Nice tidy sum," George commented.

"Well I think we have what we wanted Mr Dawse, if you will give us the duplicate, we will get out of your way," Chris smiled.

"No trouble at all Inspector, I feel sad about Mr Hogan, he seemed a pleasant man," Mr Dawse replied handing Chris another envelope.

"Thank you," Chris replied. "By the way who witnessed this Will besides yourself?" he asked.

"My Secretary Mr Larkins," Mr Dawse replied.

Chris followed by George stood, offered his hand with his thanks, and took his leave.

"Well that's a turn up for the book," Chris said to George as they made their way back to the police station. "He left his entire estate to Mrs Wright."

"Guilty conscience I expect," George replied. "He drove her daughter to suicide."

"You are probably right George, it would have been a nice sum for Peter Wright to inherit," Chris replied.

"Pity that," George sighed.

"Well it's a part of his mother's estate," Chris debated. "I can't see why her brother Mr Morrison can't get it if it's proved he is the only living relative, if he don't, then the government will, bearing in mind, if he should be guilty of murder he would not get it even if entitled."

Chapter Ten

*I*t was just striking four, as Chris and George entered the police station, sergeant Williams looked up. "Dead on time he smiled as he looked at the wall clock, I have the chap who found the body waiting," he smiled. "What do you want to do regarding the security of the house?" he asked.

"Tell the Beat Bobby to keep an eye on it," Chris replied. "Not much we can do, we can't have a man standing outside all the time, is sergeant Bloom around?"

"In the back," replied sergeant Williams.

"Tell him I would like to see him when I have finished with the man who found the body," Chris said holding out his hand. "You have the keys to the house?"

Sergeant Williams looked under the counter and brought out the keys that the constable had left and put the bunch into Chris's waiting hand.

"Thank you sergeant, now I will see this man," Chris smiled as he made for his office.

Chris looked at the young man who sat opposite to him in the interview chair, he was not outstanding, just a normal sort of man around thirty years old. Chris looked at George who sat with his notebook open and a pencil at the ready.

"Your name?" Chris asked.

"Archie Baldwin," the man answered.

"You work in the Sorting Office of the Post Office?" Chris asked.

"Yes, been there for the last six years," Archie answered.

"Good job is it?" Chris asked with a smile.

Archie shrugged his shoulders. "As good as any, it's an early start, but then you get plenty of the day off which suits me."

"So you sort the letters out into different rounds, reading the different handwriting styles must be a bit of a problem?" Chris asked trying to put Archie at ease.

"Unable to read some of them," Archie confessed. "But we have to be fast, we can't hang around trying to read the addresses, we put them aside, then afterwards when the rounds are finished, we try hard to read the addresses, we normally manage."

"Really," Chris replied. "At least letters are eventually delivered."

"That is the job of the Post Office," Archie smiled.

Chris leaned forward on his desk. "Now Mr Baldwin, I understand you found the body of your colleague Mr Wright, please tell us how that came about?"

"Well, it was gone five thirty, but there was still no sign of Peter for the Littleton round," Archie swallowed before continuing. "When a postman do not turn up without explanation, it means that another postman has to do the round, usually after he has finished his own, it means overtime for the postman, but not many are in favour of doing another man's round, especially a Littleton round which means cycling."

"So what happened?" Chris asked interrupting.

"The supervisor asked us, if one of us would go to Mr Wright's house, just to see if he had over slept, I volunteered because I had a bike, you see sometimes a postman will over sleep."

"I don't doubt it," Chris replied. "So you went to his house, then what happened?"

"I knocked the front door, which I might add flew open, I walked inside calling out Peter, then I saw Peter lying on the floor, at first I thought he was asleep, so I went over and shook him, then I realised it was more serious when he did not move."

"Why did you not call the police?" George asked who had been writing and listening.

"From where?" Archie answered. "There was no phone in the house and none nearby, I thought it would be best to go back to the sorting office and let the supervisor deal with it, on my bike it did not take me long, anyway I did not consider the police at the time, I thought he was ill."

"You thought he was ill, and you left him?" George asked.

"What could I do at that time of morning, I just thought it was best to let the supervisor handle it, which turned out to be the right decision."

"Apart from shaking him, you did not do or touch anything else?" George asked.

Archie shook his head. "No, I was out of there as soon as I could."

"Were you friends with Mr Wright?" Chris asked.

"Yes I suppose," Archie answered. "We worked at the same place, if we saw each other in the pub, we would buy each other a drink, but not what you call bosom buddies, we never met up to go for a drink or such."

"What was your opinion of Mr Wright?" Chris asked.

"He was nice enough," Archie replied. "He was good looking, the women were attracted to him."

"Was that a problem to you?" George asked.

Archie looked at George a slight smile on his face. "That is a funny question, why should it be, I have my own girlfriend."

"Just a routine question Mr Baldwin," George explained. "I just wondered why you said women were attracted to him, was there any women trouble with him at the post office?"

Archie looked down at his lap. "There was once, but it was an internal matter, I don't think I should bring it up, it is not my place."

"Mr Baldwin," Chris said looking at him. "This is a murder enquiry, I can tell you that Mr Wright was not ill, he had been murdered, now you were at his home around the time he was murdered, so anything you know about Mr Wright, you must tell us, it will not get you into trouble."

"I would not have been here if I had not been asked," Archie replied, looking worried.

"Your explanation, which I am sure your supervisor will verify, it will put you in the clear Mr Baldwin, but we have to find out who killed him, surely you would want that?" Chris said gently.

"Of course," Archie replied.

"Well," Chris said.

"If I won't get into trouble, then I will tell you what I know," Archie replied.

"Peter has only been on the Littleton round for a few months, before that he used to do Twyford. I was not there, but one day a man came storming in the office, demanding to see the supervisor, which he did. It seems that this man threatened to kill the postman who was having an affair with his wife. Rumours started and Peter's name was mentioned. Now normally when a postman is caught having an affair on his round, he is sacked, but our supervisor do not accept just one side of the story. Peter it seemed denied having the affair, the supervisor checked up by going to Twyford and seeing the woman while her husband was at work. She told him she only had to talk to a man, and her husband who was extremely jealous would accuse her of having an affair. Rumour has it that this man caught his wife at the door in her night dress taking the mail from Peter and jumped to the wrong conclusion," Archie cleared his throat.

"Postmen see more women in their night dresses than any other men, their rounds are early, and often have to knock the door for a signature, many women answer the door in their night dresses," Archie remarked.

"Do you know the name of this man?" Chris asked.

Archie shook his head. "No, and Peter never mentioned it, however the supervisor believed Peter and took him away from Twyford round and put him on the Littleton round."

"Thank you for being open with us Mr Baldwin, is there anything else?" Chris asked.

Archie shook his head. "Not that I know," he replied.

Chris stood up and offered his hand. "Thank you for coming in Mr Baldwin."

Within a few moments of Mr Baldwin leaving, Sergeant Bloom knocked and entered and sat in the interview chair.

Chris looked at his watch. "It is late now, but I have a job for you Rowland, do it when you feel the time is better. I want you to knock doors around Clifton Terrace, find out if anyone heard anything around five o'clock this morning. I can tell you that Mr Wright who you checked up on has been found murdered."

"I have heard the rumour," sergeant Bloom replied.

Chris handed him the keys to the house. "These are the keys to the house, go in while you are up there, have a look around make sure all is secure."

Sergeant Bloom took the keys. "I might do it tonight when everyone is in," he said.

"It might be a waste of time but we have to cover our backs, find out if Mr Wright was in any women trouble."

"Do you think he was?" sergeant Bloom asked.

"At the moment we do, information has reached us that he might be," Chris replied.

"I do my best," Sergeant Bloom smiled as he rose to leave. "I'll report back as soon as I can."

Chris looked and smiled at George. "I hope we are not being taken off the track," he said. "I was sure the two murders were connected, still we have to accept the fact Mr Wright was strangled not shot like Mr Hogan."

"What's our next step then?" George asked.

"Too late for anything tonight, but tomorrow morning before coming in pop and see the sorting office supervisor," Chris suggested.

Chapter Eleven

$\mathcal{G}$eorge had left the office soon after Mr Baldwin had left, and Chris had settled down to read the reports. He checked his watch, decided to give it a rest, he thought that he could still meet Elizabeth.

"I have put out the lights Sergeant," Chris smiled as he looked at the desk sergeant. "I shall be at Alresford Road if needed."

"I'll make a note of it," replied the desk sergeant.

Chris left the station, and found himself in semi darkness, that was lit with a few gas lamps here and there.

"I was wondering if I was going to see you tonight," a voice said.

Chris turned sharply and saw Elizabeth.

"I got away a few minutes early," Elizabeth smiled as she reached up and kissed him on the cheek.

"I was on my way to meet you," Chris replied as they walked towards the King Alfred Statue. "I am not fond of these dark nights."

"Oh I don't know," Elizabeth remarked. "Darkness hides a lot of things, for instance, no one would see you taking me in your arms while you have your wicked way with me," she giggled.

"I'm sure the few people passing would realise," Chris replied with a smile.

Chris very used to the way Elizabeth teased him whenever she could. Actually Chris enjoyed her teasing, and wondered just what Elizabeth would be like when they were married, at the moment he had to control himself, knowing that sex between them would only happen after they were married, due to the respect Elizabeth and for her parents.

As they reached the house in Alresford Road, Chris playfully patted her behind as he allowed her to go first. She stopped at the front door. "Quick," she teased offering her lips. "Before mother opens the door."

Olive opened the door. "You two will freeze standing outside, you have a key Elizabeth."

"I was just getting it out," Elizabeth said a smile on her face.

"Come along in, dinner is ready," she said kissing Elizabeth and Chris on the cheek.

Ron who was sitting in his armchair looked up, as Elizabeth crossed the room and kissed her father. "How are you Chris?" he asked as he smiled at his daughter.

"I am fine thanks, yourself?" Chris asked.

"Tired, done the beds, cleaning and dusting," Ron replied with a smile and one eye on his wife.

Chris smiled at Elizabeth as Olive exploded.

"You would not know how to make a bed, you would put the sheets on top of the blankets, as for cleaning I have a job to get you to clean your shoes, you would not know how?"

"Don't be angry my sweet," Ron replied trying to keep a straight face. "You have made the dinner, I know you are tired, I will wash up after dinner if you need a rest," Ron smiled.

Olive looked at Chris, she was lost for words. "Take no notice of him Chris, he gets in these funny moods sometimes, let him wash up," she laughed. "He would break more than he washed, what would happen to him if I were not here, don't bear thinking about."

"Dad only teasing you mum," Elizabeth interrupted. "I hope my husband will love me as much as dad loves you," she said with a sly look at Chris.

"We don't want to talk about these sort of things Elizabeth," Olive scolded. "Come and give me a hand in the scullery."

"How is the war going Ron?" Chris asked taking the armchair opposite Ron.

"Still about the same, I am beginning to wonder about this trench warfare, our chaps go over the top, gain about a couple hundred yards, the Germans counter attack and drive them back, it's a kind of stalemate, costing thousands of lives."

"As bad as that?" Chris asked.

"It's this Gallipoli Landing that worries me, we landed there about six months ago, we have made no headway still stuck on the beach, losing thousands."

"No hope of the war being over soon then?" Chris asked.

"I can't see it being over in the next couple of years," Ron replied.

"Come sit at the table," Olive commanded as she entered the room carrying plates, followed by Elizabeth. "No starters today, but apple pie and custard for afters."

Chris smiled at Ron, as they both rose and sat at the table.

"This looks good Olive," Chris praised as he looked at his steak and kidney pie with mashed potatoes and vegetables.

"Thank you Chris," Olive replied. "It is nice to be appreciated," she smiled looking at her husband.

"I was just about to praise your cooking my sweet, but Chris beat me to it," Ron smiled.

"That would be a first," Olive remarked looking at Elizabeth with a slight smile.

"You know dad is only teasing you mum," Elizabeth smiled. "You know he appreciates you."

"It wouldn't hurt for him to say so now and again," Olive replied as she cut into the steak pie. "Anyway Chris how have your day been?" she asked.

"Not all that good Olive," Chris replied. "Since you asked, I had another murder today."

"Dear oh dear," Olive murmured. "What is the world coming to, we have our young men losing their lives in France, one would have thought that was enough without murders being committed at home."

"Two different things love," Ron voiced. "Society will never change regardless of wars, there will always be murders, robberies, and other crimes are still committed, war do not stop it."

"In my experience, crimes in society are committed mainly for four main reasons, revenge, greed, jealousy and desire," Chris remarked as he ate his meal. "Take those four reasons away, there would be very few crimes, and I would be out of a job."

"Greed and desire could be the cause of wars," Ron said. "I mean, the greed give one country the desire to occupy and own another country's land, we do enough of that in Africa."

"I agree but jealousy could also be linked with desire," Chris remarked as he thought of Mr Wright's murder. "For instant a man could be so jealous of his wife, he gets the desire to kill any man he thinks she is interested in," Chris said hurriedly. "But the desire is always there."

Olive turned to Ron. "Do you feel that way with me?" she laughed.

"No my precious," Ron replied. "I don't feel that way at all, in my opinion jealousy is a form of distrust, but I do and always have trusted you my sweet."

"What a lovely thing to say dad," Elizabeth interrupted. "I told you he loves you mother," she said smiling at her mother.

Chris saw a faint blush came to Olive's face, he guessed she was very happy with what Ron had said.

With the meal over, with Olive and Elizabeth in the scullery washing up, Chris retired to the armchair opposite Ron. He took out his pipe, filled it and lit it, and took an enjoyable puff.

"This new murder Chris," Ron asked. "Any connection with your Littleton case?"

"It will soon be in the papers Ron, so it can't do any harm in telling you, it was the postman who found the body at Littleton," Chris told him.

"So it is connected," Ron replied.

"At the moment I can't see why, but I have a feeling that should it be the case, it could combine greed and revenge."

Ron shook his head. "I agree with Olive, we don't need this at home while our boys are dying for no good reason abroad."

It was around midnight when Chris returned to his lodgings.

Chapter Twelve

George called into the Sorting Office just before eight thirty, he thought by that time the supervisor would be free, as all the rounds would have been sorted. After a few enquiries he made to the workers walking about, he was soon confronted by the supervisor, who wanted to know his business in the sorting room.

"I am Detective Sergeant House," George introduced himself showing his warrant card. "I would like a few moments with you, regarding a Mr Peter Wright, who was found dead yesterday at his home."

"I am the supervisor Jim Blake," the man said offering his hand which George took. "It would be better to talk in my office, if you would come this way, would you like a tea," he added.

George shook his head. "Just had my breakfast," he smiled.

"Lucky you," Jim replied. "My breakfast is other people's lunches."

"Too late for me," George replied as they entered a small office at the rear of the building.

"Take a chair," Jim offered as he sat behind his desk. "Now how can I help, I know very little apart that he is dead and was murdered."

"You know he was murdered?" George asked.

"This morning I did," Jim replied. "Archie told me of his interview with you."

"I see," George replied realising that Mr Baldwin had been told he was murdered. "Yes we did tell Mr Baldwin," George admitted.

"This is a terrible crime, do you have any understanding as to why or who committed this crime?" Jim asked.

"Not at the moment Mr Blake," George replied. "We do have couple line that we are pursuing."

"Well I wish you all the best in your efforts Sergeant, now how can I help you?" Jim asked.

"How did Mr Wright get on with his workmates, I mean did he have any grievances with any of them?" George asked.

Jim spread his hands. "Not that I know of, but then again, the postmen only come in here to collect their post bags which contains all the letters of their round, then they are off, they hardly have time for grudges, unless it is outside."

"I can understand that Mr Blake," George replied. "What about on their rounds, do they get into any trouble?"

"A few people may go on to a postman who is expecting a letter which had not arrived, but I would think that is very few," Jim replied honestly.

"Do postmen get in trouble with women on their rounds?" George asked. "I would take it that they do see a lot of women on their rounds."

"If a postman needs a signature, yes they knock the door and usually women answer the knock, regarding having affairs with them, it is very rare," Jim replied. "When it comes to my notice, I investigate, and if the postman is having an affair, he is dismissed."

"Did Mr Wright ever become involved with a woman on his round?" George asked.

Jim looked at George before answering, he imagined that George already knew that Peter had once been involved with a woman. "Mr Wright was once on a Twyford round, a husband came to me complaining that my postman was having an affair with his wife, and he wanted it stopped," Jim spread his hands. "I investigated, and soon realised that it was a case of a jealous husband, Mr Wright was completely innocent."

"I am sorry Mr Blake, I have to ask these questions," George said. "If jealousy gets out of control it can be highly violent, did this husband threaten Mr Wright?"

"Not directly to Mr Wright, but he told me he would kill him if it did not stop, I remember he was really in a rage, frightened me a bit," Jim smiled.

"Tell me about the case Mr Blake if you will, we need to know all we can about Mr Wright?"

"You know he came from Somerset do you?" Jim asked.

"Yes we know all that part of his history," George replied. "But not much since he moved here five years ago?" George asked.

"I don't know much about him, he started working here about a year ago, kept good time in the mornings, and did his rounds without any complaint, until this man," Jim took a folder from his drawer and opened it.

"A Mr Mick Phillips of 5, Park Lane, Twyford, it was almost closing time when he came bursting in through the door demanding to see me. I did investigate, I saw the woman, she explained that her husband had seen her at the door with the postman, she was just giving a signature to for a package she received, unfortunately she was in her night dress, and her husband jumped to the wrong conclusion."

"Your opinion was?" George asked.

"As I said Mr Wright was innocent, the woman although quite attractive was double his age for one thing, she swore to me that having an affair with a man would not be safe for her."

"So his wife was very frightened of him?" George asked.

"Seem to be, anyway, I have heard nothing since, I did take Mr Wright off the Twyford round, and put him at Littleton, and as you know he found one of his deliveries dead."

George nodded his head.

"Do you think there is any connection between the two?" Jim asked.

"Not that we know of at the moment Mr Blake," George replied getting up not wanting to discuss the whole case. "Thank you for your time and cooperation," he said offering his hand. "I will try to keep you informed."

Chris alone in the office while George was at the Sorting Office, studied over and over all the reports he had on the murders, with Mr Hogan murder, he did have a weak suspect Peter Wright who could have had a motive and the opportunity, but in his mind he dismissed him as the killer, and now he had been murdered. There is his uncle, the landlord of the White Horse, he may have had a motive, after all it was his sister's daughter that had committed suicide, also he lives just a few hundred yards from Mr Hogan, and could have easily done the crime during Sunday night, but would he have murdered his own nephew, and for what reason. Then there was the question mark of Reggie Shepherd, he certainly had a motive, but did he have the opportunity.

Only one thing seems to stick out at the moment, Mr Hogan was killed because of the stories he wrote in the Somerset newspaper about Jessie Wright. Two questions stayed in his mind, did the murderer know about the Will, and why did the murderer wait so long before getting revenge. Chris sighed as he closed the file, leaned back in his chair, and took his pipe, which he filled, and lit drawing on it deeply.

Chris decided to visit Reggie Shepherd, who he met while interviewing Mr Wright, he wondered did he or Mr Morrison know about the murder of Mr Wright. He thought that Mr Morrison should be told, being his only living relative.

Chris walked towards to Upper Brook Street decided to visit Queens, he entered the smoke filled bar, a fire was burning which gave the bar some warmth, it was Friday lunch time and not a lot was in the bar, just a few older men were sitting and talking. Chris walked to the bar, where a chubby face woman was serving, she smiled at him, and pushing loose strand of her black hair away from her face, welcomed him. "What's your pleasure Sir?" she asked.

"I'll have a pint of your best bitter please," Chris answered, normally he would have asked for a sandwich, but looking around he did not fancy asking.

"Haven't seen you before Sir," the woman said giving Chris his pint. "Do you live around here?"

"I do," Chris replied. "Are you the landlady?"

"Yes I am, the old man is still sleeping off his hangover in his bed, last night we had a bit of a party here," she smiled. "That will be tuppence please," she added.

"Would Mr Shepherd be in?" Chris asked. "I understand he is staying here."

"He stays here," replied the landlady. "But he is out, I don't expect him back until late, at least he won't be if he follows his usual routine."

Chris smiled. "He has a routine has he?"

"He seems to have, leaves early in the morning come back late at night, he arrived here last Saturday night, and Sunday night he didn't come back at all, but mind you I told him he would have to pay for the night," the landlady laughed showing some bad teeth.

"Would you allow me to buy you a drink landlady?" Chris asked.

"Call me Vera," she replied, pushing loose strands of hair out of her face again. "I'll just have a gin and tonic."

"My pleasure," Chris smiled putting a penny on the counter as she poured from a bottle into a glass. "Cheers," she said smiling.

"Did you learn where he went on Sunday night?" Chris asked.

Vera put her glass down smacking her lips. "Just said he took a trip out of Winchester and couldn't get back."

"Really," Chris replied. "Must have been a long way out, you could walk from most villages around."

"Well it was late when he went, might have been something to do with the phone call he had, almost about closing time." Vera said. "Anyway he was back in time for breakfast, and limping, he said he slipped in the dark, how do you know him?" Vera asked.

"I have met him once only, he comes from Somerset," Chris, replied. "He comes from Crewkerne."

"He talks with a Somerset brogue," Vera replied. "Do you want me to say who called?" Vera asked.

"I was thinking about that," Chris said after taking a gulp of his bitter. "It would be best if you did not mention my visit, you see I am a policeman, and I don't want to panic you or Mr Shepherd, I think he said he will be leaving this weekend."

"That's right," Vera said. "He's booked in unto Saturday morning," the smile leaving her face. "Is he in trouble?" she asked.

"Not that I'm aware, it was just that I would liked to have spoken to him."

"I'm glad," Vera replied. "Apart from his peculiar times he is a nice man."

"I'm sure he is," Chris replied finishing his pint. "Just one more thing Vera," Chris smiled. "Early Thursday morning, did Mr Shepherd go out particularly early, say in the middle of the night?"

"Can't remember," Vera replied. "Each of our guest are given a key, we have a side entrance away from the bar which is always locked at nights, sorry I would not have know if he had."

"Never mind Vera," Chris said with a smile. "Thank you for your cooperation."

"I hope to see you again," Vera smiled.

"You never know," Chris replied as he made for the door.

Chris walked back to the Police Station, his mind was busy, Mr Shepherd's leaving on Saturday become a problem to him, he entered his office, and found George there.

"How did you get on?" Chris asked as he hung his overcoat and trilby, before crossing to his desk.

"I saw the supervisor, a Mr Jim Blake, he was quite helpful, but his story was almost the same as Mr Baldwin told us, however I did get the name and address of the jealous husband at Twyford."

"We can do a check on him," Chris replied. "What is your thoughts on him?"

"I don't know," George replied. "It was six months ago this happened, and Mr Wright has been no where near Twyford since then, six months is a long time to bear a grudge, surely jealousy continues only if the affair continues, and I don't think this was an affair, just a conclusion that a jealous husband jumped to."

"I agree George, but we must protect our backs, a check on him won't hurt, I get the constable there to do a check," Chris said.

"Where have you been," George asked.

"I have been to the Queens, Mr Shepherd was not available, but I spoke to the landlady, she calls herself Vera. She told me that last Sunday night almost about closing time Mr Shepherd had a phone call, he left in a hurry and was out all night only arrived back in time for breakfast, and was limping."

"Walking down that lane in the dark do you think?" George asked.

"Well I nearly twisted my ankle," Chris replied. "But how did Mr Shepherd get to Littleton, did he walk, remember he do not know the area, and it was pitch dark."

Chris pondered for a while before continuing. "I asked Vera if Mr Shepherd had left the pub early Thursday morning, but she could not say, it seems there is a side entrance, and all guests are given a key, she had no idea."

"Do you suspect him?" George asked.

"As far as I know he was the last person to be with Mr Wright, he was there with him when I left, my worry is that tomorrow he leaves Winchester, can I let him," Chris continued. "Seeing Mr Morrison is the only relative of

Mr Wright, I thought he had the right to know, can you get on your motorbike and pop over there, it's only just gone eleven."

"I can get his alibi for early Thursday morning," George said getting up.

"Try to see his wife, if she is there," Chris remarked as George left.

Left alone, Chris opened the file on Mr Hogan, after studying all reports again, he reached for the receiver of the phone, Sergeant Williams answered.

"Get me Constable King of Littleton," he asked.

Minutes later the phone rang. "Constable King here Inspector," came a voice.

"Morning constable, I am glad I caught you in, do you know that your postman Mr Wright has been found dead?" he asked.

"I did hear a rumour, but could not believe it, the new postman told me this morning," constable King answered. "So it's true, that is terrible, was it a natural death Sir?" he asked.

"I am afraid not Constable," Chris replied. "What we have to do now is to see if his death is connected with Mr Hogan's death."

"I can understand that Sir," came the reply.

"Sergeant House is on his way to see Mr Morrison, as far as we know he is the only living relative of Mr Wright, in the meantime, I want you to do me a little errand."

"I'm free," came the reply.

"I want you to get in touch with the Witcher brothers, Tom and Bill you know them?" Chris asked.

"Yes I know them," constable King replied. "They will probably be in the White Horse, it is opening time."

"I don't want you to see them at the pub, wait until they are home, I want you to ask them what time they left the White Horse on Sunday night, try to get them to remember, it could be important," Chris emphasised.

"Also get them relate to you what they were talking about to with Mr Hogan outside the pub that night, I do have their conversation, but just see if they alter it at all," Chris added. "Tell them it has to be in confidence, ask them if anything was said about a Will, and did they tell the landlord about it?"

"I understand Sir," replied constable King. "I'll get back to you as soon as possible."

"Thank you constable, I will be here for a while yet."

Chris replaced the receiver, leaned back in his chair, took his pipe and lit it, a smile played on his face as he puffed out smoke.

After enjoying his pipe, he opened Mr Hogan's file, taking out sergeant Bloom report, then finding the number of the Yeovil Globe newspaper, he reached for the phone and dialled the number.

"Yeovil Globe," came a voice.

"Good afternoon," Chris answered. "I am Detective Inspector Hardie, of Winchester CID, I would like to speak to your editor."

"What town was that?" came the voice.

"Winchester," Chris answered. "It's a city."

"Just a moment," the voice replied.

Chris waited for a couple of minutes when a booming voice shattered his eardrums. "Inspector Hardie, I am Mr Edwards the editor, how can I be of assistance?" he asked.

"Good afternoon Mr Edwards," Chris replied. "I will come straight to the point, I am investigating a murder, the victim I believe was a freelance reporter, who from time to time would send you stories for your paper."

"What name Inspector?" came the reply.

"Hogan, Mr Len Hogan," Chris repeated himself.

A short silence followed before Mr Edwards answered. "He was murdered you say?"

"I'm afraid so Mr Edwards," Chris answered.

Another short silence followed. "How can I help you Inspector?"

"I was hoping that you would not mind answering a few questions over the phone, it is important," Chris replied.

"Inspector I would be glad to help the police, but how can I be sure that you are who you say you are?"

Chris smiled to himself, taking no offence. "I'll put the phone down Mr Edwards, you can look up the number of the Winchester Police Station and call me back."

"I will, but give me a time while I get his document will you?" Mr Edwards said.

"Thank you Sir," Chris replied, replacing the receiver.

It was ten minutes later when the office phone rang.

"I'm sorry to have kept you waiting," came the booming voice of Mr Edwards. "I now have all his document in front of me."

"I am interested in Mr Hogan's involvement with a Miss Jessie Wright a few years back, I am told that she sued Mr Hogan for libel, then committed suicide," Chris explained.

"According to my deputy, your office have already been on the phone regarding this, but to put things right, Mr Hogan himself was not sued, it was the newspaper, we were responsible as we printed it," Mr Edwards replied.

"Was Mr Hogan in court during the trial?" Chris asked.

"No, nor was I, we fought the case on the right to print, free speech and all that, we were able to convince the court that what we had printed was the truth, we had a sign statement from one of her past suitors, that he had taken her to bed."

"Are you able to tell who gave you that statement?" Chris asked feeling excited.

"Well it was all recorded in the high court, so it would be available in the records of the case, I'm not sure it's my place."

"It is rather important Mr Edwards, I would like to clear this case," Chris pleaded. "Apart from Mr Hogan's death we have a Mr Peter Wright who has died suspiciously, and he was the brother of Miss Jessie Wright who sued your newspaper."

"My, my, Mr Edwards replied his voice a little quieter, don't you have any suspects at the moment Inspector?" Mr Edwards asked.

"To be honest Mr Edwards, Mr Wright as you can imagine was a suspect, or thought to be one, however we do have his uncle living just outside Winchester, and his friend a Mr Reggie Shepherd staying here at the moment, I need more information," replied Chris.

"My, my," Mr Edwards repeated himself. "If I remember rightly the people you have mentioned were all involved in one way or another in the libel case against our paper. The trouble with this case Inspector, they could not sue the reporter for libel because he did not print it, it was the Globe that printed it. When the case came to court it was against the newspaper, individuals were not named, we had to prove what we printed was the truth, and this statement whether true or false, helped us win the case."

"This man who wrote the statement was he in court?" Chris asked.

"Not that I'm aware of," replied Mr Edwards. "But I do know, he refused to testify in open court, but agreed to see the Judge in his chambers strangely enough."

"Did Mr Hogan produce the statement?" Chris asked.

"Oh no," Mr Edwards remarked. "It was sent to us by the solicitor of Mr Cole."

"Mr Cole is who?" Chris asked.

"The Lord of the Manor who Miss Wright sued and won a case against him for breach of promise," Mr Edwards replied.

"That was generous of them," Chris remarked.

"In a way yes, but don't forget Mr Cole wanted revenge, losing the case against Miss Wright did not help him, he was a magistrate after all, which he gave up."

"I see," Chris said. "So your case simple rested on this one statement."

"That is about it," Mr Edwards agreed.

"Would this man who furnished the statement have met Mr Hogan do you think?" Chris asked.

"I would have thought so, perhaps he negotiated it," replied Mr Edwards.

"Even if I managed to get the script of the court case then, his name would not be mentioned?" Chris asked.

"That's about the size of it," Mr Edwards answered. "By the way, as Mr Hogan was one of our reporters, is there a story here for the Globe?" he asked. "I am a newspaper man after all, and although we realise the tragedy of the case, it means a story to us."

"Well you have been straight with me Mr Edwards," Chris replied sensing a disappointment. "I can issue a statement to the press, send your reporter and ask for me, I will tell him what I am able."

"That is very good of you Inspector, I appreciate it," Mr Edwards replied. "Now how can I put it Inspector," he continued. "Although his name is very confidential, if one of your suspects come from Crewkerne, a small village near here, you could strike lucky," Mr Edward added.

"Thank you very much Mr Edwards," Chris replied a smile appearing on his face. "I will look forward to seeing your reporter."

Chris replaced the receiver, and sat back in his chair. According to Mr Edwards of the Globe, the person who supplied the statement that got the paper off from the libel case came from Crewkerne, however he had two people from Crewkerne, Mr Morrison and Mr Shepherd, one was uncle to Jessie, the other was engaged to her, out of the two the only one who could have sex with Jessie was Mr Shepherd, he was therefore the only one who could have supplied the statement to the court on behalf of the Globe, or Chris thought was there someone else involved who had not yet come to be known.

Chris picked up the receiver and spoke to Sergeant Williams. "Get me constable Shaw of Twyford, I don't have his number," he asked.

Chris put the receiver back and waited.

Chris checked his pocket watch, it was almost midday, when the phone rang.

"Constable Shaw here," came the voice as Chris lifted the receiver.

"Constable this is Detective Inspector Hardie of Winchester," Chris said.

"Nice to hear from you Sir," came the reply.

"I would like your help Constable," Chris remarked.

"That is why I am here Sir," constable Shaw replied. "How can I help?"

"I have an ongoing case, a name has come forward who just could be involved," Chris answered.

"I have heard Sir," constable Shaw replied.

"I suppose you have," Chris answered with a slight smile. "The name I refer to is a Mr Mick Phillips lives at number five, Park Lane, Twyford."

"I know him Sir," constable Shaw answered.

"What is he like?" Chris asked.

"Pleasant enough, bit moody now and again, but I have had a drink with him, suffers I am told with jealousy, I pity his wife, she is quite a nice person," constable Shaw remarked. "This is not the case about the postman is it?" he asked.

"So you know about it?" Chris remarked.

"The whole village knew about it," constable Shaw laughed. "Very little stays secret in a village."

Chris smiled to himself. "The trouble is constable, Mr Wright the postman involved has been found dead, not natural I might add."

"I personally can't see Mr Phillips being involved in murder, if he were it would be quick on the spur of the moment, admittedly he has a quick temper when he sees a man talking to his wife, but he is up one minute and down the next, we are talking about several months in between here, personally I can't believe it, but what would you like me to do Sir?" he asked.

Chris felt content with constable Shaw words. "Nothing at the moment constable, his name has been brought forward with him making a threat against the postman, but I am incline to agree with you, six months have past, it is a long time, anyway, if I need further checking I will get in touch with you."

"Anytime Sir," constable Shaw replied.

Chris smiled as he replaced the receiver. The phone rang almost immediately. "Constable King of Littleton Sir," came the voice.

"How did you get on?" Chris asked.

"I saw the Witcher brothers at their home as you suggested," constable King started. "They told me Sunday night they left the pub around closing time, there was no one else in the pub when they left, the pubs shut at ten on Sundays."

"Good man," Chris remarked. "Then what?"

"Well it seems that Mr Hogan was considerably the worse for drink, and he was crying," continued the constable.

"Really," Chris remarked.

"They told me they stopped outside the pub a long time, spending most of the time holding Mr Hogan against the wall by the door of the pub, he was relating a case to them about a girl who committed suicide, it was obvious to them that he regretted his part in it, because he could not stop sobbing and crying, it seems every time he drinks too much he talks about the case, the brothers told me they have heard the story several times. Anyway after the pub lights went out, they managed to get Mr Hogan walking towards his cottage, but it took time as he kept on stopping and sobbing saying he was bribed in what he had done, but wouldn't have done it at the cost of a young innocent life."

"I see," Chris remarked when the constable paused. "Anything else?"

"They said it was gone eleven when they eventually saw Mr Hogan walking down the lane to his cottage, they did not go with him, it was so dark, and being old they were a bit frightened I think, anyway," the constable continued. "They waited at the top, and much later they saw his light come on, so they knew he had got down the lane safely, they could see the light from the top of his lane."

"He managed to let himself in and light the light which I believe was paraffin, was he all that drunk I wonder?" Chris remarked.

"Well he is usually a bit tipsy when he leaves the pub, and he has been walking down the lane in that condition for many years," constable King remarked, and everyone knows he never locks his front door."

"Was his Will ever mentioned while they were talking?" Chris asked.

"I did ask about that, it seems that Mr Hogan did mention his WILL in the pub about a week before he was murdered, there was an argument who had the most money in the village, there are a few rich people here," constable King remarked.

"I am sure there are," Chris replied.

"Anyway, they told me that the landlord never waits for Mr Hogan to order, once empty the landlord fills his glass again, they said they never seen him pay, and perhaps he pay at the end of each week, I know it's not illegal having a slate, anyway I'm told Mr Hogan boasted that his Will and he said it will make a certain woman rich for the rest of her life, but said no more in the pub about it. The brothers told me that taking him home that night, he laughed drunkenly and said, the woman who gets his money, will make her brother jealous."

"Really," Chris remarked interested. "Did they tell the landlord about what was said."

"Not much luck there Sir, they are forgetful, they do remember that the landlord often gives them a free drink should he be interested in what was said when taking Mr Hogan home."

"You have done well constable, thank you very much, you will let me have your report as soon as possible," Chris praised.

"I will do," replied the constable. "Anything else?"

"At the moment no, but I think I shall need your help sooner than you think, but for now thank you constable."

Chris sat for a while, details from the last three phone calls going through his mind, with a smile on his face thumped his desk before getting up and going outside to the desk sergeant.

"Sergeant Williams," Chris said as he approached. "Would Sergeant Bloom still be in the building?" he asked.

"In the back typing out a report I think," sergeant Williams answered. "With one finger I might add," he said with a smirk.

"Let him know that I want to see him before he leaves the building."

Chris was about to leave the desk when he had another thought. "When he is ready, perhaps you will come in the same time sergeant," Chris added as he retreating into his office.

Chapter Thirteen

*I*t was just before midday that George pulled up outside the White Horse at Littleton, standing by his motorbike he took off his gloves, and unbuttoned his overcoat as he made his way into the bar, Mr Morrison looked up and smiled at him.

"Sergeant House, what do I owe this pleasure," he welcomed him.

"I will have a pint of your best bitter landlord," George replied. "And allow me to buy you a drink, I need to have a few words with you."

"Dear oh dear, that don't sound so good, but I will take your offer, I will have a whisky," Mr Morrison replied.

"You are empty, perhaps we can sit at a table," George said looking around.

"I will bring the drinks over," Mr Morrison offered.

George sat at the table he had occupied before and waited for the landlord, who within a few moments joined him.

"Drink up," George said as he lifted his pint and took a drink, while watching the landlord take a sip of his. "I have some bad news for you Mr Morrison."

Mr Morrison smiled, he spread his hands. "Well then Sergeant, what is it?" he said his smile leaving his face.

"Your nephew Peter Wright, was found dead yesterday morning," George said looking at him.

Mr Morrison stared back at George, he picked up his whisky glass and drank the remainder in one swallow, he got up went behind his bar, and helped himself to a double before returning. "I can not get my head around it, what do you mean found dead?" he asked.

"He was late at the sorting office yesterday morning, a chap was sent to find out the reason, and found your nephew dead I am afraid," George explained. "Did you not miss him yesterday morning delivering the post?"

Mr Morrison hesitated trying to find the words. "No, not really, I know on rare occasions he is put on other rounds, and he has a day off now and then, he works six days a week you know, I was expecting him to call in today of course, but he never came, but I felt no need to worry, what was it an heart attack, I never knew he had a bad heart?"

"He did not as far as I know, I am afraid your nephew was murdered," George informed him.

"God," Mr Morrison replied taking up his whisky glass and swallowing the lot.

"We are informing you Mr Morrison, because as far as we know you are his only remaining relative."

"I suppose I am," Mr Morrison remarked. "Of course I will take care of everything, but who could want to harm Peter?"

"We have that to find out," George continued. "We know he was well on Wednesday night, Inspector Hardie was at his house talking to him about finding Mr Hogan's relatives."

"Could it have been suicide?" Mr Morrison asked.

"Only if he was able to strangle himself," George replied. "He did have a friend with him when Inspector Hardie called, a man named Reggie Shepherd, do you know him?"

"Do you suspect him?" Mr Morrison asked without answering the question.

"Possible, he as far as we know was the last person to see your nephew alive," George answered. "Do you know this Mr Shepherd?" George asked again.

"Shepherd is a common name sergeant, I probably know many," Mr Morrison replied.

"This man comes from Crewkerne, the same place you came from, I understand it is just a small village."

"Oh yes I know who you are talking about, it has to be Reggie who Jessie was engaged to," Mr Morrison picked up his whisky glass finishing the lot. "Poor Peter," he muttered.

"You have not seen Mr Shepherd then?" George asked as he sipped his pint.

"No, never knew he was in Winchester, Peter and Reggie were close friends, I never saw Reggie a lot."

"I take it that Peter had no enemies that you know of?" George asked as he finished his pint.

Mr Morrison shook his head. "He never made enemies, he was a friendly type, certainly no one who would want to murder him, I cannot see a reason for it."

"Be sure we will find out who the murderer is, Mr Morrison I know I have brought you bad news, but do you think your wife could make me a sandwich?"

"My wife is not here at the moment, I will make you one, a bacon is it?" he asked as he rose. "Another pint?"

"I have never seen your wife, does she come from Somerset?" George asked as he pushed his glass forward which Mr Morrison took and went behind the bar.

He filled the pint glass, and brought it to him. "I'll make your sandwich now," he said leaving again without answering the question, this time disappearing by a side door near the counter.

George returned to the station, he could not think of any other questions to ask, but he pondered over Mr Morrison's attitude, he did seem shocked when he was told of his nephew's death, but did not see the grief that George expected.

Chris looked up as he entered the office. "Had a liquid lunch?" he asked.

"Had a couple, I asked if his wife could make me a sandwich but she was not there, I felt a bit mean when he told me he would make it himself, I had just delivered him bad news, anyway he gave me the drink and sandwich on the house."

"Was he upset?" Chris asked.

"More shocked I would say," George answered. "I did not see much grief, he did admit to knowing Mr Shepherd however, but he had no knowledge that he was in Winchester."

"Your opinion?" Chris asked.

"I don't think he knew of Mr Wright's death, I think it came as a shock to him, his reason for not missing his nephew delivering the post yesterday and this morning was plausible and acceptable."

Chris then filled George in on the three phones he had made, and by the time he had finished, it was half way through the afternoon.

Now Mr Shepherd is leaving tomorrow morning, he will leave after breakfast, but I cannot let him go, also I have no reason for keeping him, with the aid of Sergeant Bloom and Williams, I am going to have him arrested as he leaves his lodging, perhaps if I call the Sergeants in I can explain it in one go," Chris said, as speak of the devils, a knock came on the door, and both sergeants entered.

"Ha," remarked Chris with a grin. "Relax and sit any where," he offered.

Sergeant Bloom took the interview chair, while Sergeant Williams sat near George's desk not knowing what to expect.

"Now, as you both know I'm working on a murder that took place at Littleton, I do have a strong suspect, but not enough evidence against him, my trouble is he will be leaving the town tomorrow morning, I want him here."

"This is something not strictly to the book," sergeant Bloom interrupted.

Chris looked at him with a smile on his face. "Not quite, but I was hoping to get both your cooperation."

"You have mine," sergeant Bloom offered.

"Mine as well," sergeant Williams grinned. "Who is this man, is he suspect in both murders?"

"His name is Reggie Shepherd, at the moment lodging in B&B at the Queens in Upper Brook Street, the landlady told me he will leave tomorrow morning, before ten I expect, and yes I believe he is involved in both murders," Chris informed them. "Now this is what I want done, Sergeant Bloom, if you are able I want you to bring him here, take a constable with you, but do not stop him until he leaves the Queens, for then he will have his luggage with him."

"You don't know the exact time he will be leaving?" sergeant Bloom asked.

"That's the crunch I don't know, but I would say after breakfast, which is served between eight and nine."

"How will I recognise him?" sergeant Bloom asked.

"He is a six foot tall man, he looks like a guardsman, he is well built with dark hair, he might have a limp."

"I'll work something out," sergeant Bloom said.

"What do I do?" sergeant Williams asked.

"You have the hardest task Sergeant," Chris smiled. "But I'm sure you are up to it, when this man is brought in, I want him put somewhere until Sergeant House gets in," Chris said.

"I thought it was his day off?" sergeant Williams smirked looking at George.

"We are a team Sergeant," Chris said looking at sergeant Williams. "George will want to be in it, day off or not," Chris smiled looking at George who was nodding his head. "However when Sergeant House gets here, I want you to bring in Reggie Shepherd, but somehow keep his luggage which I want you to search."

"What will I be looking for?" sergeant Williams asked.

"A revolver, should you find one, replace it back where you found it, and give me one ring on the phone," Chris said.

"And if I don't find one?" sergeant Williams asked.

Chris spread his hands in front of him and shrugged. "I'll have to let him go, and perhaps I will not be able to solve the case."

"Well I will do what you ask," sergeant Williams said getting off the desk. "I'll have to get back to the desk now," he said.

"Good men," Chris remarked as they left the office.

Chapter Fourteen

Chris left the Police Station it was nearing six, darkness had descended some two hours before, Chris bought a paper from the paper boy standing in the archway, and put it in his overcoat pocket. He was passing the Butter Cross on the opposite side of the road when he caught the sight of Elizabeth approaching, he smiled as she came to him.

"You look nice and warm," Chris said as Elizabeth fussed with the collar of his overcoat, and doing up his top buttons.

"I'm just sensible darling," she answered, grabbing his arm. "You may think that the cold weather do not affect you, and perhaps it don't in your young age, but this cold weather getting into your bones can bring on rheumatism or arthritis in your old age, so darling please button yourself up."

Chris smiled to himself as they walked along the high street, Elizabeth holding onto his arm with both hands now, they walked towards the Alresford road.

"Christmas is just a couple weeks away, we'll write out the cards tonight darling," she said. "Mother will have a nice fire going, and we can sit by it after dinner, and write them, it will be cosy," Elizabeth smiled looking up at him.

"I have my list, not many though" Chris replied.

"It's best to get them done, I have bought the cards, we can write them out," Elizabeth smiled.

Elizabeth tightened her hold on Chris's arm. "You know darling," she said in all seriousness. "I shall be twenty six when I have my first child, I shall be getting old."

Chris looked down at her and smiled. "You will never be old in my eyes," he answered. "I'm pleased to know that we are having a child, If you have a son, by the time you reach fifty, he will be twenty four, he will adore you, he will take you out, and he will protect you."

"Do you really think so Chris?" Elizabeth asked a smile coming to her face. "That would be lovely."

"Everyone adores you," Chris answered. "Your parents idolise you, you're their child, and they think the world of you, in fact I don't blame them for disliking me because of my marrying you, I love you, and so do everyone."

"My parents idolise you darling," Elizabeth replied alarm in her voice. "And you wouldn't be taking me away from them would you, as for everyone else, I'm not sure they all like me, I do have my own mind and opinion you know," she said.

"Oh," Chris teased. "Do that mean I have to brace myself for onslaughts after we are married?"

"Don't tease darling," Elizabeth replied with a squeeze of his arm. "But getting back to our children, I want two," Elizabeth announced. "I want a boy and a girl," she giggled with a blush on her face.

"I hope you get your wish," Chris replied with a smile, wondering what it will be like to have his very own family. "Then you will have a son to protect you, and a daughter to go shopping with, and talk women's talk."

"Lovely idea," Elizabeth giggled, as they reached her house. "But I shall always be the one to look after you," she promised.

"I'm sure you will," Chris replied slapping playfully at her bottom as they walked up the path towards the front door.

The evening gone very well, after a fish meal that Olive had prepared, while Ron sat in his chair reading the paper that Chris had bought from the newsboy, Olive made herself comfortable on the sofa, knitting, while Elizabeth and Chris sat at the table writing Christmas cards, the flaps of each envelope was tucked inside rather than seal, saving half of the stamp cost.

Chapter Fifteen

Chris was in the office early on the Saturday morning. Chris looked up from the files that he was studying as a knock came on his door, Sergeant Bloom poked his head in. "Mr Shepherd is in the waiting room," he said. "I'm afraid he is not very happy."

Chris looked at his pocket watch. "Is it that time already," he said seeing that it was almost ten. "Did he have any luggage?" he asked.

"Yes a case," replied sergeant Bloom.

"Well you know what to do, keep him happy until Sergeant House gets in, before bringing him in," Chris remarked.

Sergeant Bloom retreated with a smile on his face, Chris returned to his files, hoping the George would not be too late.

It was a little after ten that George entered the office, and hung his overcoat.

"It's cold out there," he said going to his desk.

Chris smiled. "Now George I have Mr Shepherd in the waiting room, I was waiting for you before I question him, I couldn't let him go back without a few more questions," he said hurriedly as a knock came on the door.

Sergeant Bloom ushered Mr Shepherd in to the room.

"Mr Shepherd," Chris greeted him standing up. "Please forgive me for delaying your departure."

"I should damn well think so," Reggie exploded as he approached the desk. "I will now miss my connection at Yeovil junction, it means a long walk."

"It could not be helped Mr Shepherd," Chris replied as he re-seated himself.

"I need to ask you a few more questions not only about Mr Hogan, but also Mr Wright, please take a seat," he said indicating the interview chair.

"I don't know why?" Reggie again exploded as he sat. "I have nothing to do with his death, I am only here on a visit."

"You are in Winchester to see Mr Wright?" Chris asked.

"That is right, you saw me in his house Wednesday night, why would you want to ask me about Peter?" Reggie asked fidgeting in his chair.

"Mr Wright was found dead early Thursday morning Mr Shepherd, perhaps you can now understand why I had to detain you from catching your train," Chris informed him.

Reggie just stared. "I don't believe it, there must be a mistake."

"No mistake Mr Shepherd, we have informed his uncle," Chris replied.

Reggie shifted in his seat, and shook his head. "But why, whatever was the reason?" he asked. "Was he shot?"

"No he was killed by strangulation," Chris replied.

"I left him on Wednesday evening, not long after you left Inspector, he was going to retire," Reggie spoke fidgeting in his chair. "But why pull me in, you don't really believe that I had anything to do with his death, we were good friends."

"The fact that you were engaged to Miss Jessie Wright and you were visiting her brother, and you were in the area at the time of the murder of Mr Hogan, cannot be over-looked," Chris replied.

"You have no legal right," Reggie stormed. "You knew I was going home, I told you, having this copper approach me in the street was most embarrassing."

"You are right, you did tell me, but that was before I spoke to the editor of the Globe your local newspaper, I now need to ask you some questions Mr Shepherd," Chris said. "Please Mr Shepherd reply honestly, you can be sure I will find out the truth sooner or later," Chris spoke with the voice of authority. "Did you know Mr Hogan?"

Reggie hesitated for a moment. "I have already told you I did not," he replied angrily.

"I know what you told me, but I am asking you again, did you know Mr Hogan?" Chris asked, his voice was calm but authoritative.

"No I did not," Reggie replied. "And that's the last time I'm saying it."

"Would you like a solicitor with you Mr Shepherd, I have one outside if you wish?" Chris asked.

"Why the hell would I need a solicitor for?" Reggie stormed. "I'm not here under arrest, just get your questions over and I'll be on my way, but believe me I intend to complain."

"It's your decision whether you have a solicitor Mr Shepherd, you have been asked," Chris answered. "Now the Globe newspaper won their case against libel on a state-ment from a man who stated that Miss Jessie Wright did have other lovers, were you the man who wrote that statement Mr Shepherd?" Chris asked.

Reggie sat and stared at Chris with disbelief on his face. "You must have a very low opinion on me," he shouted in anger. "What sort of man would do that the girl he was engaged to?"

"I'm afraid I cannot afford opinions Mr Shepherd," Chris replied a little uneasy.

One ring of the phone came but Chris did not lift the receiver.

"Well the answer to your question is no, and the question was insulting," Reggie replied. "Now that you have had your fun, can I go?" his eyes looking towards the phone, which did not ring again.

Chris folded his arms, and leaning forward on his desk. "Do you have any luggage Mr Shepherd?" he asked.

"Yes a case, your coppers have it outside," he answered.

Chris reached for the receiver and asked for Mr Shepherd's luggage to be brought in.

"What do you want with my luggage?" Reggie shouted looking uneasy.

"Just checking every detail Mr Shepherd," Chris answered. "You won't mind me looking through it, will you?"

"I certainly will," Reggie again stormed in anger. "What can my luggage tell you?" he shouted, waving his hands around.

"I am looking for a revolver Mr Shepherd," Chris answered.

"But you can't do that," Reggie said as the case was brought in and placed on the desk in front of Chris. "You have no right," he shouted.

"I assure you I do Mr Shepherd, I am conducting a murder investigation, but I am sure with the answers you have given me, you have no need to worry."

Chris tried to open the case. "The case is locked Mr Shepherd," Chris said looking at him.

"Give it here," Reggie said angrily.

All fight gone out of him as he took a key string attached to his trousers, he grabbed the case and he turned the key in the lock towards him, and unlocked it, he lifted the lid, and fumbling with his hand beneath his clothes, pulled out a revolver.

"This is my revolver, I did not kill Mr Hogan with it," he said handing it to Chris.

Chris took the revolver, he was not worried about the fingerprints. "Well Mr Shepherd," Chris remarked. "This puts a different picture on things, I am afraid I am unable to let you go now, I am charging you with suspicion of killing Mr Hogan, anything you might say will be taken down and held against you and used in the court of law."

"You are a fool," Reggie shouted as George stood up crossing to Reggie taking him by the arm. "You will be sorry for this," Reggie shouted, throwing his hands in the air.

Chris looked at George after he had come back into the office. "Well what do you think?" he asked.

"Well it looks as though you have solved this case in less than a week, without a clue to go on," George replied. "It looks certain with this revolver."

"I'm not happy though," Chris replied. "I had to charge with suspicion, just to hold him."

"What problem do you have Chris?" George asked. "After all I bet that's the revolver that killed Mr Hogan, it would be a hell of a coincidence if it turned out not to be."

"I'm sure you're right George, but on Tuesday I shall know the truth, I want the Witcher brothers, and Mr Morrison all in this office with Mr Shepherd on Tuesday morning at ten, that will give them time to get a solicitor should they want one."

"You have something in mind, do you suspect the Witcher brothers?" George asked.

"An idea, not quite formed yet but will be by Tuesday, now George, how do we find out about this revolver being the one, it's no good worrying about fingerprints, we will only find Mr Shepherd's on it," Chris said.

"I'm thinking that the Armoury Sergeant at the Barracks would be the best bet Chris," George told him.

Chris smiled and he nodded his head with an agreement.

"Well I go up there now, I have my motorbike outside, I'll take the revolver and the bullet that killed Mr Hogan," George stood up. "How many bullets are there in the magazine?" George asked.

"Three bullets," Chris said handing the gun, and the bullet wrapped up in brown envelope.

"What about if it's needed to be fired?" George asked.

"Anything that give us an answer," Chris replied.

George asked Sergeant Williams to get him the Winchester Barracks. A few minutes later the phone rang, and George lifted the receiver.

"Winchester Barracks," the voice answered.

"I would like to speak to the Adjutant," George asked.

"I am afraid he is not in the Barracks at the moment," came the reply.

George pondered for a moment. "What about the Armoury Sergeant?" he asked.

"I will put you through," came the reply.

After a few moments of talking, George replaced the receiver with a smile on his face. "He will see me now," George informed Chris who was watching. "I have my motorbike outside, I'll get up there now."

"Thanks George," Chris replied. "Let's hope it will clear that part up."

"Do you think Mr Shepherd also killed Mr Wright?" George asked as he was about to leave.

"It's possible of course, but I have no proof," Chris answered.

Left alone in the office, Chris reached for the phone and dialled constable King.

"Inspector Hardie here Constable," Chris spoke as he heard the voice.

"I want you to go to the White Horse for me, tell Mr Morrison that I want him in this office by ten on Tuesday morning, also the Witcher brothers. You can tell him that I will be interviewing Mr Shepherd at the same time, and should they feel the need to have a solicitor, it is within their rights to have one present although they are not under arrest."

"Right Sir," came the reply after a short pause. "I will do it straight away."

"Good man," Chris remarked.

"What about if they can't make it?" constable King asked.

"Use your authority Constable, tell them if they don't turn up they will be arrested," Chris answered smiling to himself.

"I see Sir," constable King replied. "If it happens it will my first arrest in this village," constable murmured.

"The first will come one day Constable" Chris remarked. "But in this case don't worry they will be here, if any proves awkward just point out gently that their risks of arrest."

"I will Sir," constable King replied his voice brightening up. "Anything else?"

"Not at the moment Constable, thank you, but you may have to arrange transport for hem," Chris replaced the receiver.

It was midday when George returned to the office, before discarding his overcoat he took the revolver from his pocket and the envelope with two bullets in it, and placed them before Chris. "I was lucky the sergeant was in the armoury, anyway the sergeant fired one shot, and he would swear in court that both bullets came from the same gun."

"Well that's good news even though there was not much doubt," Chris muttered as George took off his overcoat.

"The sergeant did tell me that it is an older revolver, this one he believes is a Mark 3, used mainly during the Boer War, these revolvers have been updated since to Mark 4 and 5," George added.

"Anyway George off you go it is your day off, and thanks for your help this morning, I will repay," Chris smiled.

"Nothing else I can do?" George asked. "I haven't got anything else to do."

Chris looked at him with a smile on his face. "I could treat you with a pint at the Rising Sun if you are up to it."

Chapter Sixteen

*I*t was a cold Sunday Morning, Chris walked slowly down the high street, as usual the high street was busy with people dressed in their Sunday best, going or leaving church, children going to Sunday School. Soldiers were everywhere, some wearing Khaki, with others in blue dress, which signified that they were wounded. Chris felt happy, although he still had doubts, he had jumped to the conclusion that he knew the killer, but was now not quite sure, but knew that it was one of two persons he had in his mind. He walked up Magdalene Hill, his mind still turning over the evidence he already had, he did not see that Elizabeth was waiting for him just below the Blue Ball Hill Junction.

"Are you in a trance?" Chris suddenly heard a voice that brought him to a halt looking around.

Elizabeth was standing just inside the recreation ground smiling.

"I'm sorry," Chris stuttered. "I did not see you there."

"How could you, you were looking at your feet all the time," Elizabeth said as she looked around her. "There is no one around," she smiled as she offered her lips which Chris took willingly.

"Now I am warm," Chris smiled as their lips parted.

"So am I, you take my breath away, I like your kisses," Elizabeth smiled as she took his arm. "Mother has a nice fire going, but I couldn't wait, I had to come to meet you."

"What are we doing today?" Chris asked as they turned into Alresford Road. "It's too cold to do much."

"I can think of many things we could do to keep us warm had we been married, even if we are not," she added with a giggle, squeezing his arm.

"You don't make it easy for me, with your teasing," Chris replied smiling down at her. "I am a man, I do try to control my feelings," Chris said blushing.

"I know," Elizabeth smiled clinging on to his arm. "But can you hold on until we are married, you see I look forward to my marriage and my honeymoon with you full of excitement and expectation, I go to sleep at night thinking of us on our honeymoon, if we were to do things before we are married, then all that excitement and thought of our honeymoon would be gone. You know you are the only man I shall ever give myself to."

"I do love you, and yes I want you, but I am prepared to wait, because I respect you and your parents," Chris touched her arm with his free hand.

"I know," Elizabeth smiled as they stopped at the bottom of their path.

Chris smiled back at her and allowed her to go first up the path to her house with a playful slap on the bottom.

Olive was waiting for them with the front door open. "Come along you two, it's too cold to hang around, I have a nice fire going."

Ron who was sitting in his armchair greeted him with a smile. "Winter is with us I'm afraid," he said looking at Olive. "I was thinking we could go down and have a pint."

"Chris is here to be with our daughter, not to go to the pub with you, it seems whenever you see Chris you want to go for a pint," Olive scolded.

"I was just being polite to our guest," Ron replied with a wink at Chris.

"We could all go," Elizabeth suggested. "After all it's not far to walk."

Olive looked at her daughter. "You have a lot of your father in you, you don't get it from my side of the family, still I do have to cook dinner, why don't you three go, that's if you want to?" Olive advised.

It was gone twelve when Chris, Elizabeth and Ron entered the Rising Sun, being Sunday dinner time, there were already quite a few men in the bar, some sitting around the roaring log fire smoking their clay pipes, some playing darts and skittles board game, Chris glanced to where he usually sat, and was pleased to see that it was empty.

"You and Elizabeth sit there by the window," Chris said to Ron. "I will get the drinks, a whisky for you Ron?" he asked.

Ron smiled. "Suits me fine," he answered.

Chris looked at Elizabeth who was watching him. "Just gin and tonic please," she said before she was asked.

Chris faced the smiling Alfie, who already had the whisky poured. "Yours is a bitter I take it?" Alfie said having already half filled the glass.

"That will be fine," Chris replied. "And I will have a gin and tonic for Elizabeth."

"Nice to see you Miss Oborne, you look well," Alfie said as he poured her drink.

Chris put a shilling on the counter, and pocketed the change that Alfie gave him.

"That is because she is happy being with me," Chris boasted.

"I am sure it is," Alfie replied accepting his boast.

The hour and a half was enjoyable, and it was almost two pm when Olive with the front door open greeted them. "Come along Elizabeth, Chris, get your coat off, the dinner is ready."

She looked at her husband who was last to enter. "I hope you have behaved yourself," she said as Ron kissed her on the cheek.

"I have my sweet," Ron replied taking a bottle of stout out of his pocket and giving it to her. "I never forgot you," he smiled.

After a dinner of Roast Beef and Yorkshire pudding, Ron and Chris retired to their armchairs, while Olive and Elizabeth cleared the table and washed up.

"I should have bought Olive that stout," Chris remarked to Ron as he took out his pipe, filled it and lit it.

Ron smiled. "You will learn about women soon enough Chris, that small inexpensive bottle of stout meant a lot to Olive, because it showed her that I was thinking of her. Women are strange in that way, they really appreciate it when you bring them a bunch of flowers or a box of chocolates, men are not like that, I mean when have you heard of a woman bring her husband a bunch of flowers," Ron shifted in his chair. "Women like receiving, and we men like to give."

"I must remember that Ron," Chris replied. "The trouble with me is that I have so much on my mind regarding my work, that I forget everything else."

"Well don't forget the wife's birthday or anniversary, if you do prepare yourself for trouble, we men do have one problem, we do seem to forget the dates important to women, they do not."

"I will have to keep a diary," Chris replied blowing out smoke. "One thing women give us is children," Chris remarked.

Ron thought for a while. "Give us in one sense of the word Chris, when you are having words they will often say that they ruined their lives by giving us children, but it is only words not meant. Olive gave me Elizabeth so she says, but it had to be with my help, if we had separated, Elizabeth would not become my child but hers, she would fight like a tiger to keep her, my father was a tall well built sixteen stone man, while my mother was a slim nine stone woman, quite a difference one might say, but if I was being bullied, it was my mother's shirts I clung to, not my father, the female of any species are the most fierce."

Their conversation ended as Olive and Elizabeth entered the room, Ron and Olive relaxed in front of the fire, while Elizabeth and Chris relaxed on the sofa, the afternoon passed quickly into evening, and after saying goodnight to Ron and Olive, Chris accepted Elizabeth's lips at the front door before making his way to his lodgings.

Chapter Seventeen

hris left his lodgings in good time to see Elizabeth, walking down from the Westgate, Chris thought he would see Mr Dawse the manager of Barclay Bank again in the bank as he was passing, but first he would see Elizabeth.

"Are you waiting for me darling," Chris saw a smiling Elizabeth looking at him.

"I was," replied Chris getting his kiss on the cheek. "I have to call Barclays bank opposite so I thought I would wait for you first."

"I am so glad you did darling, I enjoyed yesterday, and missed you after you were gone and I went to bed," Elizabeth giggled.

"Behave yourself, I have to go into the bank in a moment, teasing this time of morning is no good," Chris scolded.

"Sorry darling," Elizabeth replied meekly with a smile on her face. "It will be different when we are married," she kissed him quickly on the cheek. "I must go in now darling, will I see you tonight?" she asked.

"I will certainly try, but you understand," Chris answered.

Elizabeth did not replied but with a smile she quickly kissed him again then walked into her bank.

Chris was shown straight into the manager's office. Mr Dawse offered his hand in a welcome. "Unexpected, but always welcome Inspector," Mr Dawse said offering Chris a chair as he seated himself. "About Mr Hogan is it?"

Chris gave him a polite smile and nod. "I'm afraid so Mr Dawse, you have helped us greatly in the past."

"Well I have of course spoken of your case to the head office again Inspector," Mr Dawse smiled at the compliment. "It's our legal department opinion that Mr Len Hogan's estate will go Mrs Wright's next of kin."

"That would have been her son, but as I have already informed you, Mr Peter Wright is dead," Chris added.

"Tricky, very tricky," Mr Dawse replied. "Anyway Inspector, how can I be at service to you this time?"

"You told me last time that you had all the documents in the vault belong to Mr Hogan, at that time I was not really interested in his property, but I have been wondering since if he had left a letter with his deed?"

"You might be right Inspector, I don't know quite what's in the envelope, it is a large one, our instruction was to give it with the Will," Mr Dawse smiled. "Head office has told me to give you all the help possible, apart from allowing originals out of the bank, of course I can give you copies."

"I can assure you that we appreciate your cooperation Mr Dawse, a look at that envelope might turn out to be helpful," Chris answered.

Mr Dawse smiled as he stood. "It will take me a couple minutes Inspector, please feel free to smoke," he added as he left the office.

Chris took out his pipe, and sucked at it unlit.

"Well here it is Inspector," Mr Dawse said entering the office and returning behind his desk. "It's a rather large envelope, I'll open it for you."

Chris watched as Mr Dawse opened the envelope, and tipped the contents on the desk in front of Chris. "There, have a look Inspector," he said.

Chris leaned forward, there were three smaller envelopes in the large envelope, and Chris picked up each one in turn. The first envelope was addressed simply with the words. "Deed to Fir Cottage, Littleton." Chris was not really interested, and placed the envelope to one side, the second envelope was addressed to Mrs Wright, at their Yeovil address, he was interested, but took the third envelope to see who that was addressed to, it was his funeral wishes.

"He seem to be a man with an orderly mind," Chris remarked looking at the three envelopes on the desk in front of him. "However it would be interesting to see what he had written to Mrs Wright?"

"I am told to cooperate with you Inspector," Mr Dawse replied. "It's rather tricky but as Mrs Wright is deceased, and it is addressed to her personally, and as it's a murder investigation, no harm can come of it."

"Thank you Mr Dawse," Chris replied. "If you would allow."

Mr Dawse carefully opened the letter and passed it to Chris.

Dear Mrs Wright,

Should you read this letter, you have been read my Will, and in case you are wondering about it, not perhaps knowing who I am, I give a short explanation.

After your daughter won her case against Mr George Cole the wealthy farmer in Yeovil, I managed to get an interview with him. I found him full of revenge, instead of getting the story I intended about his feelings. He employed me to get anything I could on your daughter that would show the public that he had suffered a miscarriage of justice. As a top reporter, I would in normal circumstances ignore his wishes, but I regret to tell you that the sum of money he offered, any ethics I had went out of the window.

Put it down to my experience as a reporter, I soon found a person who was able, at a price to relate stories of your daughter to me. These stories had to be livened up, which was done by just adding a few chosen words here and there, which would make the reader feel that she was indeed a bit of a hussy.

Then came the unexpected, you sued the paper for libel, my orders then were to get a written letter from this person, which would corroborate the stories I had sent to the paper. This was only managed by a large sum of money being offered.

You must remember Mrs Wright, Mr Cole was extremely wealthy man, owned many hundreds of acres farm land around Yeovil, he was Lord of the Manor, and a magistrate, and had powerful friends, no doubt a few strings were pulled. The letter was not presented in court, but was read by the judge in his chamber, the writer did not testify in open court, and the Globe newspaper won their case against libel on a statement from a man who stated that Miss Jessie Wright did have other lovers.

No words can tell you of my feelings when I heard that your daughter had committed suicide Mrs Wright, and since that day, remorse have weighed heavily on me daily, knowing that I played a part in her suicide, my only excuse being that at least I was a stranger to your family.

I have left you my entire estate, please think of it as my apology, I hope it will allow you to live the rest of your life in comfort.

Len Hogan

Chris read the letter, then passed it to Mr Dawse. "He seems he genuinely regretted his actions, it's a shame that Mrs Wright could not have read it, it might have eased her grief."

"You would like a copy Inspector?" Mr Dawse asked.

"Appreciate it," Chris replied as Mr Dawse got up.

"I'll get Mr Larkins to run one off for you," he said excusing himself from the office.

Chris entered the Police Station, and was greeted by Sergeant Williams.

"This cold weather don't seem to ease up," Chris remarked making for his desk. "I saw the manager of the Barclay Bank again," Chris said. "Mr Hogan had left some documents in the vault, one was the deed of the cottage at Littleton, one his funeral wishes, and this third letter to Mrs Wright," he said passing the copy to George.

"You have been busy," George replied as he started to read.

"It's a letter from a man who is truly remorseful for his actions," George said passing the letter back to Chris. "I wonder if Mrs Wright would have accepted the money had she been alive?"

"No way of knowing that George," Chris replied. "It will be interesting to know who will get his money and his cottage."

"What do you think he meant, saying he was at least a stranger?" George asked.

"My opinion is that he was trying to say that the other person was connected in someway to the family, that is obvious with this other person refusing to testify in open court," Chris replied.

"I guess you're right Chris," George muttered.

"I will have the Mr Hogan case to wrap up tomorrow, at least I hope I can," Chris smiled.

"So you know the name of the murderer?" George asked.

Chris smiled. "I rather wait until tomorrow before I tell you, I want to put things together in my mind overnight."

"You are ready with your story then?" George asked with a grin, knowing that Chris would already know who the murderer was.

Chris got up and crossed to the stand, taking his overcoat which he started to put on.

"Where you off to now?" George enquired.

"I'm going to have a walk around town, get my head cleared," Chris replied as he left the office.

Chris was passing the reception desk on his way out. "Inspector," he heard the desk sergeant say. "A young man is waiting to see you, he asked for you personally."

Chris looked around and saw a young man rise from his chair. "I am Tony Allen," he smiled. "My boss Mr Edwards of the Yeovil Globe told me to contact you."

Chris extended his hand. "I remember," he said. "But I'm afraid you are a day early."

"No problem Sir," replied the reporter. "I'll spend the night here on expenses," he replied with a smile.

"Have you arranged lodging?" Chris asked.

"I've just arrived," the reporter answered.

"Well try the Rising Sun, use my name, come to the door, I'll point you in the right direction," Chris said.

"Carry straight on," Chris said pointing the way, as they stepped outside the police station. "It's not far, over the bridge, cross the junction, and carry on for about fifty yards and you'll come to it."

"Thank you Sir," replied the reporter respectfully. "When would be the best time to call back?" he asked.

"Leave it until tomorrow afternoon," Chris replied. "By then I should have a statement for you, how is Mr Edwards?"

"As far as editors go, he's OK," the reporter answered taking a large envelope from his overcoat pocket.

"He asked me to make sure you got this," he said passing over the envelope. "As far as I know it's full of bits and pieces on what the paper know about the case in question."

"Really," Chris replied taking the envelope. "It could be useful."

The reporter smiled, and offered his hand. "Well I get my lodging fixed before it's too late," he said.

Chapter Eighteen

*C*hris entered his office early on the Tuesday morning and found George already there. Chris had deliberately missed Elizabeth on the night before, he had to think, and could not do that with Elizabeth close to him. He went to his lodgings, and spent the night there going through the envelope given to him by the reporter from the Yeovil Globe.

"Morning George," Chris greeted him as he discarded his top clothing. "Still brisk outside," he remarked crossing to his desk rubbing his hands as he did so.

"It's only what we can expect this time of year," George answered.

"I shall be playing on the death of Mr Hogan today, I hope I can solve it, I think I know the killer, it's whether or not I can get him to confess, what about the chairs George?" Chris asked.

"Sergeant Dawkins have it all arranged," George answered. "The shorthand typist will be here at nine thirty."

Silence remained for the next hour while both detectives studied their notes, until the door opened and chairs was brought in by sergeant Dawkins.

Chris looked up. "Place two here by the interview chair, and three behind, just in case they bring their solicitors, have one by George for the shorthand typist," Chris suggested. "When they are all here, bring them all in."

"And Mr Shepherd who is still in the cells has he had his breakfast?" Chris asked.

Sergeant Dawkins smiled. "He likes his food, his appetite is not affected being in the cells," he remarked.

"Really," replied Chris with a smile. "Perhaps he has nothing to worry about."

"Well certainly would be," sergeant Dawkins murmured leaving the room.

"You're not sure about him are you Chris?" George said after sergeant Dawkins gone.

"If he didn't do it he must have lent the gun to someone," Chris replied. "It will be up to him, if he didn't do it he has to give us a name, otherwise he will be charged."

The shorthand typist entered the office, a slim middle age woman, neatly dressed, carrying a notebook and two or three pencils. "I'm Mrs Saunders," she introduced herself. "I am here to take shorthand."

Chris looked at her and smiled. "I am Detective Inspector Hardie, and Detective Sergeant House," Chris said pointing George. "With whom you will sit, I shall be interviewing several people in a few moments, I want you to take down every word each of them say, can you do that?"

"I have been a shorthand typist for over twenty years Inspector," Mrs Saunders replied. "It will be no hardship, as long as it's not a race meeting, usual speed of talking is no bother."

"I will slow it down should it become a race meeting Mrs Saunders," Chris replied with a smile. "After the interview, I shall want what each person said typed up, is that OK?"

"Perfectly alright Inspector," Mrs Saunders replied moving towards George. "Is this where I sit?" she asked.

A knock came on the door, sergeant Dawkins entered.

"Mr Bill Witcher and his brother Tom, Mr Morrison and his solicitor Mr Double," he said respectfully.

Chris rose from his chair. "Thank you all for coming," he said. "Please take one of these chairs Mr Double, it's good to make your acquaintance, I don't think we have met before, please take one of the back chairs, I have Mr Shepherd coming in a moment."

Sergeant Dawkins entered holding Mr Shepherd by the arm. "Thank you Sergeant," Chris said. "Mr Shepherd will you please sit by your friends."

"I thought you were back home, I had heard you were in Winchester," Mr Morrison said as Reggie sat down by him.

"Never got as far as the station, then I was arrested," Reggie replied with a little sarcasm in his voice.

"Whatever for?" Mr Morrison asked.

Chris ignored the small talk. "Who do you represent Mr Double?" Chris asked before Reggie could reply.

"Mr Morrison has engaged me to represent himself," Mr Double replied.

"You can also represent Mr Shepherd while you are here," Mr Morrison said looking at him. "I had no idea Reggie was here, one would have thought, someone would have been informed, what sort of police force have we got."

"Mr Morrison," Chris interrupted. "I am sure Mr Shepherd will tell you that he was offered a solicitor, he also did not want anyone informed."

"Is that right Reggie?" Mr Morrison asked.

Reggie shrugged his shoulders. "I didn't want any fuss."

"Now that is all cleared up, perhaps we can get on," Chris said feeling the need to gain control of the interview.

"Now, Mr Morrison, Mr Shepherd, you are both here, so that we can clear up the murder of Mr Len Hogan," Chris waited a moment for comment but none came, all those were just staring at him.

"Now Mr Morrison, you had the motive, and the opportunity, did you kill Mr Hogan?" Chris asked.

"Of course I didn't," Mr Morrison replied in a loud voice.

"Mr Shepherd have already denied the murder," Chris continued. "Only he had the motive and the opportunity, and the means," Chris remarked. "That is why he was arrested."

"I don't get this," Mr Morrison said shifting in his chair. "All this motive and opportunity, what does it mean?" he asked.

Chris leaned on his desk, and played with his hands in front of him. "I won't ask you each again if you killed Mr Hogan, Mr Double will be sure to tell me that you have answered the questions, so I will tell you a story," Chris looked toward George, and gave a small smile.

"Almost seven years ago, Miss Jessie Wright, Mr Peter Wright's sister," he began looking at Mr Shepherd. "Was engaged to be married to Mr Shepherd here, Mr Shepherd at that time was in the army, his home leave was few and far between, and unfortunately during these long absences, Miss Jessie Wright, met a wealthy farmer Mr George Cole, she fell in love with him, and after breaking her engagement to Mr Shepherd, got engaged to Mr Cole. It seems Mr Cole promised marriage to Miss Wright just to get her into bed, after which he withdrew his proposal of marriage," Chris looked around the room, everyone was taking an interest.

"Mr Cole was a very wealthy man, he owned hundreds of acres land, he was also Lord of the Manor and a magistrate. He not only knew people with power and influence, he was also a powerful person himself in and around Yeovil.

So one can imagine the shock he must have had when Miss Wright took him to court for breach of promise to marry. Mr Cole was a freemason, and so was the Judge in the case who was also a freemason, it must have been a bitter blow to him to have to find against one of his own brothers, but the case against Mr Cole was proven, Miss Wright's reputation could not be faulted, Miss Wright was awarded the sum of two thousand pounds, a lot of money, but to Mr Cole pocket change."

"We know all this Inspector," interrupted Reggie. "Can't you get straight to the point," he shouted.

"I could if you would all tell me the truth," Chris answered.

"Why don't you believe us?" Reggie asked.

"I believe everything the people tell me, until facts prove them to be lies," Chris replied.

Chris looked around the room for any other interruptions, but none came.

"After the case," Chris continued his story. "Mr Hogan who as we all know was a top reporter, he managed to get an interview with Mr Cole, a follow up story would certainly have been in the public interest. But instead of getting a follow up story, he was given an assignment by Mr Cole, who I believe paid him a vast sum of money, he was to find out stories about Miss Wright that would make the public believe that Mr Cole's case had been a miscarriage of Justice."

Chris took a sip of water before carrying on.

"Miss Wright and her family felt so much anger over the stories appeared in the local newspaper about her and alleged her carrying on with other men, that they decided to sue the paper for Libel, with the money Miss Wright had got from her case against Mr Cole. Miss Wright stood no chance against the paper, Mr Hogan found a person who was able to provide stories about her, at a price, these stories were not true, only mislead people into believing that Miss Wright was just another gold digger and a loose woman, this person who provided the stories refused to testify in open court, but only agreed to see the Judge in his chamber and gave a signed statement to the Judge as his evidence, so the person could not be cross examined. The paper won the case, on the ground of freedom of speech, and that the stories they printed was true and in the public interest."

"If this statement was not offered as an evidence in open court, how do you know about it?" Mr Morrison interrupted. "You seem to know a lot more about the case than anyone else."

"It's my job," Chris replied. "I dig and ask questions."

"I still don't know how you know about a statement that was not admitted in open court," Mr Morrison responded.

Chris looked at Mr Morrison fully in the face. "You seem worried about this statement Mr Morrison, what the statement said is not a problem to me, but who wrote it is."

"Well as you are unable to find out, why bring it up?" Mr Morrison asked.

"How do you know that I am unable to find out who wrote it?" Chris asked.

"Well," Mr Morrison hesitated, thinking it would be best if he did not argue over the letter. "I was at the court, the statement was not read, only the Judge read the statement and he would have not mentioned who wrote it."

"I agree with what you say," Mr Morrison.

"Let me put you out of your misery Mr Morrison," Chris said. "The Yeovil Globe knew about the statement, but did not know who had written it, my own investigation led me to the bank where Mr Hogan kept his Will and other papers, amongst which was a letter to Mrs Grace Wright, Peter Wright's mother, as she was deceased, and this was a murder investigation, with the approval of the bank I read the letter, I'm sorry Mr Morrison, I now know all about the letter, Mr Hogan felt remorseful after Miss Jessie Wright's death, and in his letter to Jessie's mother explained everything, I have a copy here," Chris said indicating a few documents on his desk.

Mr Morrison looked at Chris with a straight face before speaking. "So you know I provided the stories, to the dictation of Mr Hogan?" he said.

"Mr Hogan mentioned in his letter how he had altered the stories, but he remained silent as to who supplied them, but my guess was that it was you," Chris replied.

"That's trickery," Mr Morrison stood up shouting. "You tricked me."

"I don't see how," Chris replied. "It was you admitted that you were the one who provided the stories."

Mr Morrison sat down trying not to look at Reggie who was staring at him with wide eyes. "That don't make me a murderer," he said meekly.

"It might pay you to look at your solicitor, before you say anything Mr Morison," Chris advised. "Anyway let's continue with my story, after losing her libel case against the Globe paper, sadly Miss Wright committed suicide. Mr Morrison moved to Littleton, where he was able with the money he received from Mr Hogan to become a landlord of the White Horse. Later Mrs Wright moved to Winchester with her son Peter, and bought a house in Clifton Terrace, perhaps with the money left over from breach of promise case that Jessie had Willed to her mother. Mr Hogan was so full of guilt over Miss Jessie Wright's suicide that he almost gave up being a reporter. He was a wealthy man now large sum of money he received from the Lord of the Manor, he bought himself a little cottage at Littleton, I am quite sure he did not know that his partner in crime Mr Morrison was the village landlord. When Mr Hogan walked into the pub for the first time, it must have been a big shock to Mr Morrison."

No one didn't seem to want to interrupt, Chris looked at George, who was all ears, he winked as Chris continued.

"All these moves of course took place at least five years ago, and one would wonder if Mr Hogan was going to be killed why wait this length of time. But there was a time which must have been very worrying for Mr Morrison, as Mr Hogan became known as the story teller during his visits to the pub, he would often get the attention of customers by telling them of the cases he had reported in the past. I am of the opinion that Mr Hogan never spoke about the case they were both involved with, he was well liked in the village as he kept people amused with his story telling."

"Well don't try to pin Mr Hogan's murder on me," Mr Morrison interrupted.

"He will not do that, I have already been charged," Reggie replied with a grin.

"Only on suspicion Mr Shepherd, you did have the murder weapon, and if you didn't do it, all you have to do is to tell me who could have got hold of your gun."

Reggie decided to make no comment, seeing Mr Double shake his head at him.

"Now I come to the final chapter," Chris continued. "You may think I am contradicting myself."

"Oh here we go more trickery," Mr Morrison exploded. "Never a straightforward explanation."

"Mr Morrison, I was going to tell you about the motive for this crime," Chris replied a little anger in his voice. "I'm sure the true motive of Mr Hogan's murder was Mr Hogan's Will."

"So now we have a Will, which no one knows about apart from you," Reggie spoke for the second time.

"Mr Hogan left his entire estate to Mrs Grace Wright," Chris continued without answering Reggie. "I know because I have a copy here," he said turning his head to the documents on his desk. "Mrs Grace Wright had she lived would've been a very wealthy woman, Mr Hogan's own word was that she could live in comfort for two life times with what he had left her."

"Well that should let me out, I am not a member of the family, therefore not a relative," Reggie grinned.

"That will be up to others to decide, but in this case I will agree with you," Chris answered. "Looking at it, at first Mr Hogan's death we thought was a revenge murder, it was easy to understand with the suicide of Miss Wright, but it was the time lapse that altered this thinking."

Chris felt he was getting no where, he had allowed all the suspects to ask questions during the interview, normally he would've told them, that he asked the questions which they would answer, by allowing them freedom to ask questions, he was using psychology, hoping they would slip up.

"Mr Morrison," Chris said looking at him. "Mr Hogan was known as a story teller, you however kept him sweet, you were always in fear that he would tell the story of Miss Wright which now we all know. Mr Hogan however had two devoted listeners, two brothers who most night they would stop outside the pub after closing time talking, before eventually walking towards their homes together, the devoted listeners were two brothers Tom and Bill Witcher. They would talk together outside the pub, while you were inside cleaning, once you put out the lights, they would walk together towards their homes."

"No crime in that," argued Mr Morrison.

"Of course not," Chris replied. "But you did overhear a lot of what they were talking about, and even if you did not hear the full conversation, it was easy for you the next day to get the full story from the brothers, they would tell you all for a free pint."

"I was always worried as to what he might say," Mr Morrison explained. "I was deeply ashamed of myself having betrayed my own family."

"I can understand that," Chris agreed. "But about a week before Mr Hogan was killed you heard unexpected news. Mr Hogan usually was a little tipsy when he left your pub, but this time, he had too many, because Mr Morrison you heard him talking about his Will he had left to Mrs Grace Wright, the next morning after plying the Witcher brothers with a free pint you got the whole story."

"You can't prove that," Mr Morrison muttered. "You are making this up."

"Let's see then, now Tom and Bill Witcher," Chris said looking at the brothers. "Mr Morrison always asked you what conversation took place between you both and Mr Hogan the night before did he not?"

"We don't like to offend," Bill Witcher replied nervously. "What would happen if Mr Morrison barred us, where would we go for a drink, no other pubs around there, it's unfair to ask, what do you think Tom?" he asked looking at his brother.

"It's a sin to offend," replied Tom. "How would we spend our days in a small village if we were barred?"

Chris smiled inwardly. "I'm sorry you both feel that way, but this is a murder investigation, you must answer, but you can be sure that Mr Morrison will not bar you."

"Ah, but in case if he do?" Tom asked worriedly.

"Then see the village Constable King," Chris replied.

"Well Mr Morrison knows we have to tell the truth, Tom," Bill said looking at his brother. "So we must tell, meaning no offence to Mr Morrison."

"You tell then Bill, you're better at it than I," Tom replied.

"Mr Morrison would often ask us, just as a matter of fact during the evening what story Mr Hogan had told us," Bill explained. "He would at times give us a free pint," he added.

"We took it because we don't like to offend," Tom interrupted. "We took it thinking Mr Morrison was being nice to us for being good customers, that's all."

"A couple weeks ago Mr Hogan mentioned about his Will in the pub didn't he?" Chris asked. "But made no further comment on it."

"I remember, don't you Tom?" Bill asked.

"I do remember," replied Tom.

"When you walked him home that night, did he mention anything else about his Will?" Chris asked.

"Only that it would make Mr Morrison jealous," Tom replied.

"Then the next time you were in the White Horse, the landlord questioned you and gave you a free pint?" Chris asked.

Both Tom and Bill nodded their heads looking at Mr Morrison.

Chris looked at Mr Morrison with a serious expression on his face.

"Then you phoned Mr Shepherd and told him," Chris spoke in a firm voice.

"Wrong there Inspector," Reggie spoke up. "Peter phoned me."

"Really," Chris replied.

"Yes Peter phoned me during one evening, he told me he knew a man who collects weapons from the Boer War, and he pays top price, he asked me to come to Winchester, and bring my gun, a revolver he knew that I had, that I had got from the Boer War."

"Really," Chris repeated himself.

"Yes as I said Peter phoned me and asked me to bring my revolver, naturally I hesitated, no one knew I had the gun apart from Peter. I did not want trouble with the police, but Peter persuaded me, so I came to Winchester, I gave the revolver to Peter, and booked in at the Queens, later Peter phoned me at the Queens, and told me that the man already had several of my type of revolver and did not want any more. I was at Peter's house that night you saw me to get the revolver back, during my time at his house he told me about the murder at Littleton, and told me it would be best for me to leave Winchester, I did not see any reason for this, but decided to leave at the weekend."

"Thank you Mr Shepherd, had you told this at the beginning, much of my time would not have been wasted, did you come to Winchester by train?" Chris asked.

"I did," Reggie replied.

"From where?" Chris asked.

"From Yeovil," Reggie replied.

"Then you had to change trains at Yeovil Junction?" Chris asked.

"That's right," Reggie replied. "What is all this questioning?"

Chris ignored the question and smiled. "Now you say Mr Peter Wright phoned you during an evening, ten days ago?" Chris asked.

"About ten days ago," Reggie answered.

"Did he phone you from his home?" Chris asked.

"Yes," Reggie replied. "I remember he sounded out of breath, I asked him why, and he told me he had just got indoors, it was all uphill to his house."

Chris played with his hands on the desk as he looked at Reggie. "You believe that Mr Wright murdered Mr Hogan with your gun?" Chris asked.

"Who else could have done it, you told me he was shot with my gun, and only Peter could have done it."

"When Mr Wright gave you back the revolver, did you check whether it had been fired or not?" Chris asked.

"Peter had the revolver three days, I would suppose he cleaned it," Reggie replied.

"What about the bullets Mr Shepherd, did you not check the chamber, especially after Mr Wright had told you of the murder at Littleton?" Chris asked.

"Not at that time, the revolver was neatly tied in a package, the same as I had given it to Peter, I had no reason to distrust Peter."

"When did you find out one bullet was missing?" Chris asked.

"I never knew," Reggie replied. "Not until you found the gun in my case."

Chris sat back in his chair. "I am sorry Mr Shepherd, but your story do not add up," he said.

"Inspector," butted in Mr Double. "The way I see it is that my client have given you a voluntary account of what happened, and at this point should you have any doubt as to his story, please tell your reason."

"Thank you Mr Double," Chris replied. "Please allow me to finish the story I started. Mr Morrison now knew of the Will, and his greed took over, he phoned Mr Shepherd, Mr Shepherd actually arrived two days previous in Winchester, and for this time he stopped at Littleton with Mr Morrison."

"That is not true," interrupted Mr Morrison. "You can ask my wife."

"You sent your wife away once you knew Mr Shepherd was going to arrive," Chris told him. "Your wife is at a little village near Crewkerne, called Haselbury Plucknett in Somerset staying with her sister."

"You have been busy bees," Mr Morrison replied sarcastically.

"Mr Morrison and Mr Shepherd, had both been in the Boer War together?" Chris continued. "Mr Morrison knew that he could not get his hands on the WILL while Peter was the next of kin, Peter would have to be discredited, in reality he would have to be blamed for the crime of Mr Hogan."

Chris paused, it had been a long drawn out interview, but he thought he was now getting somewhere. He looked at George, who was smiling at him.

"It was arranged that Mr Shepherd would book into a B&B for a while, until a suitable time presented itself," Chris continued. "The right time came sooner than expected, on that Sunday night Mr Morrison overheard Mr Hogan and the two brothers talking about Miss Wright and her suicide and Mr Hogan's Will, lucky for Mr Morrison, he was able to close his pub early that night because it was Sunday, he phoned Mr Shepherd at the Queens just as they were closing.

He told Mr Shepherd that if the story of Miss Wright came out it would not be beneficial, Mr Hogan had to be killed that night, and Peter who delivered the letter on Monday would be the main suspect."

"I am sorry Inspector," Mr Double spoke up. "How could my client be sure that a letter would be sent to Mr Hogan for delivery on that particular day?"

Chris smiled. "It had all been worked out, Mr Shepherd sent an envelope to him every day for a week, the envelope only contained blank pages, we found some of them, the envelope he received on the Monday morning, was sent from Yeovil Junction, it contained two blank sheets of paper."

"Surely anyone could have sent those envelopes," Mr Double replied.

"I agree but for one thing, Mr Shepherd's fingerprints was found on the blank sheets."

"Just how did you get my fingerprints to match?" Reggie shouted.

I have no doubt you used gloves while you put the blank sheets into the envelopes, but at sometime you must have touched the blank sheet without your gloves, we matched the print with the print on the your revolver," Chris informed him.

"It's a trick," Reggie shouted loudly.

Chris paused again, no one spoke, and all eyes were on him.

"Sunday night somehow Mr Shepherd got to Littleton, it must have been after midnight, he had to walk, he met up with Mr Morrison perhaps at the top of the lane leading to Mr Hogan's cottage. One of them walked very slowly and carefully down the lane, it was dark, very dark that night, but by keeping an eye on the lighted window and walking very carefully, he knew that the light from the window was in a straight line with his walking."

"A lot of rot, Peter was the only one who could've killed Mr Hogan, I did not even know where Littleton was, let alone walking there in complete darkness," Reggie shouted in anger.

"Anyway," Chris continued taking no notice of the interruption. "Mr Hogan was perhaps drowsy, and lying on the sofa, his door as everyone knew was never locked, he was shot through the head without much trouble. Some time later he was back at the main road, where they went back to the White Horse, perhaps had a whisky, before Mr Shepherd started to walk back to Winchester, arriving at the Queens about breakfast time."

"Where do you get all this stuff from," Mr Morrison asked, fidgeting in his chair. "Comic books?"

Chris continued again ignoring the interruption. "I think Mr Shepherd decided to depart from Winchester as soon as he could, when I had spoken to the Witcher brothers who told me bits and pieces about Jessie Wright what Mr Hogan had told them, but they did not tell me about the Will, perhaps because Mr Morrison you had frightened them?"

"Rot," Mr Morrison replied angrily.

"You then phoned Mr Shepherd and told him that I knew of the past, perhaps suggesting that he should contact Mr Wright, who did not know that Mr Shepherd was in Winchester."

"My client have already told you that Mr Wright phoned him," Mr Double argued.

"That Mr Double was not possible, Mr Wright has no phone in his house," Chris informed him.

"It must have been from somewhere else then," shouted Mr Shepherd.

"You told me yourself that Mr Wright said he had just got indoors," Chris reminded him.

"Perhaps I was wrong," Mr Shepherd replied.

"Had I not called on Mr Wright last Wednesday night, I might not have met Mr Shepherd, but I did, and from then on, things began go wrong with your plan. Mr Shepherd, you said you were at Mr Wright's house to collect the revolver, this is not true, Mr Wright knew nothing about you having a revolver, Mr Morrison did however."

"Not true," Mr Shepherd responded. "I told you I was collecting the revolver from him.

"It's all written down what you said Mr Shepherd," Chris continued. "You said it was neatly tied in a package, you also told me that you had not checked the revolver, when I allowed you to give me the revolver from your case at the police station, it was not in a neat package, not even wrapped in a cloth. I am sure you cleaned the gun as soon as you got back to the Queens from Littleton that Monday morning."

Mr Morrison stood up. "I'm not taking the blame," he said. "I did phone Mr Shepherd when I heard about the Will, it was all innocent, as a friend I was just giving him news, he then came up with a plan, about getting hands on the money, and I'm sorry but I went along with him, I did not shoot Mr Hogan."

Mr Shepherd looked at Mr Morrison hatred in his eyes. "You dirty conman," he shouted and spit at him.

"It was all your idea, you talked me into it, my trouble was that I was broke, the thought of getting my hands on thousands of pounds excited me, but you killed Mr Hogan, I only watched from the top of the lane."

Chris smiled inwardly. "I know who shot Mr Hogan, it was you Mr Morrison, I am sure it was you, and you will be charged with his murder."

"At least you know I did not kill Mr Hogan," Reggie commented.

"But you killed Peter Wright," Chris spoke.

"Don't be daft, how could have been me, I left Peter a short time after you had left, surely the landlady of the Queens can verify I was in my room all night," Reggie replied.

"At first I thought the murder of Mr Hogan was out of revenge, but wondered why it took so long, I eventually dismissed this idea, and concentrated on other reasons, which came to light once the Will was mentioned. I believe Mr Peter Wright was going to get framed for killing Mr Hogan. He was the one who would inherit the Will left by Mr Hogan to his mother. If Mr Wright was convicted of Mr Hogan's murder, then Mr Morrison the only living relative would get the lot," Chris commented.

"Why would I want to do harm to my sister's son?" Mr Morrison argued.

"Money Mr Morrison," Chris answered. "The same reason why you drove your sister's daughter to suicide, but I do believe you had no knowledge of your nephew's murder until you were told, you see when I met Mr Shepherd, he asked me if I suspected Mr Wright being the murderer of Mr Hogan, I replied that I did not, it was a mistake, because my words caused the death of Mr Wright, Mr Shepherd strangled Mr Wright probably before he left his house."

Reggie smiled. "I would have been daft to do that, after you had seen me with him that night."

"Perhaps that what you were hoping for me to think," Chris replied. "I thank Tom and Bill Witcher for attending,

Mr Morrison you are being charged with the murder of Mr Len Hogan, and Mr Shepherd will be charged with the murder of Mr Peter Wright."

"You will never make it stick," Reggie stormed. "You have no real proof."

Chris did not answer as George with the aid of Sergeant Bloom took the two men from the office, where they were read their rights.

With the office cleared, Chris looked at George with a weak smile.

"I thought I was going to lose that one," he remarked taking a deep breath.

"I wondered where you got all that information, I knew nothing of it," George replied.

"I didn't have time to tell you, but yesterday as I was leaving the office, there was a reporter from the Yeovil Globe, I promised to give him a statement, as Mr Hogan was one of their reporters, anyway the editor sent me down all documents he had on the case which I read last night in bed, I was able to use some of it," Chris explained.

"Did you have any idea who committed the murder before you started?" George asked.

"Only that it had to be Mr Morrison or Mr Shepherd, I never considered Mr Wright being the murderer of Mr Hogan," Chris replied. "I will say one thing however, had Mr Shepherd left Winchester on the Monday of the crime, I might never have solved the case."

"What about Mrs Morrison, we never did meet her," George remarked.

"No, and here again Mr Morrison had planned in advance, he knew Mr Shepherd would be arriving, so he sent his wife away on holiday, he didn't want her involved. When

147

I asked him about his wife that Monday, he simply said that she was in Winchester shopping, and I had to believe him," Chris answered.

"It was a good job we found the gun," George remarked.

"Yes," Chris replied. "That was a stroke of luck meeting Mr Shepherd, he could have gone back crewkerne without us knowing he had been in Winchester, and even if we had eventually found out about him, finding the gun might have been difficult, only assumptions and opinions as it was, had it not been for you finding out about Mr Wright not having a telephone, I could have believed his story about selling the gun."

"What about Mr Morrison, he was Mr Wright's uncle, I mean what sort of man was he?" George asked with a tone of disgust.

Chris smiled. "George look at his record, he had no pity when he sold stories about his niece did he so, why would he worry about his nephew, he is a man without feeling in my book, he is guilty of her suicide."

"What will happen to Mr Cole the Lord of the Manor," George asked.

"Well, when this case come to the court, Mr Cole the Lord of the Manor will be reinvestigated as to his part in the bribery," Chris replied.

"Well at least that case is over Chris," George smiled.

"Don't forget the paper work," Chris added with a smile on his face.

THE END

BOOK TWO

INSPECTOR
CHRIS HARDIE

MURDER WITH A
BROTHEL
CONNECTION

Chapter One

*D*etective Inspector Chris Hardie, leaned back in his chair, staring at his hands that was resting in his lap twisting a pencil, he was deep in thought. He heard Detective Sergeant George House. "Are you with us Chris?"

So deep in thought, it took Chris several seconds to realise that he had been spoken to, he lifted his head as he threw the pencil on his desk, and with a slight grin on his face turned to George.

"Sorry George, deep in thought, what did you say?"

George looked at him with a grin. "Just asking if you are on the planet?"

Chris pushed forward and rested his arms on his desk. "Christmas is just ten days away you know."

"Is that a problem?" George asked.

"For me it is," Chris replied. "I have to decide where I spend Christmas, I normally spend the day with my land-lords, Mr and Mrs Dobson, I have done so for the last five years, but now I have Elizabeth and her parents to consider, I don't want to hurt anyone."

"Split the day between both parties," George advised.

"Already thought of that," Chris replied. "But who do I spend Christmas dinner with, which is the main meal at Christmas."

George shrugged his shoulders. "Who's the best cook?" he asked.

"Both of them are good cooks," Chris replied. "It's a problem, but I think I'll let Elizabeth decide."

"Coward," George grinned.

"What are you doing for Christmas anyway?" Chris asked George.

"You know my friend invited me to his home in London, but then who knows, we may have a case on our hands."

"Sorry George, yes I do remember, we will work something out should there be a case, it's quiet at the moment, let's hope it keeps that way," Chris remarked.

Chris leaned forward picking up his pencil, when the telephone rang, he picked up the receiver.

"Oh Sergeant Williams," Chris spoke onto the receiver. "Good news I hope?"

A couple moments later George watched Chris replaced the receiver.

"A body has been found behind the Corn Exchange in Jewry Street," Chris informed George. "It seems that a woman has already been taken to the hospital, Bob Harvey the Police Surgeon is already there, so we better make a move," Chris said getting up and going to the hat stand to put on his overcoat and trilby.

"It's as black as the ace of spades outside," George said looking out of the window that was behind his desk. "And it's only just gone four thirty."

"It's winter," Chris replied as he buttoned his overcoat. "It will be cold up there so put your overcoat on, we might as well walk, it will only take us five minutes."

The Corn Exchange was an impressive white building, that would bring Roman to one's thoughts because of the huge stone pillars mounted on top of the steps that led to the entrance, behind the Corn Exchange there was a gents toilet and the tarmac ground held a cattle market twice a week, today was not one of those two days.

"Why do murders have to take place in the dark," George made a comment. "How the hell are we supposed to find any clues?"

"That's life George," Chris answered as a torch light beam caught them.

"This way Sir," spoke the constable holding the torch. "Mr Harvey is waiting for you behind the gents toilet."

"Lead on then constable," Chris said politely.

Approaching the scene, Chris noticed that two other constables were holding torches, with their beams playing on the body of a man, the constable leading them played his beam on the police surgeon, who was standing looking down at the body, he looked up as Chris and George came close.

"Chris, George," Bob greeted them. "Bloody dark isn't it?"

"No arguments there," George commented taking a pocket torch from his pocket and started to flash it around the area looking at the ground.

"How did you get here so fast Bob?" Chris asked.

"I was at the hospital when the call came in," Bob replied.

"Why was the hospital called first?" Chris asked curiously. "The police are usually first to be called."

"There was a young lady involved as well Chris," Bob answered. "I'm sorry I broke the rules but in this darkness I could not examine her properly, I had to have her removed to the hospital."

"I'm sure you did the right thing Bob," Chris replied. "What about the body then?" Chris asked.

"One shot with a revolver to the head, died instantly, but I will do some detective work on the body, just in case he died of other means."

"Who found the body?" Chris asked, looking towards the constables who were holding the torches.

"A chap using the toilet," one of the constables answered. "He heard what he thought was a scream, and came around to investigate, he says three men ran off, he saw the two bodies in the corner, and heard the girl moaning, so he called the hospital, then he saw me and Jack here," Chris saw his head turn towards the other constable.

"We were going off duty, he was showing us the bodies, when the police surgeon arrived, Jack here," again the constable talked looking at his mate. "Ran to a phone box and phoned the desk sergeant."

"Thank you," Chris replied. "You both did well, where is this chap who found them?"

Jack the other constable answered. "Just across the road in the De Lunn cafe," he said. "The chap was in a bit of a state, so I suggested to him to go across, I have his name and address," Jack continued. "He's a young man about twenty I would say."

"Thank you constable," Chris replied. "It was very thoughtful of you taking name and address, he could have ran off."

"Do you want me to get him over?" the constable asked.

"No, not yet," replied Chris. "I'll go over later, but you can let me have your torch, and you can go over and keep him company."

"I'll do that Sir," the constable replied as he gave Chris his torch before leaving.

Chris stooped by the body playing the torch upon it, he saw that the man was in a top coat, which was unbuttoned. Chris guessed that his age was early twenties, he pressed around where he knew pockets were normally sewn, then placed his hand inside the suit jacket feeling the inside pocket, and came away with a wallet, an open envelope fell aside, Chris played the torch on it and read the address.

"If this letter belongs to the body, then our victim is Mr Cross, number 23, Upper High Street," Chris said as he felt the presence of George at his shoulders. "Find anything?" he asked.

"Just a button," George replied. "It looks army button."

"Better bag it then," Chris advised. "Search the body, and put what you find with it."

As George stooped towards the body, Chris stood up, and taking Bob's arm walked a step away.

"Bob," Chris said. "You must have a little idea about the girl?"

"Well it is dark, and the girl was in a hell of a state, however, between us, I think she has been brutally raped, perhaps a couple of times."

"Did she take her handbag with her, no sign of it here?" Chris asked.

"I helped as she was put into the ambulance," Bob answered. "There was no handbag, perhaps it was robbery?"

"I don't think so Bob, the man's wallet is still on him," Chris replied. "You said a revolver shot, could it have been army, after all we have plenty soldiers in Winchester," Chris commented.

"Now Chris you are asking me to guess, however the time is almost straightforward, it's now five thirty pm," he said peering closely at his pocket watch. "The victim died about four pm, no more than an hour and a half ago."

"I'll have the area cordoned off for tonight, perhaps tomorrow we will find something, I know you are anxious to get to the hospital, you can take the body when George is finished, I am going to the cafe and talk to the chap who found the couple."

"Have a cup for me Chris," Bob said a grin on his face. "I'll get in touch."

Chris stooped with George. "I'm going to the cafe George," he said. "Make some arrangements for this area to be cordoned off for the night and on my way to the office tomorrow morning, I'll take another look around, come over when you have finished."

"And by the way phone the desk sergeant and get someone to the address on the envelope, tell him to send someone with a bit of sense."

Chris made his way to the cafe, and seeing the constable sitting with a young man, made his way to their table.

"I am Detective Inspector Chris Hardie," Chris said to the young man who was looking up at him. "I would like to ask just a few questions," he said pulling up a chair and seating himself.

"Constable, you may be a help to Sergeant House," he looked at the constable sitting with the young man.

"Very well Sir," the constable taking the hint, got up, nodded to the young man and left.

"Thank you for calling the hospital," Chris said to the young man. "Your quick action might have been beneficial to the young lady, I wonder would you mind relating the story to me that you have already told the constables?"

"Not at all," answered the young man.

"First can I have your name?" Chris asked taking out his notebook and pencil. "For reports you understand," Chris remarked seeing a worried look on the man's face.

"My name is John Thompson," the young man replied.

"Address?" Chris asked.

"Number,49, Middle Brook Street," came the reply.

"Are you married Sir?" Chris asked.

"No," the young man said with a smile. "I'm too young, or at least my mother thinks I am."

"What is your age Sir?" Chris asked.

"Twenty two," Mr Thompson replied.

Chris wrote the age down, then looked at him. "So you live at this address with your parents?" Chris questioned.

"Plus two soldiers billeted on us," the young man replied.

"That is the fate of most Winchester houses I'm afraid, with the thousands of soldiers in Winchester, they have to sleep somewhere," Chris commented. "Still we all have to do our bit," Chris added.

Chris put down his pencil. "Do you originate from Winchester?"

"Born here Inspector," replied the young man.

"So you're a Hampshire Hog," Chris joked with a smile.

"I understand the joke Inspector, but have never been able to understand where the name Hog came from, I know it's a pig," replied Mr Thompson.

"Can't help you this Sir," Chris replied with a grin. "If I ever find out, I'll certainly let you know, now tell me your story."

"Not really a lot to tell Inspector, I was using the gents toilet, I was busting for a wee, I thought I heard a scream, that seem to come through the wall in front of me. I tried to hurry what I was doing, then I entered the cattle market to see what was going on," the young man took a swallow, before continuing.

"My approach must have been noisy enough to frighten off whoever it was, it was quite dark, and I saw three men running away, they seem to have very funny faces, but I could not really see in the dark. The three men were lost within seconds, and I just stood there wondering, then I heard the moan, coming from the back of the toilet, I went towards the moan, and saw it was a young lady, a man was lying beside her, but a few feet away. I looked down at them, not knowing what to do, but the girl who did not speak only moan seemed to be in a bad way, so I ran to the nearest telephone box, and phoned the hospital, later after my return to the couple, I met two policemen who I notified, that's about all I'm afraid," concluded the young man.

"You did very well Sir, and thank you," Chris said. "Would you be able to recognise the persons you saw running away?"

The young man shook his head. "It was too dark, but their faces were of a bright colour, that seem to shine out in the dark."

"Strange," Chris remarked.

"I thought so," agreed the young man.

"Which telephone box did you use Sir, I mean was there one near?" Chris asked.

"In Hyde Street Inspector, there is one just pass the Brewery."

Chris who had been sitting away from but facing the door looked up as George entered.

"This is Detective Sergeant House Sir," Chris said introducing George. "George meet Mr John Thompson, who saw the crime and phoned the hospital."

"Glad to know you Sir," George replied. "You did the right thing," George said as he seated himself.

"He lives in Middle Brook Street," Chris remarked.

"Really," answered George without making the young man aware that he also lived in Middle Brook Street. "Do you work in Winchester?" he asked.

"I work for my father, he has a small shop in Upper High street," replied the young man.

"Selling what?" George asked.

"Models, medals, army buttons and such like," replied the young man.

"Sounds interesting," Chris cut in.

"Fairly," came the reply.

"Before you entered the gents toilet Sir," George questioned. "Did you hear a noise, shall we say like one of these motorcycles back firing?"

"Not that I can remember," replied the young man. "I'm sure I would have remembered that."

These men or shadows you chased, could they have been soldiers, I mean, could you tell whether they wore peak caps, soldiers wear hobnail boots, which would have made a noise running," Chris asked.

"I'm sorry Inspector, I don't think they were wearing peak caps, I remember their faces seem to shine, as for the boots, no," the young man shook his head. "I don't remember."

Chris made to get up. "Well thank you again Mr Thompson for all of your help, I will however need a statement from you, just what you have told me tonight, would you be able to call into the Police Station sometime tomorrow, and make one?"

"I will Inspector," promised the young man.

George followed Chris as he crossed the road, returning to the cattle market place, Chris did not speak. The three constables were there roping off the area, by the aid of their torches.

"The body gone then?" Chris said to the shadowy forms in the darkness.

"Yes," replied one. "Just a few moments ago."

"Jack," Chris said, and a constable a few feet from him stopped what he was doing.

"That's me Sir," he said.

"Where did you telephone the desk sergeant from?"

"From the telephone box just at the other side entrance," he replied.

"Thank you," replied Chris.

Chris turned away, followed by George. "Anything wrong?" George asked. "I used the same phone box to phone the police station."

"No, not really, just checking, I remembered the telephone box as we came here, Mr Thompson said he ran all the way down Hyde Street to phone the hospital."

Both men had now reached the other side entrance of the Corn Exchange, which was only separated from the other entrance by the width of the Corn Exchange.

"Here is the telephone box you and the constable used," Chris continued approaching the box and opening the door, then closing it before continuing their way. "It just seems strange that Mr Thompson did not know of this one, it's only ten feet or so from the Gas Lamp."

"Perhaps his mind was in panic," George argued. "His mind was not thinking correctly, and he ran to the first box that came into his mind."

"Perhaps," Chris replied as they turned into St George's Street. "Your question about the motorbike backfiring, the shot that killed the man must have been loud, someone must have heard it, not many people about and in the darkness, the noise may have been enhanced."

"Bob thought that the girl had been raped perhaps twice, how long would that take, not forgetting there was very little struggle with two men holding the girl," George remarked.

"Meaning?" Chris asked.

"Well, was the man shot straight away, or was one man holding him while the other two had their way with her," George concluded.

"Rape cannot be easy, even without a struggle, if as you say, the man might have been shot straight away, the time could be much greater between the shot and when they were interrupted, that we have allowed for," Chris answered.

Coming out of Cross Keys Passage, they crossed the Broadway almost opposite their police station.

"We will get some door knocking done tomorrow," Chris remarked opening the police station door.

The gas lighting of the police station flickered as the entrance door was opened and closed, but the warm air inside hit their faces, which made them shudder. Unbuttoning his overcoat, Chris looked at Sergeant Williams who was behind his counter.

"Cold outside is it?" he mocked, Chris ignored the remark as he approached the counter.

"Has a constable contacted the address, phoned through to you by Sergeant House?"

"Yes Inspector," sergeant Williams replied. "His remarks were that he was not up to this type of police work, it was too upsetting, he informed them that you would be calling on them."

"Thank you Sergeant, it's not an easy task, there are three constables behind the Corn Exchange still working," Chris said taking off his overcoat. "I don't know their names, but I believe a couple should be off duty, I have told them to put in overtime, I will endorse it."

"The Chief Inspector won't like that, budget you know" sergeant Williams replied with a grin.

"Thank you Sergeant Williams," Chris replied. "That is certainly nice to know, and I will keep it in mind."

The grin left Sergeant Williams face as he took the meaning, he cleared his throat. "Just joking Inspector, just joking," he murmured.

"I would also like to have Sergeant Bloom for the day tomorrow, would he be available?" Chris asked.

The sergeant picked up his clip board and looked down the list. "He's on walking duty tomorrow," sergeant Williams replied a smirky grin on his face. "But Inspector, I'll alter the list, Sergeant Bloom will be on duty tomorrow morning at seven, I'll leave instructions for him," sergeant Williams replied.

"That's what I call working together," remarked George before Chris could make a comment.

Once inside their office and had taken off their overcoats and trilby, Chris turned on the gas fire as he made his way to his desk.

"I'll get Sergeant Bloom to do the house knocking tomorrow," Chris said rubbing his hands together to get his circulation moving. "He did well on our last case."

"I agree," remarked George.

"We still have the question about the gun," Chris continued. "They probably took it with them."

"Could it be anything to do with the army?" George asked.

"Your guess is as good as mine, but to find out is your job, you will be visiting the barracks tomorrow, find out about who carries revolver could those recuperating have brought it back from France, you know the kind of questions," Chris said.

Chris saw George nod his head. "I shall go back to the cattle market first thing in the morning and have a look around," Chris raised his eyebrows and looked at George.

"Fingers crossed," George remarked getting up and crossing to Chris's desk, where he emptied the bag containing the contents of the dead man's pockets.

Chris picked up a pencil, and started to move the objects. "Not much," he remarked as he moved an handkerchief to one side. "Just a couple of keys, a few coins, a penknife and a part of a packet of woodbines, with a half empty box of matches," Chris examined the woodbine packet, and the match box, but found nothing unusual, he looked at the keys.

"Keys to his home do you think George?" Chris asked.

George shrugged his shoulders. "Front door perhaps?"

Chris then concentrated on the wallet, he did not worry about fingerprints, the crime had not been about robbery, and Chris was sure that the wallet had not been touched by the attackers. The envelope fell out as he picked the wallet up. "At least this tells us who the victim is," Chris commented as he looked inside the envelope and took out the letter.

Chris read the letter, which was no more than a note, then passed it to George.

"Looks like he was over due with a debt," George remarked returning the letter. "He must have known who it was from, there is no address above, just signed with a letter T."

"Perhaps his parents, or wife if he has one will offer us some help," Chris said.

George's face went serious.

"Trouble?" Chris asked seeing his look.

"Just thinking Chris, perhaps the woman in the case is his wife?" George questioned.

Chris fell silent, his mind testing the possibility. "You could be right George, good thinking, it never crossed my mind, I looked upon it as just a courting couple that were attacked by rapists while they were having a kiss and cuddle in privacy."

Chris stood up, he collected the items on his desk and bagged them, apart from the wallet which he put in his pocket.

"We better get around to his home and find out, at least they have been notified, so we should not be weighed down with sudden grief, I only hope the constable that saw them was tactful," Chris put the bag of items in a drawer of his desk, before moving to the hat stand.

Chapter Two

*I*t seemed darker, and was certainly colder, both men pulled the collars of their overcoats up around their heads. The high street was badly lit, little or no lighting was coming from shop windows, and the gas lamps were at such a distance from each other, that only a small area around them pieced the darkness.

"Looks like a late night for us George," Chris remarked as he kept his eyes on the beam of light in front of him that was coming from the torch held by George.

"And no overtime," George remarked grinning to himself in the darkness.

There was no traffic about, so they walked in the middle of the road, the sound of hobnail boots, and outline of peak caps, plus the swaying of small torch beam told them that there was plenty of walkers on the pavements, but mainly soldiers, they passed the Butter Cross, and Elizabeth came into Chris's mind, he often met her at this point. "I was supposed to meet Elizabeth at six," Chris remarked.

"Well you're a bit late," George replied. "It must be coming to seven now."

"I'll have to give it a miss tonight, she will understand," Chris replied.

They reached the Castle, and went through under the centre road, rather than taking the footpaths either side of the building.

"Well this is Upper High Street George," Chris said as they both stopped in the middle of the road. "All we have to do is to find number 23," he said peering into the darkness.

Piano music was coming from the dimly lit Castle public house, on the corner of Success Street, Upper High Street. "Let's try the pub side," Chris suggested moving towards the pub, with George following.

"A whisky would be warming," George muttered.

George played his torch on the terraced houses front doors as they passed each one.

"Here it is," Chris said stopping, he pulled the collar of his overcoat down, before knocking the door.

The door opened, and Chris felt the warm air inside the house, a man opened the door.

"I am Detective Inspector Hardie, and this my colleague Detective Sergeant House Sir," Chris said to the man.

"At last," replied the man. "Well you better come in."

Chris and George entered the passage and waited for the man to close the door.

"This way," the man said opening a door to the right of the passage.

It was a well furnished front room, which was lit by three gas lamps on separate walls. Chris looked at the man, who was at least six foot tall, wearing slippers and trousers, and a pullover over his shirt. His hair was dark, mingle with grey, Chris thought him about forty years old. The man sat on a sofa next to a small woman, that Chris took as his wife, she was also wearing slippers and a long dark frock, her hair was pressed back into a bun. She was holding a handkerchief to her face that was tearstained, and her eyes were red. Chris thought she might be around the same age of her husband. The man looking at them waved his hand. "Please take a seat," he offered.

George found himself an armchair, but Chris remained standing. "Before I give details, am I speaking to Mr and Mrs Cross?" Chris asked.

"I'm Tony and this is my wife Elsa," replied the man who was holding his wife's hand.

"Thank you Sir," Chris replied taking the wallet from his pocket. "Do you recognise this wallet?" Chris asked handing the wallet to the man.

Letting go of his wife's hand, Tony took the wallet, he looked at it then opened it, a cry came from Elsa who had been watching. "Martin received that letter yesterday," Elsa sobbed.

"Yes it is Martin's wallet," confirmed Tony.

"Do you have a photo of him?" George asked.

Tony got up from the sofa, and went to the sideboard, he took a framed photo from it and gave it to George. "That's Martin, taken, let's see about six months ago wasn't it Elsa?" Tony asked looking at his wife, who nodded her eyes full of tears.

George took the photograph and studied it, then eventually handed it back to Tony, then nodded to Chris who had been watching.

"What's happened to my son?" Elsa cried as her husband once again sat by her side. "We know nothing only what the constable told us, and he was not sure."

"I am sorry Mrs Cross, and I am sorry for the questions I have just asked, the truth is we are ahead of routine, normally we would not question you until after the formal identity of your son, now we are sure that the boy we saw was that of your son, I'm afraid your son is dead."

Elsa gave a howl, she buried her head into her husband, and cried uncontrollably. "No, no," she choked on her words.

Several moment passed as Elsa sobbed her heart out, Chris hated it, he had seen during his time as a detective all the terrible injuries and violence that a human could carry out on another human, he could deal with it without emotion, but he could not bear a woman crying, and was thankful when Elsa pushed herself away from her husband, she dried her eyes, then fiddling with her small hanky for a while blew her nose.

"I am sorry," she said as she again dabbed her eyes with her hanky. "Where is my son now?"

"At the hospital Mrs Cross," Chris answered. "It is standard procedure that an autopsy is performed when there are suspicious circumstances surrounding someone's death."

"When can I see him?" Elsa asked still dabbing her eyes and sniffing.

"Some time tomorrow I expect, we still want the body formally identified, a constable will come for you to take to the morgue."

"The constable said he was shot," Tony said.

"That's correct Sir," Chris replied, not wanting to tell them he was shot in the head. Chris continued. "Was your son married Sir?"

"No," replied Elsa. "Not even engaged, he was a good and steady young man."

"A young lady was with him, she was badly assaulted, and rushed to hospital," Chris continued addressing his words to both of them.

Elsa looked at her husband, as she gave another cry.

"Good God," Tony said. "What was it, a mugging of some sort?"

"What was her name?" Elsa cut in before Chris had time to answer.

"This is why we are a step ahead of our usual routine," Chris began to explain. "We did not see the lady, she had been rushed to hospital before we arrived on the scene, by all accounts she is in a bad way, however she had no handbag that could be found, so we know nothing about her yet, it was a thought by the Sergeant here, that she might have been your son's wife, but now you have confirmed that she was not, as for your question Mr Cross, I am doubtful that it was a robbery, only the lady's handbag is missing, nothing was taken from your son."

"Where did this take place Inspector?" Elsa asked. "The constable told us Jewry Street."

"Actually in a corner of the cattle market, behind the Corn exchange," Chris replied. "Between four and four thirty this afternoon."

Elsa began to cry again, and her husband took her hand, squeezing it gently.

"This is a terrible shock to my wife and myself Inspector," Tony said. "It is murder isn't it?"

"It seems to be Mr Cross, we are at the moment treating it as such, will you read the letter inside of your son's wallet for me please," Chris asked, taking the letter from the wallet and passing it to him.

Tony took the letter out of the envelope and read it. "Good God," he exploded. "I can't believe this."

Elsa took the letter from his hand and read it, tears started to flow from her eyes. "If my son wanted money, he knew he only had to ask me," Elsa sobbed. "Why, would he go to a money lender, he had a good job, he was a tailor, why?"

"I don't think it's from a money lender Mrs Cross," Chris replied. "They would send letters with their own letter headings, also it's only signed with an initial, I believe this is a private loan with a private individual."

"Then I don't understand," Elsa said.

"Nor me," Tony remarked.

"Where did your son work Sir," George asked.

"Burton Menswear in the high street, he is a tailor," Tony replied.

"Did your son have a best friend?" George asked.

Elsa looked at her husband. "I suppose Jeffery, Jeffery Mallard," she remarked. "They went to school together, they always went out together."

"Do you know where he lives?" George asked.

"Clifton Hill, I don't know the number," Tony replied.

"Thank you," George replied as he started writing.

"If I may, I would like to go back to this lady who was with your son, was there anyone special to him?" Chris asked.

"Naturally Martin went out with a few young ladies, he was a handsome lad," Elsa answered, Chris sensed a pride in her voice. "He never went out with one long term that I know of, and I don't suppose he told us of every girl he went out with."

"He wasn't short of girl friends," Tony cut in. "We often had notes put through the door from young ladies, we have had them come to the door."

"But Martin would have none of it," Elsa butted in as she sniffed and dabbed her eyes. "Some of girls were in service," Elsa's voice sounded as though she had no time for them.

"You have no time for girls in service then Mrs Cross?" Chris asked.

"Not for most," Elsa admitted. "I was in service myself, I know that some of these girls will see a man she likes, then will do anything for him so that he would marry her and take her out of service."

"Really," Chris replied.

"Yes," answered Elsa.

"What do you do for a living Mr Cross?" Chris asked.

"I carry coal from the station, me and my Shire do about five trips a day," Tony replied.

"At least it's all down hill," Chris said with a slight smile.

"That's not always good," Tony replied. "You should see the sparks coming from my Shire's horseshoes, as he tries to hold back the heavy coal cart going down North Walls."

"Only one Shire?" Chris questioned not having seen it.

"That's right," Tony replied. "Just one."

"There is a model shop in this street is there not?" Chris asked.

"Almost opposite," Tony replied. "Are you interested in them?"

"No, not at all, but it was the son, a Mr John Thompson that found your son and this lady, he called the hospital first because of the lady, it was the hospital who phoned us."

"That's a coincidence," Elsa said.

"I though so," Chris replied. "Well we won't keep you any longer, I have no words that can ease your grief, apart from telling you, we will catch who ever did this."

Chris stood up followed by George who had got quite comfortable, he replaced the letter in the wallet and put it in his pocket.

"You will get all your son's effects when the case is over," Chris assured them.

"Now don't get up, we will see ourselves out, oh by the way," Chris stopped and looked at them. "What would be the age of your son?"

"He was just twenty three a month ago," Elsa said bursting into tears.

Once outside Chris and George hurriedly pulled up their overcoat collars, it had been quite warm inside, but outside was bitter cold.

"Did we miss anything George?" Chris asked.

"Don't think so," George replied. "But I am wondering if you can keep your promise about catching the murderer."

"So am I George, so am I, come on I'll treat you to a whisky in the pub before we part for the night."

"I'm so lucky you are my boss Chris," George laughed as they entered the warmish smoke filled bar of the Castle Public House.

Chapter Three

*I*t was striking eight am, when Chris approached the Corn Exchange, he had wanted to get there early, just in case someone did enter the police cordon. He stopped in his tracks, seeing two sheep run out of the entrance he was making for, followed by a sheepdog, who ran to the front of them, turning the sheep back into the market.

"God," Chris thought to himself as he hurried his walk. "Must be a cattle market day."

At the entrance, Chris stopped and looked, he dug his hands into his overcoat pockets and cursed, the market was in full swing. The rear of the ground was full of cattle pens, cows, sheep, pigs, chickens, geese filled these pens, the noise the cattle was making sounded like a horrible chorus. Low base wagons, still with horses between the shafts stood empty, men who Chris thought were farmers because of their dress, walking everywhere between the pens, studying and examining the cattle, and the sheepdog was still trying to get the two sheep under control.

Chris shook his head, as he looked at the police cordon, the ropes surrounding the area was on the ground, Chris could tell that the area had been tampered with, perhaps with sheep that were always running amok. He cursed himself for not having found out when the market was held, he could have had a constable standing by. Chris looked at the area, he did not expect to find or see any evidence now, after a few more moments of looking around, Chris shrugged his shoulders, and with his hands still in his overcoat pockets, left the market and before making his way to the police station entered the gents toilet, while thinking that if he walked down the high street, he would have a chance of seeing Elizabeth on her way to the bank.

Chris caught sight of Elizabeth approaching as he reached Dolcis the shoe shop, he quickly stepped into the entrance and waited for Elizabeth to pass.

"Good morning Elizabeth," Chris said causing her to sidestep with alarm.

"Oh Chris, you fool, you gave me a heart attack, I was in deep thought," Elizabeth said reaching up and kissing his cheek.

"What about," Chris asked leaving the shop entrance and making his way to the kerb, so that he could walk Elizabeth to work, while protecting her on the inside.

"About not seeing you last night," Elizabeth grinned as she grabbed his arm. "I missed you."

"Sorry about that, another case came up late yesterday afternoon," Chris replied.

"I understood darling," Elizabeth said. "Was it serious?"

"A murder," Chris replied.

They walked a few paces in silence, after which Elizabeth asked. "Anything else darling?"

Chris took time to answer. "Well if you really want to know," he said squeezing her arm with his free hand. "A young lady was also involved, and the police surgeon believes she was raped."

"Oh no," replied Elizabeth. "How is the girl, is she alright?"

"No idea until I get back to the office, as I said it happened late afternoon yesterday, she was in hospital before I got there," Chris answered.

"You will catch the person responsible darling, I'm sure of that," Elizabeth said quietly as they stopped at the bank entrance. "Will I be seeing you tonight?"

"Can we play it by ear Elizabeth, I was unable to do a lot yesterday owing to the darkness, but I must start inquiries in urgency today, so I don't know where or what I will be doing."

Elizabeth let go of his arm, and pulled up his overcoat collar. "Forget me darling, just catch the man, I love you," she said planting another kiss on his cheek before walking into the bank.

Chris entered the Police Station, and went to the desk, where Sergeant Dawkins was greeting him with a smile. "Morning Sir," he greeted him.

"Morning Sergeant, although too cold to be a good one," Chris smiled undoing his overcoat buttons.

"I agree," replied sergeant Dawkins, as he looked at a list on his pin board. "We have a couple in the cells, there was a bit of a riot last night so it seems, sergeant Williams had to call the police surgeon to give them a once over, blood everywhere, so it seems."

"Are they alright?" Chris asked.

"So it seems Sir," replied the sergeant. "Sergeant Williams left me this envelope to give you," he said reaching below the counter and bring a large envelope into view. "It seems the police surgeon left it for you."

"Thank you Sergeant," Chris said. "By the way, is Sergeant Bloom in?" he asked while studying the envelope.

"Yes Sir, he's in the rest room, I'll tell him you're in," replied the sergeant with a smile.

"Tell him if there is still tea left in the pot, mine is white with two sugars," Chris said as he left to enter his office.

Chris placed the envelope on his desk, before taking off his trilby and overcoat, he was just seating himself behind his desk when Sergeant Bloom entered with a steaming hot cup of tea.

"That was quick Sergeant," Chris praised. "I can do with that, it was cold at the cattle market, just sit yourself while I read whatever is in this envelope."

Still looking at the envelope with wonder, Chris took up the cup and drank, it was hot, and Chris felt the warmth as it went down, smacking his lips, Chris put the cup down, and picking up the envelope opened it. He took out what was obviously a hasty written letter.

Chris, this is not my autopsy report, but I thought you would like to know that the man, Mr Cross was shot once only in the head, the shot killed him, I found nothing else that could have caused his death. The young woman, as far as we can tell was raped at least once, she was badly bruised and with some bleeding, she has been cleaned up, and she could go home, but she is not saying anything, not even her name, so you had best come to hospital and see her, today if possible. I dug the bullet out and enclosed it hoping it will help.

Try to keep the fighting off the streets, I need a rest sometimes you know.

Bob Harvey

Chris picked up the envelope and shook it, and a bullet fell out, he picked it up studying it, when George walked into the office.

George took off his overcoat, and hung it on the hat stand, then blew his lips while rubbing his hands, blasted cold outside he said as he made for his desk.

Chris smiled, then looking at Sergeant Bloom. "Rowland, I need your help all day today," he said.

"Sir," replied sergeant Bloom who was sitting in the interview chair, his helmet on his lap.

"Cut the Sir out, we are working as a team in the office, I'm Chris and that's George," Chris said indicating George with his head.

"Now let me put you in the picture, we were called out to a crime yesterday late afternoon, a man had been shot and killed and a woman had been raped, she is in hospital."

"I had heard the rumours around the station," Rowland interrupted.

Chris nodded. "Well those rumours are mostly true, George and myself have already interviewed the parents of the dead man late last night. I was early at the cattle market this morning, it was pitch black yesterday afternoon, we could not really look for any clues thoroughly, so I went early this morning having had the area cordoned off," Chris looked at George. "What do I find, a cattle market was in full swing, our cordon off area completely destroyed," a disappointed look came into his face.

"Bad luck Chris," George remarked.

"Yes it was," Chris agreed. "Now Rowland, I want you to look around the wall of the market inside and outside, we are missing the gun and a handbag, assuming that the woman raped carried a handbag, also I want you to search the roof of the gents toilet, I noticed this morning that the roof could hide things thrown onto it."

"Right you are Chris," Rowland said with a slight blush on his face calling his superior officer by his Christian name.

"With regard to getting onto the roof of the toilet, use your authority, then I want you to knock a few doors, as far as we are able to tell the dead man was shot around four o'clock, someone must have heard something," Chris smiled as he continued. "And sometime this afternoon, I want you to call at No 23, Upper High Street, the dead man's parents, take them to the hospital, the body must be formally identified."

"I'll get straight on to that Sir, I mean Chris," Rowland smiled.

"You can wear civvies if you like," Chris offered.

"Well Chris this uniform is very much warmer than my Sunday best, and this helmet keeps my head warm," Rowland replied with a grin on his face.

Chris smiled. "Up to you Rowland, should you find something, get back to the desk sergeant who will know where George and myself will be."

With Sergeant Rowland Bloom gone, George looked at Chris. "I bet you felt a fool this morning?" he laughed.

Chris grinned. "Not half, what a fool I was, not realising that a cattle market could be held, never crossed my mind," he admitted.

"Nor mine," George replied. "So what do we do?"

"Letter from Bob," Chris said handing over the letter for George to read.

"I'm going to the barracks then," George said giving the letter to Chris, after reading it.

"That's it George, you can take the bullet, find out what the calibre is and what sort of gun, you know what to ask,"

Chris passed the bullet to George, who examined it before putting it in one of his waistcoat pockets.

"You are off to the hospital I take it?" George asked.

"Yes, then we meet back here, we will have to leave it late to go and interview this Mr Jeffery Mallard, he will probably be working during the daytime."

"I'm using my motorbike," George said. "It's the same way, I'll drop you at the hospital if you like?"

"Save a walk," Chris grinned. "Thanks."

George waved to Chris without looking, as he drove away from the hospital main entrance, leaving Chris standing watching him go.

Chris pushed open one of the two large doors of the entrance and taking off his trilby made his way to the reception counter, when a young woman, dressed neatly in a long floral frock, her hair pressed back into a bun, was waiting for him with a smile.

"Can I help you Sir?" she politely asked keeping her smile. "We are not allowed visitors at this time of day."

"I understand that young lady," Chris replied. "Actually I am here to see a young lady brought in yesterday afternoon, my name is Detective Inspector Hardie."

The young woman ran her eyes down a list that was laid on the counter, she put her finger on a spot. "Yes Sir," she replied. "Sister Atkins is looking after her, if you will follow me Sir," she said as she lifted a flap in the counter. "I'll show you the way."

"Thank you," Chris replied, then followed the receptionist.

Chris followed the receptionist through two sets of double doors, until she stopped outside the third pair. "Wait here Inspector, I'll get the sister for you."

Chris nodded his head as the receptionist disappeared through the double doors, he had no long to wait.

"Detective Inspector Hardie," the sister said as she came through the doors. "You are looking well."

"Do you know me?" Chris asked a little bewildered.

"It seems you have forgotten me Inspector, as I remember you were a sergeant last time we met."

"Of course," Chris said with a smile as he remembered his last visit to the ward regarding a rape. "Please forgive me, yes I do remember you."

"Yes," the sister replied. "You came here to see a Miss Goldsmith if I remember correctly."

"That is correct sister, you have a good memory," Chris answered.

The sister looked at him. "This young lady you are here to see Inspector, I have kept her in a cubicle next to my office, you will be able to talk to her without being overheard," the sister continued. "I hope you are able to get her to talk, and once we know where she lives, she can go home, her ordeal has passed and she is well, but I can't say about her mind, girls deal with this in different ways."

"I agree," Chris said. "I really need for her to talk, if I am to get anywhere with this case."

The sister pushed open one of the double doors, Chris entered the small cubicle, it was made of wood and glass, the young lady sitting up in bed was very attractive, she had long blonde hair, the ends resting both sides of her shoulders, Chris could tell that it had been combed and brushed. Chris placed his trilby on the bottom of the bed, then pulling up a chair that had been specially placed for him, he sat, he smiled at the young lady, who did not smile back.

"I am Detective Inspector Hardie, how do you feel?" Chris asked gently. "You have had a nasty experience."

The young lady looked at him, but did not reply, Chris wondered how he was going to get her to talk. "I have to ask you a few questions Miss...?"

There was no response. "Please will you speak to me, don't you want your attacker caught?" Chris spoke gently.

Chris sat there waiting for her answer, and wondering how he was going to get her to talk.

"You won't catch him," the young woman suddenly said as she shifted herself in the bed.

"I might have a chance if you will answer my questions," Chris replied.

"What is it you want to know?" she asked staring at him with worry on her face.

Chris smiled to himself. "First of all I would like to know who you are, and where you live?"

My name is Miss Janet Wilson, I live at 33, Pine road, Woolston, Southampton," the young lady replied.

Chris was already writing it in his notebook. "Thank you Miss Wilson, now how are you feeling?" Chris asked, his voice gentle.

"I'm OK," she answered. "Just want to get out of here."

"You can go home if you want to," Chris told her.

"I know," she replied. "If I talk to them."

"Why won't you talk to them Miss Wilson, they only want to help you?" Chris replied.

"It's personal," Miss Wilson replied.

Chris thought it would be better to leave this question alone, after all she was speaking now.

"Tell me did you carry a handbag, we could not find one, if we had, we might have known who you were?" Chris questioned.

"I was told it was missing," Janet replied. "It had all my stuff in it, I have no money or anything now to get back home."

"Don't you worry about that Miss Wilson, I will get you home," Chris replied.

Knowing that Janet was not yet about to talk freely, Chris put other questions to her.

"What were you to Mr Cross, that man you were with yesterday afternoon?" Chris asked.

Janet thought for a while before answering. "He was a nice young man, I met him at a pub, I don't know which one, but it was somewhere near the centre, I think it was opposite an hotel."

"He offered to walk me to the station to catch my train home, it was dark, anyway we stopped at a place, he called it the cattle market, as I said it was dark, I was quite happy for a kiss and cuddle, though I can assure you it would not have gone any further."

"I understand what you are saying Miss Wilson," Chris agreed. "But then things started to happen?"

"It certainly did," replied Janet. "Torch beams fell upon us and three men I think it was, came up to us, we or at least I could not see properly because of the light in my face, then a shot, I heard Martin cry out, and saw him slump to the ground."

"You must have been frightened?" Chris remarked kindly.

"I don't know," Janet replied. "I felt my arms grabbed each side, the next thing I knew I was lying flat on the ground, the two men holding my arms and my legs spread eagle position," Janet sobbed as she spoke. "It was terrible, then the third man knelt between my legs, and raped me," Janet took a tissue, and blew her nose. "I don't know what happened to me after that, I must have fainted, the next thing I knew was a doctor touching me."

Chris allowed a few moments before he spoke again. "You went through a terrible ordeal Miss Wilson, it must have been very frightening, do you remember whether you screamed when Mr Cross was shot?"

Janet wiping her eyes shook her head. "I don't remember."

"I suppose it was too dark for you to see their faces?" Chris asked.

"I could not tell you what they were wearing, or how big they were, but I did see their funny faces, they were wearing masks like what you would put on a guy fox."

"Really," Chris asked.

"Yes they were, they were laughing faces," Miss Wilson sobbed.

"Is there anything else you can tell me Miss Wilson?" Chris asked.

Janet shook her head. "I have laid here trying to think, but there is nothing, it happened all too fast."

"Do you know a young man by the name of John Thompson?" Chris asked.

It was several moments before Janet replied, she was shaking her head. "No I don't think so, why, is he one of them?"

Chris forced a smile. "No Miss Wilson, but as far as we know, he drove the three men off."

"I'll have to thank him," Janet murmured.

"Is there anyone I can get in touch with?" Chris asked.

"I live alone Inspector," Janet replied. "I have my own small flat."

Chris found himself in deep thought, he did not really want Janet to return to Southampton, not just yet, after all he was with a murder investigation.

"Miss Wilson," Chris said. "Would you consider staying in Winchester a few more days?"

"Why?" asked Janet her face showing alarm.

"Well a case of rape is very serious, but when it is mixed up with a murder inquiry, which is more serious, I would like you to be more available if you can understand my meaning," Chris answered.

"I don't know," Janet replied. "How can I stop here no clothes, no lipstick, no nothing, I need to go home to get changed."

Chris again thought hard to come up with an answer. "I can always send a constable with you to get what you need," Chris offered. "I know a nice little pub, where I can have you put up, the landlady is very pleasant, actually it is my local, it won't cost you."

"I don't know," Janet hesitated. "I could stay in Woolston, and come to Winchester whenever you need me."

"That could create delays," Chris replied. "Should I need you for any unforeseen event, I would have to first contact, you could be out, perhaps all day, then you would have the train trip to Winchester, I would be more comfortable if you would stay here."

Janet did not want to stay, but could understand his reasons. "Oh very well, it will give me a break, but I must go home first, I only have torn underwear."

Chris smiled. "I'll arrange everything, by the way, would you mind telling me your age?"

"Twenty three, Inspector," Janet answered.

Chris left the cubicle wondering if he had done the right thing by asking her to stay in Winchester, what would the Chief Police Inspector say about the cost, he wondered.

Chris found the ward sister waiting for him, he smiled at her. "She's talking now sister, her name is Janet Wilson, she lives in Woolston, Southampton."

"Thank you Inspector," replied the sister. "I'm glad we know, I wonder why she would not talk to us?"

Chris shrugged his shoulders. "Embarrassed perhaps," he murmured.

"I'm not sure that's the reason," replied the sister. "Anyway, all is clear for her leaving the hospital."

"I would like her to stay just for tonight sister, I need to arrange lodgings for her for a few days, I need her in Winchester, this is after all a murder inquiry."

"If it's OK with Mr Bob Harvey," sister Atkins replied. "Which I am sure it will be, what time will you collect her tomorrow?"

"During the morning Sister," Chris replied. "Thank you very much for all your help," Chris added offering his hand.

Having left Chris at the hospital, George drove back towards Winchester, down Romsey Road. He slowed as he reached the junction with Clifton Road, crossed the railway bridge then slowly turned into the entrance of the Peninsula Barracks.

George came to a sign. "Stop this side of the gates." He saw two soldiers polishing small brass cannons, that was situated each side of the gate on the outside. He looked as passed the gate, and saw the sergeant, who was holding a cane, that was tucked under his armpit. George looked at him and smiled to himself, from his well polished boots to his peak cap, he was a picture of smartness. George got off his motorbike, and pushed it towards the sergeant.

"What have we here Laddie?" boomed the sergeant walking around the motorbike.

"Nothing Laddie," replied George as he took his warrant card from his pocket to show the sergeant.

The sergeant who had gone red in the face with George's reply, took the warrant card and read it.

"Detective Sergeant House," he read loudly. "What can I do for you?"

"Nothing," replied George who had taken an instant dislike to the man. The Sergeant's face seem to swell as it coloured.

"Then what is your business here, this is an Army Barracks," the sergeant barked.

He looked back at the soldiers who were supposed to be polishing, but had stopped to look back, wondering why the sergeant was shouting.

"Get back to your polishing," he shouted taking a step towards them. "I'll have bog jobs for you both after."

The soldiers turned and began polishing the cannons muttering, and George wondered if he had gone too far.

"I want to see someone in authority," George said trying to keep his voice sounding polite.

"I am the authority here," the sergeant barked still keeping himself as straight as a bean rod.

"I want to see someone higher in authority," George replied, he could not help smiling inwardly as the sergeant's face bloated, and his face went crimson.

"On what business?" barked the spluttering sergeant.

"Sorry Sergeant, I can't tell you, I want to see an officer," George replied. "And sergeant, if I am unable to see an officer, I shall leave and contact the Chief Constable of Hampshire, if that happens when I return, you may be a corporal?"

George thought the sergeant was going to explode, without another word he marched into the guardroom to the right. George stood holding his motorbike, he looked at the soldiers polishing, and could tell that they were smiling. The sergeant returned he did not look at George. "Roger," he shouted at one of the polishers, who quickly came to the sergeant. "Sergeant," Roger said standing to attention.

"Take this policeman to Captain Squire the adjutant, and don't dally, park that machine over there," he indicated the guard house with his cane.

"Thank you Sergeant," George said looking at him fully in the face. "I will inform the adjutant of your welcome, and by the way, I am not just a policeman, I am a Sergeant with full authority outside these gates, where you have none."

George left the sergeant foaming at the mouth, he was never spoken to like that, he only wished that George was a soldier under his command.

"We'll have to run if we cross the parade ground," soldier Roger said to George. "If you don't mind we'll walk around it."

"I have time," George replied. "That Sergeant of yours is full of himself."

"Yes," replied Roger. "Me and my mate Tom, we are on guard house duty with him, twelve bloody hours, he don't give us any rest."

"Will he really put you on bog cleaning," George asked.

"I doubt it," Roger replied. "He's full of bull, but he is known for helping any soldier who gets into trouble outside the barracks, I don't think he likes the police."

"I got that impression as well," replied George.

"He was wounded in the arm during the Boer War, so it's said," Roger continued. "We have several here who was in that war with him, they say he's a good man to have with you."

Chris did not answer as Roger stopped at a door, another army sergeant was seated at a desk inside, who looked up as they entered.

"Gentleman here to see the Adjutant," Roger said. "Send over by the guard commander."

"Thank you," replied the army sergeant.

"Have you any ID?" the army sergeant asked.

George produced his warrant card, which the army sergeant read.

"Excuse me a moment Sergeant," the army sergeant said as he knocked on an adjoining door, then entered, to return within a moment.

"Captain Squire will see you now Sergeant."

The army sergeant knocked the adjoining door again, and opened it for George to enter, then closed the door behind him. The office was small, with just filing cabinets and a desk, which a soldier with three pips on his shoulders sat, he rose as George entered.

"Detective Sergeant House," the Captain said holding out his hand, which George took. "Please," he said indicating a chair in front of his desk. "How can I help you?" he said handing back George's warrant card.

George began to tell the Captain his reason for being there as he pocketed his warrant card.

"The murder and the rape occurred around four thirty yesterday afternoon, unfortunately at that time it was pitch black apart from the gas lamps, our witness could not describe the three men that ran away, perhaps he only saw the shadows," George said.

"I'm sorry Sergeant," replied Captain squire. "At a pinch, I could get details of all men off duty last night, that would take time, you have to know we have soldiers billeted all over Winchester, in private houses I mean, what they do in the evenings I would have no control over, apart from knowing where they went or did."

"I can understand that Sir," George replied. "There are also many who are recuperating in Winchester."

"Yes they wear a blue uniform, also billeted in all over, so you see the problem?"

"I do indeed Sir," replied George. "However at the moment we are more concerned about the weapon used in the murder."

George took the bullet from his waistcoat pocket and placed it before the Captain, who picked it up to examine it. "The police surgeon extracted that from the victim's brain," George said, watching the Captain screw up his face.

"Nasty," he murmured. "I know how to shoot and dismantle guns and rifles, but as for anything else, I'm lost," the Captain said modestly. "Just a moment," he said putting the bullet down on his desk, as he rose and went to the door of the office, which he opened.

"Sergeant," he said loudly.

"Sir," George heard the quick reply from the sergeant outside.

"Get the armoury sergeant over here straight away."

"Yes Sir," George heard the reply before the Captain closed the door, returning to his desk.

"The armoury sergeant is a good chap, I think he'll have the answers to your questions, don't you have shootings in Winchester Sergeant?" he asked. "I mean, how do you get your information about fire arms?"

"We get very few Sir," George replied. "Being an army town we do get many fights."

"I'm sure you do Sergeant," the Captain agreed with a smile.

"The shooting we get which are few, are usually shotgun wounding, rarely revolver," George answered.

The office door opened with a knock, and a sergeant entered the room and stood at attention. "Sergeant Millard Sir," the sergeant said.

"At ease Sergeant," replied the Captain. "We have a problem here and I thought that you will be able to sort it out, come over here and look at this bullet."

"Yes Sir," barked the sergeant taking off his peak cap, and holding it under his arms before moving to the side of the desk, and picking up the bullet.

"What do you make of it Sergeant?" the Captain asked.

"Well Sir," the armoury sergeant replied still examining the bullet. "It's a 455 calibre, from a Webley revolver, it's a British Officers weapon, double action, six shots.

"Anything else Sergeant?" the Captain asked as he looked at George with a grin on his face.

"Well Sir, these revolvers were first used for active service in 1887, in 1894, 97,and 99 and in 1914, they were updated, and called Mark 1, 2, 3, 4, 5, in the order of their update, I would say this bullet came from a Mark 5 Sir," the sergeant said putting the bullet down on the desk. "But not a hundred percent sure Sir."

"Anything you would like to ask?" the Captain asked George, still with the grin on his face. "I am sure the Sergeant can answer."

"These revolver Sergeant," George asked. "Forgetting what Mark it is, would they be issued only to Officers?"

"Correct Sir," the sergeant answered. "Officers only, mainly on the field of battle in war time."

"What about Sergeants?" George asked.

"We have our rifles Sir," replied the Sergeant.

"Can they be bought outside, I mean in civvy street?" George asked.

"No Sir, the revolver is not a civilian gun, for Army use only," came the answer.

"Well sergeant that bullet you have just examined, killed a civilian yesterday in Winchester, would you say, it was most likely to be a soldier that used it rather than a civilian?" George remarked.

The armoury sergeant who was at ease, but standing almost at attention looked at George, and George could see a smile in his eyes.

"Only two ways in my opinion," replied the armoury sergeant. "Number one, if an officer sold it, which I cannot believe, number two, it was brought back by a wounded soldier."

"If an officer sold his revolver, would he be able to replace it without an enquiry," George asked.

"No Sir," replied the armoury sergeant. "There would be an enquiry, but perhaps some might buy a revolver more to their liking and get rid of army issue without informing the authorities."

"Could it have come from your armoury?" George asked.

"Impossible Sir," replied the armoury sergeant. "Impossible."

"Have any revolvers been reported missing?" George asked.

"Not to my knowledge Sir," replied the armoury sergeant.

"Well," George said looking at the Captain. "If your sergeant is right, it was probably brought back from France."

"If a soldier is brought back wounded, would it be possible to bring back a revolver without it being seen?" George asked.

The Captain smiled. "You have no idea, we have found many German souvenirs, anything from a bottle of brandy to an officer's sword, I am sure a revolver would not be too much of a challenge, wrapped up in a flannel or a bit of clothe."

George got up, he had exhausted all his questions, he held out his hand to the Captain. "You and your sergeant have been more than helpful Sir, thank you both for your frank reply to my questions."

"Have you formed any opinion Sergeant?" asked the Captain as he let go of George's hand. "You must have one."

"It seems that the question of the gun is cleared, an army officer's gun not available to civilians, it is very possible that this revolver was brought into the country by a wounded soldier, however whether it was soldier who used it yesterday, still remains to be found out. However Sir, I will keep you informed, that's the least I can do for your help, but before I go," George said taking out a button from his coat pocket. "This button was found at the scene," he said handing it to the Captain.

The Captain studied the button, then turning to the armoury sergeant put the button against his tunic. "It seems to be one of ours," he remarked, giving the button to the armoury sergeant, who also studied it turning it over in his hand.

"It's our tunic buttons Sir," he said. "However I doubt if it was on one of our men's uniform, this button needs cleaning, I doubt if it has seen any polishing for months."

"Would you say that the button could have been kept in a box or some sorts then sergeant?" George asked him.

"As a keepsake, yes, I would agree Sir," replied the armoury sergeant.

Chapter Four

It was around midday when George entered the office, Chris was seated behind his desk, he looked up as George entered and took off his overcoat.

"I'm glad that's over," George remarked going to his desk. "I had a bit of an argument with the sergeant guard commander," he said, sitting down at his desk. "I'm glad I'm not in the army."

"That bad was it?" Chris asked.

"Well the adjutant was OK, so was the armoury sergeant, he new his business," George replied and then related his morning to Chris who did not interrupt.

"Well," said Chris after George had completed his story. "It is a good thing to know about the revolver, not available to civilians, the question is, do we put all our energy into finding soldiers who have returned from France?"

George shrugged his shoulders, he did not answer the question. "The button could have been kept in a box according to the armoury sergeant, or in my opinion in a tray in a shop that sell these sort of things, anyway, how did you get on Chris?" he asked.

"I take your meaning George," Chris said before related his visit to the hospital.

"That's a bit awkward, her living at Southampton," George commented after Chris had finished.

"Well I have persuaded her to stay in Winchester for a few days," Chris replied. "But she wants to go home to get a change of clothes."

"Oh," remarked George.

"I'm going to get Sergeant Bloom to go with her," Chris said.

"What is she like?" George asked.

"Attractive, long blonde hair, seems to be slim, I only saw her with the bedclothes covering her," Chris smiled.

"Where will she stay?" George asked.

"I'm hoping Alfie the landlord of the Rising Sun will be able to help me out, he did before," Chris replied.

"Have you asked him?" George questioned.

"No but we will do about in half an hour, when we have a liquid lunch break," Chris smiled.

"Can't wait to see her?" George remarked.

"No good for you George, and it's a pity, she is really attractive, but before you came in I had been on the phone to the Southampton Police, who put me in touch with the Woolston Constable, it seems our Janet Wilson is a known prostitute."

"She would be," George remarked with a laugh.

"Anyway the constable said he would copy her records, and send it to us," Chris said.

"Are you going to tell her you know?" George asked.

"Not for the moment, let's see how things turn out?" Chris replied.

Chris followed by George entered the Rising Sun, the bar was empty, a couple were sitting in front of the large open fire.

"Afternoon Chris, George," Alfie greeted them. "Day off?"

Chris smiled as he approached the bar. "Not quite Alfie," he replied. "But I would like a word with your lady wife, whenever she is ready."

"I see," replied Alfie, putting two glasses under a pump. "Bitter I take it," he said as he started his pump action.

"That's right," Chris smiled. "Any chance of a couple cheese sandwiches."

"The wife won't say no to you will she," Alfie replied. "You sit down with these," he said after he had filled the glasses with bitter. " And I'll call her," he said.

"How are you keeping these days Alfie?" George asked. "I must say you are looking well."

"Never felt better," Alfie replied as George took his glass. "It's all down to the wife, she treats me like a baby," Alfie said with a smile.

"I think you mean she looks after you like a baby, Alfie, not treat you," Chris cut in.

"Same difference," Alfie replied taking the sixpence from the counter that Chris had put there.

Chris followed by George took their glasses to their usual seat, by the window that looked out upon Bridge Street.

"Janet Wilson is a prostitute from Southampton, do you think that she could be mixed up with this shooting in Winchester?" George asked before taking a drink of his pint.

"Hard to tell," Chris replied. "On the face of it, she could have just picked up Mr Cross in the pub, I suppose that he was a customer, perhaps she's the roving type," Chris replied.

"About the revolver," George continued. "Perhaps we should question Mr Thompson again to see if he has remembered anything more, if the revolver was brought back from France, who ever brought could have sold it off."

"I see your point George," Chris replied. "The only facts we have at the moment is that the revolver is army issue, let's hope that Mr Mallard who we shall see tonight can throw some light on the case?"

Chris who was sitting with his back to the window, saw Liz the landlady coming towards them, carrying two plates. "Cheese sandwiches, order of two," she smiled placing a plate in front of each of them.

"How are you Liz?" Chris greeted.

"Just fine," Liz replied. "Alfie said you wanted to talk to me."

"Alfie as well," George said with a smile.

"Oh dear," she smiled before calling Alfie out from behind the bar.

Liz sat next to George, and Alfie pushed himself close to Chris and waited.

"I have a little problem, that I hope you can help me out with," Chris began after swallowing a gulp of beer. "Would you Liz, with Alfie's consent of course, be able to put up a young lady for a few nights?"

"Of course we can," Liz replied without hesitation. "Who is she?"

"Her name is Janet Wilson, her home is in Southampton, at the moment she is in hospital, you see she was badly attacked yesterday."

"I heard something about that," Alfie interrupted. "At the cattle market wasn't it?"

Chris smiled at Alfie. "I expected you to tell me all about it when I entered."

"I was about to, when you said you wanted to see my wife," Alfie replied.

"Will you shut up Alfie, and let Chris finish," Liz scolded. "Now Chris, carry on," Liz said after giving Alfie a look.

"Not much more to tell Liz," Chris replied. "I am unable to tell you what happened to her, but she can if she wants to, one of our constables will collect her from the hospital tomorrow, he will escort her to her home in Southampton, where she will collect a change of clothes, the constable should bring her back here sometime late afternoon tomorrow."

"I'll take care of the poor soul Chris," Liz promised. "Have no worries."

"Thank you both," Chris replied. "I knew I could rely on you, now Liz, Alfie, let me get you both a drink."

"Not for me, thank you Chris, I have work to do" Liz said getting up. "I'll expect this young lady tomorrow then."

Chris nodded with a smile as Liz left. "What about you Alfie?" Chris asked as Alfie stood up. "Will you have a drink?"

"I'll have a bitter, if you don't mind," Alfie replied going back behind the bar.

Chris leaned back in his chair, and took out his pipe, filled it and lit it, and was soon blowing clouds of smoke out of his mouth.

"I hope you enjoy that?" George who did not smoke said between coughing.

"Sorry George," Chris answered, as he waved the smoke away from George.

"Yes I do enjoy a pipe, never used to smoke you know, but I find a pint and a pipe enables me to think more deeply, and don't ask how, because I am unable to explain it," Chris smiled.

Chris and George walked along the tree lines pavement outside the Abbey Grounds.

"Let's go to the Mr Thompson's house in Middle Brook Street," Chris suggested. "Sergeant Bloom will not be back yet, we might as well make use of our time."

"Will he be in?" George wondered.

"Well we might be able to talk to his mother," Chris answered.

They crossed the road before the turning into Colebrook street, having passed the Police Station and the Guildhall, eventually turning into Middle Brook Street. A row of bay window terraced houses came in sight all of which had a small narrow garden in front, and they found themselves behind a lady, carrying two wicker baskets of shopping, Chris studied the lady from behind, she was he thought middle class, noticing her long brown topcoat, and matching wide brim hat. Chris and George was now looking at the numbers, they wanted number 49.

Still behind the lady, they noticed that she stopped, pushed open a small iron gate, and with two strides reached the front door. She put her hand into the letter box, and pulled out a string with a key on the end, which she put into the front door lock. She turned her head back to the street, and saw two men looking at her. "Oh," she said a little flustered. "Can I help you?"

George pushed open the gate, it was number 49.

"Chris took out his warrant card, we are looking for the Thompson's residence, I am Detective Inspector Hardie, and my colleague is Detective Sergeant House, we are looking for Mr John Thompson," Chris spoke in a calm voice.

"I am Mrs Vera Thompson," the woman replied. "I am afraid my son is not at home, perhaps you would like to come in while I get rid of this shopping," she offered as she pushed open the front door.

"Thank you," Chris said taking up the offer and following her in.

Mrs Thompson put her baskets on the floor, and opened a door on the right of the passage. "Please wait in here, make yourselves comfortable, I will be with you in a moment," she said picking up her baskets, and walking towards her scullery.

Chris and George entered the room, it was the bay window room, very well furnished, a sofa and two easy chairs were placed towards the window, and matching sideboard and table and chairs were placed to the rear of the room.

"Hm mm," remarked George, they are not short of a few bob.

Mrs Thompson entered the room, she was minus her hat and coat, her dark hair was shoulder length, held in place by hair slides, Chris thought she had a matron figure.

She crossed to the sofa, and sat down. "How can I help you Inspector?" she asked.

"We called hoping to see your son, Mrs Thompson," Chris replied. "You do know that he was a witness to a crime yesterday?"

Mrs Thompson gave a weak smile. "Yes Inspector he told me."

"Where is your son now, Mrs Thompson?" George asked. "Is he at Upper High Street?"

"No, he left early for Southampton, we also have a shop there at St Denys," Mrs Thompson answered.

"Oh, I had no idea," Chris remarked.

"Is there any reason that you should know Inspector?" Mrs Thompson replied. "That would have nothing to do with what my son saw would it?"

"Not really Mrs Thompson," replied Chris slightly put off. "But we do like to know all about any witness."

"How is that poor girl that John was on about?" Mrs Thompson asked.

"She will leave hospital tomorrow," Chris informed her. "She also comes from Southampton."

"Regardless of where she comes from, the girl has suffered a rape, and I hope you catch who is responsible," Mrs Thompson said.

"We will of course do our best," Chris replied. "How is your son, it must have been a shock for him, after all it's not an every day event is it?"

"I should think not," Mrs Thompson replied. "It's dreadful that this sort of behaviour is allowed to happen."

"Your son gave us the impression that he worked with his father in Upper High Street," George commented.

"You might have got wrong what he said, or perhaps he was not thinking straight," Mrs Thompson replied. "He do work with his father, but at our shop in Southampton."

"I would think you are right Mrs Thompson," Chris replied. "After all it must have been a shock which altered his way of thinking, what time does he normally get home Mrs Thompson?"

"Normally about six," Mrs Thompson replied.

"He was early yesterday," George remarked.

"No," replied Mrs Thompson with hostility in her voice. "Tuesday is early closing day, now," she said getting up from the sofa. "Perhaps it's better if you leave now, and if you need to talk to my son, call when he is here."

"I'm sorry you seem upset Mrs Thompson, had we known that your son worked at Southampton, we would not have called, but your son promised to call at the station to sign a statement," Chris picked up his trilby and made for the door, followed by George.

"Good afternoon Mrs Thompson, and thank you for talking to us."

"That told us a lot," George remarked as they were making their way back to the police station. "She got a bit worked up didn't she?"

"She did," replied Chris. "But how did she know Janet was raped, I only knew for sure this morning that she was raped by that note of Bob's.

"Perhaps her son assumed that she was," George answered. "I thought so myself."

"So did I," Chris replied. "But I'll keep it in mind, don't forget that button could have come from the model shops where they sell these souvenirs, anyway, sergeant Bloom must be back by now, it's started to get dark."

Sergeant Bloom was talking to the desk sergeant as they entered the station. "Come along in Sergeant," Chris invited.

"Well Rowland?" Chris said.

Sergeant Bloom cleared his throat. "Sorry not a lot to tell, I checked the wall of the market, inside and out, it was difficult with the inside, cattle pens everywhere, I had to climb over a couple, anyway, I found nothing, I asked a few questions to farmers, their answers were the same, and it was the same as the outside. I checked the roof of the gents toilet, I managed to get a ladder from the stock exchange, the roof was clean apart from bits of paper, and a couple of old French letters," he said his face blushing as he saw Chris look at George with a smile.

"What did you do then?" Chris asked.

"I knocked a few doors, no one seem to have heard any-thing, one person said he saw horse and trap enter about four yesterday afternoon, but he told me that since the Market Hotel was altered into a part time cinema a year ago, the noise outside had increased especially with more motor vehicles on the road, with their back firing and he took very little notice these days, so I'm sorry, it's been a wasted day."

"No it has not," Chris replied. "It would have been nice had you discovered something, but at least we now know that we have not missed anything, that's just as important."

Sergeant Bloom smiled, he felt a little despondent.

"How did you get on at the hospital morgue Rowland?" Chris asked.

"That was positive," he replied. "I took Mr and Mrs Cross to the hospital, where Mr Harvey met us. To see that poor woman's agony when she saw her son laying there, was really hurtful, I would not like that job on a daily basis," sergeant Bloom remarked.

"So then she confirmed that the body was that of her son?" George asked.

Rowland nodded. "Yes she did."

"Have you stopped for a meal?" Chris asked.

"No, didn't have time, surprising how the time goes when you're investigating."

"Well you can knock off now, go home and rest your feet, but tomorrow, I want you to be an escort to a nice looking young lady," Chris continued picking up an envelope.

"Go to the hospital about midmorning tomorrow, a Janet Wilson will be waiting, you will escort her to Woolston Southampton, so that she can get a change of clothing, you are to bring her back, and take her to the Rising Sun, where you can leave her with the landlady, can you do that?" Chris asked.

"Of course," replied Rowland with a smile on his face. "That will make a change, go by train you mean?"

"That's right," replied Chris. "Now," Chris continued emptying the envelope.

"Here is a letter to the sister of the hospital, here is also the name and address of where Janet Wilson lives at Southampton, a return train ticket from Winchester to Southampton for two. You will have to go across the floating bridge to get to Woolston, so here is five shilling for the return fare, you will have enough for a bit of refreshment out of it."

Chris put all the items back into the envelope and handed it to Rowland. "In this job, you should wear civvies Rowland, the uniform might cause Janet embarrassment," Chris advised.

"That's alright Sir," Rowland said getting up. "I'll get Mrs Bloom to iron me a shirt tonight, I'll report back when I'm finished."

Chris looked at George and smiled, as Rowland left the office. "Takes him away from his usual routine, it will make a change for him."

Chris picked up a larger envelope that had been placed on his desk, he looked at it. "Autopsy report I think," Chris remarked as he started to open it, when a knock came.

Sergeant Dawkins poke his head in. "I have a Mr Jeffery Mallard outside Sir," he said to Chris. "He wants to see you about Mr Cross."

Chris looked at George. "Please show him in Sergeant," Chris said to the desk sergeant.

"Save us a trip later tonight," George remarked as the office door opened, and a young man was ushered in.

He was a young man, looking well groomed, his clean shaven face was smiling as he approached Chris who was already on his feet with his hand out. Chris noticed he carried a brown trilby in his left hand, his light brown overcoat was slung across his shoulders, and Chris was able to see that he wore a brown single breasted three piece suit.

"Mr Mallard," Chris welcomed. "I am Detective Inspector Hardie, and my colleague Detective Sergeant House."

"I am grateful to you for calling, we intended to call upon you tonight, thinking that you were at work during the day, won't you take a seat?" Chris offered indicating the interview chair.

Mr Mallard smiled as he flattened his dark hair with his hand. "Good job I did come then," he said. "It would have been a wasted trip for you tonight, I shall not be in."

"Don't you work Sir?" George asked trying to make up his mind whether he liked the man or not.

"Afraid not Sergeant," Mr Mallard replied. "My parents left me a small but comfortable legacy, plus the house I live in, so you see I just enjoy myself."

"How old are you Sir?" Chris asked.

"Twenty three Inspector," came the replied. "You are wondering why I am not in the army," Mr Mallard asked with a broad smile.

"It crossed my mind," Chris replied.

"It's a simple reason Inspector," replied Mr Mallard. "I have never thought of myself as a hero, in fact I hope I don't have to go over to France, I hear it's not very healthy over there, so I am waiting for conscription, sadly," Mr Mallard sighed. "I have a feeling that conscription will not be far off."

Inspector Noal flashed through Chris's mind, he was a man getting on in years, he had no need to go, but he felt it was his duty, he looked at George, who was rubbing his leg, in which he had been wounded, but Chris did not want to judge the man.

"How do you pass the time then, Mr Mallard?" Chris asked refraining from calling him Sir. "Don't you get bored?"

"Lord no," replied Mr Mallard with a wave of his hand. "I have plenty of friends all over, Basingstoke, Andover, Southampton, you name a place."

"You are a fortunate man," George replied, having made up his mind that he did not like the man.

"So you called to talk about Mr Cross?" Chris said deciding to change the subject.

The grin left the face of Mr Mallard. "Yes I called on Mrs Cross this morning, she was in quite a state I can tell you, she told me what had happened. Mrs Cross told you that I was Martin's best friend, so I thought you may have tried to contact me, as I am out mostly, I decided to call upon you, but I really don't see how I can help you?"

"It's just the process of elimination Mr Mallard," Chris replied. "As his best friend, do you know if he had a special girl friend, perhaps someone he would not tell his parents about?"

"Martin liked the girls," Mr Mallard replied. "Mrs Cross told me about a girl being involved, but for the life of me, I don't know any girl that he took serious, he was a sort of love them and leave them, if you get my meaning."

"We get your meaning Mr Mallard," Chris answered. "Was he able to pick all these girls up in Winchester?"

"No, we often went to Southampton," Mr Mallard replied. "Spent most of our weekends there."

"He spent a lot of money on women then?" George asked.

Mr Mallard screwed his lips. "Martin had no need to worry about money, if he wanted help, then I was always there."

"Did he gamble?" Chris asked.

Mr Mallard shook his head. "As far as I know, no never," he replied.

"Would you have know if he was in debt?" Chris asked.

"I would not think so," Mr Mallard replied. "We were best of friends, did most things together since school days, why do you ask Inspector?"

"Do you know a Mr John Thompson, or a Miss Janet Wilson who comes from Southampton, you might have met her there?" Chris asked ignoring his question.

Mr Mallard screwed his lips again before answering. "It's no to both I'm afraid," he replied. "But having said that, I might have met Mr Thompson without knowing his name if he lives in Winchester, I might even have met this Janet at Southampton without knowing her name, I have met quite a few," he grinned.

"Where were you between, let's see, three thirty and four thirty yesterday afternoon?" Chris asked.

"Do I need an alibi Inspector?" Mr Mallard asked shifting in his chair. "I was Martin's best friend, not his murderer."

"Everyone who was close to Mr Cross has to be a suspect Mr Mallard," Chris stated. "It's a matter of elimination, that's all."

Mr Mallard hesitated before answering. "This puts me in a difficult position Inspector, I was with a young lady, in her home, a married young lady I might add."

"Don't worry," George replied feeling a disgust. "We are very discreet."

"I certainly hope so," Mr Mallard replied. "One don't deliberately break up a marriage of a young lady who have done you a favour."

"It won't come to that Mr Mallard," Chris replied feeling the same as George. "Just her name and address please?"

"Oh very well Inspector, her name is Linda Coven, number 7, Canon Street."

"Thank you Mr Mallard," Chris said noting the George was already writing the address down. "Now what number do you live at Clifton Hill?"

"Number 7," Mr Mallard replied a slight grin on his face.

"Should I want to get in touch with you again, what would be the best time?"

"Now you have me Inspector, it will be a hit or a miss," Mr Mallard replied.

"Not to worry then Mr Mallard," Chris replied. "We will succeed."

Chris stood, calling the interview to an end. "Thank you for calling Mr Mallard, we appreciate it," he said without offering his hand.

Mr Mallard stood, he took hold of the lapels of his overcoat, making sure that it rested securely on his shoulders. "No trouble at all Inspector."

Chris blew out of his mouth as Mr Mallard departed. "I don't like that man," he commented.

"I hope conscription comes soon for him, and he has a kind of sergeant that I met yesterday, don't know what to make of him?" George replied.

"Well at least he came to us, which means an early evening for us, I can meet Elizabeth," Chris remarked, taking up the large envelope he had not yet opened.

He looked up as a knock came on the door, and sergeant Dawkins poked his head in.

"That Mr Mallard that just left, when he entered the station I was just letting those two sailors go, that's been in the cells since last night."

"That's a bit late sergeant," Chris remarked.

"Well yes Sir," replied sergeant Dawkins. "But they were in a bad way last night as I told you, they had an hangover this morning, so I let them stay a bit longer."

"That was nice," Chris replied with a smile.

"The funny thing is, these sailors had to get back to Southampton where their ship is docked, they were at my desk when this Mr Mallard came in, and the funny thing is, they knew each other."

"Really," Chris replied. "Just how do you mean?"

"Well they shook each others hand, and laughed together, but didn't say much, apart from hello, how are you, funny don't you think?"

"Yes I do Sergeant," Chris replied. "And thank you for telling us, by the way, what is Canon Street like?"

"Terrible Sir," sergeant Dawkins replied with a slight smile. "Very rough part of the town."

"That surprises me Sergeant," Chris said. "A few months ago Canon Street was involved in a case I was working on, it seemed a nice street then."

"It was Sir," replied sergeant Dawkins. "But now we believe that at least two houses are used as brothels, we seem to be getting a lot of sailors down there as well, it's a very rough street now, in fact after dark I won't allow a constable down there on his own."

"As bad as that Sergeant?" Chris asked in a surprised tone.

"It is Sir," came the reply.

"Why aren't the houses closed down?" George asked.

"Proof," replied sergeant Dawkins. "It's hard to get proof."

"Winchester girls I suppose?" George questioned.

"That's not what we hear, many of them comes from Southampton."

"Something wrong here Sergeant Dawkins," Chris remarked. "Why, would girls come here from Southampton, and then to be followed here by sailors from Southampton, I mean it just don't make sense, surely it would be a lot better for the girls to stay in Southampton, they would have at least five times the clients down there, plus no journey."

"Whatever the reason Sir," replied sergeant Dawkins. "That is exactly what happens."

"Well thank you Sergeant," Chris said as once again he picked up the large envelope.

The sergeant turned to go. "You wouldn't have any numbers of the houses you suspect would you Sergeant?" Chris asked as an afterthought.

"Yes Sir," replied the sergeant turning back. "As far as I can remember it is number seven and eight, both next door to each other."

Chris looked at George as the sergeant departed. "It seems our Mr Mallard visits a brothel if the sergeant is right, he had me fooled when he told us he did not want to break up a marriage."

"As I said," George replied. "I don't like the man."

Chris once again picked up the large envelope and this time opened it, and drew out two sheets of foolscap, and read.

The top sheet was the autopsy report on Martin Cross, Chris looked straight at his blood group. Type "O Positive."

Chris continued to read the report, which verified most of what Mr Bob Harvey had written in his hasty note last night. A single shot to the head had killed Martin, he was healthy in all other departments. There were signs that he had sexual intercourse before he died, with traces of sperm found between the buttons of his trouser flies, and spots on his pubic hair. The body was identified as Mr Martin Cross, by both his parents Mr Tony Cross and Mrs Elsa Cross. The report was signed and dated by Bob Harvey the police surgeon.

Chris passed the report to George, as he began to read the report on Janet Wilson.

Dear Chris,

My examination of Miss Janet Wilson reveals that she was subject to a brutal intercourse, Miss Wilson herself states that she was rapped, she was badly bruised with some bleeding. Sperm removed from her vagina show blood group, "O Positive." At the moment sexually transmitted diseases, or pregnancy, cannot yet be confirmed. I have given her a note of referral to Southampton General Hospital in a month's time. Hope this of help. Bob Harvey Police Surgeon.

Chris stared at the report for a while before passing it to George, who after reading it twice passed the reports back to Chris. "You thinking what I'm thinking?" George asked.

"It's a thought," Chris replied. "Then blood group O Positive, is common."

"I know, it's my group" George said. "He ruled out suicide in the autopsy report," George remarked.

"Yes simply because no gun was found, you can't shoot yourself, then hide the gun," Chris said. "Also, Janet Wilson said Mr Cross was shot before she was rapped, for the moment we have to assume that the killer took the gun with him, the missing handbag might have been used for this reason," Chris leaned back in his chair, and took out his pocket watch.

"Well it's time to go, thanks to Mr Mallard calling we are saved that trip, so I can meet Elizabeth, now first thing tomorrow, I shall be visiting the Thompson's model shop, so I shall be late, I'll take that army tunic button with me."

"Anything you want me to do?" George asked.

Chris thought for a while. "Sergeant Bloom has his work tomorrow, probably take all day, I am expecting a report on Janet Wilson from Woolston Police, you can chase up John Thompson if you want to, he has not come in to sign a statement."

Chapter Five

Chris sat at one side of the table with Elizabeth at his side, they faced Ron and Olive, Elizabeth's parents, eating a steak pie and vegetables. Chris felt happy, he was part of a family, and they were lovely people.

"Have you two made up your minds, what are you doing for Christmas?" Olive said while pushing her peas around the plate. "It's not far off now you know."

Chris looked at Elizabeth, who was looking at him with the same question in her eyes. He looked across to Ron, and saw that he was not going to be of any help.

"I was going to leave that to Elizabeth," he finally said, feeling a bit of a coward.

"Have you spoken to your landlady?" Elizabeth asked.

"I haven't seen much of her for the last couple of days, you know when I get home, she is in bed, and in the mornings, they keep out of the way so that I can wash and shave in privacy," Chris replied before eating a forkful of steak and crust.

"Well Chris love," Olive spoke. "We will have to sort it out, Christmas is a busy time."

"I know Olive," Chris replied. "It's just that I have always spent the day with Mr and Mrs Dobson, they both have been very good to me, I don't want to hurt them, all I want to do is to spend Christmas with Elizabeth."

"Oh darling," Elizabeth said putting her hand on his arm. "We will have to compromise."

"Why not come to dinner Chris?" Ron suggested. "Spend the afternoon and tea with your landlady, then come back here during the evening, I'm sure for that night, you can spend here without having to go back."

Chris looked at Elizabeth who was smiling at him. "That's a good compromise darling," she said. "Naturally I will come with you in the afternoon."

Chris finished chewing before he spoke. "OK, dinner here, tea with the Mr and Mrs Dobson, back here for the evening, sounds great to me."

"That's settled then," Olive said with a smile. "You can stay here overnight, we have a spare room."

"Thank you Olive, I don't want to cause you bother," Chris replied.

"Don't be silly Chris," Ron spoke up. "I'll have company for a drink during the evening."

"We will wait and see about that dad," Elizabeth giggled.

With the meal over, Elizabeth and her mother cleared the table, and went to the scullery to wash up. Ron retired to his favourite chair, put on his glasses then picked up the paper and started to read, the paper covering his face as he held it up, it was a usual routine with him. Chris sat in the remaining armchair, and took out his pipe, lit it and puffed contentedly, glad that the question of Christmas had been settled.

Ron lowered his paper, and looked over the top of it at Chris.

"The war won't be over this Christmas Chris," he said.

Chris took his pipe from his mouth. "I get very little chance of reading the paper," he said. "Are we in a bad way?"

"We seem to be holding our own, but it seems the cost is heavy in lives," Ron replied.

"It makes one feel guilty you know," Chris said loudly. "Especially at Christmas time, while we are here eating and drinking and having a good time, those boys are out there in mud, wet trenches, perhaps without a Christmas dinner?"

"Perhaps they will agree to a pause for the day?" Ron remarked.

"Let's hope so," Chris replied. "But they will still be laying in wet trenches, still it would be a rest I suppose."

"No sign of America coming in yet," Ron said.

"I can understand that Ron," Chris replied. "America thousand of miles away, it's not their war, you can understand, that families do not want their husbands, sons, brothers are killed in a war that they do not understand, I do not know how such a war could start over the killing of one man."

"Power, greed, and politics," Ron replied. "If the Archduke Franz Ferdinand had not been killed, something else would have started it, it's been coming for a long time."

The rest of the evening passed with all of them playing draughts, and it was natural that Elizabeth was the winner. "Well," Ron said after the eighth game. "That's my lot, it's bed time for me, come on Olive love, let's leave these two alone."

Olive smiled, and for once showed obedience, Elizabeth kissed her parents goodnight, and Olive kissed Chris. "Goodnight Chris," she said as she left the room followed by Ron.

"See you Chris," Ron said with a wink as he disappeared behind his wife.

Elizabeth was already sitting on the sofa, and she patted the space beside her.

"Come here," she said with a grin over her face. Chris did as he was told, Elizabeth grabbed his arm.

"Darling, do you know I'm counting the days," she sighed.

"What days?" Chris asked teasing.

"Our wedding of course," Elizabeth scolded and hitting his arm.

"Oh that," replied Chris smiling to himself.

"Darling don't tease," Elizabeth said hugging herself as close to Chris as she could. "Every day seems a week to me."

Chris turned towards her, he held her face in his hands.

"Every day seems a year to me," he replied, and pressed his lips on to hers in a long lingering kiss.

"Oh darling," she sighed resting her head on his shoulders so that she could look at him. "How's your case going darling?" Elizabeth asked.

"Early days yet," Chris replied. "I have that young lady involved staying at the Rising Sun for a few days," he said.

"Oh," remarked Elizabeth.

"Well she comes from Southampton, I need her here just in case I get a break."

"What will happen if this case is not solved by Christmas?" Elizabeth asked.

"Sorry darling, but we have to play with the cards given, I don't know," Chris replied.

"I hope it don't spoil our Christmas," Elizabeth murmured.

"I'm sure it won't, Chris replied. "But I am glad we sent out our Christmas cards early."

Elizabeth looked at Chris full in the face, Chris saw her lovely eyes which were sparkling, he saw the question there.

"Of course I almost forget," Chris carried on. "I do have one more to buy, but you can't do it, it's rather personal," Chris saw a smile on Elizabeth's face, he pulled her over his lap, it was a gentle loving kiss he gave her.

It was around midnight when he said goodnight to Elizabeth and he went to his lodgings.

Chapter Six

It was just striking nine when Chris pushed open the door of Thompson Model Shop in Upper High street, the tinkering of a small bell over the door sounded. Chris looked over to the counter of the shop, where a middle aged man, dressed with collar and tie, with the rest of him covered with a long brown working coat was smiling at him.

"Good morning Sir," he said still with the smile on his face.

"Morning," replied Chris. "Would I be speaking to Mr Thompson?"

"You would be Sir," came the reply. "How can I help you?"

"My name is Detective Inspector Hardie of Winchester CID," Chris introduced himself as he approached the counter.

"Oh, you called upon my wife yesterday, and upset her rather," Mr Thompson replied as the smile faded from his face. "How can I help you?" he asked. "If it's about my son's statement, he is at your station now, we have had to close our Southampton shop for the morning, I can't understand why his statement is so urgent, after all he only saw shadows."

"I'm sorry about the problem this has caused Mr Thompson," Chris replied. "Your son did promise to call in yesterday to make his statement, however, we were at that time with the opinion that your son worked at this shop, he did not mention that he worked at Southampton, had he done so, we would have certainly made it easier for him to come in. You see Mr Thompson, this is a murder inquiry, the statements made by witnesses, and others are very important, we read them through time and time again, trying to put things together, please, accept my apologies for your inconvenience."

"Fair enough," replied Mr Thompson. "Is there anything else?"

Chris took the army tunic button from his pocket, and showed it to Mr Thompson.

"You sell these sort of things Mr Thompson?" he asked.

Mr Thompson took a quick look at the button, then walked away to the far end of the counter, returning with a shoe box, which was full of army buttons. "That's my entire stock of buttons," Mr Thompson said pushing the shoe box towards him.

"Do you sell many?" Chris asked poking his fingers in the box, and touching those on top.

"Not many, people bring in boxes of stuff to sell, boxes with badges, buttons and such likes," Mr Thompson replied. "I sort them out when I get a free moment."

"It would be possible to know where this button came from?" Chris asked still looking in the box.

"Like trying to find a needle in a hay stack, if you ask me," Mr Thompson replied.

Chris looked up at the shelves behind Mr Thompson, rows of boxed models were on show, all types of farm wagons, and carriages, boxes of animals, soldiers, every thing from a ship to a fort. "You have some nice things here

Mr Thompson," Chris said. "I never get the time for it, but I can well understand that it would be interesting, I see you also have replica fire arms."

"I keep a small range," Mr Thompson said.

"I know it's a silly question Mr Thompson, but I must ask it, do anyone bring in real fire arms for you to buy, they are also collectors items aren't they?" Chris questioned.

"Yes they are," Mr Thompson replied. "And yes, I have been offered a revolver or a shotgun to buy, but I never do."

"Lately," Chris asked.

"Can't really remember, it's a rarity if I'm offered one, and as I said, I only sell replicas."

"I suppose you sell the same type of thing at your shop in Southampton?" Chris asked.

"Of course," Mr Thompson replied. "The beauty of having another shop is that if I have a stock here that don't move, then it goes to Southampton, and vice versa."

"Excellent idea," Chris confirmed, then offered his hand, which Mr Thompson took. "My apologises again Mr Thompson for any inconvenience caused."

"I understand Inspector, sorry can't help you with the button," Mr Thompson replied letting go of Chris's hand. "Is the button important to your case?"

"Could be," replied Chris as he opened the door. "It was found at the scene of the crime," Chris tipped his trilby and left.

Chris was now opposite the house of the victim, he wanted to call in, but first of all he wanted to speak to George, he wondered where the phone kiosk would be, looking around, he saw the wooden structure of a kiosk outside a shop facing Sussex street. Chris pulled open the wooden door, took the receiver in his hand and dialled after inserting a penny.

"Winchester Police Station," spoke a voice.

"Sergeant, it's Hardie here, is Sergeant House in?" Chris asked.

"Ah Inspector, Williams here, yes I think he's in the office," came a voice over the phone.

"Put me through then please," Chris told him.

A crackling came over the ear piece as Chris waited.

"George here," the words suddenly came.

"George, I have been to Thompson's Model shop, has his son been in?"

"Yes all done Chris," replied George.

"While I am up this way, I'm going to call on Mr and Mrs Cross, see if I can look around their son's bedroom, in the mean time, can you go to that Gunsmith Shop in Southgate Street, ask if anyone has sold them a revolver, you know what to ask," Chris said.

"Good as done Chris," George replied. "See you back here."

"OK," Chris managed to reply as the penny ran out.

Chris knocked on the door, and within a few moments it was opened by Elsa Cross.

"Oh, Inspector," she said.

Chris could see by her face that she was grieving badly, and he wondered if he had call too early after the event. "I know this is a bad time to call Mrs Cross, I wonder, can I come in for a moment?"

Elsa stood back inviting him in, Chris took off his trilby as he entered.

"My husband is not in Inspector," she said quietly as she showed Chris into the room.

Chris unbuttoned his overcoat as he felt the warmth. "It's cold enough for snow Mrs Cross," he said, unable to think of anything else to say.

"Would you like a cup of tea Inspector?" Elsa asked. "You do look cold."

"Please do not trouble yourself for me Mrs Cross," Chris replied.

"That's alright Inspector, I like to keep myself busy."

Chris knew what she meant. "In that case a cup would be nice," Chris answered.

A few minutes later, Elsa brought in a tray with teapot and two cups and saucers, with milk and sugar, which she placed on the dining room table, by which Chris was already sitting.

"How do you like it Inspector?" Elsa asked.

"White with two sugars please," Chris answered.

Both drank their tea in silence, then Chris put his cup back into the saucers. "How are you copping Mrs Cross?" he said gently.

"I like to keep busy," Elsa replied as her eyes watered, and she quickly took a hanky from her apron pocket and wiped them. "My husband did not want to leave me, but coal has to be delivered, especially in this cold weather."

Chris nodded his head.

"Was there something special you want Inspector?" Elsa asked as she finished her tea.

"Well yes, but it can wait until your husband is home if you prefer," Chris replied trying to sound gentle.

"What is it Inspector?" Elsa asked.

"I was wondering if I could take a look at Martin's bedroom?"

"Whatever for?" Elsa asked.

"It is a routine Mrs Cross," Chris replied. "Many times the room of the victim gives us clues, clues are often found which helps us to find the person responsible, I need all the help I can get with this case."

"Then by all means Inspector, I dearly want to know who killed my son," Elsa sobbed with tears in her eyes.

"I'll leave you to it," Elsa said as she let Chris into the her son's bedroom. "I'll be downstairs."

Like the rest of the house, the room was neat and tidy, a single bed taking up the centre of the room. Under the window of the bedroom was a marble top wash stand, with a jug and basin, next to that which occupied the corner of the room was a wardrobe, on the other side of the room was a chest of drawers, standing near by a desk.

Chris stood at the foot of the bed and looked around, he had no idea what he was looking for, he crossed to the chest of drawers, and opening each drawer, he gently searched without disturbing the contents. He looked into the wardrobe, and satisfied himself that it was hiding no secrets. He did not touch the bed, Elsa was an excellent housekeeper, anything under the pillows or mattress she would have found. He came to the desk, the one or two books that were piled on top. He opened the drawers of the desk, and began to feel disappointed, then the bottom drawer would not open it was locked. Chris smiled to himself as he took out a bunch of keys from his pocket, that had been on Martin's body, he was glad that he had thought about putting them in his pocket with the button.

He selected a key, inserted it in the lock, and it opened.

Chris took out a small black hardcover notebook that laid at the top, and flicked through it, it was some sort of address book with many girls names and addresses, at the back was a page with sums of money entered by initials. Chris placed the address book on the desk, and took out several letters, not wanting Elsa to come in, he quickly scanned through the letters, and decided he must take them back to the office to study. He felt in the drawer and satisfied that nothing remained, closed and locked it.

Chris put the black hardcover address book into his pocket, he selected one of the books on the desk and folding the letters, placed them inside the leaves. Looking around making sure that the room looked the same as when he entered, he went back downstairs.

"I've made you another cup of tea Inspector," Elsa said as he entered the room. "It's cold outside, it will warm you."

"That is good of you Mrs Cross," Chris replied sitting again at the table. "Your house is always lovely and warm, I wish my office was the same."

"My kitchen range is always burning, it gives out a lot of heat, I have no fire in this room, so my husband thought that he would build a serving hatch, just there in the wall," she pointed. "When I open it the heat fills the room."

"A brilliant idea, I'm impressed," Chris replied.

Elsa gave a weak smile. "Tony is very inventive," she said proudly.

Chris finished his tea. "I have found a couple of letters that I would like to take back to the office Mrs Cross," Chris said touching the book. "I need to study them, I feel it might help, I will give you a receipt for them, and you will get them back."

"You have no need to do that Inspector, after all you are a policeman," Elsa replied.

Chris took his small receipt book from his pocket that he always carried, and started to write. "Book and sundry documents," then signed and dated it. Chris tore it, and placed the receipt on the table. "It's just routine Mrs Cross," he said getting up. "I'm sure your husband will appreciate that."

Mrs Cross looked at the receipt without touching it.

"Inspector," she said with a pleading in her voice. "Who ever killed my son, took my life and my future happiness, I will never get over loosing my son this way, he was very special to me, also I will never have any grand children now to make a fuss of, please find who ever responsible."

Chris saw both of her eyes filled with tears and the tears flowing down on her cheeks.

"Mrs Cross, I will get who ever is responsible, it will take time, but I shall catch him in the end."

"I believe you Inspector," Mrs Cross sniffed as she wiped her eyes with her hanky.

Chapter Seven

Chris made his way back to the Police Station, the old town clock in the high street above the Butter Cross said almost two pm. He pulled up his collar, and pulled the brim of his trilby, the traffic was quite heavy not only with horse drawn vehicles but with handcarts. Many people seem to be out, and Chris thought that they must be doing their Christmas shopping. After leaving Mrs Cross he had done a few errands, and had walked up and down Canon Street before enter the station.

Sergeant Dawkins greeted him. "Getting colder," he smiled. "Snow by Christmas."

"Hope not," Chris answered as he took off his overcoat. "However you could be right, is Sergeant House back?"

"He's in the office Sir," sergeant Dawkins replied.

Chris entered the office. "Morning George," he said making for the hat stand and hanging his coat and trilby. "Cold enough to freeze the brass."

"Yes I agree," George interrupted with a smile.

Chris crossed to his desk. "A letter there for you from Southampton," George informed him.

"I was expecting one," Chris said picking up the letter without opening it. "How did you get on?"

"I went to the Gunsmith shop in Southgate street, I saw the manager, I explained my reasons, and he told me that he has been offered revolvers, but he deals mainly in 12 bore rifles. He would not buy a gun of any description unless he knew the person, anyway to cut a long story short, he said even if he wanted to buy a 455 Webley revolver, he would have been unable to sell it, it's not a gun for civilian use."

"Well we knew that, but at least we covered that side, it means that whoever had the gun, bought it illegally, unless it was an army officer that killed Martin Cross, let's examine what we have," Chris said.

"We have a body, we have a woman who was raped, we are told by the woman that the man was shot before she was raped. We are told that three men were involved, all of them were wearing masks, we have a witness who said he chased the men, his words however do verify what the woman said, there was three men," Chris paused and looked at George.

"That is the case, but what else do we have, we know he was shot by a revolver, not for civilian use, finding the gun will prove a problem, if we ever find it, then the motive, as yet we are no where near one, but there must be one," Chris sighed as he finished.

"Everything is conquered by perseverance," George replied.

"In this case I have plenty of that," remarked Chris as the face of Mrs Cross came to him. "Still perhaps my morning work will throw some light, I saw Mr Thompson senior this morning, he could not help with the button, I never expected that he could," Chris continued. "You know he has two shops one here and another at Southampton, I am surprised, how can people afford to buy models, I was looking at some of the prices, they were a weeks wages."

"A lot of people find pleasure in them," George remarked.

Chris did not reply. "Anyway, I then called in at Mr Cross, only his wife was there, she allowed me to have a look at her son's bedroom, I think I might have struck lucky," Chris said with a smile taking out the black notebook from his pocket, and putting it on his desk.

He took the letters from the pages of the book he had also brought and gave them to George. "Have a look at those letters see what you can make of them, I'll study this address book, it looks interesting."

The first six pages contained names and addresses of women, at least three of them lived at Southampton. He moved to the back of the address book, and by each initials several sums of money was written. Checking the names of the women in the front of the book, Chris realised that the initials represented each one woman at the back of the book. "What is the money entered for," he muttered to himself. "Could they be loans or what?"

"There's a solicitor letter here," George broke the silence. "You won't guess who used to own number seven in Canon Street?"

Chris was only partly listening, and without looking up from the address book. "Who?" he asked.

"Martin Cross," replied George.

Chris looked at George, he forget about the address book as he leaned back in his chair.

"Really," he said a little shocked. "That's Mr Mallard's alibi address, he was there when the owner was getting killed."

"Seems that way." George agreed.

"Mr, nor Mrs Cross not mentioned that their son owned a house," Chris ventured. "I wonder if they knew?"

George shrugged his shoulders. "Don't forget that Sergeant Dawkins said that the place was being used as a brothel."

"That's right," Chris agreed, as his mind went back to the address book. "This address book must be an account book, it has six women names in, and beside their initials a sum of money written, that money must represent what the women earned as prostitutes," Chris commented.

"You are saying that Martin Cross was running a brothel?" George asked.

"For Mrs Cross sake, I hope not," Chris answered. "But it looks that way, and another thing, three of these women comes from Southampton, and our only witness runs a shop there, coincidence do you think?" Chris passed the book to George, who returned the letters for Chris to read.

Chris studied the letters while George studied the address book.

These letters from the solicitor who represented Martin Cross in buying the house, are dated August 1914, that's over a year ago, I was hoping to get something regarding that letter he had in his wallet," Chris remarked.

"Well he wasn't broke," George replied. "These girls are earning fifty pounds a week for him according to this book."

Chris leaned back in his chair. "It looks as though we have a prostitute situation here," he said. "I noticed that Janet Wilson was not mentioned in that book."

"No," replied George. "Perhaps she's not involved, and that Martin Cross only met her in the pub?"

Chris leaned forward, took the receiver from the phone.

"Sergeant Dawkins, when you have a few moments, will you come in?" he spoke onto the receiver.

"Ah, Sergeant," Chris said moments later as Sergeant Dawkins entered. "You told us yesterday that you were keeping an eye on a couple houses in Canon Street, number seven I think you said."

"That's right Sir," replied sergeant Dawkins. "We have reasons to believe that the owner is keeping a disorderly house."

"Is that the only house Sergeant, I thought you said one or two?"

"That's right Sir, number seven and number eight, next door to each other."

"Have any action been taken about them?" Chris asked.

"Not to my knowledge Sir," sergeant Dawkins replied. "Our Chief Inspector wants proof before he takes action, and we can't get that."

"Is there a file open on them?" George asked.

"No," replied sergeant Dawkins. "They only came to our notice with the fights that happens around them mostly at nights with soldiers and sailors, it's mainly hearsay the evidence we have."

"Thank you Sergeant," Chris said. "In future any trouble in that area let us know will you?"

"No problem Sir," sergeant Dawkins smiled as he left.

"Well let's see what we have from Woolston," Chris spoke as he picked up the envelope and opened it. Chris read the letter enclosed.

To Inspector Chris Hardie of Winchester CID.
Sir,
The woman known as Janet Wilson owns a three bedroom house, on the West End Road, Woolston in Southampton. There are two women, known prostitutes also

living at that address, although we have questioned a couple men caught coming from the house, they have told us that they do not pay for sex, it is between consenting adults, free of charge, you will understand why we are unable to act.

There is a minder otherwise known as a pimp, goes by the name of Mr T, an average built man so we believe, never seen him, we believe that Janet Wilson is the madam, also we think Mr T has his fingers in other pies, but no proof, hope this been of some help, I am always here.

Sergeant Worthy, Woolston Police House.

P. S. The names of the other two women living at Miss Wilson's house, Susan Mitchell and Leslie Wicker. Janet Wilson also owns a small flat near by in Pine Road, number 33, Woolston in Southampton.

Chris passed the letter to George.

"That's a turn up for the book, so Janet, if our case is all about prostitution could have known Martin Cross?" George stated. "Sergeant Bloom should be back soon, it will be interesting what he has to say."

"The interesting thing is that we know who T stands for, Martin Cross it seems owe him money but how, or why?" Chris replied. "Also we must find out who owns number eight in Canon Street?"

"I can do that Chris," George replied. "Are you inform-ing Mr and Mrs Cross?"

"Not yet until I know everything, if the worse comes to the worst, I'll eventually have to break her heart," Chris answered. "I want to look in number seven in Canon Street first."

Chris had taken out his pocket watch, it told him it was four thirty, he was about to remark on the time when a knock came on the door and Sergeant Bloom entered.

"We have a stranger in our midst," George remarked.

"Don't you go on," sergeant Bloom murmured.

"You look very presentable Sergeant," Chris said.

"Thank you Sir," he replied touching the knot in his tie, then unbuttoning his grey overcoat.

"Come and sit down and tell us how you got on?" Chris offered.

Sergeant Bloom sat in the interview chair, and Chris saw as his overcoat fell apart that he was wearing a single breasted three piece suit.

"I picked Janet, that is Miss Wilson," sergeant Bloom said a colour creeping into his cheeks. "From the hospital as you said, we caught the ten forty five train from Winchester, we took a cab from Southampton station to the Woolston floating bridge, it's a long time since I had a ride in a horse drawn cab, I enjoyed it, mind you I asked the fare first."

Chris smiled to himself, it was obvious that Sergeant Bloom had enjoyed himself.

"Miss Wilson has a nice well furnished flat, it's in a side road, anyway, she collected her things, and she told me I was the first man she had taken to her flat," he continued colouring again.

"You must have been honoured," George remarked.

"I find her very attractive, well dressed, pleasant, and she smells nice," replied sergeant Bloom again showing a slight colour.

"Anyway, as we left her flat, we returned along this long road to the floating bridge, then she stopped outside a really fancy house, you could tell only posh people lived in it," sergeant Bloom added. "Anyway, she asked me to look after her case, which I was carrying, while she called at this house for a while, she went inside, and was out again within ten minutes, then we carried on to the floating bridge. I asked her if they were posh friends of hers, she replied that they were. We caught the train back, and I took her straight to the Rising Sun as you told me."

"She's there now?" Chris asked.

"That's where I left her ten minutes ago," sergeant Bloom answered.

"Thank you Sergeant, you done well," Chris said.

"Can you get the bobby on the beat, what they know about a Mr Jeffery Mallard of Clifton Hill, it must be kept confidential of course, also what you can find out about a shop in Upper High Street, called Thompson Model Shop," Chris continued.

"I can do that," sergeant Bloom replied. "I must say I have enjoyed the last two days."

"You have been a great help to us, by the way, you got on well with Miss Wilson so it seems, did she act like a woman who was raped just two days ago?" Chris asked.

"To tell the truth, we got on so well that I completely forgot about her ordeal, I hope she don't think that I was insensitive," sergeant Bloom replied.

"I'm sure she won't," Chris smiled. "Now you can go home now, and while you are dressed, take your wife out for a treat."

Sergeant Bloom smiled. "It would make a change for Mrs Bloom, by the way," he said putting his hand in his trouser pocket. "I have two shilling and twopence left."

"That means you can at least take your wife for a drink tonight," Chris smiled. "Now off you go, and thank you."

"How old is the Sergeant Bloom do you think George?" Chris asked.

"Over forty I would say," replied George. "Still he likes the young ones by all accounts, she's nice and she smells nice," George mimicked.

"He's useful to have around anyway," Chris said dismissing the subject.

Chris met Elizabeth just after six, both of them wrapped in their topcoats, walked up Magdalene Hill, towards Elizabeth's home.

"Do we do the Christmas tree on Sunday?" Chris asked.

"Yes," Elizabeth answered. "Dad will have the tree by then, and I hope you will be off."

"It's my day off," Chris remarked as they crossed the Blue Ball Hill.

"You're lovely and warm," Elizabeth said smiling in the darkness, with both her hands clutching the left arm of Chris. "Are you warm in bed?" she teased. "Only I suffer with cold feet."

"I'll suffer the cold feet, as long as the rest of you is warm," Chris replied, wishing that they were already married.

"I'm burning for you darling," Elizabeth replied as they crossed St Johns Road.

Chris stopped at the bottom of the pathway leading to Elizabeth's home.

"Stop teasing, my will power is very weak where you are concerned, so if you want me to be a good boy, stop teasing."

Elizabeth looked up at him smiling. "I love you so much," she said offered her lips, which he accepted willingly.

The house was well lit with flickering gas lighting, and a glowing fire was lit in the front room. "You must be freezing," Olive said. "Sit by the fire while I lay the table."

Chris took the easy chair, opposite the one that Ron was snoozing in.

"I'll help you mum," Elizabeth offered. "I had the warmth of Chris around me coming home, I'm not cold."

Olive looked at Chris and smiled.

Ron stirred in his chair and opened his eyes and saw Chris sitting opposite, he straightened up.

"Sorry Chris, I must have dozed off."

"It's the fire," Chris replied. "Makes one drowsy."

"I suppose so," Ron replied moving himself. "How are you Chris?"

"I'm good," Chris replied with a smile. "I will be glad when the winter is over, I don't like these dark nights, especially when you have an investigation."

"I hear that there is some scheme to alter the clocks, so that we get more daylight, I'm not quite sure how it works," Ron said.

"It's daylight in the evenings that I want," Chris replied.

"How is your case going?" Ron asked. "Elizabeth is always worried when you are on a case."

Chris smiled inwardly, he did not want Elizabeth to worry, but it gave him a morbid kind of pleasure, knowing that someone worried about him, having no family, no one had ever done that.

"She must not, investigations are dull, not dangerous," Chris remarked.

Elizabeth and her mother Olive both came into the room with plates and cutlery, both were smiling and talking, both wearing a white pinafore over their long dresses. Elizabeth looked at Chris, her eyes was full of love, she smiled at him. "Come along you two, get to the table."

Chris and Ron looked at each other, as with a smile they both took their place at the table, and for the next few minutes were fussed over by the ladies, who filled their plates, later Chris pushed his dessert plate away from him.

"You know Olive," he said leaning back in his chair, and placing his hands on his stomach. "Mr and Mrs Hardie, who were my adopted parents were good people, my landlady and her husband Mr and Mrs Dobson are also good people, in fact it seems that I have lived with good people all my life, but when I sit here, I feel that I am really and truly a part of a family, and it's nice."

"Darling," Elizabeth said her eyes watering. "You have a family now, one you can call your own."

"I know, that's why I miss now having one," Chris replied.

"It's a crime," Olive said. "No child should be without its blood parents during their upbringing regardless how the adopted parents are good."

Chris knew that Olive was religious. "Don't blame God," Chris said. "I always believe that everything that happens have a purpose, even if we do not know what it is."

"Do you know anything about your parents Chris?" Ron asked.

"Not a thing," Chris replied. "I could have found out I suppose, but I did not know that I was adopted until I was eighteen, and then I thought it's too late, after all I knew that they were both killed, so I knew I could not find them."

"You poor darling," Elizabeth remarked.

"It's alright Elizabeth," Chris replied. "I don't hurt, having never known them, but at times like this, I wonder."

"Perhaps darling if your parents had not died, we might never had met," Elizabeth said quietly as she touched Chris's hand.

"Perhaps that was the reason," Chris said. "if so, there is someone I need to thank even though it sounds dreadful."

"Do you think your father could have been a police-man?" Ron asked.

"No idea Ron," Chris answered. "I was born in 1886, did we have policemen then?"

"Bow Street Runners, London's first professional police force I think," interrupted Olive. "Now no more of this sad talk, what are you two doing tonight?"

"Just a lazy night mum," Elizabeth replied.

"I'll have the Christmas tree here tomorrow or Friday," Ron remarked.

"Chris is off on Sunday, we will dress the tree then," Elizabeth replied.

Ron looked at Chris with a smile. "That's me told," he said, as Chris returned the smile knowingly.

Chapter Eight

Friday morning was cold and brisk, and Chris turne up his collar as he made his way down the high stree He was late, it had been almost midnight when h had left Elizabeth's house the night before. He passed w dressed women in their heavy top coats, and their fancy ha displaying feathers and birds, and even fruit. Chris looked the bank where Elizabeth works as he passed, he would ha loved to have seen her. His mind tried to grasp the reason how or why two perfect strangers could come toget adore each other to the extent, where each would willi give their own life for the other. He smiled as he entered police station, he knew what his old sergeant, Serg Willett would have said. "It's just love."

"Morning Sergeant," Chris said to Sergeant Will at the desk. "I'm not a lover of this cold weather," he unbuttoning his overcoat. "Where's Sergeant Dawkins?

Sergeant Williams looked at the large brown c clock on the wall behind him. "I thought it might warmed up by this time," he replied without a smile. off for Sergeant Dawkins."

Chris ignored the remark. "Everything alright he a: making his way to his office.

"Another fight at Canon Street last night," s Williams replied. "Uniform sorted it out, apart fro just a couple of drunks."

Chris stopped at his office door, and looked back at the sergeant. "Was anyone hurt?" he asked.

"Not bad enough to keep them," the sergeant Williams answered. "In a fight you are bound to be bruised."

Chris nodded his head in agreement. "Civilians?" he asked.

"No, this time a couple of soldiers, we have their names."

"Thank you Sergeant," Chris replied. "I might need to see them later," he said as he entered his office. He took off his overcoat and hung it on the stand, his trilby following, he saw George at his desk looking at him with a smile on his face. "Had a late night?" he said as he sat behind his desk.

"What are we doing today?" George asked. "Have we come to a full stop?"

"It often seems that way, then something turns up," Chris answered. "There was a fight at Canon Street again last night, so Sergeant Williams said, that will give us an excuse to call at the house this morning."

"Better give the girls time to get up," George remarked with a grin. "They also had a late night."

"Alright," Chris murmured.

Sergeant Williams knocked and came in with two hot cups of tea. "Thought you would like a warm up," he said placing a cup before the two of them.

"Tell me Sergeant," Chris said after thanking him for the tea. "Did these soldiers come from Winchester barracks?"

"I've only read the report left by Sergeant Dawkins," sergeant Williams replied. "The soldiers are based at Winchester, awaiting transit but they are billeted in Winchester."

"Do we know where?" George asked.

"I have the addresses on the report list," sergeant Williams answered. "Is it important, Sergeant Dawkins allowed them to go because they will soon be in France."

"Sergeant House and myself will be at number 7 or number 8, Canon Street this morning," Chris remarked. "Have those soldiers addresses on my desk by the time we get back please."

"I will," sergeant Williams promised as he left the office.

"Those soldiers will be at the barracks now," George remarked. "What do you think?"

"Better to see them in their billets," Chris answered. "If we see them at the barracks, they will have a superior with them, and perhaps they won't be free answering questions."

"I agree," replied George nodding his head.

"When we have finish the tea, we'll go to Canon Street," Chris said taking a drink.

Half an hour later Chris found number seven, just a little way down Canon Street, on the left hand side, there was a school on the right hand side.

"Is that a mixed school I wonder?" Chris remarked as they stopped outside number seven.

"No idea," answered George following Chris, there are a few young girls playing in the playground. "Maybe all girls school."

"Whatever," Chris remarked turning towards the door of number seven. "It's not a nice place to run this type of house," he said knocking the door.

The door was opened by an attractive blonde young woman, her blond hair resting on the shoulders of her light blue house coat, she looked however that she had not been up long.

"Morning," she smiled.

"Morning," George answered with a smile. "I hope we haven't got you out of bed?"

The young woman looked at them for a few moments, then her smile faded. "What can I do for you?" she asked.

"Are you the tenant of the house?" Chris asked.

"I live here," the woman answered.

"Are you the tenant?" Chris repeated himself. "I am Detective Inspector Hardie, and this is Detective Sergeant House," Chris informed her. "And I would like to see the tenant please."

A slight smile came back to the woman's face. "You will have to wait here while I see if she is in her room," she said closing the door, but leaving it ajar.

"She looks a bit of alright," George remarked as they waited on the doorstep with their hands deep in their coat pockets.

Chris was smiling, but had made no comment when the door opened.

"You had better come in," the same young woman said. "The tenant will see you in a few moments, she was having a lay in."

"Thank you," Chris answered taking off his trilby and following the young woman inside, Chris noticed the passage they were in was a long one, the house seemed narrow from the street, but obviously was built a long way backwards. The woman opened a side door left of the passage. "Perhaps you would wait in here," she offered. "It is warm, please make yourself at home."

Chris and George entered the room, furnished only by four sofas placed in a square, and low table in the centre of the square, with a few magazines on it.

"Looks like a waiting room," George remarked as he selected a place to sit.

"Perhaps it is," Chris answered.

Ten minutes had gone before the door opened, and a smartly dressed woman of about thirty entered.

"I'm sorry to have kept you waiting gentlemen," she said as she closed the door behind her, and touched her dark hair that was somehow built into a high display on top of her head.

"My apologies for disturbing you," Chris replied as he stood. "I am Detective Inspector Hardie, and my colleague Detective Sergeant House," he said indicating George with a look. "And you are?"

"Mrs Ellen Bliss, please Inspector be seated and tell me how I can help you?" she replied making her way to a sofa.

"Are you the tenant of this house Mrs Bliss?" Chris asked.

"Yes I rent this house Inspector, can you tell me why that is of interest to you?" she replied.

"We are having to deal with fights, Mrs Bliss, and they simple have to stop."

Mrs Bliss smiled. "Inspector I know that there are fights outside, many of these are overspill from the pub a few yards further down. Canon Street is a very rough street, I never go down the street, I feel it's not safe to do so."

"We have reports that the fights starts from here," George spoke up.

"Can I be held responsible for any fight that take place outside my house?" Mrs Bliss asked innocently. "We are only women in this house you see."

"Mrs Bliss, you must forgive me, but we know that there are young women here that seems to entertain men in the forces," Chris spoke gently.

"Entertain is the right word Inspector, but it has different meanings, and I hope you do not suggest the wrong meaning?" Mrs Bliss replied, her face sober.

"Yes we entertain men of the forces here, my house is open twenty-four hours to any young soldier or sailor that may feel lonely, I have four young woman here, who will sit with them in here," she said indicating the room. "They sit in here talk, spill out their problems and troubles, we make them tea and sandwiches, and sympathise with them, many times this room is full, it's a happy room, many sad beings leave here smiling," Mrs Bliss commented.

"How do these young ladies of yours earn their living Mrs Bliss?" George asked. "They need money to live don't they?"

"The four young women I have lodging here are all married, and get their husband's army pay. When their husband went off to France, the army pay was so low that it was hard to keep the roof above them, so the five of us decided to live together, entertaining the lads was just an afterthought, it passes the time, but we are glad to do it."

"Besides entertaining the men as you told us Mrs Bliss, would any of the girls go farther with their entertainment do you think?" George asked.

Mrs Bliss thought for a while. "That's a brute of a question Sergeant," she said with a shrug of her shoulders. "As far as I'm aware the answer is no, but who can tell, who can tell what two people gets up two, women are sentimental, how can I say whether one might give comfort out of pity in that way, but I can assure you, not in this house."

"You say you rent this house Mrs Bliss," Chris said. "Who do you rent it from?"

"I rent it from a Mr Martin Cross, he's a Winchester man, he's a very hard man, he would only rent it on a six monthly term of payment, I paid him just two weeks ago."

"Have you a receipt Mrs Bliss?" Chris asked, a bit shocked.

"Yes I have," Mrs Bliss replied. "But why are you so interested in my rent agreement?"

"Mr Cross is dead Mrs Bliss," Chris replied.

Mrs Bliss looked at Chris bewildered, Chris thought her shock was genuine.

"I only saw him two weeks ago," she muttered. "I must say this is surprise news, how did he die?" she asked.

"He died three days ago," Chris replied ignoring the question. "We found an address book in his belongings Mrs Bliss, do you recognise these names, Sue Hayward, Neil Dower, Linda Coven and Blanche Criddle?" Chris asked taking the address book from his overcoat pocket.

"Yes they are the women lodging here, but then he knew all the women," Mrs Bliss answered.

"At the back of the address book Mrs Bliss, he has their initials with a sums of money entered by the side of the initials, can you explain that?"

Mrs Bliss took the address book, and studied the page, she shook her head as she handed it back to Chris.

"You better asked the girls Inspector, I see my name is not entered."

"No it's not," replied Chris. "Why would you suppose that is?"

"Again Inspector, you should ask the girls," Mrs Bliss replied.

"What do you pay in rent Mrs Bliss?" George asked.

"Thirty pounds every calendar months on a six monthly term of payment," Mrs Bliss replied. "What are your thoughts on it Inspector?" Mrs Bliss asked Chris.

"My first thoughts are that it represents money paid to Mr Cross by each woman," Chris replied. "I can't believe that Mr Cross was paid from each of the woman that much, it runs into hundreds, where would they get it from?"

Mrs Bliss shrugged. "I have no idea," she replied.

"I'm afraid I will have to see all the women mentioned here," Chris informed.

"I will get them for you," Mrs Bliss replied, getting up and leaving the room.

"Mrs Bliss do not seem too concerned," George remarked.

"No, I noticed that," Chris replied. "Baffling."

The door opened and four sober dressed young ladies followed Mrs Bliss into the room.

"I am Sue," said the first blond hair girl to enter, then sat on a sofa.

"I am Neil," smiled the second girl, a striking dark hair woman, who went and sat by Sue.

"I am Linda," smiled the third young lady, who held her hand over her mouth, unable to stop giggling.

"I am Blanche," the blonde woman who had answered the door to them announced as she sat by Linda.

"These young ladies lodge here with me Inspector," Mrs Bliss spoke. "You can now ask them."

"Thank you Mrs Bliss," Chris replied, a bit taken back, and a bit nervous, he had never interviewed such a large group of striking women before, he looked at George, who was sitting up in his chair, eyeing each one.

Chris cleared his throat. "Ladies, I am here because the owner of this house is dead."

A chorus of, "Oh no," came from the young ladies.

"I'm sorry ladies," Chris apologised. "I thought that Mrs Bliss would have told you."

Chris saw the ladies shook their heads and look at Mrs Bliss, who remained silent.

"Well I am afraid it's true," Chris continued. "He died three days ago, and among his belongings we found this address book," he said holding the address book in front of him for all to see.

"With all your names in it except Mrs Bliss, now at the back of this address book, your initials have been written, and by the side of each initial a sum of money is written, I need to know the meaning of this?"

"Why do you really have to know Inspector, what would a few names in the back of an address book do with his murder?" Mrs Bliss asked.

"I'm sorry Mrs Bliss," Chris remarked. "I can't remember saying he was murdered."

Mrs Bliss looked straight at the Inspector. "I took it that he was murdered, why else would the police worry what he had written down in an address book, if he died of natural causes."

"You are quite right of course Mrs Bliss, this is a murder investigation, so I need the truth from each of you."

"He has £72 written down for me," Blanche was the first one to speak, Chris looked at the book.

"That is right Mrs Criddle," Chris replied.

"£54 for me," volunteered Sue Hayward.

"£44 for me," Linda Coven murmured.

"And £62 for me," Neil Dower replied.

Chris checked the amounts as each lady told him, he nodded his head. "All seems correct, can you now tell me the reason why Mr Cross would have this information?"

"It's our combine savings," replied Blanche. "We are saving for the house next door, this house is a bit small for all of us."

"Is the house next door, number 8, up for sale?" George asked a little taken back with their explanation. "Only we have reasons to believe that there is activity at number eight."

"That might be me," Mrs Bliss answered. "I do have the back door key to the house, to keep an eye on the house just in case, you see the owner is abroad somewhere, he's been gone at least three months, and I have no idea when he will return."

"I see," Chris replied wondering what his next question would be. "Why would Mr Cross have these details at the back of his address book?" he asked.

"Mr Cross would be dealing with the buying number 8 as soon as the owner comes back," Mrs Bliss answered. "After all, we are just women, it's far easier for a man to represent us in these matters."

"So Mr Cross have your money as written in the book?" George asked. "You might have a job to get it back."

Murmurs started between the girls, who eventually looked at Mrs Bliss for her opinion.

"I'm sure everything will be alright girls," she said. "We have his signature on the amount he has of yours, and that book is also proof."

"Not really," replied George. "Money is entered beside your initials it do not say you gave it to him, it could be that you owed it to him?"

Another murmur went up between the girls, but no one spoke out, they seem contented to let Mrs Bliss do the talking.

"You are not with the ladies in their wish to buy next door Mrs Bliss?" Chris asked. "Your name not on the list."

A smile came to her face. "You might as well know Inspector, I'm sure you will find out anyway, but if Mr Cross is dead, then this house comes to me, you see I knew him before he bought the house, this house was on the market as I was looking for one, but I only had half of the asking price, I asked to Mr Cross to buy the other half, on condition that I could live in the house for as long as I wished, and in the event of a death, the house would go to the survivor. He insisted that a rent was paid however, otherwise it would be of no use to him, and I agreed."

"I am not without sadness over his death, but business is business, it could have been the other way around," Mrs Bliss commented.

"But how do you know, that he has not altered this agreement you say you have?" Chris asked.

Again Mrs Bliss smiled. "There is a clause that controls that situation, it can only be altered by both signatures."

"Very wise," Chris remarked. "So let's get this straight, you, Mrs Bliss will become the owner of this house through Mr Cross's death, he owes these young ladies a sum of £232 combined, he would be dealing with the buying number 8 as soon as the owner comes, what is the asking price by the way?"

"£545, a ten percent deposit has already been paid," answered Mrs Bliss.

"So £54 has been paid, that leaves £490, that's a lot, can you get it?" Chris asked.

"We hope to, you may think I'm bad to say this, but I can now get a mortgage for the rest on this house if we need it by the time the owners come back from abroad."

Chris decided he did not want to pursue the interview on the same subject.

"Do you know a young woman by the name of Janet Wilson?" Chris asked.

The young ladies were shaking their heads. "No," replied Mrs Bliss.

"What about Susan Mitchell, Leslie Wicker?" Chris asked.

Again the young ladies shook their heads. "Should we know them Inspector?" Mrs Bliss asked.

"Just enquiries Mrs Bliss," Chris remarked. "You say you entertain lads from the forces, would you entertain civilians as well?"

"Not as a rule Inspector," Mrs Bliss answered. "Sometimes however, a soldier might have a civilian with him, many lads are very shy Inspector, the need to be accompanied, we would not bar him from entering."

"That's very charitable of you," George remarked. "How can you afford to give out sandwiches and tea, if you are open twenty four hours a day, and also save for the house next door?"

Mrs Bliss gave George another black look. "We manage Sergeant, these lads are good lads, many bring a tin of spam or a packet of tea, we manage, it cost very little."

"If you don't have civilians in as a rule," Chris said altering the subject again. "I suppose you would not know a Mr Jeffery Mallard, or a John Thompson?"

Mrs Bliss hesitated before answering, Chris thought he saw a slight fear enter her eyes. "I'm afraid I know none of the people you have mentioned Inspector, we don't often know their surname."

"Miss Coven," Chris said looking at the girl. "Do you know Mr Mallard?"

A shade of pink appeared on Linda Coven's face as she stammered to answer. "Should I Inspector?"

"He told us he was with you during the hours when the crime was committed."

Linda looked at Mrs Bliss. "What is this man like Inspector?" Mrs Bliss asked.

Chris described him as best he could, he saw a smile come to Linda's face.

"Dandy," she said. "Yes he was here with us, we call him a Dandy, always ware his overcoat over his shoulders."

"That's him," Chris replied. "So you can alibi him that he was here, between four and five o'clock three days ago?"

"We all can Inspector," answered Mrs Bliss.

"But he is a civilian," George remarked. "Did he come with a soldier, only calling him Dandy implies that he is not a stranger here?"

"He was a friend of Mr Cross," Mrs Bliss replied. "He did not call regular, but when he did, he always brought a supply of rations, you could say, he was a one off."

Chris looked at George, then stood up. "Thank you ladies for your time, and your answers, you may have helped us a lot, because of your names being in the address book, I might need statements from each of you."

"We will be here Inspector," Mrs Bliss replied getting up and opening the door of the room. "Please feel free to call whenever you want to."

Once outside Chris put on his trilby, and buttoned his overcoat, he felt the cold, he looked up Canon Street, and he looked at his watch. "It's gone twelve George," he said. "Let's have a sandwich in the White Horse."

Before passing number eight, Chris looked in the window, then stepped back into the road, and studied the upstairs. "All the windows have blinds," he remarked moving on. "Still one would expect that if the owner is away."

They entered the White Horse, Chris looked around, it had been several months since he had been in the pub, he knew he would not see the landlord he knew, he was in prison.

"Afternoon gentlemen," the man behind the bar greeted them. "Not a very warm day is it?" he smiled. "What can I get you?"

"Two pints of bitter please," Chris replied. "And a couple of cheese sandwiches if you have them."

"That we can do," replied the smiling barman, as he took two pint glasses in one hand, and turning his back, held them under a barrel that was on a stand behind him, he turned on a brass tap, and the beer started to filled the glasses.

"There we are Sir," he said turning back to them and placing the glasses on the counter. "With the food, eight-pence please."

Chris paid the man and looked around the bar for a chair. "Let's sit over there by the window," Chris suggested taking his pint and moving towards the table, with George following.

"Well, what is your opinion Chris?" George asked putting his glass down.

Chris took a drink of his beer and smacked his lips, felt angry. "That was the most brilliant load of nonsense that I have ever heard in my life, if the police station think they will get a case of a disorderly house against them, they will need two things, catch a man in the act of paying a girl for sex, or get a man to confess that they paid for their entertainment that it was sex, Mrs Bliss have every situation covered, it must have taken some thinking."

"When I entered," George replied. "It smelt like a brothel, all powdery and smell of perfume."

"I wouldn't know George, never been in one but at least they gave Mr Mallard an alibi," Chris replied.

"They were certainly nice looking," George remarked. "I could have fancied them myself."

Chris did not answer, as the barman came over with two plates each holding a sandwich.

"Thank you," Chris said.

"Enjoy," replied the barman.

"I was watching you, George, your tongue was hanging out," Chris remarked with a grin.

"That's youth for you I suppose," George answered with a laugh as he picked up his sandwich.

"Did you believe this merry go round they told us the truth about the money and the house?" Chris asked looking at his sandwich.

"When you think of it, they did very well with our questions, they said the money by their initials was money being saved for the house next door, they did not seem all that concerned about the possibility of losing it?" George replied.

"Yes," Chris replied biting into his sandwich. "Why would you give money to a landlord to save for you, why not put it in a bank, also Mrs Bliss said Mr Cross was a very hard man, yet she loans him money, it don't add up, but we will look into it."

Chris refused the second pint. "I want to call into the Rising Sun before they close," he said.

"We have it down there then?" George replied.

"Not you George," Chris said with a smile. "Too many girls in one day is not good for you, I want you to find out who Mr Cross had for a solicitor, he must have had one for the house."

"You keeping this Janet Wilson all to yourself then?" George said with a grin on his face.

Chris smiled. "You will see her soon enough, but at the moment she don't know you, and I want it kept that way."

They both drank the remains of their pints, and left. "We'll cut through the Cathedral Grounds," Chris remarked. "It's quicker."

They soon found themselves in Colebrook Street, they crossed the road and entered Abbey Passage. "Well here we are," Chris said stopping outside the Fire Station. "I'll leave you to it, and see you back at the office."

"Don't drink too much then," George answered as he passed the front of the Fire Station, and entered the police station next door.

The Rising Sun was not busy, just a couple of men smoking clay pipes and sitting by the roaring log fire, which gave the whole pub warmth.

"Hello Chris," Alfie smiled. "This is unexpected," he said taking a pint glass and holding it below the pump nozzle. "Bitter is it?" he asked as he started to pump the pump.

"Do I have an option?" Chris replied with a smile noticing that the glass was already half full. Chris put the cost on the counter. "How is the young lady?" Chris asked as Alfie gave him the pint.

"Lovely young thing," Alfie replied. "She's upstairs at the moment, do you want to see her?"

"In a moment Alfie," Chris replied taking a sip of his pint. "Did she come down to the bar last night?"

"Just for a moment, she wanted to make a couple telephone calls, she said they were both to Southampton, she paid me sixpence afterwards, told me to keep the change, she is a lovely girl," Alfie concluded.

"You might see Sergeant House in here perhaps tonight or tomorrow, if she is around, don't let on that he is a policeman."

Alfie put a finger to his lips. "Not a word," he promised with his usual grin.

"I'll take my pint to the table then Alfie," Chris replied. "Would you ask her if she can spare me a moment at the bar?"

Chris saw her as she entered the bar, through the side door that separated the bar from the private dwelling, she smiled as she approached him.

"Inspector," she said. "What a lovely surprise."

Chris stood, and offered her a seat. "Will you have a drink?" he asked.

"Thank you," Janet replied. "A drop of gin perhaps with tonic."

Chris went to bar, and within a few moments placed her drink before her. "Mother's ruin," he remarked.

"I wouldn't know," Janet replied. "I'm not a mother."

Chris settled himself opposite her. "Lodging alright?" he enquired.

"Great," Janet replied. "Alfie and Liz are very nice people, they have made me feel very welcome."

"So you are happy here?" Chris remarked.

"Who wouldn't be, it's a change for me lodging in a pub, free of charge as well," Janet replied with a smile.

Chris watched as Janet poured some tonic on top of the gin, then taking a sip. "Do you often come to Winchester?" Chris asked.

"Whenever I can," Janet replied. "Believe it or not, but I have a boyfriend at the barracks, in Winchester, a Lance Corporal," she added.

"That is not hard to believe," Chris replied honestly. "Will he be going to France?"

"I'm sure of it," Janet replied. "Although I don't know when, I'm sure it won't be long."

"You will miss him," Chris said.

Janet took a sip of her drink, then nodded her head. "He will be better off than most, his officer will look after him."

"Favouritism?" Chris asked.

"No, he's a batman to a Captain," Janet said with a smile.

"I see," Chris replied his mind racing as he took a drink.

"Looking after a Captain, could reduce the number of times he has to go over the top, as they say," Janet smiled.

"Please forgive me Miss Wilson, it was rude of me for not asking, how are you feeling from your ordeal?" Chris altered the subject, not wanting her to think he was prying.

"Can't you call me Janet," she said grinning at him. "I'm just sore," she answered his question.

"You said you don't live with your parents Janet, live in a flat on your own, you must work?"

Janet grinned. "I could have been a shop girl," she replied. "I could have gone into service, but I would not have been able to rent a flat on my own, believe it or not Inspector, I clean houses, and shops, I'm a Miss Mop."

"That sort of work gives you a good income?" Chris asked.

"For me it does," Janet replied. "Inspector, I would like to be home for Christmas, it's only a week away you know."

"Yes I do," Chris replied. "I am not making a lot of progress at the moment, but coming Tuesday, you can go home, however I will need a statement before you do."

"To clear things in my head Janet," Chris remarked after taking another sip of his drink. "It was the first time you had met Mr Cross wasn't it, I mean, you said you met him in the Bell Inn, and you allowed him to walk you to the station, but on the way, you stopped for a kiss and cuddle."

Janet sipped her drink, she looked at Chris and smiled. "Inspector, firstly, I don't remember saying I was in the Bell Inn, secondly, yes it was the first time I had met Mr Cross, and thirdly, I did stop for a cuddle, my boyfriend had let me down, I felt miserable and lonely, I just wanted a hug, I was not going to give Mr Cross something that Albert thinks he owns."

"You told me that you were in a pub, in the centre of the town, which you didn't know the name, but it was opposite a hotel, well the only hotel opposite a pub in the town is the Suffolk Arms Hotel, and that's opposite the Bell Inn, almost."

"You are clever Inspector," Janet said as she finished her drink.

"Would you like another one?" Chris asked with a smile.

"I have nothing better to do," Janet replied. "Yes please."

Chris went up to the counter taking his half empty glass with him.

"Same again for the lady Alfie, and I'll have a half, mustn't have too much, I have work to do," Chris said.

"Why, did your boyfriend let you down?" Chris asked as he placed the new drink in front of her. "I mean how did you know he let you down?"

"He was supposed to meet me at midday under the King Alfred Statue, by half past one he had not appeared, so I decided to have a drink, I think I went in two or three pubs, can't remember," she said grinning at Chris.

"I expect his Captain needed him," Chris replied.

"No, it's something else," Janet replied. "The Captain is on leave."

"Have you made contact with him since?" Chris asked curiously.

"He knows where I am," Janet replied taking another drink.

Chris leaned back, took out his pocket watch.

"You got to go?" Janet asked.

"Afraid so," Chris replied pocketing his watch. "I do have work to do you know, will you be alright?"

"Will I see you again?" Janet asked.

"Before Tuesday, I promise," Chris answered.

With his collar up and his hands dug deep into his overcoat pockets, Chris slowly walked back to the Police Station, his mind going over the interview he had with Miss Janet Wilson. Most of what she had said, he already knew, apart from her boyfriend, a soldier name Albert. He wondered who she had phoned at Southampton, he would like to know.

He entered the station, the desk sergeant was missing, he went through to his office, and was greeted by George.

Chapter Nine

"Any luck George?" Chris asked as he took off his overcoat and his trilby. "With the solicitor," Chris added crossing to his desk.

"I phoned the solicitor who dealt with his house, I got the number from the documents you brought back from Mr Cross's bedroom, it seems that the solicitor Briggs and Briggs, Mr J. Briggs, he was in court, he won't be at the office today, so I made an appointment for Saturday morning."

"Saturday?" Chris remarked. "Your day off."

"I know," George replied. "But I'm quite happy to come in, I have no plans."

"It would be a great help George," Chris answered. "I can't pay you back this week however, I am decorating a Christmas tree on Sunday."

"It's no problem Chris," George replied.

"Good man," Chris replied, then related his meeting with Janet Wilson.

"Any plans for tonight George?" Chris asked.

George shook his head. "Usually go for a pint in the Barleycorn, or the Robin Hood," George answered. "No big deal."

"Can you have one at the Rising Sun tonight?" Chris asked. "Play it by ear, keep an eye on Janet Wilson."

"I can," George replied. "But I do not know her?"

"She will stick out like a sore thumb," Chris remarked. "Anyway, Alfie will give you the nod."

"Expenses?" George asked with a grin.

"I'll try," Chris replied with a smile. "Then tomorrow you can see this solicitor, after then, if it's necessary spend the lunch time in the Rising Sun."

"This job is getting better all the time," George laughed. "What will you be doing?"

"My next job is to phone the barracks, to try to find out more about Janet's boyfriend, then," Chris said picking up a piece of paper from his desk. "I'm going to the billets of those two soldiers that were in a fight last night, you never know."

"What do you want me to do?" George asked.

"Janet Wilson, according to Alfie, made two phone calls to Southampton last night, is it possible to find out who those calls were made to?"

"I'll have a go," George replied. "Where is the exchange?" he asked.

Chris shrugged. "I know the General Post Office is in Parchment Street."

"That's where I will ask," George replied taking his overcoat from the stand, and leaving the office.

"On your way out George, get the sergeant to get me the peninsula barracks will you."

It was some five minutes later when the phone rang, Chris took the receiver.

"Hello," Chris spoke onto the receiver.

"Peninsula barracks here," Chris heard a voice say.

"Good afternoon," Chris spoke into the receiver. "I am Detective Inspector Hardie of Winchester CID, I would like to speak to the adjutant, I believe his name is Captain Squire."

"Just a moment Sir," came the reply.

Chris tapped the top of his desk with a pencil that he held in his hand while he waited.

"Captain Squire," a voice said suddenly.

"Oh, Captain Squire, I am Detective Inspector Hardie of Winchester CID, you may remember my colleague Sergeant House called on you regarding a revolver?"

"I certainly do Inspector, I hoped his visit was a help?"

"It was Sir," replied Chris. "I was wondering if you can assist me further?"

"If I am able Inspector," replied the Captain.

"The woman who was raped Sir, it seems she had a boy-friend, a Lance Corporal station at your barracks, all I know about him is that his name is Albert and he is a batman for a captain, who is now on leave, I wondered if you could fill in the missing information."

"Can't you ask this woman inspector?" Captain Squire questioned.

"In a murder investigation Sir," Chris replied. "Everyone is a suspect, ask a direct question, people tend to clam up, so one has to draw the information from them."

"Inspector, let me speak to my sergeant in the other room, can you hold?" replied the Captain.

"Certainly Sir," Chris replied.

Chris started to tap the pencil, he looked absentmind-edly around his office, looking at nothing in particular, when the phone crackled again.

"Inspector," came the voice of Captain Squire. "We have a Captain Dobbs on leave at the moment, he is the only one with a lance corporal for a batman, I believe the soldier you are interested in is Lance Corporal Albert Foster, he comes from Birmingham."

"That could be him Sir," Chris replied.

"I'm afraid he's on jankers at the moment Inspector."

"Jankers being a punishment?" Chris asked.

"That's right Inspector," replied Captain Squire. "Have you not been in the service Inspector?"

"Tried, but I have the policeman's complaint, flat feet," Chris answered. "Would it be possible for you to tell me, why, he is on jankers?" Chris asked.

"It's only minor Inspector, he was overdue, and got four days punishment," the Captain replied.

"What day was that Captain?" Chris asked. "When he was late?"

"Tuesday night Inspector," captain replied.

"Thank you very much Captain, I appreciate your cooperation," Chris replied.

"Inspector, you do know that if your investigation involves a soldier, you will go through the Army won't you?" Captain Squire asked.

"Well the revolver is incline to involve the Army, but as yet I have no proof as to where it came from, because I cannot find it, but be assured Sir, if my investigation was to involve the Army, I would let you know," Chris promised.

"Thank you Inspector, so Lance Corporal Foster I take it is not involved?"

"At the moment Captain, I am only filling the gaps in stories," Chris assured the Captain. "However, he was late in barracks, on the night the murder and the rape was committed, I would like to know his whereabouts of the night."

"Anything else Inspector, I will try to get the information for you," replied the captain.

"It would be interesting to know, if the Captain had a webley revolver, and whether the Captain took it on leave with him, by the way Sir, do you know when this Captain went on his leave?"

"Last Monday," came the reply. "I know him personally."

"Can you keep the police out of it Sir?" Chris asked. "You might gain more information if you do."

"Leave it with me Inspector, I'll get back to you as soon as possible, this will be interesting, no direct question you said, thank you for ringing Inspector," replied the Captain.

"Thank you Sir," Chris replied.

Chris smiled to himself as he replaced the receiver, he wondered how the Captain would go about it, but already an idea was forming in his mind. He picked up the address of the two soldiers that had been fighting, they were both billeted together at number 6, Wales Street.

It was close to five pm when George entered the office. He smiled at Chris who was watching him hang up his overcoat.

"I got them," he said. "Janet Wilson phoned Southampton 3526 first, it's a house at Woolston, on the West End Road number 94, that probably where Susan Mitchell and Leslie Wicker hangs out, George sounded excited. "But wait until you hear who else she phoned."

"Thompson Model Shop, in St Denys," Chris interrupted.

George stood there with his mouth opened. "How the hell did you know that?" George asked.

"Just a guess," Chris replied smiling at George. "Very few private phones around, people tend to use the phone box, it's mainly businesses that have phones."

"She could have phoned to a phone booth?" George said a little angry, that he felt his surprise was spoiled.

"In that case she would have had someone at the other end waiting, which would have meant arrangements, she has had no time to do that, don't forget she's been in hospital," Chris remarked.

George went back to his desk, without answering.

"You did well George getting the details anyway," Chris praised, before he related his phone call to the barracks.

"Captain Squire, he's not a bad bloke," George replied. "I shall find his answers interesting."

"Won't we just," Chris replied. "Fingers crossed, now George you better get off and have some dinner, you can't drink on an empty stomach."

George got up, and took his overcoat. "I would rather do my duty than yours," he said with a grin putting on his overcoat.

"See you in the morning, after you've been to Briggs and Briggs," Chris said with a smile. "Mr Cross might have made a Will, if J. Briggs allowed to disclose the contents?"

"I'll see you then, it will be late in the morning," George replied, leaving the office.

Chris entered Wales Street from Water Lane, one gas lamp was burning at this end of the street, which enabled Chris to see the numbers, number 6 was almost opposite the Ship Inn, Chris knocked the door.

A tall thin woman, her dark hair cut to ears length, opened the door. She wore a long dark dress which was covered with a white apron, in which she was wiping her hands.

"Yes?" she asked.

"I am Detective Inspector Hardie," Chris answered. "And you are?"

"Mrs Morgan," the woman replied, stepping out onto the pavement, and looking both ways. "You had better come in," she said grabbing his arms and almost pulling him in.

Chris was pushed straight into the front room.

"Don't you know, it's unsafe for a copper around here, especially after dark," Mrs Morgan said. "Now tell me what's my Peter been up to now?"

Chris could not help smiling. "Policemen not liked around here Mrs Morgan?" Chris asked.

"No way, Bobbies usually walk in pairs along here," Mrs Morgan said pushing a odd hair away from her face.

"I am not in uniform Mr Morgan, anyway it's not your Peter I want," Chris assured her with a smile guessing that Peter was her husband.

"If it's not my Peter you want, what do you want?"

"I understand you have two soldiers billeted with you," Chris replied.

"That's right," answered Mrs Morgan. "What they been up to?"

"Nothing serious Mrs Morgan," Chris replied. "I would like a word with them."

"Well they are playing cards in the scullery, you better come through," she said opening a door at the far end of the room.

The two uniform dressed soldiers looked up from their cards as Chris led by Mrs Morgan entered the scullery.

Chris turned to Mrs Morgan. "Thank you," he said. "Would you mind if I spoke to these men in private, I'm sure you will understand Mrs Morgan," Chris said pleasantly.

"If you must," Mrs Morgan replied, retracing her steps into the front room and closing the door.

Chris smiled at the two soldiers, as he pulled a chair up to the table.

"I am Detective Inspector Hardie of Winchester CID, I need to ask you a few questions, but nothing you have to worry about," Chris said hoping to put them at ease. "I would like you to answer my questions as honest as you can."

The two soldiers looked at each other, the soldier sitting next to Chris shrugged. "OK, ask away," he said.

"You were both in a fight last night I believe," Chris began. "In Canon Street."

Chris saw them smiling at each other.

"Sorry about that Inspector," replied the soldier sitting opposite. "We always fight each other, we are best of friends."

Chris smiled. "I don't understand."

"It's the way we are, we fight each other, but bear no grudge, we might fight over something tonight if we go out, but we normally fight over women between ourselves, but I normally win," the soldier sitting next to Chris said with a grin.

"In your dreams," remarked his friend. "In your dreams."

Chris felt bewildered, he certainly did not want them to fight now, even if they remained friends.

"Were you fighting over a woman last night?" Chris asked.

The two soldiers looked at each other. "What about coming to the point Inspector?" the soldier sitting opposite asked.

Chris thought for a moment, his usual way of getting information was asking questions in different ways, he would often ask the same question differently.

"Aren't we under military command being soldiers?" the soldier sitting next to Chris asked before Chris had made up his mind what to say.

"Partly," Chris replied. "Your Adjutant, Captain Squire know all about my investigation."

Chris saw the two look at each other. "Let me tell you about it, if you are honest with me, I will not mention your being picked up last night for fighting."

"Then you will want to know our names," answered the soldier opposite.

"You gave your names to the police officer last night," replied Chris.

"So we did," replied the soldier.

"I am investigating a murder," Chris started. "You two have nothing to do with my investigation, apart from you visiting that house last night, which might be involved, what I need to know is did you pay the girls for their service?"

"You are asking us to grass Inspector," the soldier sitting next to Chris spoke.

"You know Inspector hundreds of men come here, ready to go to France, to fight for king and country, we all volunteer, when we get to France, we get trenches, wet and full of mud, no comfort at all, now you want us to grass on the girls who gave us soldiers that bit of comfort before we go?"

"I do sympathise with that," Chris replied. "It's not my wish to stop it, but this particular house might be mixed up in murder, and that I cannot let go."

"What is it you want to know then Inspector?" asked the soldier sitting next to him.

"I want to know, did you pay them?" Chris replied.

"Not directly," he replied. "We buy a ticket off the touts, two bob for a quickie, if you pay ten bob, which many of us can't afford, you can have an hour, anything goes."

"Who are these touts, do you know them?" Chris asked.

"No, they are around town, they stop you and ask, they are street vendors," replied the soldier opposite.

"When you call at the house, do they let you in?" Chris asked.

"Oh yes, tea and cake is provided, and the girls will come and talk to you, but if you can't show a ticket, that is all you get."

"I see," replied Chris. "You would be allowed in, and the ladies will talk to you, if you show them a ticket, then they will take you upstairs?"

"That's it Inspector, anything more I can't tell you," replied the soldier sitting by him.

"Who were you fighting over last night, I do know all the ladies of the house," Chris asked smiling inwardly over his own curiosity.

"I wanted a girl named Blanche, and so did he," replied the soldier sitting by Chris, in the end I got Neil, and he got Blanche, so we fought."

"Well don't fight any more," Chris remarked. "When you are in France, you will find your best friend more important than a bit on the side," Chris said getting up.

"Thank you for being straight, and don't worry, your names will not go to the barracks."

Chapter Ten

Saturday morning was cold, and cold made worse by a brisk wind blowing all the time, Chris dug himself as far into his overcoat collar as he could, his hands were deep in his pockets. He wondered if he would see Elizabeth, but he was a little early.

Chris stopped outside the Suffolk Hotel, to allow a wagon loaded with sacks of corn to enter Middle Brook Street, with the wagon passed, he crossed to the other side, and there was Elizabeth, smiling at him. She was in an all light brown outfit, her dress was a foot longer than her coat, she had a scarf around her neck, partly hidden by the collar of her coat that was turned up.

"You look lovely as well as warm," Chris smiled at her as he reached her. "Come on I'll walk with you."

"No you won't darling, you get to your office," she answered as she kissed him on the cheek, and then checked the collar of his coat making sure it was fully turned up. "It's too cold, I don't want you walking all the way back."

Chris smiled, she always fussed over him, and he liked it, but mainly because he had never had anyone to fuss over him before. "Keep close to the buildings," Chris advised. "You won't find the wind so biting, you're half day today?"

"That's right darling," Elizabeth replied. "You're off tomorrow, and we have the Christmas tree to decorate, mum and dad put the paper chains up last night."

"I was making enquiries in Wales Street last night," Chris remarked. "I kept thinking of you."

"I thought of you while I was in bed, wondering how you will keep me warm," Elizabeth teased, as she again kissed his cheek. "I'll see you, if not tonight, tomorrow morning early," she said with a smile as she left him before he could answer her teasing.

Chris entered his office, and straight away put on the gas fire, he shivered as he took off his overcoat and trilby, and hung them on the stand. The desk sergeant had told him that it had been a quiet night. "They don't go out much in this weather, anyway, most are saving a little for Christmas," sergeant Dawkins remarked.

Chris sat rubbing his hands briskly, his eyes fell on a envelope laying on the desk, he picked it up and examined it, it had been hand delivered, he torn it to open, and looking at the signature at the bottom, smiled to himself, it was from Captain Squire.

Inspector Hardie,

I am off on a long weekend leave, I tried my detective ability out, and have come up with the following, which I hope may be of help to you. Lance Corporal Albert Foster excused for being AWOL, he went to Southampton, and missed the train back, that is all.

I had the armoury make a gun checked, it's not an unusual happening. Mr Foster's Captain did not take his revolver home with him, his revolver was in perfect condition, all bullets were accounted for. Best of luck Captain Squire.

Chris read the letter again, and felt disappointed, however, Lance Corporal Foster's excuse did not back Janet Wilson's excuse for being in the Bell Inn, and meeting Martin Cross.

It was gone eleven when George entered the office, he took off his overcoat and hung it, rubbing his hands as he crossed to his desk.

"It's freezing cold outside, Chris," he remarked. "Nice and warm in here."

Chris smiled. "You should have stayed in bed," he teased.

"Well I have seen solicitor Mr J Briggs of Briggs and Briggs," George said with a smile. "He was cagy at the start, only to be expected I suppose," George continued.

"Anyway after I told him I was on a murder enquiry and his client Mr Cross was dead, he relaxed a bit, asked me how I knew Mr Cross was his client. I told him because of the house, and the letters he had wrote him. I then asked him if I could see the Will, if he had made one. He wondered of course why Mr Cross's parents had not contacted him, I told him they probably did not know about their son having a Will, let alone a house."

George paused for a while, as he got his thought together. "He showed me the Will, it was simple, if he left any money go to his parents, the house which we are interested in go straight to Mrs Ellen Bliss there is no question, no one can fight it."

"That is all?" Chris asked.

"Simple as that," George replied. "He did say he would contact Mr and Mrs Cross. I told him it may come as a shock to them, knowing that their son half owned a house with a woman, and I asked him to delay his contact with them for a couple of days."

"What did he say to that?" Chris asked.

"He said he would, at least until we contact him again."

Chris picked up the letter he had received from Captain Squire and passed it to George. "This was hand delivered this morning," he said.

George took the letter and read it, he shook his head. "Not promising is it?" George said handing the letter back. "We badly need that gun."

"I agree," replied Chris. "Did you notice the boyfriend's excuse for being late, he went to Southampton, and missed the train back to Winchester that night."

"One of them is lying," George remarked. "Are you going to ask her straight out about it?"

"I'll let it lie for the moment," Chris replied. "I'm puzzled though."

Chris then related to George his interview with the two soldiers.

"Crafty," George remarked after hearing the story. "It will be a job to find the touts, they don't approach civilians do they?"

"Wouldn't think so George, but at least apart from the tickets, they told me about the street vendors," Chris answered. "But we are investigating a murder, and we end up investigating prostitutes, how did you get on last night at the Rising Sun?"

"Almost forgot about that Chris," George replied with a smile. "Silly me, I went in and stopped until nine thirty, you were right, she stuck out like a sore thumb, also Alfie gave me the nod. Alfie told me that she was meeting a friend in the pub, so I waited. A smart looking girl came in, every bit as attractive as Janet. I sat where we usually sit, but they sat near the fire, I could not hear what they were speaking about, but they both can sink gin and tonic, God knows how many they had."

"She probably came up from Woolston?" Chris remarked. "We know she made a telephone call there."

"You are wrong," George replied with a grin. "When she left I followed, it was hard work, it being dark, and me having to keep well behind, I lost her in Canon Street however," George remarked.

"Did you indeed," Chris remarked interested.

"I walked by the house we visited, and loitered for a while, I saw a couple soldiers go in and out, but never saw the woman," George replied.

"She could be spending the night there?" Chris questioned.

"Could be," George agreed.

A knock came on the office door, making them both look towards it, Sergeant Bloom entered carrying his helmet under his arm.

"Morning," he said with a blush on his face. "Just thought I'd let you know that the bobby on the beat around Clifton Terrace told me that the people living there call Mr Mallard a Dandy because of the way he dresses. He is not at home very much, and when he is, there is no noise. It is widely thought that he has some kind of business."

"Probably right," George answered.

"Anything else Rowland?" Chris asked.

"The Thompson family are well respected, pleasant people I'm told, as for the shop opposite, people wonder how he makes a living, it's always empty."

"Thank you Rowland," Chris answered. "I thought that myself, still keep your ears open won't you."

"I'll do that Sir," sergeant Bloom answered, taking himself from the room.

Chris turned to George. "You know George, all the information we have, just takes us around in circles, I am wondering, if this is one case I'm not going to solve."

George smiled. "You win some and lose some," he said.

Chris thought about what George had said, and he did not like it, but thought that he might be right. "Well George, you might as well take what is left of your day off, we are stuck at the moment, I don't know which way to go?" Chris sighed.

"I am off to the Rising Sun," George replied. "One never knows?" he said getting up and putting on his overcoat. "I will also pop in there tonight, something might turn up."

"Thanks George, I appreciate it, what we need is another constable in this office, I think I'll have a talk to Chief Inspector Fox about it."

"I agree Chris," George answered as he left the office.

Chris was doodling with a pencil when the telephone rang, he lifted the receiver.

"Detective Inspector Hardie," he spoke into the mouthpiece.

"Sergeant Worthy of Woolston police Sir," came the reply.

"Yes Sergeant," Chris answered. "How are you?"

"Quite well Sir," sergeant Worthy answered. "I thought I would let you know, we brought in Susan Mitchell last night, she was one of the known prostitutes I put in my letter to you."

"I remember Sergeant," Chris answered all ears.

"It seems she had been to Winchester for the evening, she caught a late night train to Southampton, but the ferry had stopped running, so she took a horse cab, who had to bring her to Woolston, the long way to go to Woolston by road, anyway she could not pay and offered the horse cab driver her special service, if you get my meaning, but the cab driver would have none of it, so he drove straight to me Woolston Police Station."

"Surely she could have got the money from someone in the house?" Chris asked.

"She was not driven to West End Road, but to Pine Road," he said. "With Janet Wilson with you, the place is empty?" the sergeant added.

"That was lucky," Chris remarked.

"That was more than lucky Sir," replied the sergeant. "It's a long drive for a horse cab, also the driver must have been very faithful to his wife, Susan is quite striking."

"So I believe," replied Chris.

"Anyway Sir," continued the sergeant. "She was very chatty, seems she had more than enough to drink, and she slipped a little information."

"Such as," Chris asked.

"Well Sir, it seems that their pimp comes from Winchester, and it's a house use as a brothel in Winchester controlled by the same pimp, I know it's not a lot, but it's something."

"I agree Sergeant, and thank you for thinking of me," Chris replied. "Perhaps I can give you a little information in return, visitors to the brothel do not pay the girls, my information is that visitors buy a ticket from touts, mainly member of the forces were approached by those touts in the streets," Chris added.

"That's handy to know Sir," replied the sergeant.

"You are quite welcome Sergeant, it's a pity that she did not give the name of the pimp," Chris remarked.

"It is Sir," came the answer just as the phone went dead.

Chapter Eleven

*T*here was no let up in the cold weather, but by the time Chris arrived at Elizabeth's house, he was sweating, he had walked briskly and Alresford Road was all up hill.

Olive opened the door to him, and welcomed him with a broad smile, she was fussing with his overcoat, when Elizabeth rushed downstairs. They looked and smiled at each other, and Elizabeth rushed up to him, and planted a kiss on his cheek.

"You're nice and early," Elizabeth said leading Chris into he front room.

Ron looked over the top of his paper. "Cold outside Chris?" he asked.

"A bit," Chris replied looking around the room. "Someone has been busy," he said looking at the paper chains.

"Mum and dad did those," Elizabeth replied still holding on to Chris's arm. "This is our job," she added looking at the bare Christmas tree as high as the room, which stood left of the scullery door. "I have all the trimmings," she smiled looking up at Chris. "It will be fun."

"If you say so," Chris replied feeling comfortable with the warmth of the room.

"You have a cup of tea before you start Chris," Olive said.

"Put a spot of whisky in it," Ron remarked looking over the top of his glasses. "It will warm him."

"It's nice and warm in here," Chris remarked, as Elizabeth let go of his arm so that he could sit in the easy chair facing Ron.

"I'll help you mum," Elizabeth said as she followed her mother from the room.

Moments latter, Olive brought in cup of tea, and gave it to Chris. "I have a nice beef roast for dinner," she smiled. "I hope you have a appetite?" she asked.

Chris smiled his reply.

"I'm taking him for a pint before dinner," Ron interrupted.

"Only if we have finished decorating the Christmas tree dad," Elizabeth butted in.

"You better get a move on then," replied Ron looking at Chris with a smile.

Chris felt very comfortable as he sat sipping his tea, he watched as Elizabeth brought in a few boxes into the room placing them by the side of the Christmas tree, while Olive followed her in carrying a small wooden step ladder. "I can do that for you," Chris said about to get up.

"Sit where you are, and finish your tea, it's all very light stuff," Olive remarked.

The next hour passed quickly as Chris on the instruction from a giggly Elizabeth, about decorating the tree. Silver and gold tinsel were evenly spread over the tree branches, colour glass balls were threaded on to the branches by means of a ring attached to the balls, Elizabeth wanted a cracker placed here and there between the branches, and at the end of the long branches, a small clip on candle stick was placed, Elizabeth having placed a birthday cake candle in each.

"When do you light these candles?" Chris asked enjoying himself.

"Christmas day," replied Elizabeth. "We have to be careful that the tree don't catch fire, now all we have left is the fairy, that goes on the very top," Elizabeth smiled.

"I had better do that," Chris replied putting the step ladder in a position that would enable him to reach.

"I would like to do that," Elizabeth smiled.

"You could fall," Chris remarked a bit worried.

"Not with you holding me," Elizabeth teased.

Chris looked towards Ron and Olive, who had been watching their progress.

"You might as well give in Chris," Ron remarked looking over the top of his glasses and smiling. "She will get more enjoyment with you holding her than she will with just planting that fairy."

"Since when have you been an expert on what women want?" Olive said looking at Ron.

"You taught me all I know love," Ron replied with a grin.

"Ronald," Olive scalded, and crossing to him, pushed him playfully.

Elizabeth was already half way up the ladder. "Hold my legs," she giggled as she looked down upon Chris. "Don't let me fall."

Chris put his arm around her thighs, he smelt the lavender water on her, and felt her wriggle.

Elizabeth climbed down from the tree and stood back. "There darling," she said. "It's a beautiful tree, now during the week, we have to put presents under it."

"Just in time," Ron remarked.

Elizabeth looked at her father with scolding eyes. "You make sure Chris don't drink too much."

"That's one thing women are good at," Ron remarked.

"Oh, what is that?" Chris asked innocently.

"Orders," replied Ron. "They are very good at it," he said teasingly looking at his wife.

"Dinner will be on the table by one thirty," Olive said looking at her husband. "Now don't lead Chris astray."

"Of course they do have their good points," Ron carried on while in the hall way, with his wife helping him on with his overcoat, and making sure his scarf was tidy around his neck.

"I'm sure they do," Chris replied as Elizabeth was helping him.

Elizabeth pulled on the lapels of Chris's overcoat, brought him nearer to her lips. "Yes we have," she whispered giving him a quick kiss on the lips. "By the way Chris, will the young lady be there?" Elizabeth asked.

"What young lady is this?" Olive asked.

"Oh just a young lady involved in a murder, nothing for you to worry about mother," Elizabeth replied, looking at Chris and smiling.

"You do see the seamy side of life Chris," Olive replied, as she stood back from her husband satisfied that he was done up warm. "I have no idea how you stand it?"

"It's just a job Olive," Chris answered, smiling down at Elizabeth. "Someone has to do it."

"I think you are very courageous Chris," Olive said giving her husband a kiss. "Now don't be late for dinner," she added as Ron opened the front door.

"Who's this girl Elizabeth is on about?" Ron asked as they made their way down Magdalene Hill, towards the Rising Sun.

"It's a Southampton girl who was raped, beside a man who was shot dead," Chris replied. "She will probably talk to me if she is in the bar."

"Will I be in the way?" Ron asked understandingly.

"No way Ron, I'm off duty today," Chris replied with a smile.

The large log fire in the Rising Sun threw out the heat that hit them as Ron and Chris entered, Chris saw that the people in the bar area were crowding close to the fire, apart from them playing darts. Chris approached the bar, where Alfie as usual grinning held two glasses in his hands.

"I think it's two bitters Alfie," Chris said as he looked back at Ron who nodded.

Sensing that Ron had taken their usual seats behind him, Chris watched as Alfie started his pump action. "Is she in?" Chris asked.

"Upstairs," replied Alfie. "George was in last night," he added as he placed the two pints before Chris.

"One for yourself Alfie," Chris offered.

"I'll have a half bitter, that will be fivepence please," Alfie said. "Do you want me to call her?"

"No Alfie," Chris replied. "I am on my day off."

Chris took the drinks to the table at which Ron was sitting unbuttoning his overcoat. "That fire really warms the place up," Ron remarked, making himself comfortable. "I'm glad you came today, I don't get a lot of chances to have a pint."

"Glad to be of service," Chris smiled. "I don't think Elizabeth appreciated it."

"You would only be sitting around while they were in the scullery cooking dinner," Ron replied. "Praise their cooking when we have dinner, and all will be forgiven."

Chris smiled as he took a drink.

"What's this case you're on Chris, are you near solving it?" Ron asked.

"Stuck I'm afraid, I have a lot of the puzzle, but nothing fits yet," Chris replied looking up and seeing Janet Wilson entering the bar, she made straight for him.

"Inspector," she smiled.

"Miss Wilson," Chris replied standing up.

"Janet, please Inspector," she smiled teasingly.

"Janet," Chris replied feeling colour come to his cheeks. "This is my future father-in-law, Mr Oborne."

Ron smiled at her. "Nice to know you," he said.

"Can I get you a drink?" Chris offered.

"Well I'm helping Liz with the Sunday roast, but one small gin and tonic would be nice," Janet replied keeping her smile.

Chris went to the bar.

"Please be seated Miss Wilson," Ron offered her a chair. "Are you staying here?"

"For a few days as a guest of Winchester police," Janet replied with a grin. "I am enjoying it."

Chris returned with her drink and sat down.

"I always wondered if you were married Inspector," Janet said looking down her eyes hidden by her eyelids.

"It's my day off," Chris replied ignore the remark.

"I had no idea policemen had days off," Janet teased as she sipped her drink.

"Very few I can assure you," replied Chris. "Anyway how are you settling in?"

"It's nice here," she replied taking another drink. "I wish I had my handbag however."

Chris looked at her, he saw her remark as a question, wanting to know if it had been found.

"Did it contained anything of value?" Chris asked.

"You don't know much about women Inspector," Janet replied. "A handbag is a secret place, where no man should go."

"Really," replied Ron. "I wonder now what my wife has in hers."

"Don't go there," Janet grinned in answer before speaking to Chris. "I was wondering would it be OK for me to pop to Southampton this afternoon, I want to see a friend, I promise I'll be back by this evening, you are off duty, and it's Sunday, if I catch the three pm train I can be back before you miss me."

Chris thought for a while. "I'm sure that's alright Janet," Chris replied. "I will take your word for it that you will be back tonight."

"I will," Janet replied. "You have my address anyway if I'm not," she grinned.

Ron finished his drink, and got up. "Can I get you another?" he offered Janet who had finished hers.

"No thank you," Janet replied as she also got up. "I must go and help Liz, but I wish you a Merry Christmas should I not see you again."

"Thank you very much, I wish you the same," Ron replied taking Chris's glass and going to the bar.

Janet smiled, then turning to Chris. "I'll be back, perhaps you will be in again later tonight?"

"Play it by ear," Chris remarked. "I hope you have a safe journey."

Ron brought back the drinks. "That's quite a looker," he remarked placing the pint before Chris. "You are a lucky dog," he grinned.

Chris smiled as he sip the new pint. "Is there a telephone box on the way back?" he asked.

"No, Chris, the nearest one is in the Broadway."

"I'll have to use it before going home," Chris replied.

"Can't you use Alfie's?" Ron asked.

"I want to be out of earshot of Miss Wilson," Chris replied. "In fact I like to do it now, would you excuse me for a few moments."

"You carry on Chris, I'm happy here," Ron replied wondering.

George crossed to the phone as it rang. "Sergeant House," he spoke into the receiver.

"George," answered Chris on the other end. "I am at the Rising Sun."

"Lucky you," George replied with a grin on his face. "What's up?"

"I have just given Miss Wilson time off to go to Southampton, she's catching the three pm train from Winchester, I would like to know if she really goes to Southampton?"

"You want me to spy?" George answered.

"There is a nice pub just outside the railway station George," Chris remarked.

"Well nothing going on here, it will be a break, leave it with me," George replied.

"Don't drink too much," Chris smiled as he put back the receiver.

"That didn't take you long Chris," Ron remarked as Chris returned to the table and sat down.

"I needed to phone George," Chris replied.

"Is he good?" Ron asked.

"I don't have to tell him what to do, sometime I think he knows before I ask him," Chris answered with a smile. "He is the right man for the job that make it a lot easier for me."

"I'm sure it is Chris," Ron replied. "We better get along after this one."

Chris smiled. "Olive is alright Ron, you are lucky to have such a woman."

"Chris I have known that, even before we married," Ron grinned picking up his pint and taking a drink.

Chapter Twelve

*C*hris had not gone straight to the office on the Monday morning, he had called in on Mrs Cross.

"How are you coping Mrs Cross?" Chris asked as they sat in the front room.

"Life goes on Inspector," she answered, her face full of sadness. "But it is a struggle."

"I'm sure it is Mrs Cross," Chris replied sympathetically. "And your husband, is he bearing up?" Chris asked.

"Tony keeps everything inside," Mrs Cross replied. "It is no good for his health, I wish he would let go."

Chris sat forward twisting his trilby with his hands. "I am sorry for having to call, reminding you of your loss Mrs Cross, but I do have just one question that I need to know the answer," Chris said softly.

Mrs Cross looked at Chris, her face was sad, and Chris saw that her eyes were watery. "I'll help if I can," she replied with a kind of sob in her voice.

"Did your son have a bank account Mrs Cross?" Chris asked.

Mrs Cross looked at her lap, and shook her head. "I have his post office book here," Mrs Cross replied. "There is just over thirty pounds in it, why do you ask?"

Chris looked at her, he was trying to choose his words very carefully before he spoke, he did not want Mrs Cross worried, he didn't want to cause her more grief after everything she had been through.

"You remember the letter we found on your son about a loan he had queried, it's quite possible that the writer of that letter may come out in the open and try to get the money from your son's estate."

"If my son leaves any debts Inspector, we will honour it," Mrs Cross replied. "But truly I can't imagine Martin have any debts."

"You have not found a bank account apart from the post office account, no statements or such likes?" Chris asked gently.

Mrs Cross shook her head, Chris could see she was on the verge of crying. "His post office book is on the mantel piece there," Mrs Cross said looking up at the mantel. "You can see it if you want."

"I haven't found any other form of saving, but then again, you are the only one who has been in his room since," she sobbed. "I can't bear to go in there yet."

"Don't worry about it Mrs Cross," Chris answered. "I'm sure it's not important, just us in our muddling way trying to tie all the loose ends up."

"You're very kind Inspector, please, when can we start arrangements for my son's burial?" Mrs Cross asked.

Chris got up to leave. "Straight away Mrs Cross, your undertaker will be able to collect your son from the hospital, you know you can have him home should you want," Chris replied. "If I can be of any help, please get in touch with me at the station."

"Thank you Inspector," replied Mrs Cross getting up and moving to the door. "Thank you again for your kindness, my husband will be pleased, perhaps now he will release his feelings."

Chris entered the police station, and was greeted by Sergeant Williams. "I have just taken your tea in, told Sergeant House to drink it himself if you should not come in," he said unsmiling.

"Well I am in now Sergeant," Chris replied. "If my tea is cold I'll let you know, I'm sure you won't mind replacing it."

Chris smiled at George who was behind his desk, he took off his overcoat and trilby and hung them on the stand. "This cold weather don't seem to ease up," Chris remarked making for his desk.

"I have been to see Mrs Cross this morning," Chris said touching the cup of tea that was on his desk, and felt satisfied it was hot enough. "I wanted to know if Martin had a bank account, but all Mrs Cross knew was that he had a post office book with about thirty pounds in it."

"If the money in his book represents what we think, he must have money somewhere, perhaps he didn't use a bank?" George voiced his opinion.

"So many alternatives," Chris replied after he had taken a drink of his tea. "He could have it stashed away in a bank box, one thing however, if he has a bank account, it will be hard to find out which bank he uses?"

"Janet Wilson, bought a return ticket to St Denys," George said while he was thinking about what Chris had just said.

"So now we know she did not go into Southampton, I'm not familiar with the geography, the question is, is it easier to go to Woolston from St Denys than going from Southampton, or would she be calling on a certain shop in St Denys, wonder where Mr Thompson was yesterday?" Chris spoke as he finished his tea.

"I phoned Alfie," George said. "Alfie said she arrived back just before closing time."

"At least she's back, I would like to know where she went?" Chris remarked.

"Who of those we know, would you consider to be a pimp?" Chris asked George.

"Why do you ask me, Chris?" George replied.

Chris smiled. "Well, you have more experience than me in these matters."

"With that vote of confidence, I would have to say Mr Mallard," George replied.

"Has he got the muscle?" Chris asked. "I mean don't you have to be the bully type?"

George shrugged his shoulders.

A knock came on the door, and Sergeant Williams entered and closed the door behind him. "I got a gentleman to see you Inspector, his name is Mr Troop, he has a car outside, he must be rich." sergeant Williams said excitedly.

Chris looked at George wondering. "Send him in Sergeant, don't keep him waiting."

Mr Troop entered the room, he was a large built man dressed in a overcoat with fur around the collar, and carrying a blue grey trilby, Chris noticed that he had spots over his well polished brown shoes.

Chris stood up and offered his hand. "I am Detective Inspector Hardie, and my colleague Detective Sergeant House," he said indicating George with his head.

"Please," Chris offered the interview chair, he waited until he was sure that Mr Troop was comfortable. "What can I do for you Mr Troop?" Chris asked.

"For me Inspector, very little, I am here with the expressed wish of Mr J Briggs my solicitor," Mr Troop replied.

"Is that Briggs and Briggs solicitors?" George asked.

Mr Troop nodded his head. "From my solicitor I learnt that a Mr Martin Cross had died, although I can't see why my dealings with the man is any business of the police, but I have taken my solicitor's advice, and I am here."

Chris smiled to himself. "Perhaps you can tell us the reason your solicitor advised you to call upon us?" Chris asked.

Mr Cross owes me a large amount of money, when I heard that he was dead, I asked my solicitor to put in a claim against his estate. Mr Briggs told me that he was aware that Mr Cross had died in suspicious circumstances, and I may be of some help to you?" Mr Troop answered.

"We found a letter on Mr Cross's body, it was simply signed T, would that be you?" Chris asked.

"It would," Mr Troop replied.

"Are you a money lender?" George asked.

Mr Troop managed to smile. "No way, but I will give a loan to people I know."

"You knew Mr Cross?" Chris asked.

"I should do, he made all my suits, having a good tailor is very important to me," replied Mr Troop.

"Can you tell us why he borrowed from you?" George asked.

"I'm not quite sure what you mean Sergeant," Mr Troop replied.

"We understand he has a rich friend who he could borrow off, had he wanted money," George spoke.

Mr Troop grinned. "You are not talking about that Dandy Mallard are you?" he asked. "He would not have lent Mr Cross a penny, he treated Mr Cross as a dog, and Mr Cross took it but Mr Cross was a different man when he was not under Mallard's influence."

"Really," Chris said.

"I can tell you a lot about that man, but it has nothing to do with my loan to Mr Cross," Mr Troop remarked.

"May I ask what type of work you are in Mr Troop?" Chris asked.

"I'm into property business Inspector," Mr Troop replied. "I have several properties all over."

"Do you own any in Winchester?" Chris asked.

"Well I do now," Mr Troop smiled. "If you contact my solicitor you will find that I have the deed signed and sealed for number 8, Canon Street."

"According to Mr Cross's solicitor," George remarked, astounded at what Mr Troop had said. "That number 7, go to Mrs Bliss who lives there at the moment, she and Mr Cross were partners, and as far as number 8 is concerned the house was on the sale and she has paid a deposit on the house."

Mr Troop grinned again. "I suppose it's very difficult for you to grasp business, I bought number 8 from the owner who was in France at the time, I bought it, I paid cash, and as far as I know Mr Cross had received his deposit back, number 7 of course do go to Mrs Bliss as you say."

"Then why send Mr Cross a letter asking him to pay the money he owed you?" Chris asked.

"That was a different loan Inspector, one that I intend to claim for, I loaned him the money to buy his girl friend a flat in Southampton, Woolston, you see Inspector, number 7, Canon Street was a gamble, and I was promised good returns which I got, it was only a matter of a couple hundred pounds that I loaned Mr Cross, and I have had more than back already, the loan was more of an investment, it did not have to be paid back, just a weekly income from it."

"So you have now lost your income from number 7, but own number 8," Chris tidied it up.

"You're getting there Inspector," Mr Troop grinned broadly.

"Then Mr Cross took out another loan from you, in order to buy his girl friend a flat in Southampton, Woolston, and a part of this money is still owing," Chris again added.

"Well the income from his last loan was good, and still coming in, why would I refuse him?"

"So just how much was Mr Cross paying you Mr Troop?" Chris asked, still not in control of his thoughts. "It must have been a good sum?"

Mr Troop thought for a while. "My answer to that, would it be of help to your case Inspector?"

"It could be, and it would be appreciated," Chris replied.

Mr Troop thought for a moment again. "Very well," he replied. "On number 7 Canon Street, he would pay me fifty pounds a week, consider that he has five ladies living there, that should not have been a problem to him," Mr Troop smiled. "As far as his girl friend's flat is concerned, he had to pay me fifty pounds a month, and this is the debt he fell down on."

"How much does he still owe you then?" George asked.

"Unable to say correctly, my accountant could tell you, but I think it's somewhere around eight hundred," Mr Troop replied.

"How do you think he was getting that type of money Mr Troop, after all, he was a tailor, getting perhaps five pounds a week," Chris spread his hands across his desk.

"If that," chimed in George. "And you were getting two hundred and fifty pounds a month from him Mr Troop," he said.

"Where did you think that a modest paid tailor was getting that amount of money to pay you Mr Troop?" Chris asked.

Again Mr Troop grinned. "Inspector, where people who owe me get their money to repay me, I've never concerned myself with, as I have said I was doing very well with my investment in number 7 Canon Street, I'm just sorry that Mr Cross is dead."

"You mean because of income loss," George remarked.

Mr Troop shrugged his shoulders. "Partly," he replied. "I did like the man, he had great personal charm."

"Do you know Mr Cross's girlfriend?" Chris asked.

"I've met her," Mr Troop replied with a grin. "Before you go on about her, I am aware that she rents one of my better houses in West End Road, Southampton."

"We understood that she was the owner of the house?" Chris replied.

"Well she is, in a way," replied Mr Troop. "You see, she leases the house under a seven year term."

"We are talking about Miss Janet Wilson here?" George asked.

"That is correct Sergeant," Mr Troop replied.

"According to Mr Cross's solicitor, he did not own any other property, if you loaned him the money to buy Janet Wilson a flat, then he must have put it in her name?" George remarked.

Mr Troop grinned. "Mr Cross was not stupid Sergeant," he replied. "I myself have four solicitors, like any other profession, they have different expertise, however my claim should bring out all the details."

Chris could not think of another question to ask, he looked at George who was keeping quiet. "Well thank you

Mr Troop for making time to see us, you have helped a lot, but before you go, how can I get in touch with you should the need arise?"

Mr Troop put his hand under his top coat, and brought it away holding a small card. "That will find me Inspector, I'm glad I was able to help," he remarked standing as he offered the card to Chris and he left the office.

"Well, how has his information helped us?" George asked Chris when Mr Troop had left. "Mr Cross and that Lance Corporal Foster both having an affair with Miss Janet Wilson."

"I'm wondering if she had any others?" Chris muttered. "Still we must get on, it is Christmas next weekend, and I want this case out of the way before then, I have still got to buy a couple of presents and a special Christmas card for Elizabeth."

"What is our next step then?" George asked.

"I want you to get on to the Land Register Office, wherever, and find out about number 33, Pine Road, Woolston, who the solicitor was in the buying of the place, also whose name it is in, then you can go and interview Mrs Bliss again, find out just what Mr Cross was like in character, you can also tell her that she will not be getting number 8, it might help."

"I want to interview Lance Corporal Foster, if Captain Squire will allow it," Chris said.

George got up and took his overcoat from the stand. "I'll interview Mrs Bliss first," he said putting his overcoat on.

Chapter Thirteen

Captain Squire, who had just returned from a long weekend leave, was only too happy to oblige Chris with his request about interviewing Lance Corporal Foster.

"I will have to be in the room Inspector," Captain Squire had explained on the phone, to which Chris agreed.

"I may have to frighten him a bit," Chris replied, pussying around is not getting any results.

Captain Squire laughed. "Not to worry Inspector, I'll have him here within the hour," he hung up the receiver.

Chris entered to the Captain's office, a sergeant sitting at a desk looked up, Chris also noticed a Lance Corporal Foster sitting to one side.

"Inspector Hardie," asked the sergeant, to which Chris nodded.

The sergeant got up, and knocked on the door behind his desk, he opened it and looked into the room, only to withdraw his head, before asking Chris to enter.

Captain Squire was already standing, he had his hand outstretched and a smile on his face.

"Inspector Hardie," the Captain said as Chris took his hand. "I must say I expected an older man."

Chris smiled at the compliment. "Promotion is quite quick these days, many of our lads at the front defending our country's honour."

"I wouldn't say that Inspector, naturally I have made enquiries, and I'm told you are a top man," replied the Captain.

Chris smiled, he was a modest man, but still felt pleased with the compliment.

"Well Inspector, how do we work this?" the Captain asked. "But please take a chair."

Chris smiled as he sat. "I have had no luck with finding the gun Sir," Chris said. "Of all the people involved, the only one who had access to the gun is your Lance Corporal, but even if he did not supply the gun, he is involved with the young lady who was raped, and therefore I do have to interview him, it's more beneficial if he would be relaxed during the interview."

"You do what you have to Inspector," the Captain smiled leaving his desk, and opening his office door. "Sergeant," he ordered. "Bring Lance Corporal Foster in."

Chris heard the sound of hobnail boots hitting the floor.

"Left right, left right," shouted the Sergeant as he marched the Lance Corporal into the room.

"Thank you Sergeant," Captain Squire said as the sergeant brought the Lance Corporal to a halt in front of the Captain's desk.

The sergeant came to attention for a moment before turning and leaving the room.

Captain Squire looked at the Lance Corporal still at attention in front of him.

"Lance Corporal Foster," the Captain spoke. "This is Inspector Hardie of Winchester CID, he has requested an interview with you, which I have granted, during this interview I shall be in the room, and will act on your behalf, should it be necessary, do you agree?"

"Yes Sir," the Lance Corporal replied almost in a shout.

"Very well Lance Corporal, be at ease and take that chair."

With a slight look of surprise, Lance Corporal Foster sat in the chair a couple feet away from Chris, and waited, he seemed nervous.

"All your Inspector," the Captain said sitting back in his chair.

"Thank you Sir," Chris replied looking at the soldier. "Lance Corporal Foster, I am here on a murder investigation, plus a rape, now I understand from the rape victim, that you and her are going out together, so you will understand I have to speak to you."

"You mean Janet, Janet Wilson Sir?" questioned the soldier.

"That's right Lance Corporal, I wonder can you tell me the last time you saw her?"

The Lance Corporal thought for a moment. "It must have been the Monday before last Sir," he replied.

"Where was that?" Chris asked.

"At Southampton Sir," came the reply.

"At her house in Woolston?" Chris asked.

"Yes Sir," came the reply.

"Miss Wilson also states that she was expecting to meet you during Tuesday afternoon in Winchester," Chris remarked.

"Not possible Sir," replied the Lance Corporal. "I would have been unable to leave camp until four pm Sir."

"Tuesday was the day she was raped, and the person she was with was shot dead."

"So I understand Sir," the Lance Corporal replied a nervousness entering his voice.

"Where were you on Tuesday, shall we say after you left camp?" Chris asked.

"I went to Southampton Sir," came the reply.

"Knowing that your girlfriend was in Winchester, waiting for you at midday under the King Alfred Statue," Chris answered.

"I didn't know she was in Winchester Sir," the Lance Corporal replied.

"So when you saw her on the Monday, you made no arrangements for the Tuesday?" Chris asked.

"We did Sir," replied the Lance Corporal. "But we must have got it mixed up, I am sure she said we would meet at Southampton."

"Can you provide proof that you went to Southampton, or did anyone you know see you on the train or in Southampton?" Chris asked.

The Lance Corporal shook his head. "Not that I can remember Sir, the ticket collector took my ticket."

"I see," Chris replied slowly. "Now please answer me truthfully, did you kill Mr Cross, did you somehow see them having sex at the back of the Corn Exchange and shoot him?"

"No Sir," replied the Lance Corporal, his face going red. "Anyway she was raped by three men."

"Did you have access to the weapon that was used in the crime?" Chris asked.

"If you mean the Captain's gun who I am batman to, that would be impossible, anytime a check can be made on them."

"So, you got your lines mixed up as far as your next meeting was arranged, you went to Southampton, and Miss Wilson was in Winchester, have you seen her since or contacted her?"

"No Sir, I was late getting back to camp on Tuesday, I missed my train, I was put on a punishment, I haven't been out of camp."

Chris looked at the Lance Corporal, Chris could tell he was all tensed up.

"Lance Corporal, I am investigating a murder because of the gun used, anyone connected with the crime in the way of help, is as guilty as the person who pulled the trigger, now unless you want to chance being under a noose, tell me honestly, who did you give your Captain's gun to?"

"I told you I had nothing to do with it," the Lance Corporal stood up almost shouting.

"Sit down Foster," ordered Captain Squire, then turning to Chris. "He has answered your questions Inspector."

"I am sorry Captain," Chris apologised. "But the Lance Corporal is lying."

"How can you tell that Inspector?" Captain Squire asked. "He seems he answered all your questions honestly."

"When I asked him had he access to the weapon used, he did not asked what sort of weapon was used, he straight away referred to his Captain's gun."

"Well that could have come straight to mind," replied Captain Squire.

"He told me that Miss Wilson had been raped by three men, when I asked if he had any contact with Miss Wilson since her ordeal, he said he had not, so how would he know about the three men?"

Captain thought upon what Chris had said, then spoke to the Lance Corporal. "It seems to me that lies are being said Lance Corporal, if you are in any way connected with this crime, I would advice you to come clean, I have no doubt that Inspector Hardie will eventually get to the truth."

"What will happen to me?" the Lance Corporal asked hesitantly.

"It will remain as to how serious your involvement is, tell the truth, save police time will always be an advantage," Chris replied.

Lance Corporal Foster, looked down at his lap. "I'll tell you truth Sir," he said quietly.

"Are you going to make a confession Lance Corporal?" Chris asked. "If you are, I would like it written down so that you can sign it," Chris said looking at the Captain.

Captain Squire understood the meaning of the look Chris gave him, he left his desk crossing to the office door. "Sergeant, bring in a notebook, I want you to write something down."

"Sir," Chris heard the reply, and the sergeant entered holding a notebook.

"Take a chair Sergeant," Captain Squire ordered. "Lance Corporal Foster will be making a statement, I want you to copy every word."

"Understand Sir," the sergeant replied taking the last chair in the office.

"Carry on Lance Corporal, and this time tell the truth," Captain Squire ordered sitting again behind his desk.

"On the Sunday before," the Lance Corporal began. "I had met Janet at Southampton, she took me over the floating bridge at Woolston, I don't know where but she took me to a nice house, there were a couple of other women there. Janet took me upstairs to a room, and there was drinks in the room, and we had a couple each. She asked me how I liked the other women downstairs, and naturally, I told her they were nice looking, which they were," the Lance Corporal emphasised.

"Anyway, we were mucking about on the bed, then Janet ask me if I could get a gun, she wanted to frighten someone, however she was very nice to me throughout the evening, and I told her that my Captain was going on leave, and he might leave his revolver behind."

"She offered herself and the two women downstairs in a foursome if I could let her have the gun for just a couple of hours," Lance Corporal Foster swallowed, and looked at Chris. "It was a temptation Sir," he said, a pleading for understanding in his voice.

"I'm sure it must have been," Chris answered thinking of Janet Wilson. "But please go on."

"I knew that my Captain would be going on leave, and because he has children, I knew he would leave his revolver. I told her I could get it for her, but I could not allow it out over night in case of an inspection, but eventually I agreed to it being out overnight. I was to get the revolver back some time after four thirty on Tuesday outside the Oriole Hotel in City Road. It was almost six pm a man came along, asked me if my name was Albert, and gave me the gun, it was in a small purse," Lance corporal swallowed again before continuing."

"I don't know what made me do it, but I felt afraid, I looked at the revolver in the purse, and putting the purse up to my nose, I knew the revolver had been fired. I decided to take a train trip to Southampton, just to get an alibi you know, not even knowing why I should need one, but I did, and came back late on purpose, knowing I would be on a punishment," Lance Corporal Foster swallowed again. "I really cleaned that revolver, even the shells, by the time I had finished, no one could have told whether or not it had been fired."

"Who told you about the three men have raped Miss Wilson?" Chris asked.

"The man who gave me the purse holding the gun."

Would you recognise this man Lance Corporal?" Chris asked.

Lance Corporal Foster shook his head. "It was dark, but he was average built I would say, and that's about all."

"Is that the lot Lance Corporal, you haven't left anything out?" Chris asked.

"No Sir," replied the Lance Corporal. "That's the lot."

Chris looked at the Captain. "I would like him to sign his confession Sir," he said.

Captain Squire looked at his sergeant. "Finished?" he asked.

"Yes Sir," replied the sergeant.

"Let him sign it then," the Captain ordered. "Then have Lance Corporal Foster taken to the guard room, he will have to stay in the cells over night until the commanding officer is informed."

With the room cleared, Chris looked at the Captain. "Sorry Captain I never expected a confession when I came here."

"What will happen now?" Captain Squire asked.

"The way I see it Sir, he will have to appear before the court when the case has been solved," Chris answered." "Then again, I suppose the army will have a say as well."

"No doubt about it Inspector, the commanding officer will go crazy, bad for the regiment you know," replied Captain Squire. "But I am pleased to have some police work," he smiled.

George was sitting having a cup of tea, when Mrs Bliss entered the room, George made to get up.

"Don't get up Inspector," she said with a wave of her hand, while her other hand was holding together the top of her sleek black housecoat together.

"I'm a Sergeant Mrs Bliss," George answered falling back on the sofa.

"Oh," replied Mrs Bliss. "Well you should be," she replied with a smile. "Now Sergeant what can I do for you?"

"Just a few questions Mrs Bliss, first, what was Mr Cross really like, you must have known him as much as anyone?"

"Well Sergeant," Mrs Bliss said sliding herself on to the sofa opposite. "To be fair, he was good looking, he was charming, he had no trouble getting women, I had the feeling during the last few months that he had a worry on his mind."

"Any idea?" George asked.

"No Sergeant," Mrs Bliss replied. "Just a sense."

"Did you know, that he borrowed money from a Mr Troop to buy his half share in this house?" George asked.

Mrs Bliss shook her head. "I can't recall," she answered.

"Did you know Mr Cross was paying fifty pounds a week to Mr Troop?" George asked.

"God," replied Mrs Bliss sitting up, with her mouth open. "How would he get such a sum?"

"We suspect only by one way Mrs Bliss," George remarked. "You must know that we suspect this house to be disorderly."

"That was clear with your last visit Sergeant," Mrs Bliss replied. "But you have no proof."

"No Mrs Bliss, we have no proof," George replied with a smile.

"Then what do you wish me to say Sergeant?" Mrs Bliss asked sweetly.

"Mrs Bliss, I am open minded regarding brothels, I am young myself, and when I see your young ladies, all extremely good looking and desirable, I understand our lads going to the front wanting to be with them."

"Look Sergeant, I can't tell you that this is a brothel, but I do know that if you get proof, I shall face a court case, and my girls will start some place else, and a lot of young men will die, many of them virgins, not ever having known a woman."

"I guess you are right Mrs Bliss, but I have to find out where Mr Cross got this sum of money from every week, remember, it is really the people who make a living from immoral earnings and make money out of these poor girls that we are really after."

"Sergeant, you are looking in the wrong place, I can assure you, he did not get the money from this house, in fact he only got the rent from here."

"I believe you," George replied. "But it ponders the question of where?"

"All I can tell you honestly Sergeant is no money comes into this house," Mrs Bliss replied.

"What will you be doing with the house now that it's yours?" George asked.

"If we get the next door house, it will be handy, at the moment I have five of us sleeping in a three bedroom house, we are on top of each other."

"I can tell you that number 8 has already been sold, and as far as we know, Mr Cross has had the deposit back you paid."

"How do you know, who has bought it?" Mrs Bliss almost screamed getting up from the sofa. "I mean the owner is abroad, how could that happen?"

"Mr Troop bought it for cash from the owner in France," George replied.

"That's torn it," Mrs Bliss replied. "All my dreams out of the window."

"I hope you weren't thinking of expanding this business?" George remarked. "We know how the money is paid to the girls."

"Do you really Sergeant?" replied Mrs Bliss as she settled down after the shock news. "Just how is it paid?"

"We know that tickets are bought from touts, we know that only forces personnel are approached by these touts, we know that if a caller is not holding a ticket when the front door is open, you know it's not a client."

"My, my Sergeant, you have done your homework."

"This is a murder enquiry Mrs Bliss, had it not been for the murder, we would have taken very little notice of this house, we would have left it to uniform," George answered. "The murder of the part owner of this house, brought in the Criminal Investigation Department."

"That bloody murder," Mrs Bliss swore. "Brought all this trouble to us, well Sergeant what I say to you I will of course deny should you try to involve me."

"Treat me like your priest," George said with a grin.

"A couple of my girls originated from Southampton, they have told me that one house is in trouble in Southampton, too much money is being taken out of the income."

"Can you enlarge on that Mrs Bliss?" George asked.

"Only that the person taking the money was Mr Cross," Mrs Bliss answered.

"Thank you Mrs Bliss," George replied thankfully. "Now just one more question, this Mr Mallard, when he was here, did he seem to have a hold over Mr Cross?"

"Now that you have asked," Mrs Bliss replied. "There was a strangeness between them, they were supposed to be best friends, but they did not act that way, I would not say that Mr Cross was frightened of him, but Mr Cross would always go to great lengths not to upset him."

"I see," George remarked. "Apart from that?"

"That's the lot," Mrs Bliss replied.

George closed his notebook, and put it away into his pocket, he got up. "Thank you for the tea and your time Mrs Bliss, you have been very helpful."

"Always happy to help the police, Mrs Bliss replied with a grin. "Will you call again?"

George shrugged. "It's where our investigation leads us," he replied.

"Perhaps when the case is over," Mrs Bliss said invitingly.

"It's certainly a temptation," George replied as he went out of the front door with a smile. "It certainly is, a Merry Christmas to you should I not see you before," George said as he left.

By one pm, Chris and George were both in the office, where each was relating their mornings work.

"I called in with the off chance of being able to see John Briggs the solicitor, of Briggs and Briggs," George smiled. "I told him what I needed to find out, he made a phone call, and got a result. The solicitor that dealt with the flat, number 33, Pine Road, in Woolston, is Mr Warwick. John Briggs was very helpful, he got his number and phoned him for me, I spoke to him. Mr Warwick told me that the flat was in the name of Mr Martin Cross, he had a Will in his safe, made out by Mr Cross, at his death the flat would be left to a Miss Janet Wilson. That was all that the Will contained, apart from the fact that the flat did not have a mortgage, it was bought by cash."

"You know George, we did more today to close this case, than we have during the week."

"Yes but are we any closer to catching the murderer?" George asked.

Chris did not reply, he was busy with his pencil. Captain Squire and Lance Corporal Foster, Mr Troop, Mr John Thompson, Miss Janet Wilson, Mr Jeffery Mallard, he wrote the names on a paper and he passed the paper to George. "I will contact Captain Squire, and Mr Troop, will you see the other three are in this office, by eleven tomorrow morning, use your authority if you have to."

"So one of these are the murderer?" George asked.

Chris smiled. "I rather wait until tomorrow before I tell you, I want to put things together in my mind overnight."

"You're ready for your story then?" George asked with a grin, knowing that Chris would already know who the murderer was.

Chris got up and crossed to the stand, taking his overcoat which he started to put on.

"Where you off to now?" George enquired.

"I'm going Christmas shopping," Chris replied. "When you have completed that chore, you can use the phone and contact your friend in the MET in London, tell him you will be with him Christmas and Boxing day."

"Are you sure?" George asked with a broad grin.

"I shall be on duty Christmas day, I'm hoping to spend it with Elizabeth, but I shall be easily found if I am needed, you are off on Christmas day anyway, I'll stand in for you on Boxing Day which is Sunday, just be back by Monday lunch time," Chris smiled taking his trilby.

"That's great Chris, thanks," George answered. "I only hope Christmas remains quiet."

"Don't worry George," Chris smiled as he left.

Chris spent the afternoon buying several presents for Mr and Mrs Dobson his landlords, for Mr and Mrs Oborne Elizabeth's parents, a present for Mrs Noal, a special card and a present for Elizabeth. Chris found shopping tiring, and was glad he did not have any shopping to do on a daily base, most shops were crowded with people buying last minute Christmas presents and cards. He saw all the shops decorated, some had small Christmas trees standing in the shop or outside, butchers had rows of fowls hanging outside the shops, try tempting all that passers. By the time Chris had finished his shopping darkness had fallen, carrying two large brown carrier bags, Chris turned towards the police station, where he intended to wrap his presents.

"Can I carry your bag?" a voice said behind him, Chris turned and saw the smiling face of Elizabeth.

"I never expected to see you," Chris smiled as Elizabeth kissed him on the cheek. "What are you doing out so early?" he asked.

"Early," Elizabeth replied. "It's gone six."

"Has it?" Chris replied taken back. "God I hate shopping."

Elizabeth smiled. "It's nice at Christmas with all the lighted shop windows," Elizabeth remarked. "I love Christmas, what have you got in the bags?" she asked.

"Just a few bits and pieces," Chris answered not wanting her to know. "I was about to drop these at the station, would you like to come?" he offered.

"Darling I have never been in your office, I would love to," Elizabeth replied.

A few moments later, Chris having shifted one bag to the other hand, opened the door of the station, and allowed Elizabeth to enter.

"It's warmer in here," he said as he closed the door and looked at the desk sergeant who was smiling.

"Sergeant Dawkins, this is Miss Elizabeth Oborne," he introduced.

Sergeant Dawkins offered his hand which Elizabeth accepted. "Nice to know you Sergeant," she smiled.

"You don't have to be a detective to know why he has kept you all to himself," sergeant Dawkins flattered.

"That's very kind of you Sergeant," Elizabeth replied taking the compliment.

"That's enough of that," Chris grinned. "Is Sergeant House still in?"

"No he's out Sir," sergeant Dawkins replied respectfully. "Would you both like a cup of tea, the young lady must be cold."

Chris looked at Elizabeth who smiled her acceptance.

"That's great Sergeant," Chris accepted the offer. "I'm taking Elizabeth to the office."

"This is where my man spends his time," Elizabeth said looking around the room.

"Most of my work is done in this office," Chris replied putting his bags down by the side of his desk, and then turning on the gas fire. "The room will get warm now," he smiled. "It's certainly nice to have you here to myself."

"Naughty," Elizabeth teased. "It's a good job that nice sergeant is making tea for us, and will be coming in any moment."

"Why?" Chris asked.

"We are alone darling," Elizabeth smiled.

Chris went to her, and put his arms around her waist, she offered her lips which Chris took eagerly, only to be interrupted by a knock on the door.

"Now drink this while it's nice and hot," sergeant Dawkins said bringing in a tray with two cups of tea on it. "I have brought a few chocolate biscuits, in case the young lady is hungry."

"Thank you Sergeant," Chris said as he sergeant left the office.

"Thank you," Elizabeth added as the door closed.

Chris sat behind his desk, Elizabeth sat in the interview chair, they faced each other while they drank their tea, Elizabeth nibbled a biscuit.

"Are you going to show me your shopping?" Elizabeth asked between nibbles and sips of tea.

"Some of it," Chris answered. "I have bought wrapping paper and string, I was on my way here to do the wrapping, when you saw me," Chris said.

"You were not going to meet me tonight then," Elizabeth sulked.

"Yes I was," Chris replied quickly. "It's just that I mislaid the time."

"Don't be silly darling, I know you would have met me," Elizabeth smiled. "What have you bought?"

Chris leaned down and fumbled into the bags.

"I bought this for your mum," Chris said handing Elizabeth a oblong box. "It's a dressing table set, mirror, brush and comb to match, to tell the truth, I didn't know what to buy."

"It's lovely Chris," Elizabeth said as she lifted the lid. "Mother will be very pleased with that."

"I hope so," Chris replied a little downhearted.

"She will darling, even I would like that," she said sincerely.

"I bought this for Ron," Chris said taking another box from the bag. "I thought he would like it," Chris said passing it to Elizabeth, who took off the lid.

"Oh I'm sure dad will like this, I know he don't have one," she said as she held the shaving mug up and looked at the figure carved on the outside.

"I've bought this for Mr Dobson, I always buy him the same, a box of a hundred Players Cigarettes and for Mrs Dobson I bought these two pinafores, she likes pina-fores," Chris said passing them to Elizabeth.

"They are lovely darling," Elizabeth said.

"I bought Mrs Noal this box of chocolates."

"That's nice," Elizabeth replied. "She will be glad of the thought, with her husband away."

"I hope so," Chris replied. "Shall we wrap them?"

"No more?" Elizabeth asked pouting her lips.

"Not for your eyes anyway," Chris replied with a grin. "You young lady will have to wait until Saturday."

"Just a clue then darling," Elizabeth pleaded. "How can I wait another five days?"

"With patients," Chris grinned.

For the next hour, Chris and Elizabeth was wrapping the presents. "Well that's the last one," Chris remarked. "Do you think can you take your mum's and dad's present home and put them under the tree?" Chris asked.

"Of course darling, but aren't you coming with me?" Elizabeth replied.

"Elizabeth darling," Chris said reaching across the desk for her hand. "I will of course walk you home, but I want to solve this case tomorrow, I have a lot of thinking to do."

"That means a quiet seat with a pint in your hand," Elizabeth sulked teasingly. "In the Rising Sun?"

"Not this time, I don't want to see Miss Wilson who is staying there tonight," Chris answered.

"Dad said she was strikingly beautiful," Elizabeth remarked.

"Darling," Chris said squeezing her hand, thinking that Elizabeth might be a little jealous. "Beauty is in the eye of the beholder, so to your father she might look attractive with all her makeup, but you are beautiful without the use of all that rouge and powder to me, she is not a patch on you."

"Darling, you say the nicest things," Elizabeth giggled.

"The real beauty of a woman is her inner beauty, and that is shown through the eyes of a woman, I have never seen eyes like yours always sparkling, and glowing with warmth."

"Darling, I love you so very much," Elizabeth replied with a smile across her face.

"I love you as well," Chris replied, getting up and coming around to where Elizabeth was now standing, he took her in his arms and their lips met.

Chapter Fourteen

Chris looked at the people all seated before him, he saw Captain Squire sitting next to Lance Corporal Foster, both smartly dressed in their uniforms, sitting towards the back of the room. Miss Janet Wilson and Mr Jeffery Mallard was sitting nearer to him, and just behind them Mr Thompson and Mr Troop was sitting. George was sitting behind his desk waiting expectantly for Chris to commence. Near George's desk a woman was sitting with pad and pencil, Chris had dispensed with the typist in the past, it made too much noise, a shorthand secretary had been brought in today.

"Thank you all for attending," Chris opened the meeting.

"As you know this meeting is about the murder of Mr Martin Cross at the Corn Exchange, Jewry Street, 14th December 1915."

"I would like to tell you a story," Chris paused, and looked around the room, all faces were looking at him.

"Mr Cross was a young man of just twenty three years old, he was a tailor by profession, and I am told his work was excellent, in fact we have among us Mr Troop, who had all his suits made by him."

Chris waited until the rustling of movement had died down, as those in the room turned to look at Mr Troop, who had a grin of pleasure on his face.

"Mr Cross was also pleased by nature, he was a handsome and charming young man, and women it seems were attracted to him," Chris continued.

"Lucky him," Mr Mallard interrupted.

"I would say lucky you Mr Mallard, after all you were his best friend," Chris said in a serious voice.

"That I was," Mr Mallard replied.

"He satisfied your sexual appetite with a supply of women didn't he?" Chris spoke with disgust in his voice.

"I have no idea what you are on about?" Mr Mallard replied with anger in his voice. "I am quite capable of getting my own women," he said his face bright red.

"I am sure you are Mr Mallard," Chris replied smiling to himself. "It must have been a year ago, while Mr Cross was keeping company with a war widow a Mrs Bliss, she wanted to buy number seven at Canon Street in Winchester but she only had half of the asking price, she asked to Mr Cross to buy the other half, however, although Mr Cross an expert in his work, did not have that type of money, but again he was lucky, one of his best customers Mr Troop loaned him the other half, but not as a loan, but an investment which he demanded a good return fifty pound a week. Mr Cross bought the house in his name, making an agreement with Mrs Bliss, that the house would be left to the surviving partner."

"That's business Inspector," Mr Troop interrupted.

"I'm sure it is Mr Troop," Chris replied. "I just wonder how you expected such a sum to be paid, unless of course you knew what sort of house it would be used for."

"My terms were agreed, it's not my problem how the money is made for returns on my investment," Mr Troop replied.

"Would you have loaned the money, had you thought that Mr Cross was just going to live in the house?"

Mr Troop flustered. "Should I have a solicitor here?" he asked.

"Why Mr Troop?" Chris asked.

"Well this interrogation," Mr Troop replied.

"You are not under arrest Mr Troop, you were asked to come, and you came at your own free will, only if you were arrested with suspicion of committing a crime you would be interrogated."

Mr Troop was feeling uncomfortable, the grin had left his face as the people in the room were looking at him.

Chris getting no reply carried on. "During the year, although they continued being partners, Mr Cross and Mrs Bliss finished their affair, Mr Cross had met someone else, a Miss Janet Wilson."

Chris noticed that as the people looked towards her, she lowered her eyes to her lap. "Now Miss Wilson was renting a large house at Southampton, which the house has several girls, Miss Wilson was the Ma'dam."

"That is slander Inspector," Janet screamed angrily. "You have no right, I agree with Mr Troop, we should have a solicitor with us."

"It's only slander without proof Miss Wilson," Chris replied. "A solicitor would be of little use, I am only asking questions, in response to your own questions."

"Now," Chris continued. "Miss Wilson rented this house from Mr Troop."

"From my agent Inspector, I have no idea what the house I let out is used for?" Mr Troop interrupted.

George sat behind his desk was keeping quiet.

"Miss Wilson however was living at the house she rented," Chris continued. "But she wanted a place of her own, somewhere private away from the disorderly house, which she was known to the police as a prostitute at Woolston, so using her charm, she got Mr Cross to buy one for her," Chris paused to let what he said sink in.

"Mr Cross bought a flat a little away from her rented house, he borrowed the money again from Mr Troop."

A muttering filled the room, and once again everyone stared towards Mr Troop.

"Mr Cross kept the flat in his own name, but Willed it to Miss Wilson should he die," Chris continued. "We must remember here, that Mr Cross was already paying a weekly sum to Mr Troop, but his income from the Canon Street house just enabled him to do this, but the repayment for the second loan for Miss Wilson's flat began to fall behind with his monthly payments and arrears began to build, his income from his employment was of no use with the amount of money he had to pay out, he began asking Miss Wilson for loans to enable him to meet his payments to Mr Troop."

"You are just guessing Inspector," Miss Wilson responded. "How could you possibly know?"

"He had a list of names in a little black book, of money he had borrowed," Chris replied.

"You fool," Miss Wilson stood up and shouted. "That was money he had to pay the Winchester girls," realising what she had just said, Miss Wilson looked around, and sat down feeling very uncomfortable.

"Thank you Miss Wilson, I had no idea, I did not say your name was entered however," Chris answered.

George smiled to himself, at least it cleared one question up.

"The young ladies in both these houses, the one in Winchester and the one in Southampton were never paid directly for their services, you could say it was a ticket service, touts mainly around army camps and dockyards would approach anyone in uniform with the offer of sex ticket, they paid the price for the length of time they wanted, then at their own convenience called upon the house, the ticket would be given to the young lady providing the service, who would collect her earnings every week, the amount would only be paid by the tickets she held."

"Where is all this getting us Inspector?" Mr Thompson asked. "I thought we were here because Mr Cross was murdered, and all we seem to speak about is brothels."

"I will be coming to the point soon Mr Thompson, but as you are so keen on getting to the point, I can tell you that you organised the touts, and printed the tickets," Chris replied.

"But, but," Mr Thompson stuttered. "I only knew Mr Cross perhaps by sight, I certainly did not know Miss Wilson here," he said pointing at her. "What makes you think I had any part in this, you know I was a witness, as for organising touts and printing tickets, where do you get all this stuff from?" he asked spreading his hands and looking angry.

The telephone rang, Chris took the receiver and listened. "Thank you," he finally said and replaced the receiver, he sighed.

"I apologise for the interruption," Chris said. "Now Mr Thompson, I'm afraid you knew both of them, Mr Cross would call upon you every week, he would provide you with tickets that had been used, and you would pay him the total, less of course commission for the touts and yourself. He kept account of which girl had which tickets and put the amount he had to pay them, less the partnership commission, by each of their names."

"Rubbish," replied Mr Thompson. "Utter rubbish, where do Miss Wilson come in?"

"Miss Wilson herself has told us the meaning off this money in the back of Mr Cross's notebook, and she phoned you as soon as she got out of hospital," Chris answered.

"That was only to thank me for helping her when she was raped," Mr Thompson replied.

"Then I apologise," Chris replied. "But how did she get your telephone number?"

"I don't know," from the book or the exchange Mr Thompson replied. "How do I know," he replied angrily.

"You told me you never spoke to Miss Wilson that night," Chris said.

"That's right," replied Mr Thompson.

"She went to hospital," Chris answered. "You did not see her or speak to her after?"

"That's right," Mr Thompson almost shouted.

"You live in Winchester Mr Thompson, how did she know your phone number in Southampton, how did she know you had a shop in Southampton?" Chris asked.

"I," Mr Thompson could find no excuse. "It's still rubbish about the tickets anyway," he finished.

"Mr Thompson, that telephone call I have just had, was from the Southampton Police, they searched your model shop this morning, and found hand press number of tickets already printed at the back of your shop."

A slight murmur went up, and Chris noticed that Miss Wilson was looking at Mr Thompson, a frightened look upon her face.

Chris took time to look at George, who was shaking his head and smiling.

"Hang on there Inspector, you're not accusing me are you, remember I was the one who suffered a rape," Miss Wilson spoke loudly.

"I'm not forgetting that Miss Wilson," Chris answered hoping that he could be heard above the murmurs that was going on.

The murmurs fell silent as Chris continued. "I believe that Miss Wilson spoke to Mr Thompson about having Mr Cross killed, he was getting a liability with the money he was paying out to Mr Troop, also Miss Wilson wanted the sole ownership of her flat."

"Now you're accusing me," Mr Thompson stormed standing up.

"Only one question remained to be answered, how would they do it?" Chris continued ignoring Mr Thompson. "Miss Wilson gave the answer to that."

"Really Inspector," Miss Wilson shouted.

"You knew a soldier Miss Wilson, Lance Corporal Foster, you knew he had a crush on you, in fact he had been out with you several times," Chris replied.

"So what," Miss Wilson came back. "I've been out with many soldiers."

"Miss Wilson, I have a sworn statement in front of witnesses, made by Lance Corporal Foster that you asked him to get you a gun."

"Then he's lying," Miss Wilson replied angrily as she looked at the back of the room where Lance Corporal Foster was sitting.

"I'm afraid not Miss Wilson, the one problem remaining for you to get a revolver, you asked Lance Corporal Foster to get you a revolver while his Captain was on home leave, then you had to get it done within days, he was frightened, but he agreed to let you have it over night."

"Please Inspector who murdered Mr Cross?" Mr Mallard asked.

Chris smiled, he thought perhaps he had made his story a bit long, he continued.

"Miss Wilson met Mr Cross in the Bell Inn, she was to get him to the Corn Exchange market area after dark, it was a very dark evening, Miss Wilson was able to get Mr Cross in the darkest part of the market, which was behind the gents toilet, she was able to do that with the promise of sex, Mr Thompson, who was on a half day from his shop in Southampton was keeping watch unseen, after sex Miss Wilson put the gun to Mr Cross's head and shot him."

Miss Wilson screamed out loud, she had her hands over her mouth and a look of fear on her face.

"Mr Thompson who heard the shot, then came from the gents toilet, put the gun in Miss Wilson's small purse, he was about to leave and give the revolver back to Lance Corporal Foster at a prearranged spot, but Miss Wilson stopped him, she wanted sex, the shooting of Mr Cross had unleashed a sexual urge in her. Mr Thompson was angry but obliged, but in his anger he was brutal in his performance. Had this urge of hers not happened, they could have just walked away together, no one would have known."

"You silly bitch," Mr Thompson growled at Miss Wilson. "You had to do it?"

"The army button we found at the scene, probably fell from Mr Thompson's pocket while he was making sex, in a way, it helped us, Mr Thompson's father having two model shops, which these sort of items are sold."

"You can't prove that," Mr Thompson shouted angrily.

Ignoring the outburst Chris continued. "After the delay by the sex, things went wrong, a horse and buggy entered the market area and stopped, but not near enough for the driver to see them unless they move or make a noise. Miss Wilson was perhaps too frightened to move, but Mr Thompson knew he would have to do something, not knowing how long the horse and buggy would remain. He came up with an amazing story, which he quickly explained to Miss Wilson."

Chris continued, the conversation must have gone like this. "I must take this gun back, you stay quiet here, if anyone comes, you say three men came, shot Mr Cross and raped you and say they were wearing masks. When I get back, the buggy may be gone then we will be alright, we just walk away, but this gun must be given back, if not it could ruin our plans, Miss Wilson was perhaps too frightened to disagree. Mr Thompson met Lance Corporal Foster at a pre-arranged spot and gave him back the revolver, but Lance Corporal Foster, who should have gone back to camp, he cleaned the gun, decided to give himself an alibi, he took a train to Southampton, came back to camp too late on purpose, and was put on a charge, no contact could have been made with him. Mr Thompson after gave the gun back, then made his way back to Miss Wilson, all seemed to be going well, he told Miss Wilson to walk behind him until they were out on the street, but he bumped into two constables walking off duty. Miss Wilson must have heard Mr Thompson talking to them, she quickly returned to where Mr Cross was lying, and was pretending to moan as the two constables shone their torches on her, Mr Thompson did phone the police, but not where he said, he phoned the police station outside the Corn Exchange."

When Chris finished, the room remained quiet, each one looking at each other.

"So Miss Wilson shot Mr Cross," Mr Mallard interrupted the silence. "Arrest her then we can all go home."

"Mr Mallard," replied Chris annoyed. "You are lucky had Mr Cross your best friend, I would have had you for blackmailing, you knew how close Mr Cross and his mother was, and you used this in order to be supplied with sex, I think you are disgusting, but be aware, I shall be watching you from now on, and don't you dare go near Mr and Mrs Cross."

Chris looked at Mr Troop and continued talking. "This murder took place because of greed, Mr Mallard was greedy for sex, you Mr Troop were greedy for money, and the harsh amounts you wanted from Mr Cross did partly caused his murder, I shall be sending a report to the various authorities regarding the loans you made and the interest you charged, and I am sure you knew your house at Woolston was being used as a brothel, also what Mr Cross would use his house for, so in a way you were living off the immoral earnings of women."

"Lance Corporal Foster, you supplied the weapon used in a murder, I don't know whether you knew it would be used as such, but you did arrange an alibi for yourself. I am not arresting you, you are already under arrest by the Army, until you are call to a civilian court, you will remain in custody of the Army.

"Mr Thompson, and Miss Wilson, my Sergeant will read your rights, you are both charged with the murder of Mr Cross and taken into custody."

"How did you know our story about the three men were false?" Miss Wilson asked between sobs.

"You told me yourself Miss Wilson," Chris replied. "When I said I would catch the rapist, you answered that I would not catch him, no one would accidentally say him, when three men was involved."

"How did you know about my house?" she asked.

"Woolston police know all about you and your house, I even have the names of the girls you employ there. You had remained silent while you were in hospital, you would not tell the staff anything about yourself, not even your address, you did not want the police to nose around, you only opened up when you realised you had made a blunder by saying him, instead of them."

Still sobbing Miss Wilson stayed in her chair, as Sergeant House approached her.

"Mr Mallard had left followed by Mr Troop, Chris went up to Captain Squire, and thank him for all his help."

"It was a pleasure Inspector, I shall remember this meeting, you can get more out of a story than you can get at an interrogation," Captain Squire praised him.

Chris smiled and shook his hands, he watched as they left, thinking what a fool some men make of themselves over a woman, thinking Lance Corporal Foster.

He watched as Mr Thompson and Miss Wilson was taken out to the cells, and wondered about the shock coming to Mr Thompson's parents.

Chris turned towards George who was looking at him smiling.

"You're going to see Mr and Mrs Cross now aren't you?" George asked.

"Yes, this is the one person in this case that I really feel sorry for, I shall call on them tonight, at least they will know who killed their son."

"One thing remains," George queried. "Why no one heard the shot, it must have made a noise?"

"Just one of those things," Chris replied with a shrug."Unexplainable."

THE END

INSPECTOR
CHRIS HARDIE

MARRIAGE

Chapter One

 owland Dummer rubbed his hand over his chin, as he looked at his reflection in the mirror of the small tin cabinet that was fixed above the scullery sink. Satisfied with his shave, he turned on the tap, and washed his cut throat razor before drying it on a nearby cloth, closing the razor he then opening the tin cabinet door placed the razor on the small shelve inside then closed the cabinet, once again looked at his reflection in the mirror.

He did not smile at himself, as he took a neck scarf from the side, and put it around his throat over his collarless shirt. Satisfied with the knot, he sat down on a wooden kitchen chair, and started to put on his heavy hobnail boots, as he was lacing them up, the scullery door opened, he did not look up but continued to lace his boots.

"You're up early misses," he said pulling the laces of his boots tight. "I told you I would be away early to the woods, you could have slept in."

"I'll make you tea before you go, it's not five yet, still dark," his wife answered as she entered the front room, and took the simmering kettle off the range.

"I see you have stoked the fire," she said as she entered the scullery again, and prepared making the tea.

"It's nippy these morning," Rowland replied standing up and stamping his feet. "At least my feet won't be cold."

Rose Dummer, sat sipping her tea, she watched as her husband picked up a biscuit, and soaked it in his tea. "You have changed in the last three weeks," she said to him. "Are you in trouble?"

Rowland took a sip of his tea, and picked another biscuit from the biscuit tin without looking at his wife. "Not that I'm aware of," he answered soaking the biscuit in his tea. "What makes you think so?"

"You're drinking more now, when you went poaching you always brought the rabbits home so that we could have meat on the table, the last few weeks, you have sold them and drank the money away," Rose replied, holding her cup with both hands, just to fill the warmth, she only had her nightgown on.

"So now you accuse me of not giving you enough money for the housekeeping," Rowland said with anger in his voice. "I gave you ten and six on Friday, you can't have spent that already."

"I'm not saying that," Rose replied. "But the rent, bills etc takes most of that, what is left I buy food with."

"So what are you moaning about misses?" Rowland asked drinking the last of his tea.

"It's young Tom," Rose replied. "He's five years old now, and growing fast, he grows out of his shoes before they are warn out, he needs trousers that fit him, and a coat, it's cold these mornings for him going to school."

"You pamper that boy," Rowland replied.

"He's our son, of course I do the best I can for him, you might remember I nearly lost my life having him, to me he's precious, the first time I saw my son, he was a day old, you were so excited while I was carrying, of late however your attitude towards him seems to have changed."

"Look love," Rowland said with a little tenderness in his voice. "You had a bad time at his birth, that is why I am not chancing my mind having another, if as you say my attitude towards him as changed, then I don't know how, he's a good lad, I'll always remember the glow on your face when you first held him," Rowland continued smiling to himself with the memory. "I knew then that even if I could have given you anything in the world, nothing would be greater than the boy you held."

"You're an old softy Row," replied his wife with a smile. "That is why I worry, you would tell me wouldn't you if you're in trouble?"

Rowland smiled at his wife as he stood up. "You're the only one I would tell love," he said putting his hands in his trousers pocket. "Here's four and sixpence, would that help?"

Rose took the money with a smile. "I can go to the second hand clothing shop, see what they have to fit Tom, it's Sunday today, I doubt that they will open, I'll go first thing tomorrow," she replied after a moment thought.

"Well I better make a move, I have twenty minutes cycling to do," Rowland said making for the hall where his jacket hung. "I'll bring home a rabbit if I'm lucky."

Rose followed her husband into the hall, and watched as he took his special jacket, which had a large hidden pocket on the inside.

"You get back to bed misses," he said. "It is Sunday, try and get a little sleep, I'll be home early."

Rose kissed her husband on the cheek, she watched him as he went back into the scullery, and out of the back door, where she knew he would collect his bike.

Chapter Two

*D*etective Inspector Chris Hardie, cycled along the gravel path towards the farm house, followed closely by Detective Sergeant George House. Both dismounted at the front door, and placed their cycles against the wall of the house.

"Phew," Chris said with a half smile at George as he knocked the door. "I'm getting too old for this game, I'm sweating," he said unbuttoning his overcoat. "It's a brisk wind so I'm glad I wore this overcoat."

George smiled back. "It's only about seven miles, you're only thirty, you'll have to do more exercise, specially as you are getting married in a few weeks."

The door opened and a housemaid appeared in a long blue dress, covered in front by a white apron and on her head a matching cap. Chris explained who he was, the maid stepped outside and pointed to a small wood a hundred yards to the right of the gravel path, in front of which a man could be seen plainly waving his arms. Chris thanked the maid, and with George following made their way across the field towards the man.

"You are the police I hope," greeted the man as they approached.

Chris looked at the man, he looked about forties, clean shaven, he wore a tweed plus four suit, his polished brown brogue shoes stood out, as did the knee length woollen socks that was correctly turned below the knee.

"Sorry we are late Sir, we cycled, we got here as fast as we could, I am Detective Inspector Hardie, and this is Detective Sergeant House," Chris introduced themselves. "I take it you are the owner of this farm, Mr Reginal Shawcroft?"

"That I am," replied the farmer. "It seems I have been standing here for ever."

"Did you find the body Sir?" Chris asked looking at the body of a man.

"Actually no," replied the farmer. "One of my maid was cleaning the inside of the windows almost facing the wood, she saw him fall as he came out of the woods, she told me so I made my way over here, he was not moving, I did consider he could be dead with that knife sticking out of him, anyway I thought the best course of action was to phone the police, so I phoned you, after that I came back here, I felt I had to watch over the body until you came," he added.

"Thank you Mr Shawcroft, all your actions were correct, I will need to speak to the maid later," Chris replied as he watched George searching the ground around the body and ignoring the farmer's last remark over their lateness.

George who had knelt by the body looked at Chris and shook his head. "Dead as a dormouse," he said.

"Tell me Sir, would you know the man, I mean is he one of your workers?" Chris asked without taking his eyes from the body.

"I don't employ him exactly, and to be truthful I hardly know him, I knew his father very well, worked for me and my late father," Reginal Shawcroft answered.

"What do you mean, not exactly?" Chris asked.

"Well," replied the farmer taking a deep breath. "Because of his father, I have given my permission which allows him to catch rabbits in that woods," the farmer pointed with his head, Chris looked towards the woods that was about fifteen feet away.

"He keeps the rabbits down for me, he keeps what he catches, but he usually drops one or two in the kitchen for me, I find he's a good man, has a wife and a child I believe, the wood itself is about one and a half acres," again he indicated the wood with his head. "I only have a couple small plots on my land, so I do not employ a game keeper, hardly worth it."

"What is his name?" George asked his notebook already out.

"Rowland Dummer," replied the farmer. "He lives in Union Street, don't ask me the number."

"Thank you," replied George.

"Aren't you going to look at the body?" Mr Shawcroft asked. "I read detective books, and it's more or less the first thing that they do."

Chris smiled. "Sergeant House has already searched the ground, he has already examined the wound, we know he is dead, most likely because of the knife wound, before I turn him over, I am waiting for the Police Surgeon," he said looking at George. "Should be here at any time now."

The banging and clatter of a motorbike, made all three of them turn towards the gravel path leading to the house, Chris waved his arms, and was thankful when the motorbike came to a halt.

The Police Surgeon Bob Harvey carrying his bag walked across the field towards them. "Chris, George," Bob greeted them. "Got here as soon as I could, had to ask directions of course."

"No worries," Chris replied. "This is farmer Reginal Shawcroft," Chris introduced. "He owns the farm, and more or less found the body."

Bob Harvey shook hands with the farmer. "Not a pleasant thing to find Sir," he commented.

Bob looked down at the body. "Looks like a scarecrow that has fallen on his face," Bob remarked. "Still let's have a look," he said kneeling beside the body and studying the knife.

"It's in deep, right up to the hilt, I'm wondering did hit an artery, have you tested it for fingerprints?" Bob asked Chris.

"No I'm incline to leave the knife in until you have him on the table, can't really dust for fingerprints with this wind so I decided to wait for you," Chris replied.

"Do we know who he is?" Bob asked.

"We have his name, and know where he lives that's all at the moment, can we turn him?" Chris asked.

"Only on his side, we don't want the knife disturbed, I'll tell you one thing," Bob continued. "He must have been died on this spot."

"My maid saw him stumble out of the wood," Mr Shawcroft interrupted.

"Then you are looking at a very strong person," Bob replied looking towards the wood. "He could not have walked far, the knife must have gone in at the edge of the wood, I don't know how he stumbled this far?"

"I'll check it out," George offered, as he started to walk slowly towards the wood.

"Good man that," Bob remarked.

"He knows what to do," Chris agreed. "Now let's turn him on his side."

Chris turned to the farmer. "No need for you to stay Sir," he said politely. "We shall be here for a while, I can always come to the house and see you."

"That's quite alright Inspector, I will stay," replied the farmer.

Chris and Bob, carefully turned the body onto its right side, his jacket was unbuttoned, and the bottom side of his jacket fell open.

"What have we got here?" Chris asked himself. "Looks like he had a pocket sewed inside," Chris said aloud.

"All poachers have one," remarked the farmer. "You will find his catch in it, looks like he caught a couple rabbits," he added.

Chris carefully pulled the pocket open, and saw it contained three rabbits. "Can't take fingerprints from rabbits," he said as one by one took each dead rabbit by the ears and placed them on the ground, three dinners there," he remarked.

"Will you be seeing his wife?" the farmer asked.

"As soon as we have finished here," answered Chris searching the other pockets.

"Then perhaps you can take the rabbits to her," suggested the farmer. "She now has no man, and a son to bring up, the rabbits will at least feed them for a few days."

Chris finished his search. "Not much in the pockets," he said. "Just a hanky and a penknife and a couple of coppers and a key, possibly his house key."

Chris looked at Bob who was kneeling beside the body. "I suppose now I should ask you Bob about the time of death," Chris said while he was putting the contents of the pockets into a small brown bag.

Bob looked at the farmer. "What time did you report your find?" he asked.

Reginal Shawcroft shrugged. "Between seven and seven fifteen in the morning I guess," he answered.

"Well it's now nine fifteen," Bob said looking at his pocket watch. "I would say he has been dead for about two and a quarter hours."

"In this case I agree," Chris replied checking with his own pocket watch.

George came from the woods a little later. "Nothing out of the ordinary, found two cigarettes butts behind a tree about twenty feet in, found nothing else, although the undergrowth was a bit flatten as though someone had been standing there."

"Apart from a hanky and penknife, he had nothing on him," Chris said as he opened the small bag, for George to put the cigarettes butts in.

"Tenners by the way," George said as he dropped the butts in. "We are looking for someone who smoke Tenners."

Chris smiled. "That won't be easy, it's a popular brand," he replied.

"Well Bob," Chris said as Bob rose from the body. "I think we have finished here, is your wagon coming?" Chris asked.

"On its way I hope, because of that knife, I better wait here for them, make sure it's not touched," Bob replied.

"In that case Bob, I'll go to the house, I want to speak to Mr Shawcroft's maid, if that is alright with you?" Chris said turning towards the farmer.

"Quite so," replied the farmer. "Let's carry the rabbits across, I'll have them wrapped for you."

"Mr Harvey, it's a bit nippy here, I'll send you a flask," the farmer spoke looking at Bob.

"Thank you very much," replied Bob with a smile.

The farmer followed by Chris and George, each carrying a rabbit by its ears walked to the house, as they reached the house, the door opened immediately.

"Follow me, it's warmer in the kitchen," remarked the farmer. "While you are having a cup of tea I'll fetch the maid."

They entered the large kitchen, copper pots and pans hung from hooks around the range which was well alight, and was sending out a welcomed warmth. Chris was surprised when he saw the cook, a slender very attractive woman of about forty, his mental picture of a cook was a stout woman with a jolly face, but the cook he saw was a very attractive woman, she was standing next to the large range cooker.

"Cook, make these gentlemen a cup of tea please, and send someone with a flask to the gentleman near the wood, it's bitter out there," the farmer ordered.

"Sit yourself down, it will take a moment," the cook said with a good natured smile on her face.

"Then cook, will you wrap these rabbits up so the gentlemen can carry them on their bikes," the farmer requested.

"Certainly Sir," replied the cook politely seeing the three rabbits that had been placed at the other end of the table. "Do we know who the body belongs to?" she asked.

"I'm afraid it was Rowland Dummer," replied the farmer knowing that his cook knew him well.

"Oh my God," moaned the cook, her smile vanishing from her face. "Oh my God, he was such a nice young man."

Chris and George enjoyed the tea and cake that the cook had placed in front of them, she did not speak, but the occasional sniff told them she was upset. The farmer's absence from the kitchen was long enough for Chris and George to enjoy their tea and cake in peace, and when he did enter he brought the maid with him.

"This is the maid Inspector," the farmer informed him.

"Thank you Sir," Chris said, then looking at the maid who he considered about thirty and very pretty. "Please don't be frightened, please sit," Chris said indicating a chair by George.

"Would you mind telling me your name?" he asked watching the maid sit.

"Molly Atkins," replied the maid nervously.

"Where do you live?" Chris asked gently.

"Oh Sir, I live in," she replied.

"You mean you live here all the time?" Chris asked.

"Apart from my day off Sir, then I go to my mother's," the maid replied.

"Where do your mother live?" Chris asked with a smile. "Don't be nervous, these questions are just routine, as I'm sure Mr Shawcroft will tell you."

Molly looked at her employer, who was nodding his head. "Well Sir, my mother lives at number 7, Colson Road, Winchester."

"So apart from your day off, you live here?" Chris asked making sure.

"Yes Sir," replied Molly nervously playing with her fingers.

"It's five miles to Winchester, how do you get home?" George asked wondering.

"My father collects me and bring me back," Molly replied. "My dad won't let me walk all that way alone."

"Very commendable," Chris murmured remembering the distance of his cycle ride to the farm. "Now Molly tell me in your own word, what you saw while you were cleaning the windows?"

"Well Sir nothing much, I was cleaning the inside of the windows almost facing the wood, I saw this man come out of it, he was almost stumbling as he came out of the woods, his arms was out each side of him as though he was a scarecrow, then all of a sudden he fell forward, flat on his face so to speak, and that's all I'm afraid Sir," Molly took a deep breath.

"Did you see any movement behind the man who fell, perhaps at the edge of the wood?" Chris asked.

"No Sir, I saw nothing else, my eyes were on the man who fell," Molly replied.

"Then you told Mr Shawcroft, who went across the field to see what was happening," Chris asked.

"That's right Sir," replied Molly.

"Can you remember the time?" Chris asked.

"Well I started the windows at seven in the morning, I would say just after, I was still on the first window," Molly answered.

"The dead man is Mr Rowland Dummer, did you know him?" Chris asked.

Molly gave a cry, and put her hand to her mouth. "Only when he came to the house," she replied a sob in her voice. "He often called with a rabbit."

"Thank you Molly," Chris smiled. "You have been helpful, now I want you to sign a statement what you have just told us but it can wait until your day off, would you call at the police station on that day and sign it?"

"Of course Sir, my dad will bring me," Molly replied.

"That will be in order," Chris replied wondering why a woman around thirty would need an escort.

"Will that be all Sir?" Molly asked.

"Yes Molly, and thank you," Chris answered.

With Molly gone, the cook placed the rabbits before Chris neatly wrapped, Chris thanked her. "Cook I'm sorry, I do not know your name," Chris said apologetically.

"Mrs Doris Burton," she replied. "I also live in, I am a widow."

"I'm sorry," Chris replied.

"It's alright, my husband died a few years back," she replied.

"Would you mind if I ask you a few questions Mrs Burton?" Chris asked.

"Mr Shawcroft would expect us to cooperate, what can I tell you?" she asked.

"You knew Mr Dummer, he brought you the occasional rabbit I believe?" Chris asked.

"That's right, at least once a week, sometimes twice, I would make him tea, he was a very nice man," Mrs Burton sniffed in her hanky.

"Did you talk much, I mean did he tell you he found signs of other poachers in the wood?" Chris prompted.

Mrs Burton thought for a while. "He might have told me he found the odd trap that did not belong to him, I think he kept the trap, but it was a rare occasion, he mainly spoke of his wife and his son, they seem to be his life."

"You said as we came in that he was a nice man," Chris continued. "Would you say he was a man who did not make enemies?"

"We all have annoying quirks that could upset other people Inspector," Mrs Burton remarked. "But to answer your question, I would say he did not make enemies."

"Thank you Mrs Burton, and allow me to say, you make a lovely cake."

"Thank you," Mrs Burton replied with a smile.

"This is a large farm house?" George said. "Do you have many staff?"

Mrs Burton walked towards the range, and took a saucepan from a hook. "Well there's Molly, and we have Beatrice another maid, she's at church at the moment, I have a kitchen maid who do not live in, she is also at church, and once a week a washer woman comes in to do the laundry that's about it."

"Is there no Mrs Shawcroft?" George asked.

"Mrs Shawcroft passed away in childbirth some five years ago," Mrs Burton said pumping water into the saucepan. "The child also died."

Mr Shawcroft entered the kitchen. "Well gentlemen," he said as he watched the detectives stand. "Anything else I can do?" he said as he led them to the front door.

With the door open, Mr Shawcroft shook hand with the detectives. "Would you give this letter to Mrs Dummer when you meet her," Mr Shawcroft said handing Chris a envelope. "It's just a couple of quid to help her over the next month, and an offer to help with the funeral," he said with a shy smile on his face.

"I'm sure it will be appreciated Mr Shawcroft, it's very kind of you," Chris replied.

Both Chris and George put on their cycle clips, and buttoned their overcoat before getting on their cycles to ride back to Winchester.

"He seems to be surrounded by attractive women," George said as they rode side by side.

"The cook is certainly attractive," Chris remarked deep in thought. "I played with the idea that another poacher was responsible for Mr Dummer's death, it may still be true, but I would like to know a bit more about Mr Shawcroft,

338

whether or not he has always been a gentleman farmer?"

"What's your thinking Chris?" George asked as they cycled along the country lane.

"Nothing firm, just possibilities," Chris answered. "Let's see what Mrs Dummer has to say, God I hate having to do what we are about to do."

"Me too," George remarked.

Chapter Three

ose Dummer sat at the kitchen table, staring at the two detectives sitting opposite her, her mind full wondering.

"Has my Row had an accident?" she asked in a nervous murmur.

"Mrs Dummer," Chris spoke in a gentle tone. "I know of no good way of telling you this, but please try to be strong, your husband was found dead at Manor Farm this morning."

Rose sat looking at the detectives, no emotion showed on her face, as she took in what she had just been told, then tears streamed down her cheeks like water.

"No, no, no," she screamed shaking her head. "Not my Row," she cried as she started to rise.

"I must go to him," she said with tears in her eyes.

George quickly went around the table to her, and laid his arm across her shoulders. "Please Mrs Dummer, your husband's body is now at the hospital, is there anyone I can get for you?"

Rose sat down, visibly shaking, she took her hanky and wiped her eyes, but the tears still running down her cheeks. "Did he have an accident on his bike, it was a new one?" she sobbed.

"Again Mrs Dummer, please try to be strong, I am afraid your husband was murdered."

"Oh my God," Rose cried. "Who would want to do that, Row never had any enemies, he is a kind and gentle man."

Chris looked at George who was still comforting her. "Have you someone we can call Mrs Dummer?" Chris repeated George's question.

"Mrs Ewing, across the street," Rose sobbed sniffing and wiping her eyes. "I would like her here."

George gently patted Mrs Dummer's shoulders and left the house.

"Did he die in pain?" Rose asked.

Chris, who could only imagine the grief Mrs Dummer was feeling, he silently cursed his job, he never did relish this part of it. "I don't think so Mrs Dummer."

The front door opened with a bang, and a young woman followed by George rushed into the room, she was about the same build and age of Mrs Dummer, seeing her friend's distress she rushed to her.

"You poor dear," she said as both embraced. "What a terrible thing to happen to your Rowland, I am so sorry Rose."

Chris and George looked at each other, they felt uncomfortable, watching the two women crying, after several minutes Chris spoke in a gentle voice.

"Mrs Dummer, because of the serious nature of your husband's death, we do have questions that needs to be answered, if you feel you are not up to at this moment, we can leave it for a day."

Mrs Ewing gently broke away from the embrace, she held Rose's hands and looked into her face. "Rose these men want to ask you questions, do you feel up to it?"

Rose wiped her eyes. "I know," she murmured. "I heard, better to get it over with, while Tom is at Sunday School," she sobbed.

"Oh what's going to happen to us now?" Mrs Dummer sniffed.

"We'll take each day as it comes," replied Mrs Ewing. "Shall I make you a cup of tea?"

Rose nodded her head, then she looked at the detectives, her eyes were now red. "What can I tell you?" she asked.

"What time did your husband go out this morning Mrs Dummer?" Chris asked noting that George was already with his notebook.

Rose sniffed and dabbed her eyes. "A little after five," she replied.

"I take it he went by bike?" Chris asked.

"That's right, it's a long way to the wood," replied Rose half sobbing. "He had just bought that bike, his old one was years old."

"So you knew where he was going?" Chris asked.

"Of course," Rose had anger in her voice. "We were married we did not have secrets, in any case he had permission from Mr Shawcroft," Rose sobbed.

"I understand that he had permission Mrs Dummer," Chris said kindly. "Had he ever told you that he had found other traps in the wood?"

"If he had, he would never said," Mrs Dummer continued. "Even if he had he would never had told the farmer, because he might take them to court, my Row was not a man to get other people into trouble."

"I'm sure he wasn't Mrs Dummer, he seems to be a very likeable man without enemies," Chris said as he watched Mrs Dummer nod.

"Can you think of any reason why someone would want to harm your husband?" Chris asked, unprepared for the burst of sobbing that the question brought as she shook her head.

Chris wondered what to ask next, he was running out of questions, the answers getting him nowhere, he already knew most of them. "Did your husband have any worries that you know of Mrs Dummer?" Chris asked, as Mrs Ewing came from the scullery with a cup of tea that she put down in front of Rose.

"Drink that love," she advised. "It might help."

Rose said a weak thank you, and took a sip then putting the cup down looked at the detectives. "As far as I know, his only worry was keeping a roof over our head and food on the table, he did that, but over the last couple weeks, I did sense there was something bothering him, he changed a little, had a few extra drinks when he could afford, I asked him, but he told me it was nothing."

"Really," replied Chris his mind racing. "I wonder what was worrying him?"

"I would tell you if I knew," Rose replied.

"Where do your husband work?" George who had been keeping quiet asked.

"He's a porter at Winchester Train Station," Rose replied. "We can manage on his wages, and sometimes customers tipped him a few extra coppers when trolleying the passengers luggage."

"He's not mean to you then?" George pressed.

"No, not my Row, he would give me all he had, he gave me his last four and sixpence, before he left this morning," Rose replied showing a smile.

Chris looked at Mrs Ewing who was holding Rose's hand. "Will you be stopping with Mrs Dummer for a while?" he asked.

"Of course," she replied. "I'll stay overnight if she needs me."

"I'm thankful, Mrs Dummer has a friend like you, should you need anything that we are able to help with, please call the police station and ask for a detective either one of us should be in," Chris said.

"We will go now, should there be any more I need to ask you Mrs Dummer, I will have to call, I will let you know about your husband. Now before I go, we searched your husband's body, he only had a hanky, a penknife, a key and two pence on him, which we keep for the present, however," Chris said pointing to the wrapped parcel. "He had three rabbits in his inside coat pocket, Mr Shawcroft the farmer asked us to deliver them to you."

A sob came from Mrs Dummer, and Chris waited a moment before continuing. "Also," he added handing Rose an envelope. "Mr Shawcroft sent you this."

We have to try to find out what Mr Dummer had on his mind for the last few weeks Chris said to George as they rode their bikes to the police station.

"Nothing makes any sense at the moment, we need a starting point, and at the moment I can't see one, any way George, it's your Sunday off, thanks for coming along, you will have to put in overtime," Chris smiled.

"That will go down well," George laughed. "No, it's OK I had nothing else to do but stay in bed."

Chapter Four

C hris left his lodgings early the next morning, he wanted to see Elizabeth outside her bank. It was a dry morning, but the March winds were bitter. He pulled his overcoat collar up around his chin as he made his way down the high street towards the bank. He saw Elizabeth as he approached the bank, she was looking towards him smiling.

"Glad to see you're wrapped up," she greeted him, clinging tightly to his arm after planting a kiss on his cheek.

"It is a bitter wind," Chris replied.

"Just seeing you, makes me warm," Elizabeth giggled. "You make my heart beat faster, I keep wishing it was six weeks in the future, we would be on our honeymoon," she smiled.

Chris looked at her. "If your parents heard you talk like that, they would be shocked," he said shaking his head.

"I know," she giggled holding onto his arm with both of hers. "I missed you last night."

"Had a case yesterday," Chris informed her.

"Oh dear," Elizabeth replied looking at him with concern on her face.

Chris knew she was worried about the wedding. "Don't worry, it should be cleared up in time, even if it's not, it will not stop our wedding."

Chris felt her grip on his arm tightened. "It's the first murder since Christmas, I'll have to get my brain working again," he added.

"You'll solve it darling," Elizabeth said. "Will I be seeing you tonight?" she asked as they stopped outside her bank.

"Only if you go inside, out of this cold," he teased. "You have a way of distracting my thoughts," Chris replied.

"I'm glad," she smiled as she kissed his cheek.

Chris entered the police station, it was just after nine, he felt the warmth and saw the Sergeant Dawkins who was smiling at him as he entered.

"We find it cold outside?" sergeant Dawkins asked sarcastically in his usual way.

"I am used to all kinds of weather Sergeant," Chris answered taking little notice of his tone. "Now is Sergeant House in?" he asked.

"About ten minutes ago," replied sergeant Dawkins a smirk playing on his face. "Had a call out yesterday I hear."

"Yes you missed all the fun Sergeant," Chris replied as he took off his overcoat. "Now you are on desk duty, I shall need your help, but first a nice cup of tea would be welcome," Chris said making for his office.

"You can rely on uniforms," Chris heard the usual reply from sergeant Dawkins.

"Morning George," Chris greeted as he hung his trilby and overcoat. "A bit nippy out there," he remarked rubbing his hands as he made for his desk.

"I'll not argue with that," George replied. "I came in a little early to write the report of yesterday," he said looking at Chris with a smile.

"Yes, sorry about that," Chris replied.

"Glad you did call me in, can't miss the experience of a murder, anyway what's the drill?" George asked.

"I puzzled right through the day, still could not make head or tail of it, no apparent motive," Chris replied. "Thought perhaps you would like to take a trip to the Railway Station where Mr Dummer worked, you might get some information from his mates?"

"It's our only hope at the moment," George agreed. "I'll go as soon as I've finished here."

"No need to rush, I have tea coming in," Chris said as the office door opened and sergeant Dawkins entered carrying two cups of tea on a tray, and placed a cup before both detectives.

"Sit for a moment Sergeant," Chris said after he had taken a sip of his tea. "I have questions," watching the sergeant sit, Chris took another sip of his tea before putting the cup down.

"Nice cup of tea that Sergeant," Chris flattered. "Now who do we have near Couch Green on the Alresford road?" he asked.

"We have two Police Houses near, but not at Couch Green, we have one at Easton and one at Itchen Abbas," replied sergeant Dawkins.

"I know the constable at Easton," Chris replied. "They are both on the phone I take it?"

"They are," sergeant Dawkins replied.

"Well I'm going to leave it in your hands Sergeant," Chris said watching a smile come to the sergeant's face. "I know they are capable."

"Uniforms hands are always capable Inspector," sergeant Dawkins replied.

Chris smiled to himself, he always expected that answer. "Get hold of one of them, you choose, tell to go to Manor

Farm at Couch Green, and search a small wood above the farm house, he will be looking for a bicycle, should he find it, I want it brought to the police station."

"I'll get straight on to it," replied the sergeant.

"Tell whoever you select to make himself known at the Farm House, and I want you to phone Mr Shawcroft the farm owner and let him know," Chris said.

"I'll do that," replied the sergeant getting up. "Anything else?"

"You might ask the constable if he know of another way to go to the farm without using the lane," Chris added.

"By the way," George butted in. "Tell him to be careful, there might be traps in the wood."

Chris picked up his cup as the sergeant left the room, he looked at George who was smiling. "You have made his day Chris," George remarked.

"I know," replied Chris. "He'll do a good job."

Chapter Five

George entered Winchester Railway Station about eleven, although the station front was wide open, he found the warmth a degree higher, he pulled down his overcoat collar as he approached the ticket seller pigeon hole.

Explaining who he was, George asked to see the Station Master.

"You'll have to wait ten minutes," replied the seller. "There is train to London on platform two, that's where the station master is at the moment."

"I see," George replied.

"He won't be long now," the ticket seller added. "The train is due out."

George moved to one side, as a man and woman who were standing by him asked for two singles to London.

"You might make it," the seller smiled. "The train is in and due out."

"Thank you," replied the man grabbing the tickets and change. "Come Mildred we don't want to miss it," he said almost dragging the woman towards the steps. "Every time we leave home we have to go back, because you are not sure whether or not you have done this or that."

George smiled as their voices faded, he watched the couple descended the steps, and wondered if they would catch the train.

"The station master will see you now Sergeant," George turned back, saw the ticket seller who was smiling at him. "Go through that door on the right," he directed him to the station master's office.

The station master's office was quite spacious but barely furnished. The station master was sitting behind a desk near the window that looked out onto the platforms. He had a mop of white hair, a pleasant face, his white collar with a black tie was noticeable under his black station master uniform.

He rose from his desk offering his hand as George entered. "Please take a pew," he smiled indicating a chair one side of his desk.

"Thank you," George replied.

"Now how can I help you Sergeant?" the station master asked. "Although it's not hard to guess."

George grinned. "I'm amazed with this small city," he replied. "People know the things that have happened here before the police."

"That's because it is a small place, everyone knows everyone," smiled the station master. "So, I take it your visit is about Rowland Dummer?"

"How much do you know?" George asked interested. "After all nothing has been printed about it yet."

"Only talk, but Rowland being murdered is unbelievable, he was a likeable man and a good worker, doubtful if he had any enemies that could do this, was he really murdered Sergeant?" the station master asked.

"I'm afraid so," George replied.

The station master clasped his hands in front of him, shaking his head. "Unbelievable," he muttered.

George seeing him upset kept quiet, he understood his sadness.

The station master cleared his throat. "Well Sergeant how can I help you?" he asked his voice a little shaky.

"Mr Dummer was killed by being stabbed in the back," George replied intending to put the station master in the picture. "It happened at a farm about six miles out of Winchester, I believe he was there catching rabbits."

"Poaching you mean?" interrupted the station master.

"No not really," George replied. "He had permission, we cannot find any motive for the crime, the murder makes no sense at the moment."

The station master pulled open a desk drawer, and took out a packet of tenners.

"Do you smoke Sergeant?"

"Never started," George answered.

"After what you have told me, I need one," the station master said taking one out of the packet and lighting it, he took a deep puff, blowing the smoke towards the ceiling. "What can I tell you Sergeant," the station master sighed. "I only really knew him as an employee, he was a likeable young man, with a wife and a son I believe, but he did have a mate he was very friendly with, he's also a porter here, perhaps he can tell you more."

"Yes, I would like to see him," George replied.

The station master looked at his watch. "I have a train this side in five minutes, perhaps if you would like to come with me now, I'll have time to take you across."

"I appreciate it," George answered getting up.

George followed the station master to the end of the platform, looking both ways he followed the station master across the lines which had sleepers between them.

"Porters with their trucks come this way," the station master remarked. "Public of course are not allowed, they use the underground pass."

The station master stopped looking at his watch. "Look, I'll have to get back," he said looking up the platform. "The porter you want to speak to is John Lewis, he has ginger hair, in fact there he is, talking to the ticket collector."

A tannoy announcement echoed around the station building, announcing the arrival of the Southampton train stopping at Shawford, Eastleigh, St Denys and Southampton Central.

"I'll manage," George said over the noise.

"Call in on your way out if I can be of further service," the station master replied as he started to walk back across the lines.

As the sound of doors slamming came to his ears, George approached the porter standing with the ticket collector at the exit.

"I am Detective Sergeant House from Winchester CID," George said looking at the ginger hair porter. "I believe you are Mr Lewis, the station master have given me permission to speak to you."

"Well OK," replied John. "Shall we go to the refreshment room, it's empty at the moment."

"Great," replied George. "Perhaps I'll be able to get a cup of tea," he said hoping to keep Mr Lewis calm and relaxed.

"I'll get you one on the house," John smiled. "How do you take it?" he asked as they entered the warm refreshment room.

"Milk with two sugars," George replied looking around the room, and deciding to sit at a table in the corner of the room.

"There you are," smiled John placing a hot cup of tea before him. "I told them you were a guest of Tony," he added still smiling.

"Tony who?" George asked.

"Tony Martin the station master," John replied sitting down. "Now what can I do for you?"

"Have you heard of Rowland Dummer's death?" George asked.

John lowered his eyes and seemed to be staring at the table top. "Biggest shock of my life," John replied almost in a whisper. "I still can't believe it."

George took a sip of his tea before replacing the cup, he looked at John, saw the sadness in his eyes.

"Are you aware of how Mr Dummer died?" George asked.

"Everyone seem to have a different version," John replied. "Some say a heart attack, others say he was murdered, though I think murder is a bit far fetched."

"Why do you think that?" George asked taking out his notebook.

"Well, who would want to kill Row, he was harmless," John replied with a weak smile.

George decided to come straight to the point. "Mr Lewis, before I ask you a couple of questions, I have to tell you that your friend was murdered, and this is a murder investigation."

"Oh God," John replied nervously. "Who the hell would do that, Row had no enemies as far as I know."

"I understand that you and Mr Dummer were good mates, why don't you tell me about him."

John spread his hands. "What can I say, we were good mates, in fact he was my only mate, I have a wife and two kids, my wages go to my wife unopened, so I don't get out to socialise, we have worked together on this platform for several years now," John continued after swallowing as though his throat was dry.

"We pop to the pub over the road at least twice a week and have a pint before we go home, there is not a lot to tell you I'm afraid, we were just good mates."

"Did he seem to have any worries lately?" George asked.

John thought for a while. "Funny you asking that, he had been quiet for the last couple of weeks, no idea why, I thought he and Rose his wife were having a row, so I didn't ask questions."

George was beginning to feel that he was on a dead end and this interview was not going to bear fruit. "Do you smoke Mr Lewis?" George asked.

"Yes I do," John replied looking at him. "Why, do you want one?" he asked putting his hand in his jacket pocket.

"No, no," George replied with a smile. "I was just interested."

"It's up to the passengers of course when I get my first packet," John said taking his hand from his pocket.

"How do you mean?" George asked.

"Well my wife have my wages, she needs them, I rely on tips, when a passenger gives me extra couple of coppers, I go to the station shop and get my packet of five woodbines cigarettes."

George smiled. "What about Mr Dummer, did he smoke?"

"Only other people's," John smiled. "To be honest I have never known Row to buy a packet, and to be honest again, I have only seen him smoke when we are having a pint, and they were mine."

"When was the last time you saw Mr Dummer?" George asked busy writing in his notebook.

"Saturday night, we had a pint together across the road."

"How was he?" George asked.

"Come to think of it, I felt he was angry, I asked him if he would be going rabbiting on Sunday, he said he was, then he said it might be his last time, and on a rare occasion he asked me for a fag, he usually waits until I offer," John said.

"No idea why he was angry?" George asked.

"No," John replied. "I could have been mistaken, I only felt it, he was saying he had learnt of a situation that would put him on easy street, give him financial comfort and if it did he would not go rabbiting any more, but I didn't catch all what he was saying, the bloody accordion player was very loud that night and with all the chatter going on I didn't catch every word, I do remember that he was expecting some kind of certificate to verify what he had learnt."

"Pity," George remarked. "Then when you both left the pub?"

"Row went home so did I, we live in the opposite direction to each other, he lives at Union Street, I live at Greenhill Road."

"What number?" George asked busy writing it down.

"Number 36," John replied.

It was early afternoon when George returned to the police station, and as he related his visit to the railway station, Chris leaned back in his chair, listening without interruption.

"Well that's about it," George finished closing his notebook. "Not much I'm afraid."

Chris leaned forward, he clasped his hands resting them on the desk. "I was beginning to think that Mr Dummer found a poacher in the wood, a fight between them broke out and got out of hand, I had manslaughter in mind rather than premeditated murder, however what you learnt knocks those thoughts."

"How do you mean?" George asked.

"Well let's take everything you have told me is the truth, that means that Mr Dummer did not smoke apart from an odd one when drinking."

"Right," replied George.

"That means there was someone else in the woods Sunday morning besides Mr Dummer, the butts you found proof that, whoever it was, was waiting rather than poaching."

"But they could have laid there for days," George argued.

"No," Chris replied. "I checked the weather for that morning, it was very damp, the ground was wet, the butts you found were fresh, no sign of being out in the weather very long."

"OK," argued George. "But we have always known that someone was in the wood, otherwise how was he stabbed in the back?"

"I agree," Chris replied. "Poachers know their own tracks in a wood where they lay their traps, when they return to their traps, they are quick and quiet, they do not stand under a tree for an hour smoking."

"So how do that help us?" George asked wondering.

"At least it will save our time," Chris answered. "We are not looking for a poacher who accidentally killed in a fight, but someone who had a reason for killing, your other notes tell us that."

"Carry on," George urged.

"Well, Mr Lewis told you that Mr Dummer said he had learnt of a situation that would put him on easy street and if it did he would not go rabbiting any more, which might mean he was expecting a pay off, he wanted to get hold of a certificate seemingly as proof of what he had learnt, which gives us five problems," Chris commented.

"Why would this be his last week going to the woods for rabbiting, what was the certificate he was expected, why would this certificate bring him a large pay off, who has the certificate, and who was the victim that's going to be blackmailed, one can assume he expected the certificate or whatever this weekend," Chris concluded.

"The way you say it means we are getting the beginning of a motive," George replied. "But why do you say blackmail, it means that Mr Dummer is not the nice person he's made out to be?"

"My thinking at the moment is that this certificate is a serious paper to someone, who would pay to get it back, Mr Dummer did not have it, and was expecting someone to deliver it to him."

"If your thinking is right," George replied thinking that Chris's thinking was plausible. "Perhaps he was expecting someone to give him the certificate yesterday in the wood, but unknown reasons the plan went badly wrong."

"Exactly," Chris replied picking up his pipe and sucking on it. "But what do we do now?"

Chapter Six

*A*knock came on the office door, and Sergeant Dawkins entered. "Constable Elkins is here," he said walking to both desks collecting the empty tea cups.

"Really," replied Chris. "Who is Constable Elkins?"

"Itchen Abbas Constable, you asked me to send someone to Manor Farm to look for a bicycle," the sergeant smiled making for the door.

"Oh right, let's have him in then," Chris replied looking at George with a smile on his face.

Constable Elkins was a man in his middle forties, he was tall and well built with greying hair, he had a pleasant face, with eyes that gave his face the look of kindness. Chris rose as he entered and offered his hand. "Constable Elkins," he said as they shook hands. "It's nice to meet you, please have a seat."

"Likewise," replied the constable taking the interview chair. "I did meet you once a few years back, you were with Inspector Noal."

"Really," Chris replied trying hard to remember but could not. "Have you met Sergeant George House?"

Constable Elkins who was sitting half facing both desks, smiled at George.

"Haven't had the pleasure," he said getting up and offering his hand.

"Now Constable, I take it you have been to Manor Farm, just tell us in your own words how you got on, will you?" Chris asked.

"I made myself known at Manor Farm," the constable started. "I informed Reg, I mean Mr Shawcroft my reason for being there, he insisted on coming with me," the constable spread his hands.

"What could I do, it's his land, anyway, we searched the whole wood, but found no sign of a bike I'm afraid, and that about it."

"You know Mr Shawcroft, Constable?" Chris asked.

"I know everyone who lives on my patch," the constable smiled. "If someone new moves in, then I present myself to them a little later."

"Commendable," Chris remarked. "So tell me what do you know of Mr Shawcroft?"

The constable shifted in his chair. "Well it must be eight years since I took over the Police House at Itchen Abbas, when I met Mr Shawcroft his father had recently died and as his mother had died much earlier, he was what I called a struggling farmer, he had a large farm house, plenty of ground, but only two or three chaps working for him. He seemed a pleasant sort of bloke, he must have been in his late thirties around that time," the constable smiled as he continued.

"His fortunes however changed when he got married around six or seven years ago, changes began slowly for the best of course," the constable continued, his eyes showing sadness. "He lost his wife and child in childbirth about five years ago."

Chris nodded, he knew of this but made no comment and waited for the constable to continue.

"After it seemed good fortune hit him as his farm did start to prosper," the constable stated. "He seemed to have plenty of money, he took on servants for the house, and extra men, and he became what we call a gentleman farmer."

"What would you put that down to?" George interrupted.

"Well it is said that he married a rich woman, she, it's said to be the daughter of a rich Yorkshire Farmer, this Yorkshire Farmer shortly after their marriage he died, and leaving all he had to his only daughter."

"What's your opinion?" Chris asked.

"Well," replied the constable spreading his hands. "I met the lady once, and what is said could be the truth, she was a Yorkshire Lass."

"Thank you constable," Chris smiled. "Now Manor Farm is at the end of the lane, no road goes by it, when you get to Manor Farm, you have to turn around and come back to main road again."

"That's right," agreed the constable.

"Are there any other path that you can reach Manor Farm without using the lane?" Chris asked.

"As far as I'm aware, just the bridle path, where Mr Shawcroft rides his horses, the path comes out on a narrow unkept path, turn left, and you're on the Basingstoke road."

"How far is that from the Cart and Horses Pub at Kings Worthy?" Chris asked never having been along the road.

"A good couple miles I would say," replied the constable.

"Do Mr Shawcroft have riding horses?" George asked.

"Two or three I believe," replied the constable. "Along with his shires."

"Any rumours flying around about Mr Shawcroft?" George asked curiously.

The constable smiled. "Nothing serious, they do say he has an eye for the ladies," he smiled.

"Constable," Chris spoke. "You have been very helpful, can you do me one more favour?"

"Anything," the constable replied.

"Can you go home via Basingstoke road, and the bridle path, it may be a waste of time, but you never know?"

"No problem at all Sir," replied the constable.

With the constable gone, Chris leaned back in his chair sucking his unlit pipe.

"You're thinking whoever was in the woods that day, took the bicycle and made his escape down the bridle path?" George asked.

"Well it is a possibility," Chris replied.

"What's your thinking on this George?" he asked.

George looked down at his desk, and clasped his hands. "With what the constable has just told us, we have to think of the possibility that the killer entered the wood by using the bridle path, also took the bike making his escape the same way, I mean the lane to the farm from the main road is about half mile, fields either side until you reach the farm, no place to hide should you meet anyone," George added.

Chris looked at George. "Sound plausible," Chris remarked. "Perhaps you are right but we also have to consider the time factor," Chris continued leaning forward to his desk.

"We know that Mr Dummer left just after five early in the morning, we also know that he was dead just after seven am, let's be generous and say that Mr Dummer arrived at the wood at five thirty, whoever killed him must have got there earlier, perhaps an hour earlier because of the cigarettes butts, whoever it was might have been there at least an hour before."

"Agreed," George remarked.

"There are no lighting in the lane," Chris replied. "And around half past five it must have been black as the ace of spades, the murderer after he had done his deed, it was much lighter and very risky to go back via the lane so he took the bike and went by the bridle path."

"Do it help us which ever way he went?" George asked.

"Not a lot George," Chris replied. "But if the murderer knew of the bridle path, then he must have known the area, someone local perhaps."

It was getting on towards five when the phone rang, George looked up as Chris answered it.

"Ah Constable Elkins," he said, then a few moments later spoke again.

"Any chance of transporting it?" he spoke into the receiver. "Really, thanks," Chris said putting down the receiver.

Chris smiled at George who was looking at him. "Constable Elkins found the bike, or a bike thrown in the bushes as the lane meets the Basingstoke road, the front wheel is missing and he will arrange it to be transported to us, but perhaps not today, it do now seem he escaped by the bridle path," Chris smiled.

"Not only that but constable Elkins said along the path a few feet from the road, he found a clear impression of what he thought was a motorcycle, he said the tyre impression was too wide for it being a bicycle."

"But that gives us another problem?" George remarked.

Chapter Seven

*I*t was getting dark as Chris reached the Butter Cross, he saw Elizabeth coming towards him wearing a long yellowish brown top coat, on her head she was wearing a hat of the same colour, and around her neck a woollen scarf of the same colour but brighter was wrapt with the ends flung back over her shoulders.

She kissed him on the cheek, then started to fiddle with the collar of his overcoat.

"You must keep yourself warm darling," she smiled as she took his arm. "I don't want you ill on our honeymoon."

Chris smiled at her remark. "You look warm, a nice outfit."

"Thank you darling, it is very warm, by the 19th of April I shall be warm as toast," she teased, smiling up at him as they walked downtown.

"You are wicked Elizabeth," Chris replied with a smile. "What would your mother say if she heard you?"

"Don't you ever fantasize about me darling?" Elizabeth asked with a giggle.

Chris felt himself blushing at the question, but smiled to himself. "It would be unnatural if I didn't and I'd be lying," he said.

Elizabeth squeezed his arm. "I would be disappointed if you did not, I fantasize about you all the time," she giggled looking up at him as they walked.

Chris looked down at her, he saw that her lovely eyes were glistening with her smile. "I love you," he said patting her arm with his free hand.

"I know," Elizabeth murmured.

Walking on in silence, they had passed the Rising Sun before Chris spoke again.

"I'm a bit worried about the wedding," he said. "I'm afraid I have not been much of a help."

"Don't worry darling, you have other worries to contend with," Elizabeth replied.

"You have your suit, the transport is arranged so is the reception and church, the only things remaining are my dress which has to be completed and the bridesmaids dresses, for which I have ordered the material, so don't worry darling all is in hand."

"What about the money side?" Chris asked.

"You have paid the deposits where it was necessary," Elizabeth replied. "You know mother is enjoying arranging my wedding as much as I am," she replied putting a little more pressure on his arm.

They reached the path leading to the front door. Elizabeth let go his arm, and looking up at him offered her lips which he took, then pulled away from him and started to walk up the path. "Mother might want to chaperon us on our honeymoon," she giggled.

Chris was about to give her a playful slap on the rump as the front door opened, and Olive appeared.

"Come on in both of you," Olive greeted them. "It's warmer inside, and dinner is on the table."

Elizabeth greeted her mother with a kiss on her cheek, as she went inside and immediately took off her coat and hat, Chris who followed her with a smile did the same.

"How are you Chris?" Olive asked as he kissed her on the cheek.

"Very well thank you Olive," Chris replied smiling. "I think I'll have to take control over your daughter after we are married, she is out of control."

"She adores you Chris," replied Olive. "You have made her so happy."

"She has certainly changed my life," Chris replied as he hung up his overcoat. "I shall treasure her, I only hope my Job do not interfere in our marriage."

"It won't," Elizabeth said interrupting and pulling Chris into the dinning room where her father was sitting in his armchair reading the paper.

Elizabeth went over and kissed him on the cheek. "Hello dad," she smiled.

Ron looked over the top of his glasses at Chris. "Having trouble with her already?" he asked with a smile.

"Come along Ron and sit at the table," Olive commanded before Chris could answer. "I have shepherds pie and veg, it will be filling."

The meal was eaten in almost silence until Ron asked Chris what he thought of the war.

"Don't get much time to read the papers," Chris admitted. "I did read about our retreat from Gallipoli in January I think, lots of young lives lost there."

"It's you men, you think war is like playing soldiers, but it's not, war only brings death and grief, and in the end achieve nothing," Olive commented.

"I know," Ron agreed. "But a country has to defend itself."

"If women ran the government, there would be no wars," Olive remarked.

"Mum's right, women would not want to see their husbands, sons or fathers killed in some silly war," Elizabeth remarked her eyes on Chris. "Why should they, governments starts war not the people, and who is the government, a lot of sit around rich people."

"My, my," Ron said looking at his daughter. "I have never heard you voice off like that before," he said.

"Perhaps not dad," Elizabeth replied tear swelling in her eyes. "I have never had anyone to lose before."

"I understand you Elizabeth, your father forgets how I suffered in agony every day when he was out in Africa in the Boer War," Olive remarked. "Now forget the war, we have no power in what may happen, just hope that there are not many young lads dying."

Chris looked at Elizabeth who was dabbing her eyes with her hanky, he felt his love for her. "By the way, I'm still looking for a man," Chris said as all around the table stared at him.

"One of your cases Chris?" Ron asked.

"No I mean a best man for the wedding, I have to have one don't I?"

Elizabeth stood up, she leaned over and kissed Chris on the cheek. "Oh Chris you are silly, I love you very much."

"I thought your old Inspector to be your best man?" Olive asked.

"Inspector Noal yes," Chris replied. "But he is unable to come, I did think about my Sergeant George, but with me away, he will be on duty."

"Have you no other friends?" Elizabeth asked curiously and gave him a slight smile.

"I know some men, but not exactly friends," Chris replied. "In my job I don't get much free time to be sociable, the only men I really know are in the police station."

"Ask one of them darling," Elizabeth advised.

"Well I have a few weeks yet, perhaps I shall think of someone," Chris replied pushing his plate away from him.

"That was a lovely meal Olive, thank you very much."

"You got to have regular meals," Olive replied.

"Don't worry mum, I'll see to that," replied Elizabeth.

Ron looked at Chris and smiled. "That's you told Chris."

While the two women were in the kitchen, Chris sat in an armchair smoking his pipe.

"I was surprised with the outburst of Elizabeth," Ron said. "It's unlike her."

Chris took his pipe from his mouth. "It's good that women should voice their opinion, in this case I think she had me on her mind."

"I'm sure she did," Ron answered as the women came into the room.

Ron looked at his wife who started to speak. "Ron and I have been discussing your wedding," Olive began.

"Now it's only right that we pay for your reception or wedding breakfast as it is called, but both Ron and I would like to give you a present as well."

Chris took his pipe from his mouth. "Olive, Ron," he looked at them both. "You have both done more than I have with our wedding, I am very grateful to you both, but I am sure that Elizabeth will agree with me, the reception will be looked upon as your present."

Olive cleared her throat. "Thank you Chris, but as I was saying we have discussed your wedding present, we have put an offer for the empty house two doors up from here, however we do not want to upset any plans you might have made regarding this, we would like your acceptance before we purchase."

Elizabeth with tears in her eyes got up and going to her mother kissed and hugged her. "I love you mum, she then went to Ron and hugged him."

"Mum, Dad," she said sniffing. "No one could have better parents, but really mum you and dad must not spend all your money on my wedding, you have done enough already."

"Don't worry yourself Elizabeth, buying that house for you will not alter our way of living, no parents have been prouder of their daughter than us, you have been a good daughter, and I am sure you will make a good wife, like your mother," Ron added, which brought a smile to Olive's face.

Elizabeth looked at Chris who was speechless.

"We really want to do this, if it should meet with your plans Chris?" Ron assured Chris seeing that he was uncomfortable.

Chris got up, he crossed to Olive, he kissed her cheek and shook her hand. "I don't know how to thank you both," he said with a choking voice. "Never I met such a nice people like you before, if you really want to do this, then Elizabeth and I will certainly accept, and one problem will be solved for me."

"What's that then? "Elizabeth asked still sniffing.

"When I am out on a case late at night you will have mum and dad near by," Chris replied. "But you have not given your opinion yet darling?" Chris said.

"I am overwhelmed," Elizabeth answered. "Honestly Chris I knew nothing of it, but if mum and dad can afford it, we would be crazy to refuse it."

Chris crossed to Ron who rose as Chris shook his hand. "There are no words I can find Ron, like Elizabeth I am overwhelmed."

"No need for thanks Chris, in five weeks you will be family, what we have will be yours and Elizabeth's sooner or later, now I will go ahead and purchase the house, you will get the deeds on your wedding day, but," he continued with a smile. "You have to decorate before then, make it ready for when you get back from your honeymoon."

Chapter Eight

*G*eorge looked at Chris who was doodling with a pencil. "You look happy this morning Chris," he said.

"I'm always happy," Chris replied. "We were in Elizabeth's home last night, and the evening turned out to be full of surprises."

"Planning a wedding usually do bring surprises," George answered.

Chris smiled at him. "Yes, but not like the one I got, my future in-laws have bought us a house as a present, and I could not find the words to thank them."

"That is certainly a present," George was saying as the office door opened and Sergeant Dawkins entered.

"Sorry to interrupt," he said. "But a body has been found in a field at Morn Hill," he looked at Chris. "About a hundred yards down from where your young lady lives."

"You mean the field by the first bend in Alresford Road, there's a horse in the field?" Chris asked his mind visualising the field.

"That's right," sergeant Dawkins answered.

"Any other information?" George asked not knowing the area.

"A chap delivering two bales of straw to the field found her, it seems every so often he delivers straw there, the horse has a sort of lean to in the field which gives him shelter."

370

"So it's a woman," Chris murmured.

"So I'm told," the sergeant replied. "I sent a constable up there to secure the scene, and told the delivery man to stay there."

"Thank you Sergeant," Chris answered getting up from his chair, crossing to the hat stand. "How did you get the message?" he asked putting on his overcoat.

"From the big house facing Blue Ball Hill, the field belongs to the house."

Chris looked at George. "It's only a five minute walk George," he remarked. "No need to bike."

"Whatever you say," George replied having followed Chris to the hat stand. "What about the police surgeon Bob Harvey?"

"Taken care of," replied the sergeant with a slight smirk.

Chris and George reached the field within the five minutes, and to their surprise the horse drawn meat wagon was stationary along side the field.

"Bob must be already here," Chris remarked. "How the hell did he get here so quick, I'll have a word with that sergeant when I get back."

George smiled to himself, as Chris pushed open the five bar gate at the entrance to the field. The field was not flat, it had a steady slope to it, and it felt slippery underfoot, it had rained during the night, but now a brisk wind was blowing.

Bob Harvey the police surgeon rose from examining the body as they approached.

"Chris, George," he greeted them, his face was serious. "Unless there is a way for someone to strangle themselves from behind, you have another murder on your hands," Bob commented.

While George looked around, Chris looked down on the body, it was a woman in her forties, quite attractive, then the uniform she was wearing made him look at Bob.

"Do you know her Bob?" Chris asked.

Bob nodded his head. "Margery Wilson, she is the senior midwife at the hospital." "I've known her about ten years."

"I'm sorry Bob," Chris replied gently. "I wonder how she came to be here?"

Bob looked around the field. "That's her horse," he said nodding to the other side of the field. "That horse was the love of her life, saw him every night I believe before going home."

"Do you know her address Bob?" Chris asked.

"She lives at Bar End, not far from here, I don't know the number," Bob answered.

"Was she married?" Chris asked.

"No," Bob replied shaking his head. "Widow I believe, you know this woman spent her working life bring new life into this world," he gave a long intake of breath. "Take no notice of me Chris, you have your job to do, and I will help you all I can."

"You always do Bob," Chris replied. "You say she was strangled from behind."

"The red marks around her throat tells me that, it was some sort of thin rope, the pressure point is clearly recognisable on the back of the neck," Bob replied.

"Was it a sex attack?" George asked.

"I'm not sure at that point," Bob answered. "Her elastic waistband of her bloomers were down around her thighs, but the leg elastic had not moved, she could not have been raped with her bloomers placed like that, but it might have been a sex assault," Bob remarked. "Rape of course could have been the intention of whoever committed the crime, could have been disturbed for some reason?"

Chris looked around, saw the horse on the other side of the field, all he could see were open fields stretching across Winnall, he looked towards the road, some ten feet away, he could only see the far side of the road, the near side covered by rows of tall trees.

"How long has she been here Bob?" George asked. "Her clothing seems to be in a bad way."

Bob scratched his head. "I won't know for sure until I get her on the table, but a guess, I would say at least since Saturday night."

"Over two days then," Chris remarked. "What about the big house who the field belongs to, don't they ever come up here?"

"There wouldn't be much need for them to do so, they rent the field to Margery," Bob replied.

"I talk them later," Chris said. "Did you find anything George?"

"No sign of anything not even a struggle, no handbag," George answered.

"Not surprising George," Chris muttered. "Being two days old, and in this weather with the March winds it would have surprised me," Chris looked at the constable who was talking to the delivery man. "I'll speak to the delivery man," he said.

"Feel free to take the body Bob, and George have another look around, the handbag could have been thrown in any direction," Chris advised.

"I'll take her straight to the mortuary," Bob replied. "I was there when your call came in."

"That's how you beat me here then," Chris smiled to himself. "What about relations?" he asked. "Do we have anyone to inform?"

"I don't know," Bob replied. "Phone up record department at the hospital, they should know if she had a next of kin, get any trouble let me know."

Chris left Bob to prepare the body for removal, and walked across to the constable.

"Morning Sir," the constable said politely. "This is Mr Clay, works for Gliffords in St Georges Street, he found the body and reported it."

"Thank you Constable," Chris replied. "Mr Clay," he said turning to him. "Sorry to have kept you waiting, but thank you for letting us know, would you tell us how you came to find the body?"

Mr Clay took off his cap, and scratched his head then replacing the cap. "I had two bails of hay to deliver, I usually leave them at that lean to over there," he pointed to the top end of the field.

"Have you delivered them?" Chris asked.

"Yes they're delivered," Mr Clay replied. "I took the shortest route across the centre of the field when delivering, they're heavy you know, after the last one I walked back around the hedge by the trees, there was a bike by the lean to, with a handbag and a doctor's bag in the handlebar basket, I wondered where she was, I mean leaving her handbag like that, that's when I saw her."

"Did you touch her?" Chris asked.

"Oh no, no, even if I wanted to I wouldn't, she looked very dirty," Mr Clay remarked.

"Well the body had been there a long time," Chris answered.

"Constable would you mind bringing that bicycle here," Chris asked. "So what did you do when you saw her?" Chris asked turning back to Mr Clay.

"I told my mate to take the cart back, and tell the boss I would be late, and tell him why, then I went to the big house there," he continued. "I knocked the door and a maid answered, she told me that the owners were abroad, but I could use the phone to phone the police station, the policeman on the other end told me to wait at the field until an officer arrived letting no one near the body, and that's what I did."

"No sign of a handbag," George said approaching Chris.

"We have found it I believe," Chris replied nodding towards the constable who was returning pushing the bike.

Chris turned back to Mr Clay. "Thank you Mr Clay, you have been very clear and a big help, please give this officer your name and address, and I would be obliged if you will call in the police station and sign a statement."

"That I can do," smiled Mr Clay.

"If you're in trouble when you get back to work, let me know," Chris added.

Mr Clay tipped his cap and left, Chris turned to the constable who had returned with the bike, he looked at the basket in front of the handlebars, there was a handbag, and a doctor type bag pressed together in the basket.

"No good searching them in this wind George, better to wait until we are back at the office," "Chris suggested.

"I agree," replied George.

"Constable take this bike to the station, don't touch anything, put the bike in my office."

"Very well Sir," replied the constable politely.

As they watched the constable leave, the body was being taken to the wagon, Bob came over to them. "This has been an upsetting day for me," he said. "I can't quite believe it."

"To be called out on someone you know can't be easy," George remarked understandingly.

"I'm now concerned about Mr Adams," Bob replied.

"Mr Adams?" Chris said with a question.

"Yes he is a Gynaecologist, the head of maternity, and Margery have been his senior midwife for years, I'm sure he will take it badly."

"I may have to speak with him Bob," Chris remarked.

"I'm sure he will obliged Chris," Bob answered. "Anyway I better be on my way, I get you the result as soon as possible.

"Not forgetting Mr Dummer," George remarked.

"I have already done his post-mortem," Bob replied. "He was killed with the knife, I will send the report with the knife," he said with a weak grin.

"Thank you Bob," Chris said as he watched Bob leave with a wave of his hand.

"Her death hit him really hard George," Chris remarked as they watched him shut the five bar gate.

"Now what we want to know," Chris said as he walked back to where the body was found. "Did she know her murderer, or was he hiding from her?"

"Where would he hide?" George said. "It's wide open behind us, the road is much lower than the field."

"You're probably right George, but it must be considered, I'm also wondering what was the motive?" Chris replied looking at the ground where the body had been found. "If someone was hiding among these trees, how did he know that Mrs Wilson would walk along them, the horse

I would say normally stay in the centre of the field, however seeing his owner, he might walk towards her."

"It seems a nice horse," George remarked looking at the horse who was taking no notice of them.

"About seventeen hands I would say," Chris replied. "But, I think whoever murdered her was known to her."

"At least, I can't see any connection between Mr Dummer's murder and this one," George remarked.

"Certainly don't look that way George," Chris agreed. "I can't explain it but I have a feeling that there are similarities," Chris took a deep breath.

"We won't find any clues here, three days of this weather would have destroyed any that might have been, so let's pop into the house and talk to the maid, then go back," Chris suggested.

The maid repeated what Mr Clay had said, she said she knew the nurse used the field for her horse, the lean to was put up by the owners, the field could not be seen from the house, Mr and Mrs Bradley were abroad on holiday.

"Well that was straightforward," Chris said as they walked down St John Street. "I think we have two difficult cases to deal with, they would come at this time, when I have the wedding on my mind," he continued looking at his pocket watch. "However it's lunch time, let's have a liquid one, I think better with a pint."

George smiled as they entered the Rising Sun.

Chapter Nine

*C*hris and George entered the police station, and was greeted by the smiling face of Sergeant Bloom. "Afternoon Inspector, Sergeant," he greeted them both.

As George went to the office, Chris stopped and spoke to Sergeant Bloom. "Nice to see you, I have two murders on my hands."

"So I understand Sir," sergeant Bloom replied. "You know you can always call on my help."

"Thank you Sergeant," Chris replied. "Give me ten minutes, then if you will phone the hospital, I want to speak to a Mr Adams, he's a Gynaecologist."

"Will do," replied sergeant Bloom.

Chris entered the office, he took off his overcoat and trilby, he noticed a bike standing behind the hat stand, but more or less ignored it crossing to his desk.

"We didn't check the lean to," George said.

"No need to check George," Chris replied. "Whoever it was, did not go to it."

"Can you be sure of that?" George asked.

"Well if he did, he didn't touch the handbag or doctor's bag, they were still in the bike basket," Chris replied looking at the bike.

"Also had he done so, he would have taken the risk of exposing himself, you see as you walk across the junction of

Morn Hill walking up Alresford Road, you can see the lean to quite clearly," Chris said as the phone rang.

"Inspector Hardie," he spoke onto the receiver.

"Mr Adams from the hospital here Inspector, I have been expecting your call, Mr Harvey has put me in the picture, what a terrible tragedy, I am still unable to accept it."

"Murder is always a tragedy Sir," Chris replied politely. "I now have to find out who is responsible, and to do that I have to ask questions, I am told that you have known the victim for many years, I would be grateful for a few moments of your time."

"I will do all I am able to help you Inspector," came the reply. "I am in Winchester about three this afternoon, I can call if this is suitable?"

"Most suitable Sir," Chris replied. "I wonder while I am on the phone to you, are you able to put me through to your record department."

"Mr Harvey explained to me about her next of kin, I have it all in hand Inspector, I will bring the records with me," Mr Adams replied.

"Thank you very much Sir," Chris answered. "Around three then."

"I'll be there," Mr Adams assured putting the phone down.

Chris replaced the receiver with a smile and looked at George. "That was Mr Adams from the hospital it seems our friend Bob Harvey have already spoken to him, Mr Adams will be here around three, that's in about an hour," Chris continued looking at his pocket watch. "He will also bring hospital records of Mrs Wilson."

"May give us the next step?" George voiced his opinion.

"Hope so George," Chris replied. "But now let's look at the handbag and doctor's bag."

Chris felt frustrated looking at the contents of the doctor's bag, obviously it contains the tools of a midwife's trade, none of them known to either Chris or George.

"No clues here George," Chris said pushing the articles to one side as George repacked them.

"The two small apples here must have been for the horse," George remarked as he put them in the bag.

"That means she did not have time to feed the horse," Chris said looking at George.

"I suppose," George remarked with a shrug.

"It holds up with my thought," Chris replied. "Who ever it was, waiting for her, he let himself be seen or he called out to her, and she crossed the field towards him."

"Do it help?" George asked.

Chris shrugged. "It's all a part of the final picture, anyway let's see what she has in her handbag."

George emptied the contents of the handbag on the desk, and while Chris looked at them, George examined the inside of the empty bag.

"Hairbrush, comb, powder compact, purse," Chris looked into the several compartments of the leather purse. "It was not robbery anyway George, she has over three pounds in her purse."

"A few weeks wages," George commented. "She was a smoker," he said picking up a packet of players weights cigarettes."

Chris picked up a bunch of keys. "Must be the key to her house here," he remarked, if Mr Adams knows the number of her house, we will pay it a visit."

"Looking for what?" George asked.

Chris shrugged. "We will know when we see it," he replied.

Chapter Ten

Chris lifted the receiver as the phone rang. "Thank you Sergeant," he said after a moment. "Show him straight in."

"Mr Adams is here," he said turning to George as the office door opened.

Mr Adams was tall and slender with dark hair that was greying around the temples, smartly dressed in a white shirt and tie, wearing a single breasted brown suit, an overcoat was over his arm, and he held a trilby by the rim.

Chris who was standing held out his hand. "Thank you for calling Sir," he smiled as Mr Adams took his hand. "I hope it is not inconvenient, I am Detective Inspector Hardie, and my colleague Detective Sergeant House."

"Let me take your coat and hat," George offered as they shook hands.

"Thank you Sergeant," Mr Adams replied handing the coat and hat to George who hung them on the hat stand.

"Please Mr Adams take a seat," Chris offered indicating the interview chair. "It's good of you to come to us."

"No bother," replied Mr Adams taking the chair. "As I told you I had to be in town this afternoon, in any case I would like to help, Mrs Wilson was not only a colleague but she was also a friend."

"Our first problem Mr Adams, is that we know nothing of Mrs Wilson, what we do know comes from Mr Harvey, we know she is a widow, and lives alone, we do not even know her address as yet."

"All your worries are over Inspector," Mr Adams said taking out from his wallet a sheet of folded paper. "I was unable to bring the hospital files with me, but I did have them copied for you," he said handing Chris the paper.

Chris took the paper and started to read aloud.

"She was born in 1872, that would make her about 44 years old," Chris muttered. "She became a qualified nurse in 1896, that would have made her twenty four," Chris said looking at Mr Adams, who nodded. "She married in 1892, and widowed in 1901, her husband Mr Wilson being killed in South Africa while fighting the Boers. In 1904 she was transferred from a ward nurse to midwifery. Her last known address is number 9, Bar End Road Winchester, her next of kin," Chris continued. "Charles Dowling of 2, Hyde Abbey Road, he's her brother," Chris ended reading, passing the paper to George.

"That information Mr Adams is most helpful, I can't thank you enough, would you mind if I ask you a couple questions?"

"Fire away," Mr Adams replied. "I'll answer what I am able."

"I understand Sir that you have known Mrs Wilson some ten years, you must know a bit about her as a person?" Chris said.

"Oh I do," Mr Adams replied. "Margery was an impressively competent midwife, that's why she became senior midwife, she always brought the welfare of the mothers first, she did not have a selfish bone in her body," Mr Adams paused for just a second then continued."She carried out her duties with confidence, I can tell you, I shall miss her as well as her expertise."

"That's a glowing reference," Chris remarked. "What about boyfriends, did you know of any?"

"I was one once," Mr Adams volunteered. "About five or six years ago we had an affair, I might add, an affair with no ties, went on for over a year, then I met a woman I thought I would like to marry and the affair stopped, which Margery accepted."

"Did you marry the woman you met?" George asked with a smile.

"No, sadly no," Mr Adams replied. "It fizzled out after a year, we were not made for each other I'm afraid. Anyway that was five years ago, I was promoted to head of my department, Margery became senior midwife, we both had more responsibility, we never did get back to the affair state again, but somehow we came closer, we worked a lot together, but I am still single."

Chris smiled. "What about recent boy friend, any idea?" he asked.

"I did hear she was friendly with a man in our clerical office, don't ask me who, it's only a rumour as far as I'm concerned," Mr Adams replied. "Apart from that Margery kept pretty much to herself, her true love was her horse, she always talked about him," he shook his head with a grin as he remembered.

"Did Mrs Wilson's attitude, had it changed lately?" Chris asked.

Mr Adams shook his head. "Not that I can put my finger on," he replied. "She was always a jovial sort of person."

"Mr Adams, I'm afraid I have to ask everyone, can you tell us where were you between five and say seven pm last Saturday night?"

Mr Adams look towards the ceiling a slight smile on his face then looked at Chris.

"It's hard to say about the precise time Inspector, Saturday I was off, spent most of the day doing little jobs around the house, don't get a lot of time to do things, anyway I was called to the hospital because of a difficult birth that night just after seven."

"You were called from the hospital to your home?" Chris asked.

Mr Adams nodded. "All calls are recorded Inspector."

Chris looked at George who shook his head, telling Chris he had no questions.

"Well thank you Mr Adams, it was good of you to come in, and the information will be very helpful," Chris got up and held out his hand, while George retrieved his coat and hat."

"Not much I could ask," George remarked when Mr Adams had left. "After all I did not want to seem rude, he did come in on his own free will."

"I know George," Chris replied. "But his information could be helpful, it amazed me why he told us of his affair with Mrs Wilson, men in his position would normally try to hide it."

"Perhaps he expected us to find out," George replied.

"But this affair ended five years ago," Chris remarked looking at the paper that Mr Adams had given him. "We now know her next of kin, who we can see today, I wonder if her husband Mr Wilson had any family, we can check on that."

It was just after five pm that the detectives knocked on the door of 2, Hyde Abbey Road, Chris had already phoned Elizabeth telling her he would be unable to meet her. A well built man opened the door, he was about six foot, and he had a bald head, Chris found himself trying to judge his age, but found it difficult, nature had not been kind to him with looks.

"Mr Dowling, Mr Charles Dowling?" Chris asked.

"That's me," replied the man. "Who are you?"

"I am Detective Inspector Hardie of Winchester CID, and this is Detective Sergeant House, are you the brother of Mrs Margery Wilson living at 9, Bar End Road, and working as a midwife at the hospital?"

"You could say that," replied Mr Dowling unsmiling.

"Then if we can come in we would like to talk to you," Chris replied.

Mr Dowling did not answer, but stood aside for the detectives to enter. "First door on the right," Mr Dowling said as he closed the front door and followed them.

Chris saw straight away that the house was a bachelor house, in the room there was a sofa, and two armchairs, a sideboard, table with two chairs, and a radiogram, all of which hugged the walls of the room leaving the centre empty.

"You're a bit of a wood sculpture I see," Chris remarked pointing to a pile of wood chips and a shaped piece lying with a knife on newspaper on the table.

"I mess about with it a bit, take a seat," Mr Dowling offered, sitting himself in one of the armchairs. "What do you want?" he asked.

"You are Mrs Margery Wilson's brother?" Chris asked again.

Mr Dowling smiled. "Not by blood," he replied. "I was adopted by her parents."

"Really," Chris replied looking at George who was also surprised.

"When were you adopted?" George asked.

"I was ten years old," Mr Dowling answered. "I have always known I was adopted, anyway, you don't want to know about that, why are you here?"

"I'm sorry to have to tell you Mr Dowling that Mrs Wilson have been found dead," Chris replied gently.

Mr Dowling sat for a moment staring at Chris, then got up went to the sideboard, where he took a cigarette from a packet and lit it, on which he drew deeply.

"I had no idea that she was ill," he said picking up an ashtray as he returned to his chair. "I saw her during last week on her way to see her horse, she looked OK to me."

"Your sister was not ill Mr Dowling," Chris answered. "She was found dead in the field in which she kept her horse, we are treating it as murder."

Mr Dowling gave a grin. "Really Inspector who would want to kill Margery, she had a very kind heart."

"How did you get on with your sister?" George asked.

"We tolerated each other," Mr Dowling answered. "I always thought that when I was adopted Margery looked upon me as an intruder, however she was very kind after I had my accident."

"What accident was that?" George asked.

"I was riding a bike down a hill when the brakes failed, at the bottom I went straight into a telegraph pole, I was lucky to save my eyesight, but as you can see I am disfigured around the eyes, also I broke my nose," he said with a slight grin. "It's roaming all over my face anyway Margery was very kind to me then."

Not knowing what to say, Chris shifted in his chair. "Life has not been kind to you Mr Dowling, it's a good job that you have a caring sister."

"I don't know about that," Mr Dowling answered. "Yes things went alright until our parents died, both died within three years, we were both in our twenties then, Margery had married, her husband had bought a house in Bar End, and I stayed here. My parents left a small Will in which we were treated equally, but Margery resented this, as I told you throughout she considered me as an intruder, but she was kind when I had my accident."

"That was the nurse in her," George remarked.

"Perhaps," replied Mr Dowling puffing his cigarette.

"She lost her husband in the Boer War, I believe," Chris said.

"Yes, by that time she had qualified as a nurse, the house was hers so she was able to manage, but she had a hard ten years with her parents and her husband dying."

"What did Mr Wilson do for a living?" George asked. "I mean before he enlisted?"

"He was an office worker, he worked at the hospital."

"Really," Chris remarked. "So husband and wife worked at the same place?"

Mr Dowling shrugged. "Well it must have worked well for them, they managed to buy their house."

"Do Mr Wilson have any family?" George asked.

"If he did, I'm not aware of any, he had no time for me, I was only invited to the wedding because of my parents, had my parents died before they were married, I'm sure I wouldn't have been invited."

"I have to ask you Mr Dowling, where were you during last Saturday afternoon and evening?" Chris asked.

Mr Dowling got up and crossed to the sideboard when he took another cigarette and lit it, and returned to his seat. "During the day I was digging trenches at Flowerdown, just outside Winchester, during the evening I was in the Three Tuns pub, don't ask me times, I came home from work, got myself a bite to eat and went to the pub, in any case it would have been after seven."

"Is that your work Mr Dowling, digging ditches?" George butted in.

"Sometimes," Mr Dowling replied. "I hire myself out daily, some days I don't work, but as a jack of all trades, and master of none I don't do too bad."

"You mean you do anything in other words?" Chris asked.

"That's right, farming, building, decorating, gardening, I am well known and often people come to me offering a day or two work, I do alright," Mr Dowling said with a smile as he puffed his cigarette.

"Have you ever been to the field where your sister kept her horse?" George asked.

"It seems when Margery was given permission to use the field, it had no gate, so she asked me to put one up," Mr Dowling replied. "I bought two railway sleepers for a couple shillings, put them upright in concrete opposite each other, then slung the gate between them, it was a sturdy job even if I say so myself."

"I can vouch for that," George replied visualising the gate. "What about the lean to?"

"One job comes from another," Mr Dowling said. "While I was erecting the gate, the owner asked me to build a lean to at the top of the field under the wall, which I did."

"When was that?" George asked.

"Oh five years back I would say," Mr Dowling replied as he dubbed out his cigarette in the ashtray. "It wasn't long after Margery got made senior midwife."

"Have you been to the field since?" George asked.

Mr Dowling shook his head. "No need," he replied.

"You say you do farm work?" Chris asked. "Have you ever worked for Manor Farm at Couch Green?"

"My work on the farms are seasonal," Mr Dowling replied. "Such as harvest time, I have often been a beater, but Manor Farm, yes I have worked a few days for them, but not recently, it was a good job, my drinking friend Rowland Dummer was murdered there a few days ago, so I'm told."

"Mr Dummer was a friend of yours was he?" Chris repeated what he had already been told.

"Often had a drink together," Mr Dowling replied. "Nice chap, are you on that case as well?" he asked.

Chris ignored the question. "Did he confide in you?" Chris asked.

"We talked about his work at the railway station, and things like that, that's all," Mr Dowling answered. "However he must have known Margery, only last week he asked me how she was doing, I was a bit surprised that they knew each other, because Margery is so much older."

"That was all he said about Margery?" Chris asked hoping for more.

"That's all," Mr Dowling replied.

Chris looked at George, both knowing that the questioning was over.

"Mr Dowling you are Mrs Wilson's next of kin," Chris told him. "We have your sister's bike and handbag at the station, which we will return to you after our investigation is over. In her handbag we found keys, one of which we believe is her house key. We will visit the house tomorrow, would you be free to accompany us?"

"I'll make myself free," Mr Dowling replied. "About eleven would be ideal for me, by the way what is next of kin, I have often heard it said but never understood it."

"Most firms record had the next of kin written," Mr Dowling. "Who is to be notified should the person be taken ill or die while at work. Next of kin has to be a blood relation, if there are none then the person dearest to the person, in your case, your sister made you her next of kin."

Having taken their leave, Chris and George stopped at the Junction of North Walls.

"Opinion George?" Chris asked taking out his pipe out and sucking it.

"Plenty of background," George replied.

"Yes," Chris replied thoughtfully. "We know a lot about Mrs Wilson's background, but little about herself."

"We know that she knew Mr Dummer," George added.

"Not surprising George, Winchester is a tight community, everyone lives within a short distance of the town, everyone knows each other," Chris replied.

"I agree," George replied.

"Let's go in the Three Tuns for a pint, and check Mr Dowling's story," Chris suggested.

"I'm in no hurry to get home Chris," George replied. "It's a pub I haven't been in yet."

Chris pushed open the bar door, and entered a large smoke filled room, in which twenty odd men were sitting or standing around, some playing darts, push halfpenny, or dominoes. Most of the men wore caps, and many had coloured handkerchiefs tied around their necks, while others just had open collarless shirts.

"I wouldn't be comfortable in this pub," George remarked as they entered.

"We can at least check Mr Dowling's alibi," Chris answered. "There is room at the far end," he said making his way across the room to the space at the far end.

"What's your pleasure?" asked the barman.

"Two pints of your best bitter please," Chris answered.

"Are you the landlord?" Chris asked as the barman placed the two pints in front of them, and Chris paid.

"Yes, I am," replied the man.

Chris introduced himself and George. "I need to know if a Mr Dowling was in here Saturday night?" Chris asked.

"Just a moment," replied the landlord, who left them and walked to the other side of the counter where he spoke to a man sitting by himself. Chris took a sip of his pint, and watched as the man nodding his head, got up and carrying his glass approached them.

"I am Roger Webber," he introduced himself. "The landlord cannot be seen talking to policemen, at least not in this pub, he would lose half his customers," he smiled. "But perhaps I can help you?"

"Thank you Mr Webber, but who are you exactly?"

"I'm a ganger, foreman of a group of workers, I run gangs of workmen for different firms, I give most of these men work, just a day or two here and there, I have my regular gangs but if I need extra, I get them from this lot," he said looking around the room. "That's why they are here in the hope of getting a days work."

"Really," Chris remarked taking another drink. "Do you give work to a Mr Dowling who lives in Hyde Abbey?"

Roger took a drink of his pint. "He's a brute of a man, but a good worker, strong as a ox, works as hard as two men, yes I gave him two days work last Friday and Saturday at Flowerdown, is he in trouble again?"

Chris ignored the question. "What was his hours?" he asked.

"As always with my workers," Roger replied. "Seven am until five pm."

"You can vouch for him being at Flowerdown at five Saturday night?" Chris asked.

"Yes," Roger replied.

Chris looked at George.

"Does he come in here a lot?" George asked.

Roger smiled. "It's about the only pub he can enter, he's been barred from most, he's incline to fight a lot you know."

"What about Saturday night, was he in here?" George repeated Chris's question.

"I always pay the temporary labourers in here Saturday nights, Dowling was here, he had two days paying, he was in here around seven o'clock, that's for sure."

"Tell me Mr Webber," George continued. "If Mr Dowling is such a good worker, why don't you have him full time?"

Roger put down his pint and laughed. "No way," he replied. "If I did that I wouldn't have a gang left by the end of the week, he would've fought them all. Dowling is a loner, don't mix, has a temper to suit his looks, even though he can't help them. I always give him work when I can put him on his own, as I said he works like two men. Last week I had several trenches that had to be dug along the road for about a mile, I was able to leave him to it, on his own."

"That bad," George muttered.

"Afraid so," replied Roger. "When you speak to him, he seems pleasant enough, but a wrong word can upset him, then you have a fight," Roger smiled.

George finished his pint, and nodded to the landlord. "Same again landlord," he said as he turned to Mr Webber. "Will you have one with us Mr Webber?" he asked.

"Never been known to refuse a pint," Mr Webber answered with a smile. "Don't want my reputation to be ruined, thank you," he said draining his glass.

"Do you supply transport for your workers?" George asked taking a sip of his new pint.

Roger laughed. "Not likely, they have to be at the site on time, seven in the morning, with their shovel and picks."

"You don't supply their tools?" Chris asked surprised.

"No way, Mr Dowling is lucky he has a motorbike, but most have to walk or cycle," Roger replied.

"Bit harsh don't you think?" Chris asked.

"That's life," replied Roger with a shrug. "Of course it's easier for the regular gangs, they only carry their tools on the day they start, and leave them over night on the job."

"If they have to cycle how do they carry their tools?" Chris asked.

Roger took a gulp of his pint, then put the back of his hand across his mouth before answering. "The tools are tied together, and carried on their shoulder, they ride the bike with one hand."

"Seems dangerous," George butted in. "How would Mr Dowling do that on a motorbike?"

"Your guess is as good as mine," Roger smiled. "But he manages somehow."

"Do you go to many pubs?" Chris asked.

"Quite a few, you see I also clear building sites, and knock down old buildings, sometimes I have two or three different gangs working at the same time."

"That keeps you busy then?" Chris commented.

"It certainly do," replied Roger with a smile.

"You have different gangs working at the same time at different places, how do you keep track on them all?" George asked.

"By motorbike, I spend my day going from one job to another, I need a motorbike."

"I'm sure you do Mr Webber," George replied.

"Do you visit the pubs riding your motorbike?" Chris asked.

"No I use my bicycle," Roger smiled. "Mine's outside against the wall now."

"I wondered who it belonged to, I nearly hit myself on it," Chris remarked.

Roger smiled but made no remark.

"Have you ever met Mr Rowland Dummer on your travels?" Chris asked.

"Yes I know Row, never employed him though he has a steady job at the Railway Station," Roger replied. "Funny you asking about him, he was in here, let me see," Roger said thinking for a while. "Yes he was in here Friday night, it wasn't Saturday, he was standing where we are now, talking to a chap who I did not know."

"Really," Chris replied. "Can you describe him?"

Roger looked at Chris. "Why are you interested?" he asked.

"Well you must know that Mr Dummer died Sunday," Chris replied.

"I heard a rumour that a bloke had been found murdered, they say at a farm outside Winchester, but I did not know it was Row," Roger replied losing his continued smile. "Poor old Row," he muttered taking a drink of his beer.

"So you see I would be interested in anyone who saw Mr Dummer before his death," Chris explained.

"Sure, I'm sure you would be," Roger replied solemnly. "Well he was about as tall as you, wore a cap and overcoat which he did not take off, and seem to keep his back to the bar, so I did not see a lot of his face, however he wore glasses, the cap he had on was pulled well down I remember, I would have judge him as being around forty."

"You have a good eye for observation, you ought to be in the police force," Chris flattered. "Anything else?"

"Not really," Rodger replied. "I left earlier than they did, but like you two he stood out in this crowd."

"How do you mean?" Chris asked.

"He wore a collar and tie," Roger remarked. "Anyway," Roger continued. "Are you thinking that Dowling had something to do with his death, is that why you are asking about him?"

"Do you think he is capable of murder?" George asked.

Roger took a sip of his drink before answering. "I believe he is capable of manslaughter with his temper," he replied. "Premeditated I would be hard press to give an opinion, but you know what the experts tell us, we are all capable of murder."

"Did you know Mr Dowling had a sister?" Chris asked.

"Yes I knew, but I would not know her if I saw her," Roger replied, "But what do you mean had a sister?" Roger asked.

"His sister has been found dead, and we are asking you questions so that you can verify where he was during Saturday evening."

Roger Webber did not answer straight away, he sat looking at the floor. "As I have told you he was in this pub on Saturday evening," he finally replied." Before that he was working at Flowerdown," Roger said without rising his head.

"You will swear to that?" George asked.

"Of course," Roger replied rising his head. "First Margery then Rowland," he muttered shaking his head, he reached in his pocket bring out a packets of Players cigarette and lit one without offering them around."

"Expensive cigarettes," George remarked.

"Why not," Mr Webber replied. "I do quite well, I can afford the best."

"With regards to Mr Dummer, were there anyone that you can think of that was not friendly with him?"

Roger shook his head slowly. "Row was a likeable person, it would have been hard for anyone to dislike him, no doubt a few did, we all have people who do not like us, we all have our little quirks that some people take offence to, but I can't think of anyone."

Chris drained his glass followed by George who knew there were no more question to ask. "Thank you very much for your help Mr Webber," Chris said as he stood. "What you have told us will be very helpful."

"Will I have to go to court?" Roger asked.

"No idea at the moment Mr Webber, should that time come we will contact you, thanks again for all your help, and just in case your address would be helpful," Chris replied.

"Anytime," Mr Webber murmured as he reached into his pocket, and produced a card with his address written. "I use these when I am seeking new contracts," he said handing George the card who studied it.

"Are you married Mr Webber?" George asked as he put the card in his notebook.

"I was but she died a few years back, don't intend to get married again," he smiled.

Chapter Eleven

*C*hris tossed and turned during the night, he had very little sleep, his thinking kept him awake. He got up early, shaved and dressed, and ate the breakfast that his landlady had prepared for him.

"You need your overcoat today son," she smiled at him as she was about to leave the room. "Eat your breakfast it will help keep the cold out."

"I will, thank you," Chris replied with a smile picking up the knife and fork." I didn't get much sleep last night," he admitted.

"You need a holiday lad," she replied opening the kitchen door. "You work too hard."

Chris pulled the collar of his overcoat up around his neck, and his trilby down to his ears, he walked briskly, he looked at the clock that jutted out from the wall a few yards up from the Butter Cross, and saw it was just coming eight thirty, the high street was busy, the people were rushing to get to work, he dug his hands into his overcoat pockets, his mind still working overtime on the cases he was working on.

It was in front of the hotel at the corner of Middle Brook Street that he met Elizabeth.

"Hello darling," she said with a glint in her eyes as she kissed him on the cheek, then started to mess with his overcoat collar, and checking his buttons. "It's cold today,

I can't wait until I have the warmth of you to wake up to," she smiled.

"Now you're teasing again," Chris smiled gently easing her to the wall of the hotel. "Miss me last night?"

"I miss you day and night," Elizabeth replied. "But I think about the nights a lot," she giggled.

Chris smiled to himself. "I may not be able to meet with you tonight," Chris said seriously. "I had another murder yesterday just below your house, in that field where the horse is."

"I heard about it darling," Elizabeth said with feeling. "How dreadful that sort of thing can happen so close, it frightens me."

"You must not worry darling," Chris replied putting his arm on her shoulder. "No reason to, she was murdered in the field because it was an opportunity for the murderer whoever it was, whoever did this knew what he was doing and had the opportunity, so no need for you to worry."

Elizabeth lean up and kissed him. "I know darling, but I do get nervous."

"That's understandable," Chris spoke gently trying to comfort her. "Now look darling I might not be able to make it tonight, should I be able I'll meet you outside the bank, but don't rely on it."

Elizabeth smiled. "That's alright, mother has had the material for the bridesmaids dresses," she spoke excitedly. "So mother and I will be measuring the girls, and as a man you will only be in the way, we are sending dad down to the Rising Sun."

Chris smiled. "Well I'm glad you have other things to think of instead of night times," Chris laughed loudly.

"I won't stop thinking of those until you are by my side darling," she murmured with a cheeky glint in her eyes.

After another kiss on the cheek, Chris watched as Elizabeth walked away from him, and eventually lost from view. Chris smiled to himself, as he dug his hands into his overcoat pocket, looked both ways before cross the road making for the Police Station.

Chris looked up as George entered. "Morning Chris, a bit brisk out there," he said taking off his overcoat, he was rubbing his hands. "You're early?"

Didn't get a lot of sleep, tossed and turned all night, so gave up trying," Chris replied.

"When you get home you got to put work at the back of your mind Chris," George said.

"Really," Chris replied looking at him with a smile. "Are you able to do that?"

George grinned. "No, not really," he answered.

"Our Mr Dowling seems to have a violent nature," Chris said as George seated himself at his desk. "We have a file on him, he has been in our cells overnight several times for fighting."

"Not surprising after what Mr Webber told us last night," George answered.

"I wonder what makes a man violent like that, I was thinking perhaps his accident damaged him?" Chris said.

"Possible I suppose," George answered.

"Still," Chris said closing the file. "He's violent, no other sort of crime against him, but being violent is enough to make us believe he could be capable of murder, according to these files, he has put at least two men in hospital."

"I'll study him more when we meet this morning, speaking to him last night, I thought him pleasant enough," George replied.

Chris folded his arms leaning on his desk. "Let's go over what we have at the moment George, we know that Mr Dummer left his house between five and half past last Sunday morning, we also know that by seven or just after he was dead, that would mean that he was in the wood one and a half hours before being killed."

George nodded his head. "Agreed," he said.

"We are also led to believe that although he regularly poached in the wood, this time he was expecting to meet someone who was going to give him some sort of document that would bring him money from somewhere?"

"That's a puzzle," George remarked.

"Now we know by the cigarette ends, that someone was waiting in the wood and we assume that it was the murderer," Chris commented.

"We also know that he was there some time, he did smoke two cigarettes, why did he wait over an hour?" George asked.

Chris gave a weak smile. "The wood is just over an acre, do not sound very big, my own opinion is that Mr Dummer entered the wood quite away from where the murderer was hiding, don't forget Mr Dummer had already opened a couple traps having three rabbits in his poacher pocket."

"Yes, I was forgetting that," George admitted. "So the murderer was waiting for Mr Dummer to come his way, when Mr Dummer eventually did, the murderer came out and stabbed him in the back."

"On the other hand we believe Mr Dummer was meeting someone, perhaps the murderer made no effort to hide, and just confronted Mr Dummer as he approached," Chris added. "Still either way we won't know until we find the killer, if only we knew what this document was?" Chris continued. "Then again who is in the frame that have enough money to be blackmailed?"

"Farmer Shawcroft," George remarked.

"Right," replied Chris. "But did he know he was about to be blackmailed, don't forget Mr Dummer was waiting to be given the document before he could put his intentions into action, I think we are correct to assume that the murderer arrived at the wood via the bridle path, and left the same way riding Mr Dummer's bike which he must have found, and from the end of the track on the Basingstoke road made his get away by means of a motorbike."

"We never checked the prints?" George remarked.

"I think Constable Elkins is confident enough to know the difference between cycle and motorbike tracks, Mr Dummer's murderer knew the area, not many outsiders would know of the bridle path or where it leads."

"I suppose," remarked George.

"Now Mrs Wilson, perhaps we will know more about her when we visit her house this morning, we hardly know anything about her, her adopted brother Mr Dowling did not tell us much, but her murderer was someone who knew her habits."

"What we know about Mr Dowling," George remarked. "To my mind he seems more in the frame for Mr Dummer's murder than his sister's, I mean he smokes tenners, he has a motorbike according to Rodger Webber, not a lot of motorbikes around, we don't know where he was during Sunday," George quickly added. "But still it's a thought, I mean he do have the strength it seems to plunge a knife into a body right up to the hilt."

"No disputing what you say George," Chris remarked. "You are implying that the two murders are connected, which if it's true we will have to find some connection between Mr Dummer and Mrs Wilson, we know that they both knew each other, but not how well," Chris took out his pocket watch. "In just over an hour we will ask him where he was Sunday morning."

A knock came on the office door, Bob Harvey poked his head inside. "Can I come in?" he asked smiling.

"Anytime Bob," Chris replied indicating the interview chair. "I was wondering about you?"

"I thought I would drop the autopsy reports in for you," Bob said taking the seat, after he had placed two large envelopes and a brown bag on the desk.

"Thank you Bob," Chris replied.

"How are the cases going Chris?" Bob asked.

"Not well," Chris replied. "Perhaps your reports will help, your Mrs Wilson seem to have had a secret life, we know very little about her."

"Did not Mr Adams give you any leads?" Bob asked. "He told me he had hospital records for you."

"It told us she had a brother, who turned out to be an adopted brother, he told us little or nothing regarding her private life."

"Have you heard of any romances shall we say that she have had?" George asked.

"You get lots of rumours flying around the hospital," Bob smiled. "No, I haven't heard of anything like that, I did hear we have a clerk in our records office missing, can't be found it seems, still nothing to do with your case, I think the police have been informed."

"Didn't know," Chris replied. "But I will ask the desk sergeant, anyway Bob, now you are here tell us in plain English about the autopsy, I'll read later."

"Well," Bob began shifting in his chair. "I'll tell you in plain English, you will find all the medical names in the report, Mr Dummer was killed by the stabbing, the knife penetrated just below the heart, cutting the artery that supplies the blood to the heart."

"The knife, had a blade of seven inches and very sharp, it had to tear through Mr Dummer's clothing before entering the body, and don't forget Mr Dummer had on a very thick poaching Jacket, whoever it was, had to be very strong," Bob indicated the brown bag on the desk.

"Not a woman then?" George interrupted.

"Hardly," Bob replied with a slight smile. "I have tried to think how he managed to get out onto the field where he was found, my only explanation is that he did not fall when he was stabbed, the force of the plunge could pushed him forward enough, and he stumbled out on the field before he died," Bob commented. "Anyway, apart from that he was quite healthy, I found nothing else, time of death I would say around seven am."

"And Mrs Wilson?" Chris asked.

"She was strangled from behind," Bob continued. "Strangled with something like a thin piece of rope or a thin piece of cloth like a tie, calculation of her time of death is more difficult, but knowing her normal habits helped a bit, I would put the time of her death down as between five thirty and seven Saturday evening."

"Her underclothing was disarranged Bob, was she sexually assaulted?"

"No, but then as I told you, with her bloomers down just below the thighs, this would have been very difficult," Bob answered.

"So," Chris urged.

"Well," replied Bob with a smile. "Mrs Wilson had a large pocket sewn on the inside of her bloomers, large enough I would say for an envelope, I have not seen one before."

"Really," remarked Chris. "Then she could have been carrying a document in the pocket, and the murderer was after it, still one would think that a woman carrying something near to her skin in her underwear, it would have been as safe as the Bank of England, I mean who would know that?" Chris looked at George knowing that they both knew the answer. "Perhaps someone she had an affair with," Chris remarked.

Bob stood up. "Well you can discuss between yourselves, I know you will close the case eventually, but I am busy thanks to you two, so I'll bid you both good day, hoping not to hear from you for a long time," Bob smiled as he made for the door.

"Have we been helped?" George asked as he watched Chris carefully take out the knife from the bag and lay it on the blotter in front of him.

"We can make plenty of assumptions, with these assumptions we can easily make a connection between the two killings," Chris replied studying the knife.

"The pocket she has inside of her bloomers could have contained the document, also if Mrs Wilson was the carrier of the document, then it was not found on her, or she could have sewed the pocket there to keep her paper money safe, when she went on holiday, however I will agree that very few people would know about the pocket, she might have told a female friend, but Bob ruled women out, the only other person that could be considered as knowing would be a lover," Chris continued.

"This is a nasty looking weapon, be careful dusting the handle for fingerprints," Chris said lifting it over to George on his blotter.

"Don't worry," George smiled taking the blotter, before getting his detective bag from under his desk.

Chris took out his pocket watch. "Mr Dowling will be here soon," he muttered. "I'll study the autopsy reports after we have been to the house, I don't like to rush things."

Chris lifted the telephone receiver. "Ah, Sergeant Bloom," Chris spoke into the receiver. "Have you had a missing person reported regarding a clerk at the hospital?"

"It came here on Friday, I believe," came the answer.

"Any result?" Chris asked.

"Usual routine still being carried out," sergeant Bloom replied. "Mr Charles Chalker, he is unmarried and lives on his own at 22, Andover Road, the hospital told us his next of kin was his sister, she do not have any idea where he might be, she said her brother visits her very rare. Neighbours have been spoken to, they say he keeps to himself, they consider him friendly enough."

"Has his flat been entered?" Chris asked.

"Not that I know of," sergeant Bloom answered.

"Who exactly reported him missing?" Chris asked.

"The hospital," sergeant Bloom replied. "The hospital is worried, he has not been to work since Thursday, and with all their trying they have been unable to contact him."

"Well keep me up to date please Sergeant?" Chris asked.

"Certainly Sir," came the polite reply.

"By the way I am expecting a Mr Dowling any time now," Chris said.

"He is already here, I was about to come in when the phone went," sergeant Bloom answered.

"Tell him we will be out in a moment please," Chris said putting the receiver down.

"Any luck George?" he asked.

George was dusting the handle of the knife for fingerprints, he shook his head as he blew away some powder.

"No not a sign of one," he replied. "Still I don't think we expected any did we?" he smiled. "Nasty weapon however, wouldn't like it in me, looks like it's been grinded," he added.

Plenty of street knife grinders about George," Chris remarked.

"Anyway George one step at a time, Mr Dowling is waiting, we will examine the knife later after we have been to Mrs Wilson's house."

Chapter Twelve

*H*aving shook hands with Mr Dowling, all three made towards the station door.

"I will be at Bar End for the next hour Sergeant," Chris said looking at sergeant Bloom.

"Very well Sir," replied sergeant Bloom. "May I have a quick word?" he asked.

Chris looked at George. "Carry on I'll catch you up," he said.

Once outside Mr Dowling took out his cigarettes, and stopped a step, while he struck a match to light it.

"Are you a heavy smoker?" George asked.

"Twenty-two, twenty-five a day," replied Mr Dowling as he blew out a cloud of deeply inhaled smoke. "Do you want one?" he offered the packet.

"I've never smoked," George replied.

"I wish I didn't, but there's not a lot in life for me, I'm a bit of a loner, take away my fag and pint, my life would be very dreary."

"What brand do you smoke?" George asked as they walked past the Abbey Grounds.

"Tenners," Mr Dowling replied. "I've always smoked them."

"Don't you have any hobbies?" George asked smiling.

"Not really, I do enjoy riding my motorbike," Mr Dowling smiled. "I can get at least twenty miles an hour out of her."

"That's pretty good," George remarked. "Where do you go, around the country lanes?"

"Anywhere, I point the machine in one direction and take off, but not very often, I suppose I see more of the countryside with the odd jobs I do, the machine comes in handy then."

"You are able to make a living doing odd jobs?" George asked.

"Yes, better than most in a regular jobs, but you have to be able to do most kinds of work."

"I expect it is," George replied looking behind him as they crossed the bridge, and seeing Chris catching them up. "But you don't work Sundays, I suppose that is when you go out for a drive?"

"No, never go out on Sundays, that's my house cleaning day, I don't touch it through the week, but Sundays I give it a good going over, I don't make it dirty really, but I have washing and dusting to do."

"How are you coping with the death of your sister?" George asked.

Puffing at his cigarette, Mr Dowling looked straight ahead, George thought he saw a bit of anger show on his face. "If I find the bastard that strangled my sister, I'll strangle him," he replied.

"The law will do that for you Mr Dowling, but how did you know she was strangled?" George asked.

"I don't know," replied Mr Dowling without hesitation. "Didn't you tell me last night?"

"We told you she had been murdered but not how, and you did not ask," George replied.

"Well I must have heard it somewhere?" Mr Dowling smiled looking at George. "If you are thinking I done it, you are barking up the wrong tree, we may not have been close, but there was a kind of bond between us, she only had to ask, and I would have done most things for her."

"I'm sure you would Mr Dowling," George replied as Chris caught up to them.

"I can't see why you need me?" Mr Dowling remarked. "After all I would suppose going to my sister's house is a part of your investigation?"

"It is," Chris replied. "But you are the next of kin, and unless she has made a Will to the contrary, you will inherit the house, so as it is our first visit if we need to take an item or two, you will be able to sign that we took them."

"I see," remarked Mr Dowling.

They stopped outside number 9, at Bar End Road, Chris took out the keys he had found in Mrs Wilson's handbag.

"Let's hope one of these fits," he said trying the first one that did fit.

"Mrs Wilson is not in," said a voice making them turn to the neighbouring cottage where a small woman stood looking angry. "If you enter I will call the police," she said.

Chris smiled to himself as he saw the determination on the woman's face. "It's commendable of you protecting your neighbour's home," he said politely. "I am the police, Detective Inspector Hardie of Winchester CID, my colleague Detective Sergeant House, and Mrs Wilson's brother Mr Dowling, may I ask you your name?"

Clearly taken back, the woman stuttered a little. "I am Mrs Hanks," she replied. "I have seen Mr Dowling before," she informed.

"Well then Mrs Hanks, you don't have to worry, but if you will talk to Sergeant House, he will have a couple of questions he would like to ask you, and perhaps explain what is happening?"

"Well he better come in then, I'm not standing out here in the cold," she answered regaining her composure.

Chris looked at George and smiled. Seeing George follow Mrs Hanks into her house with the door slamming behind them, Chris unlocked the front door of number nine and entered followed by Mr Dowling. The front door led straight into the front room, and Chris looked around the room shaking his head.

"It's not like my sister keeping a messy place like this," Mr Dowling commented.

"I'm afraid she didn't Mr Dowling," Chris answered. "This place has been searched," he said seeing that every cupboard and drawer was opened, the contents thrown out on the floor. "It's likely that upstairs will be the same," Chris muttered.

"Who would want to search my sister's house, I mean what were they after?" Mr Dowling said with anger. "She did not have anything worthwhile, this is to do with her murder I suppose?"

Chris looked in every room in the house, every room was in disarray. "Do you know if your sister had any secret hiding place?" Chris asked Mr Dowling who was following him around the house.

"No, I wouldn't," he replied. "I hardly ever came here."

"Pity," Chris muttered. "The question now is whoever searched the house did they get what they were after?"

The question was left unanswered as George entered the house. "God, someone been busy," he remarked looking around the room.

"I've had a look around, without knowing what I am looking for, more searching would be a waste of effort," Chris answered. "How was Mrs Hanks?"

"Sweet old lady really," George said with a smile. "As soon as I was in, she made me sit, and placed a cup of tea and biscuits in front of me."

"Can't do anything here," Chris said. "We might as well get back to the office."

Having thanked and said goodbye to Mr Dowling outside the police station, Chris and George sat at their desk. "How did you get on with Mr Dowling while you were walking alone?" Chris asked.

George smiled. "I did not ask any direct questions," he replied. "As you said keep him relaxed, however he is a heavy smoker of tenners, he has a motorbike, and likes going out for rides in the countryside. I brought the conversation about Sundays, and he said he never goes out on Sunday as this is the only day he cleans his house, however he did say that should he get hold of whoever strangled his sister, he would strangle him."

"Really," Chris said putting his pipe in his mouth, and leaning back in his chair thoughtfully.

"When I questioned him how he knew she was strangled, he said someone must have told him, adding that if we suspected him, we were barking up the wrong tree," George added.

"Well he do fit the bill," Chris replied. "We are looking for a person who smokes tenners, who also has a motorbike, if Mr Dowling drives around the countryside, it's quite possible that he knows the bridle path, we know he has worked on the farm."

Chris took the pipe from his mouth and leaned forward. "You know George, I am beginning to think you might be right, when we interviewed Mr Dowling, it was because of his sister's death, nothing to do with Mr Dummer's death, now he is more in the frame over Mr Dummer's death, than that of his sister's."

George shrugged. "Well he did know his sister's habits," he argued. "And we know he knew the field, anyway how was he with you?" he asked.

"Normal I think," Chris answered. "He seemed angry when we entered the house and saw the mess, but after he followed me from room to room like a puppy, he did nothing that I can put my finger on."

"Well the morning was not a complete waste," George smiled. "Mrs Hanks told me she saw Mrs Wilson leave for work Saturday morning, it seems that when about to cycle off Mrs Wilson always wave to Mrs Hanks, that was the last time she saw her. She told me no one enters the front garden without her knowing, but she said her water works have been playing her up in the last few days, she was running to the toilet more often than usual, so that why she did not see the man who entered about eleven on Sunday morning, she only saw him leave, thinking he had knocked the door, gone away because of no reply."

Chris looked up. "I hope she was able to describe him?" he almost pleaded.

George smiled. "Well Mrs Hanks described him with his cap pull over his ears, wearing glasses and wearing an over-coat with the collar pulled up," George added.

"It seems to be the same man Mr Roger Webber told us," Chris admitted. "I wonder who it can be, anything else?" he asked.

413

"He rode away on a motorbike," George smiled.

Chris looked at George. "We have to find this man, obviously he was the man who searched Mrs Wilson's house, let's assume for the moment, that he caught Mrs Wilson at the field, where he strangled her and searched her," Chris continued. "Another problem however, how did he get inside Mrs Wilson's house, he must have had a key, whoever this man is, I am sure of one thing, he had his own key to the house."

Sergeant Bloom knocked and entered. "Thought you might like to know, we have exhausted our missing person routine of the clerk from the hospital," he said.

"Do we know his name?" Chris asked.

"Yes, it's Charles Chalker, he is called Whitty by most people," sergeant Bloom replied.

"What's he look like?" George asked.

"About five foot, ten inches, slender, pleasant looking, has dark hair and is forty five years old, single living in a flat at Andover Road," sergeant Bloom said as though from memory.

"Has his flat been entered?" Chris asked.

"No Sir," Sergeant Bloom replied.

"Is it a block of flats?" George asked.

"No it's a flat within a house," sergeant Bloom replied.

"Do the owner live in the house?" George asked.

"I believe so, yes," came the reply.

"Very well Sergeant," Chris said. "We will look into it, perhaps the owner will let us in, not a good thing to break in, this Mr Chalker could have a very good reason for being out of town without realising the trouble he is causing, thank you sergeant," Chris said as sergeant Bloom left.

"George, this missing Mr Chalker links to the hospital with our Mrs Wilson the midwife, it's strange that this happened within a few days of each other, but I can't see any connection, still we must explore every avenue, so let's see," Chris said taking out his pocket watch. "It's now almost one, we will go to Andover Road, and try to get into the flat, when we get back, I want you to go back to Mrs Wilson's house, take a constable with you and bag all the letters, bank books, photos, that sort of stuff that you might find, I should have done it while we were there."

"Will we need permission?" George asked.

"From whom?" Chris queried.

"Her brother perhaps?" George argued.

"We don't know yet if the house is Willed to him," Chris replied. "We will play ignorant on this one."

"What are you going to do?" George changed the conversation.

"I'm going to take Mr Dummer's bike back to Mrs Dummer," Chris answered. "It's no value to us, and she may be able to sell it."

George smiled. "It has a wheel missing," he said.

"I've had a new one put on," Chris answered with a smile.

George smiled to himself as he got up to reach for his overcoat.

Chapter Thirteen

*C*hris and George looked up at number 22, Andover Road, then mounted the steps leading to the front door, and knocked. The door was opened by a woman, wearing an apron over her dress, she looked pleasant, looked on the tubby side with black hair.

"Yes?" she asked.

"I am Detective Inspector Hardie, and my colleague Detective Sergeant House, from Winchester CID," Chris said politely. "We are enquiring about Mr Charles Chalker who we are told lives here."

"He has the basement flat," replied the woman looking down at the steps that led from the pavement down to the basement. "Anyway I have already told the police that."

"You are?" George asked.

"Mrs Walker," came the reply. "Look I'm sorry I can't tell you any more than I have already told the police."

"So you have not seen Mr Chalker since the police were last here?" George questioned.

"I would have informed them had I," Mrs Walker replied.

"I'm sure you would have Mrs Walker," Chris assured her noticing that she was somewhat irritable. "Have we called at a bad time?"

"I am in the middle of my housework," Mrs walker responded.

"We would like to see his flat Mrs Walker, do you have a spare key?"

"Of course," she replied. "But I'm not sure that I can allow you to enter his flat."

"Mrs Walker," Chris replied politely but sternly. "Mr Chalker has now been missing for several days, not only from his home but from his work place, I need to know if he has gone away, checking his clothes will tell us, we would of course want your presence."

"Oh very well," Mrs Walker replied realising that she had no way out of the request. "I'll get the key."

Mrs Walker unlocked the front door of the flat that was situated under the steps of the house above, it was a one bedroom flat with a large front room and a kitchen and bathroom.

"This is ideal for a single man," Chris remarked opening the bedroom door.

He walked over to the heavy single wardrobe and opened it, suits, trousers, and even shirts were hanging there, he closed the wardrobe door satisfied in his mind, that Mr Chalker had not moved from the flat. He crossed to a chest of drawers and pulled open the drawers one by one, socks, underwear, woollen garments were all neatly packed. Chris closed the drawers, looked around the room, he saw a suitcase on the top of the wardrobe.

"Well," he said looking at George and Mrs Walker who had been watching him. "He certainly have not vacated the flat, all his clothes seem to be here, even his suitcase is here, he is a very tidy man, perhaps he's away for a few days." Chris remarked.

"That would be breaking the clause of his contract," Mrs Walker informed them. "He has to notify me whenever he is away even for one night, fire precaution you know, if a fire should break out."

"Very wise," Chris agreed.

"Could he be in hospital?" Mrs Walker asked.

"I am sure he is not," Chris replied. "Checking would be a part of our routine, also in Mr Chalker's case he works at the hospital and would have been known."

"How does he pay his rent?" George asked Mrs Walker as they made their way out of the flat.

"Fortnightly," Mrs Walker replied as she locked the door. "Due next Monday."

Chris tipped the rim of his trilby as he thanked Mrs Walker. "Please let us know if you are paid the rent on Monday, do you know if he had any family?" Chris added.

"Not that I'm aware of," Mrs Walker replied. "But then I'm not one to pry."

"Strange case," Chris remarked to George as they made their way pass the Eagle Hotel into City Road on their way back to the station. "He certainly have not vacated the flat leaving all his clothes behind, but wherever he is, let's hope he's there on his own accord, we don't want another body turning up do we?"

George shook his head, then smiled. "I pity him if he has gone off without telling Mrs Walker, she will certainly slap his wrist."

Chris was settled behind his desk before he spoke his thoughts.

"George, change of plans, I want you to go to the hospital, verify Mr Chalker's next of kin, as we know he has a sister who lives in Weston Road, also while you are there, find out the addresses of the other midwifes that work at the hospital, all midwifes must be on a register somewhere?"

"You want me to interview them?" George asked.

"We need to find out more about Mrs Wilson, you know what to ask, strange, both Mrs Wilson and Mr Chalker seem to be loners, very little is known about either, I will go to Mrs Dummer as planned, also I'm going to have Mrs Wilson's house searched again, no reflection on our search, but you never know," Chris smiled.

"Fair enough," George replied putting on his overcoat. "I'll see you tomorrow."

Chapter Fourteen

With the exit of Sergeant House, Chris picked up the phone. "Sergeant Bloom," he spoke into the receiver.

"The constable, he is here waiting," came the reply.

"You are sure he is capable?" Chris asked.

"Stake my life on it," came the reply.

"Good man, send him in," Chris put the phone down, and within seconds a knock came on his office door, and a constable entered. He was a slender man, with a pleasant face, he was not wearing his helmet, and Chris envied his thick light brown hair, unlike his own that way getting a little thin.

"You wanted to see me Sir, I'm Constable Cam Streeter," he introduced himself.

"Yes Constable, come in and take a seat, I have a little job for you, Sergeant Bloom recommended you," Chris said as he watched the constable take the interview chair. "I believe you are on the beat at Bar End?"

"That's right Sir," replied the constable politely. "I have the beat the hill side of Bar End Road, Chesil Street and St John Street."

"Quite a walk then Constable," Chris remarked. "You cover Alresford Road as well?"

"I do Sir, I complete my beat twice a day, people on my beat know me, I pass their houses twice a day."

"How long have you been on the beat in that area constable?" Chris asked.

"Four years now Sir," replied the constable.

"Do you know Mrs Wilson of number 9, Bar End Road?" Chris asked.

Constable Streeter shifted in his chair, and blushed a little. "I was in the field when Mrs Wilson's body was found Sir, I brought her bike to your office."

"Of course you were," Chris replied suddenly remembering. "Forgive me constable, at that time my mind was on other things, and you do look different without your helmet on."

Chris saw the Constable smiled. "Anyway Constable, I want you to go and search Mrs Wilson's house, take your time, and make a good job of it, search every nook and cranny, even the floor boards if you have to, but don't rush it even if it takes all tomorrow, Sergeant Bloom will have your beat covered."

"What will I be looking for?" the constable asked.

"I expected you to ask that," Chris smiled. "The truth is I don't know, just bring all you find, albums, bank books, letters that sort of things, Sergeant House and myself have had a quick look, we found nothing, the house is in a mess, we found the house had been searched before we got there, whether the intruder found what he was looking for, I don't know, but events have led me to believe he did not."

"I will do my best Sir," replied the constable.

"Good man," Chris replied handing him a key that was laying on his desk. "Don't let that out of your sight, the house is a part of a murder investigation you understand."

"Guard it with my life," replied the constable with a smile.

"Did you know Mrs Wilson before her death Constable?" Chris asked.

"I have spoken to her once or twice," replied the constable. "I found her pleasant, always cheerful, smart and very attractive."

"Yes I have heard the same, by the way you will meet her neighbour no doubt who is always on the lookout, a Mrs Hanks," Chris smiled.

A grin came to the Constable's face. "Mrs Hanks is a dear old soul, but I believe very lonely, she spends all her time at her window watching people as they pass, she waits at the gate sometimes when I'm due, she likes to talk, and tries very hard for me to have a cup of tea with her."

"And do you?" Chris asked.

"On occasions, but only if I am early," the constable replied.

"Does she ever say anything about Mrs Wilson?" Chris asked.

The Constable shifted in his chair. "She praises her highly," he said. "Nothing seems too much trouble to her, but Mrs Hanks did say that she had a number of gentlemen callers come during the dark hours, but she added that Mrs Wilson a hard working single woman she had the right to have a man friend."

"Really," Chris replied deep in thought. "Did you have any thoughts on that statement?"

"Well Sir," replied the constable feeling a little uneasy. "One could take it the wrong way, but having met Mrs Wilson, she don't strike me as a loose woman."

"Thank you Constable," Chris smiled. "Well you have a job to do, make a good job of it won't you?"

"I will," replied the constable getting up to leave. "I'll report to you tomorrow then."

"Good man," Chris smiled as the constable left the room.

It was late afternoon when Chris knocked on Mrs Dummer's door in Union Street.

"Oh Inspector," Mrs Dummer remarked as she opened the door. "Please come in."

"I have brought back your husband's bike Mrs Dummer, where would you like me to put it?" Chris asked.

Mrs Dummer opened the front door wide. "Thank you Inspector, at the moment please bring it into the hall."

"Would you like a cup of tea?" Mrs Dummer asked, as Chris rested the bike against the passage wall.

"Love one Mrs Dummer," Chris replied entering the kitchen.

"Make yourself at home," Mrs Dummer said from the scullery. "I was just making one for myself, so it's ready," she said bringing a tray.

"How are you Mrs Dummer?" Chris asked as she poured the tea, he could see there was sadness in her face, and her eyes told him she was not sleeping well.

Sitting at the table facing each other, Mrs Dummer passed a cup and saucer to Chris. "Please help yourself to milk and sugar," she offered. "I still expect Row to walk in," she said her eyes watery. "I laid his dinner plate out yesterday, I must be out of my mind," she spoke softly with a weak smile.

"It's natural Mrs Dummer," Chris consoled her. "Mrs Ewing, has she been helpful?"

"She has been a God send," Mrs Dummer sniffed.

"And Tom your son?" Chris asked.

"I have a best friend at Compton, we went to school together, she is married with two children, she insisted on taking Tom with her for a while, but he will come back for the funeral," Mrs Dummer brushed her eyes with her hand.

"I see," replied Chris.

"What a terrible world we live in Inspector, I will never get over the way my Row met his end, on top of that I'm told that Margery Wilson went the same way, what's the world coming to," Mrs Dummer took her hanky from her apron pocket and dabbed her eyes.

"Did you know Mrs Wilson?" Chris asked gently.

"We lived opposite each other in Hyde Abbey Road, she is about ten years older than me, but we knew each other, I went to her wedding, as my parents were invited."

"Really," Chris remarked. "I did not know that, did Mr Dummer know her?"

"When I was carrying Tom, I met Margery in town, she was a midwife, it was her that arrange for me to go into hospital, I was going to have Tom at home, but she insisted, she said should things go wrong I would be in the best place, as it turned out she was right, I had a difficult birth, that's why my Row would not let me have another child, I would have liked one for Tom's sake, anyway Row met her when she called, they seem to get on alright."

"Did you know Mr Dowling, Mrs Wilson's brother?"

"I knew him, but had very little to do with him, I was told he was a nice, good looking boy until he had his bike accident, but I remember him most after the accident, I didn't like him, perhaps because of his looks, which is really unfair on him, he could not help looking like he do, but people are people, perhaps if he had not been such a nasty person, I might have liked him."

Chris looked at his watch, and was surprised that it was almost six pm.

"Thank you Mrs Dummer for the tea, now is there anything I can do for you?"

"Thank you Inspector, and thank you for calling, at the moment I am well off, Row's work has sent me money, and Mr Shawcroft don't seem to be able to do enough for me. He is going to pay for the funeral, and tells me he will be sending some money each week, I don't know why, but it's very kind of him."

"Well he did allow your husband to catch rabbits on his land, and I hear that Mr Dummer's father worked for Mr Shawcroft's father and himself, perhaps he is that kind of man, after all he has had a lot of grief himself losing his wife and child in childbirth."

"I know," replied Mrs Dummer. "I was in hospital with his wife."

"Really," Chris remarked.

"Yes it was the first time I knew Mr Shawcroft, when he visited his wife."

"Still you were in good hands with Mrs Wilson taking care of you, I suppose she was there at the birth?" Chris asked.

Mrs Dummer thought for a while. "I'm not quite sure, I took it that she was, as when that nice man Mr Adams injected me, then I was asleep for a long time and when I awoke my husband and Mrs Wilson was at my bedside telling me I had a lovely baby boy."

"Is it usual for a mother to be given an injection?" Chris asked out of interest.

"I have no idea Inspector," Mrs Dummer replied. "But Mrs Wilson did get me into hospital thinking that I may have a difficult birth."

Chris stood up. "I must get going now Mrs Dummer, please call the station if you have any problems."

"I will inspector, and again, thank you for calling," Mrs Dummer replied as she followed Chris to the door letting him out.

Chris decided to call in the Rising Sun, he knew that his future father-in-law would be there, as he walked his thoughts pondered over what Mrs Dummer had told him, and was now sure that the two murders were connected, he was wondering how the constable was getting on searching Mrs Wilson's house as he entered the Rising Sun. The heat of the roaring log fire hit him, he regretted that he had not worn his overcoat when returning the bike to Mrs Dummer. Several men were sitting around the fire, who glanced for a second in his direction as he entered.

"Ron," he said, looking at his future father-in-law, who was already sitting there with a broad grin on his face. "I expected to see you."

"Hello Chris," Ron greeted. "Partly your fault, the girls have kicked me out, dress fitting."

"Yes I know," Chris replied standing in front of the small pub table. "Elizabeth told me, how is Olive?"

"She's fine, happy as a sand boy, you see them together like a couple of kids, I wonder sometimes who's wedding it is, they are more like sisters than mother and daughter," Ron replied.

"It's nice to be like that, Elizabeth worships both of you, anyway Ron, I get you one in," Chris said as he turned towards the bar.

"Not long to go now until your wedding Chris," Alfie smiled, taking payment for the drinks. "Everything is going to plan?"

"I believe so Alfie," Chris replied. "To be honest I have done very little."

"Women always take over," Alfie smiled. "After all it's a big day for the bride, so everything has got to be perfect."

"Tell me about it," Chris replied picking up the drinks and returning to Ron.

"I was telling Alfie that I have done very little towards to preparations of the wedding," Chris said as he sat down by Ron.

"Have you done everything that Elizabeth have asked you to do?" Ron asked.

Chris took a drink while he thought. "Well I have my suit ready, I have paid deposits here and there, but I have not yet got my best man," Chris replied.

Ron smiled. "That's all you are expected to do, the way I see it, let the women get on with it, just do what they want you to do without moaning, then you have a happy woman, we men get under their feet, that's why I am down here tonight. Elizabeth has a very long list of things to do, and every time she ticks one off that is done, others are added to the list," Ron laughed. "A lot of work goes into planning a wedding, but one chore that women do not moan about."

Chris smiled taking another drink. "You know Ron, I still can't get over your gift of the house, I can't find the words to really tell you how grateful I am, you see my work keeps me out very late some nights, and I would worry about Elizabeth being alone, and she's bound to carry fear when she is alone at night, however knowing she will only be a door away from you, allows me to relax a little."

"I completed the house yesterday Chris, when are you coming up again?" Ron asked.

"Tomorrow, I hope," Chris replied.

"Well when you do, we will enter the house, as I said no reason why you can't decorate before the wedding," Ron said.

Chris smiled. "Will I get any say in that?" he asked.

"Only if you agree with the women Chris," Ron smiled back

Chapter Fifteen

*C*hris arrived at his office late, he had missed Elizabeth, and felt annoyed. He had left Ron around eight last night, gone his lodgings, ate the meal that his landlady had left for him and gone to bed, only to toss and turn all night.

He had gone over the case all night long, and this morning he felt frustrated, knowing that he was getting nowhere.

He had thought about Mr Adams the hospital gynaecologist, could he be a suspect, his only involvement so far was that he had an affair with Mrs Wilson five years ago, and he was her boss, his affair could have allowed him to know about Mrs Wilson's secret pocket, but then did this pocket have any meaning as far as the case is concerned, Mr Adams had anything to do with Mr Dummer's murder, did he know Mr Dummer would be at the woods that Sunday morning, and did he know the area well enough to know of the bridle path, Mr Adams was a man who had spent his working life bring new life into the world, it was hard for him to believe, he also took life.

He thought of Mr Dowling, Mrs Wilson's adopted brother, who knew Mr Dummer through drinking, he was a quick tempered man, who could have murdered anyone on the spur of the moment with his temper, Mr Dummer however was not murdered on the spur of the moment, his murder was premeditated, Mrs Wilson's death could have been on the spur of the moment. Mr Dowling also knew the Manor Farm, having worked there, he could have known the bridle path, and he did have a motorbike. But what could Mr Dummer have that could possibly have made him pay out blackmail money, even if Mr Dowling had the money to pay.

His mind turned over the missing clerk at the hospital, did he for some reason murder them both, and whoever murdered Mrs Wilson he was sure searched her house the Sunday Morning, meaning that he either had a key or knew where it was kept, however Chris argued in his mind, did Mr Chalker know Mr Dummer, did he know him well enough to know his movements on that Sunday morning.

Chris knew he must be dealing with a man with a nerve of iron, if the same person killed Mrs Wilson then the following morning killed Mr Dummer.

Chris looked up as George entered, and hung his overcoat.

"Still brisk out there Chris," he said making for his desk. "Well I have done all that was required of me," he smiled. "You look as if you need sleep, did you have a pint last night?"

"I had a couple drinks in the Rising Sun with Ron, the girls getting the dresses ready for the wedding, kicked him out, however I was home around eight, but I couldn't sleep."

"It shows," George smiled. "Anyway I went to the hospital, Mr Adams was just leaving on his motorbike when I arrived, but I managed to speak to him. "His motorbike is far better than my old clanger, he has a 1915, 550cc, considered by many to be the first modern motorcycle."

"Really," Chris said with a smile, not being very mechanical himself.

"I thought you might be interested," George continued. "The army has thousands of these machines, because they are capable of driving over soft muddy ground, I was just wondering if Mr Adams is the person we are looking for, why he did not drive his motorbike up the bridle path, the machine is capable of doing it."

"My old Inspector Noal would have given you full marks for that George," Chris said with a smile. "Solving a murder one needs to know every single detail, regardless of its value, constable Elkins told me that at the corner of the bridle path, there is a access where walkers can get over the wire fence to go right around that particular field, although it seems that Mr Shawcroft uses the path riding his horses, it is actually a right of way, you could lift a cycle over but I doubt if you could lift a motorcycle over."

"It was just a thought," George replied.

"A right thought," Chris replied. "Anyway George did you see any midwifes?"

"The hospitals have four midwifes, three at the moment without Mrs Wilson, I saw two of them, both said the same about Mrs Wilson, competent at her job, a generous friendly person. They did tell me that Mrs Wilson was promoted over them, Mrs Wilson I understand was the newcomer, they thought it was her relationship with Mr Adams at the time that got her the promotion, however the relationship ended five years ago, and as far as they knew, Mrs Wilson was seeing Mr Chalker of the record office, who has disappeared. I did ask them to let the other midwife know that I would like to see her," George said after an afterthought.

Chris then related his call on Mrs Dummer. "At least we know that both victims knew each other, which helps us a little in trying to find a connection."

"If they are connected," George voiced his thoughts." Mr Dummer seems to be the odd man out."

"Meaning?" Chris asked.

"Well so far everything seem to revolve around the hospital in some way, Mr Adams, Mrs Wilson, the missing Mr Chalker, only Mr Dummer has no connection with the hospital," George said. "Apart from them who else do we have in the frame?"

"It has not escaped my notice George," Chris replied taking out his pipe and sucking on it. "Mr Adams, his affair with Mrs Wilson was over about five years ago, since then he has only been her boss."

"Have you any thoughts yet?" George asked.

"I do," Chris replied leaning back in his chair. "I believe the motive is simple, I believe that Mrs Wilson had some sort of document that she was going to give to Mr Dummer, I also believe that someone found out and was desperate to stop it, I believe that Mrs Wilson was strangled on the spur of the moment, but Mr Dummer was deliberately knifed. I also believe that whoever the murderer is, he did not get what he was after, because after stabbing Mr Dummer he came back and searched Mrs Wilson's house," Chris paused for a seconds. "I know it is only an assumption on our part, but these assumptions represent the raw material, the opinions, beliefs and although these assumptions seem unrealistic, but they give us a starting point."

"But had she been carrying the document, surely her murderer would have found it, you believe yourself that he did not," George remarked.

"She wasn't carrying it," Chris replied. "Don't forget she went to her horse after leaving work early evening, Mr Dummer was at work that time, my guess is that she had it at home, and perhaps she was going to call on the Dummers later that evening, where she would give it to him, she was not a stranger to the Dummers."

"What would your Inspector Noal do in this case?" George asked.

Chris smiled. "Inspector Noal had his own way of investigation, he would sometimes go over the work I had done, and get more results, it was all in his questioning, many a time I have been with him while he questioned and I thought many of his questions were irrelevant to the case, but many seem to pay dividends. He used to say, keep asking questions, sooner or later if they are hiding anything a small flaw will turn up in their answers that will enable you to move on."

"I have heard he was good," George remarked.

"I learnt all I know from him," Chris replied. "That's what we are going to do, start again from the beginning." Chris spoke. "The beginning of this case was Manor Farm. Get everything you can on Mr Shawcroft, I expect the maid Molly Atkins to come in and make her statement soon, it's getting on for a week now, we will question her again before she makes her statement, it might be worth talking to her away from the farm. Anyway, phone up your friend in the MET, ask him if he can get Mr Shawcroft's dead wife's Will, she was rich she must have left one."

"I can do that," George said finishing writing down the instructions. "How much it will help us?" George shrugged his shoulders.

"It don't matter George," Chris replied. "Mr Shawcroft is not really a suspect, based on the words of his staff, also he had no obvious reason."

A knock on the office door made them both look towards it as Sergeant Bloom entered.

"Constable Streeter is here Sir," he spoke looking at Chris.

"Good," replied Chris. "Let's have him in."

"Constable Streeter," Chris smiled as he entered. "You know Sergeant House?"

Constable Streeter nodded his head.

"Take the chair Constable," Chris indicated the interview chair.

"Well how did you get on?" Chris asked as the constable seated himself.

"Well I spent a couple hours there last night, and I was there early this morning, as you said the place had been gone over, drawers had been emptied, clothes, board games and books were all over the place, but I checked every inch, walls, floor boards, inside and out of the cupboards, everywhere possible I'm afraid without luck. However before getting ready to come here, I went outside the call of nature," the constable smiled blushing a shade.

Chris looked at George who was taking an interest.

The constable smiled. "Anyway, the wooden seat of the toilet stretched the width of the toilet, and a wooden ceiling had been put up, perhaps to hide the toilet flashing system, a hole was drilled which allowed the chain to drop. I was sitting there looking absently at the ceiling, I saw one plank that was not fitting right, when I had finished, the plank not fitting properly still annoyed me, I don't know why," the constable smiled again.

"So I just pushed it up to allow it to drop in place, all it was that one edge was overlapping another, but then I felt that something was above it, so I pushed the plank up, felt with my hands and came away with this package, which I have not open," the constable bashfully gave the package to Chris. "I hope it will be what you are after."

"Good man," Chris really meant it as he handled the package.

"Did you spend your own time on it constable?" Chris asked.

The constable shrugged. "I had nothing else to do, anyway I was interested, it was good to do something constructive, walking on a beat really becomes boring at times."

"Put yourself in for four hours overtime, I'll endorse the overtime," Chris smiled.

"Thank you Sir," replied the constable getting up to leave. "I must get on my beat now," he smiled.

"Did you have a chance of talking to Mrs Hanks?" George asked as the constable who was walking towards the office door to leave.

"This morning I did, I was about to enter Mrs Wilson's house when she opened her front door, she offered me a cuppa, which I accepted, however, I got no more out of her than what I have already told you."

"Thank you constable," George replied. "She probably done you a good turn, that cup of tea she gave you might have been the reason for you wanting to use the toilet?"

"Possible," the constable replied leaving the office.

Chris untied the string, and opened the wrapping paper, a small pile of small books and papers appeared, Chris took the top book up, it was a post office saving book.

"She seems to make plenty of deposits," Chris said looking at each page. "Look at this George," Chris said holding the book to one side enabling George to see. "She has been depositing a weeks wages two or three times every week, she has quite a bit of money."

"It's not her first book," George said fingering the pages to bring them back to the first page. "There is an amount of three thousand, one hundred and fifty."

"Right George, with several thousand, one must wonder how she came by it, she could never have saved it from her salary?" Chris asked.

"Perhaps there is some truth in what Mrs Hanks was saying to the constable," George replied.

"I know what you mean George, but it would certainly go against what we know about Mrs Wilson," Chris murmured.

Chris put the post office book to one side, and picked up the next. "Names and addresses with several telephone numbers," Chris said looking through the notebook.

"Friends and relatives?" George replied.

"Could be George, apart from names and addresses outside of Winchester, which one would not call local, look here," Chris offered the book to George. "Andover, Alton Southampton."

"As far as relatives go, we believe she has none but her adopted brother," Chris answered, still turning the pages. "However should be easy for us to verify."

Chris scanned through the rest of the packages, which was mainly paper, birth certificate, copy of her Will, a few personal letters and such like. "Not much here after all George," Chris remarked disappointed. "I was hoping for more, however according to the copy of her Will, Mr Dowling gets everything."

"Do you think that the house was searched after Mr Dummer was killed?"

"I'm sure of it George," Chris replied with confidence. "I'm sure that the house was searched after Mr Dummer was killed, Mrs Hanks has told us that, she saw a man Sunday morning leaving the house."

"So you think the man in the overcoat and pulled down cap, and wearing glasses is our man?" George asked.

"I'm sure of it George," Chris replied again with confidence. "We know he was speaking to Mr Dummer in the Three Tuns pub, he perhaps in small talk learnt all about Mr Dummer's activities, and knew where he would be on the Sunday morning," Chris looked at George who was taking an interest.

"This man, knew whatever he was after, he first had to see if Mrs Wilson had it, on Saturday evening he went to the field where he knew that Mrs Wilson went every night to see her horse, not finding what he wanted, he concentrated on Mr Dummer, he knew his whereabouts on the Sunday morning, he got there earlier than Mr Dummer and waited, after murdering Mr Dummer he then came back and searched Mrs Wilson's house."

"Are you convinced that's what happened?" George asked.

Chris leaned back in his chair, and smile played on his face. "I believe that's the way it happened," Chris remarked. "But there is a flaw, Mr Dummer was stabbed from behind, and managed to keep walking or stumbling for several yards out of the wood onto the field in sight of the farm house, where he was seen by the maid."

"So," George remarked.

"Well don't you see George, if Mr Dummer kept on stumbling forward until he was out of the woods, whoever it was could not have searched him, and could not have been sure that Mr Dummer did not have the document what he wanted so badly," Chris continued. "He took a awful chance of going to Mrs Wilson's house, he could have been seen, and would have been if Mrs Hanks had not gone to the toilet, but it perhaps the only option he had left of getting what he was after."

"Any idea who it could be Chris?" George asked.

Chris shook his head. "None as yet George, I do believe that overcoat, pulled down cap and glasses are a disguise, I also believe he is not a well known man around the centre of Winchester."

"What about this clerk that is missing from the hospital?" George asked.

"Mr Chalker you mean," Chris replied leaning forward. "I have no idea, I am waiting for Monday, to see if his rent is paid, we have to remember he disappeared before Mrs Wilson was murdered, but I am not saying he could not have been responsible, he would have known Mrs Wilson's movement, but the question on my mind is did he know of Mr Dummer's movement, or did he even know him, the only thing we know for sure, is that whoever we are after, knew Mrs Wilson intimately, also had a key to her house, or knew where she kept it."

"If as you say, this chap with the overcoat and cap, he was wearing a disguise, and not known a lot, it could have been Mr Chalker, he fits the bill, and he would have got his information about Mr Dummer's movements in the Three Tuns Pub, also we are told he was seeing Mrs Wilson, well he could have been intimate with her?" George argued.

"While I agree with you George," Chris said as he leaned back in his chair. "Why did he disappear three days before Mrs Wilson was murdered, and why before Mrs Wilson was murdered he had to disguise himself to go into a pub?"

George shrugged. "Well let's see if her address book tells us anything, she knew a lot of men, but then we have a problem taking that line," George replied.

Chris shrugged. "Well we will have to wait, until we get some sort of break, anyway George, you have quite a bit to do."

George smiled going back to his desk. "Unless someone opens up, this is a case we may never solve, I get straight on with my chores," he smiled making for the hat rack and taking his overcoat. "You know I may not get results until Monday at the earliest, with the weekend coming up."

Chris grinned at him as he left the office. "If I don't see you before I'll see you on Monday."

Chris looked at his pocket watch, it told him it was almost midday. He got up and went to the hat stand, where he stood with his mind concentrated of the small address book of Mrs Wilson's as he put on his overcoat. "I'll have a bite to eat, and spend the afternoon on it," he thought to himself as he left the office.

Chris was away from his office barely a half hour, and spent the rest of the day examining the address book. He made several phone calls on the numbers entered, most of which was outside of Winchester, and as each call ended, he had a satisfactory look on his face, so engrossed in what he was doing, he completely forget the time.

A knock came on the office door, Chris looked up as Sergeant Dawkins entered.

"Hello Sergeant," Chris smiled. "Where is Sergeant Bloom?"

"He went off duty a couple hours ago, I just wondered if you wanted a cup of tea?"

"Damn," Chris remarked snatching his pocket watch out. "It's five to six, I'm late," he said putting the address book into the desk drawer.

"Thank you for the offer sergeant, but I am really late," Chris remarked putting on his overcoat as he hurried out.

Sergeant Dawkins smiled as he closed the office door. "The joy of young love," he sighed as Chris hurried out of the police station.

Dodging a couple horse and carts, Chris crossed the Broadway, and walked quickly towards the bank, a barrel organ was blasting out. *It's a Long Way to Tipperary.* Chris crossed the entrance of London Bazaar, he saw Elizabeth coming towards him, and he slackened his speed, he felt breathless.

"You look out of breath," Elizabeth said as she stood in front of him, planting a kiss on his cheek, and fumbling with his overcoat collar. "Have you been running?" she asked her eyes smiling.

"I forgot the time," Chris murmured.

Elizabeth leaned on Chris's arm as they walked towards Alresford Road.

"I have missed you these last couple of nights," Elizabeth giggled looking up at Chris.

"I thought you were busy with the dresses," Chris replied.

"I mean at nights silly," Elizabeth replied. "I can hardly wait until our wedding."

Chris shook his head disapprovingly, knowing full well he had felt the same many times. He was almost proud of himself however that he had been able to keep the trust that Ron and Olive had in their daughter, he knew if he had insisted, Elizabeth would have given away to his wishes, but he knew she would have regretted it.

"Whatever am I going to do with you," Chris said with a smile. "After we are married, you will start suffering from headaches I suppose?" Chris teased.

Elizabeth squeezed his arms and giggled. "We will have to wait and see darling, I know you are a kind and generous man, but during the night when we are holding each other close, sharing the warmth of each other, you must be dominant, after all I do have to say I obey you when we get married."

Chris looked at her as they passed the Rising Sun. "What am I going to do with you," he remarked with a smile shaking his head. "I would hate for your parents to hear you."

Elizabeth giggled again as they made their way homeward.

"Dad wanted us to see the house tonight," Elizabeth said as they reached the Alresford Road, I hope you don't mind darling but I told him Sunday in full daylight would be best, you are on your day off. If we go tonight after our meal, it will be dark, on Sunday we can take our time, and after dad has shown it to us, we can be alone there, perhaps discussing what decorations we will have," Elizabeth giggled again.

"What do you mean perhaps?" Chris asked knowing full well what she meant, he playfully slapped her bottom, as he allowed her to go first up the path to her front door.

Olive was at the door to greet them, who received a kiss on the cheek from both Elizabeth and Chris. "Dinner is almost ready," she remarked watching her daughter and Chris discard their top clothing on the pegs just inside the front door. "You can have a glass of beer with Ron before dinner Chris," she said with a smile. "I have already put it out."

Chris smiled and thanked her as he made his way into the front room, where he saw Ron sitting in his chair reading the paper.

"Hello Chris," he said looking over the top of his paper with his glasses on. "I heard what the boss said," he smiled. "Pour me one out as well," he said folding the paper and taking off his glasses. "It seems that trouble is brewing in Ireland, we could do without that with this war carrying on."

"I agree with you, we have trouble enough in France," Chris replied pouring out two glasses of bottle beer, and handing one to Ron.

"Elizabeth wants me to show you the house on Sunday," Ron said with a smile. "Perhaps she is right, it's almost dark now."

"Perhaps this putting the clocks back in May will give us lighter evening," Chris replied.

"I did hear something about it, but did not grasp the full meaning," Ron smiled. "Yes I've read about it, it seems that we will put the clocks back in the spring, and forward again in the fall, we'll just wait and see how it works," Ron said as Elizabeth and his wife entered with the food.

The evening went well for Chris, his work was not mentioned, because Olive was becoming upset when the talk was about murder. Olive's meal was a rabbit stew thickly integrated with vegetables and potatoes, it was very moorish, but Chris forced himself against having a second helping, because he knew his favourite of spotted dick and custard was to follow. With the radio on with bands playing music, the four of them passed the evening playing snakes and ladders, and Elizabeth giggled with happiness as she won game after game.

"Do you think Ron," Chris remarked with a smile. "Is your daughter cheating?"

"Perhaps we are cheating Chris, letting her win," Ron replied.

When Ron and Olive retired, Chris and Elizabeth indulged in snuggling, it was what both were waiting for, a time alone together.

"Can I ask you a question, a serious one to do with the case I'm investigating," Chris said as Elizabeth cuddled up to him. "It's a bit personal, I'm asking you because I don't know who else I can ask without causing offence?"

"Don't be silly darling," Elizabeth replied. "Ask me anything you want."

"Do you have a pocket sewed to inside the leg of your bloomers?" Chris asked blushing a shade. "Or is it normal for a woman to have such a pocket?"

Elizabeth smiled to herself as she cuddled down in Chris's arms, she knew he was shy in this department. "You can buy them with little pockets in them darling," she replied with a smile on her face.

"What would a woman keep in the pocket, as a rule I mean?"

"It would depend on where she is going," Elizabeth replied. "All women carry a handbags which they carry their bits and pieces, however should an occasion arise where a handbag is a problem, in her bloomers small inside leg pocket might be used for a small hanky or a powder puff," Elizabeth explained.

"What about having a large pocket inside the bloomers?"

"It seems a strange place to have a pocket, how big is this pocket we are talking about?" Elizabeth asked her mind now serious.

"You could put an envelope in it," Chris replied.

"You can't put much in the small pockets inside the leg," Elizabeth said. "As I said a small scented hanky or a powder puff, both these items are made of material and would only have a slight chance of falling out of the pocket, paper or coins etc could easily fall out, especially if you are cycling, I take it we are talking about this midwife was found dead?"

Chris nodded his head.

"Wouldn't these articles fall out of the pocket?" he asked.

"Could do, but not to the ground, you see the elastic leg of knickers are very tight, stop anything falling to the ground," Elizabeth replied thinking hard.

"What we are saying then," Chris said. "Whatever she was carrying in her pocket, was very important, so important that she would not trust it in her handbag."

"It looks that way," Elizabeth commented. "It would be as a safe, or should be.

"Well it's an explanation," Chris admitted. "Our thoughts are that she was carrying important papers in it."

"Of course she could have darling," Elizabeth agreed once again cuddling in his arms.

"Thank you darling," Chris said leaning down and kissing her forehead, you might have given me a part of the jigsaw puzzle."

Chapter Sixteen

Knowing that George would be off, Chris was early at his desk, he had been relaxed during last night, and the case had been out of his mind, he had slept well, and he felt as fresh as a daisy.

Sergeant Bloom entered with a cup of tea and a couple biscuits.

"Thanks Sergeant," Chris smiled. "By the way this Constable Cam Streeter, how long has he been in the force?"

"About ten years," sergeant Bloom replied. "Was he useful to you?"

"He certainly was," Chris replied. "Sit a while," he offered.

Chris watched as Sergeant Bloom sat. "I want an extra man in here, my cases are getting more difficult, and more work is piled upon just Sergeant House and myself, perhaps the crooks are getting more intelligent, I don't know, but I do need extra help."

"I'm always ready," sergeant Bloom replied with a smile.

"I have already voiced my desire to have you sergeant, but I was told that you only have three or four years before your retirement on a sergeants pay, if you are transferred to CID, you would lose them stripes and start as a constable, it would not be right or fair on you, your pension would be much lower."

"I see what you mean," sergeant Bloom replied, looking at his lap. "But if I can help in anyway, just ask."

"You can be sure that I will Sergeant even if I get an extra man, that is why I'm asking about Constable Streeter, he has let's say, twenty more years to serve, pleasant to speak to, and alert, he might make a good CID officer."

"I'm sure he will," sergeant Bloom replied. "I can make some discrete enquiries if it might help?"

"Good man Sergeant," Chris answered. "You know exactly what I want, let me know what you find out, but remember, I haven't the OK yet."

"Don't worry Sir," sergeant Bloom replied as he got up to leave. "I know what to do."

Sergeant Bloom left the office, and within a few moment entered again.

"I have a Mr Atkins and his daughter here," he said. "The daughter is here to make a statement, there is also a Mrs Steward waiting, she is a nurse, Sergeant House left word that he wanted to see her."

"Seems like a busy morning," Chris replied. "You will have to help me here if you can, take the statement from Miss Atkins, while I see Mrs Steward, then later I see the Atkins and go through the statement."

Sergeant Bloom nodded, and moments later ushered Mrs Steward into the office. She was a handsome woman, tall and slim, perhaps in her late forties, wearing a sister's uniform, and a large felt hat.

Chris stood and offered his hand. "I am Detective Inspector Hardie," he introduced himself. "Sergeant House is out at the moment, but I am well aware of him asking you to call, please take a seat," he offered indicating the interview chair.

"I have no idea what your Sergeant wanted," Mrs Steward said as she took the seat. "What I hear however it's about Mrs Wilson, I will help on anyway I can, it is a dreadful way for anyone to lose their life."

"I agree with you there Mrs Steward, and thank you for calling in," Chris replied with a slight smile on his face.

"I am off this morning," Mrs Steward replied.

"What Sergeant House wanted was, what you can tell him about Mrs Wilson, she seems to have been a loner, her only relative as far as we know being her step brother, and he did not know much about her, perhaps as they have lived apart for many years."

"So would have I," Mrs Steward replied. "I could not have lived in the same house as that man, he makes me shiver."

"You knew him then?" Chris asked.

"When Mrs Wilson first came over to our department we were all very friendly, we used to meet up for a cup of tea every now and then, even help each other out in a difficult home birth, she introduced her brother once, and I have seen him several times during the years, he do have a bad reputation you know, anyway that all stopped once she was made senior."

"Did you object to her promotion?" Chris asked.

"Well, yes I have to admit, I always thought seniority counted," Mrs Steward replied.

"Ability also," Chris added.

"Of course it do," Mrs Steward replied. "Mrs Wilson was a very capable midwife, when she first came, the other two and myself took her under our wings so to speak, and taught her the practical side, much of which you can only learn through experience, however, Mrs Wilson became a very capable and competent midwife, but I can say the same for all of us."

"I see," Chris replied slowly. "Then what is your opinion, she was made the senior above the rest of you who had served longer?"

"I have my opinion Inspector" Mrs Steward replied. "But the poor woman is now dead, I will not speak ill of the dead."

"Mrs Steward," Chris said after a few moment silence. "You can only speak ill of the dead should you lie, that is also true about the living, lies lead to other lies to cover the first lie, in this case however we are talking about a person is unlawfully killed, and if you don't tell us what you know, could allow the person responsible walking away without being punished, now you don't really want that do you Mrs Steward?"

"Of course not," Mrs Steward replied clasping her hands on her lap. "I'm here to help if I can."

"How long have you been a midwife Mrs Steward?" Chris asked.

"I became a midwife after the 1902 midwife act came into force, getting on for fifteen years now," Mrs Steward replied.

"Really," Chris replied. "Did we not have midwifes before then, I am an orphan, I know nothing of my birth."

Mrs Steward smiled. "Your mother either had a doctor, or a woman known to do that sort of work, there were no professionals, most towns and villages had one or two of these handy women, even after the act, many were still carrying on doing it, but now all midwifes are trained."

"Well we live and learn," Chris smiled. "So Mrs Steward, Mrs Wilson's promotion over yourself was a bit of a slight on your pride?"

"It hurt naturally, after all apart from her midwife train-ing, it was me who taught her the practical side, yes I resented it."

"Do you think her promotion had anything to do with her courtship with Mr Adams?" Chris asked.

Mr Steward smiled. "No not really, her affair with Mr Adams was over before Mr Adams got promotion himself, but it seems that there was a mix up in two babies, and one blamed the other for it, however secrecy prevailed about it while they worked together, their relationship was over, months later Mr Adams was promoted, soon after he promoted Mrs Wilson to senior midwife."

"About the mix up with the babies, you don't have a more fuller picture?" Chris asked."

"I'm afraid not Inspector," Mrs Steward replied.

"So as I understand it," Chris continued a little disap-pointed. "Although the relationship was over, they contin-ued to work together, as you said he appointed Mrs Wilson senior over your good self."

"It seemed that way," Mrs Steward volunteered. "I have very little to do with Mr Adams, but about a fortnight ago I did pass his office door which was slightly ajar, he was talking to Mrs Wilson, there seemed anger in his voice."

"Really," Chris remarked.

"I have no idea what it was about, but I did hear Mr Adams say, that it would upset a lot of people, and I caught Mrs Wilson's reply, which was, I know, I have a friend that will be heart broken, that's all I heard, I did not want to stop outside the door," Mrs Steward paused for a moment before continued.

"One of the nurses told me that had seen Mrs Wilson and Mr Chalker from the record office having what seemed to be an argument in the hospital grounds, just two days before he disappeared."

"Really" Chris replied interested. "She did not hear what was said?"

"She said she was too far away, but saw they were both angry."

"Well thank you Mrs Steward, you have been very helpful, and thank you again for calling in," Chris rose and walked to his office door.

"No problem," Mrs Steward smiled as Chris opened the door for her. "You know where I am should I be wanted again."

Chris closed the door behind her and wondered just how the interview had helped him. He sat down and quickly scribbled the main points of their conversation, the phone rang, it was Sergeant Bloom telling him that the statement given by Miss Atkins was finished.

"Good man," Chris replied. "Bring them in with the statement if you will," Chris replaced the receiver.

Few minutes later Sergeant Bloom entered followed by Mr Atkins and his daughter.

"Thank you Sergeant," Chris said as the sergeant retreated.

He looked at Mr Atkins, he was a youngish man, clean shaven, standing about five foot, ten inches, Chris offered his hand.

"I am Detective Inspector Hardie, I have already met your daughter," he said smiling at her. "Please," he said indicating the chairs as he went to his own chair. "Take a seat, I won't be keeping you long, just give me a few moments to read this statement."

Chris read the statement slowly, eventually put it down. "How are you Mrs Atkins?" he asked to Molly with a smile. "Thank you for coming in and making this statement, it seems OK."

"I am well," Molly replied looking at her dad, there was nervousness in her voice.

"My daughter just like her mother has a very nervous nature," Mr Atkins responded. "But I can assure you she is completely honest."

"I'm sure she is," Chris replied. "And you are a very protective father."

"One needs to be these days," Mr Atkins replied.

Chris smiled at him, then looked at Molly. "Just a few points to clear up Molly, you said you cleaned the windows starting at seven am, how did you know the time, I see you don't wear a watch."

"I saw the time by the grandfather clock in the hall as I crossed to reach the stairs, I saw it was almost seven, as I was climbing the stairs the clock chimed the hour."

"Thank you Molly, it's a question I should have asked when we last spoke, then you went and got Mr Shawcroft?" Chris questioned.

Molly nodded her head.

"Where was Mr Shawcroft when you found him?" Chris asked.

"He was outside the kitchen door," Molly replied.

"Really," Chris replied. "Was he doing anything in particular?"

"Just cleaning his shoes Sir," Molly replied.

"Really, is that usual for him to be doing?" Chris asked. "After all, I would have thought a man in his position would have his shoes polished for him."

"It's cook's rule," Molly replied nervously clasping her hands together in her lap. "No one is allowed to walk through her kitchen without first cleaning their shoes outside, there is a H scraper outside so that any mud can easily be scrapped off."

"It's all very muddy around the farm house," Mr Atkins interrupted.

"I'm sure it is Sir," Chris replied then again looking at Molly. "When you went looking for Mr Shawcroft you found him outside the kitchen door, if he was cleaning his shoes, he must have been out for a stroll?"

"He could have gone to the loo," Molly said quickly wondering if she had said too much. "And he do collect the eggs from the chickens," she added.

Chris noticed that Molly was becoming upset. "I'm sure you are right Molly," Chris said gently.

"Will her statement have to be altered and re written?" Mr Atkins asked.

"No, but I will add a note regarding Mr Shawcroft being outside the kitchen door," Chris smiled. "You see Mr Atkins in a murder investigation we need to know all facts, being inside or outside the house, may seem unimportant, but we have to know them so that we have every possible fact."

"I can understand that," Mr Atkins replied.

Chris turned to Molly with a smile, intending to ease her nervousness. "What do you do with yourselves during the evenings?" Chris asked in an interesting manor. "I mean you are a long way from anywhere, the house I saw was lit by lamps and gas, don't you get bored?"

Molly smiled for the first time. "Not really, sometimes I lay on my bed reading a book, I do go to the kitchen a lot, the cook teaches me how to cook, but we do work long hours, and we are normally very tired and fall fast asleep, we have to be up by six the next morning."

"Really," Chris replied trying to imagine the life. "But at least you will be a good cook, and some man will be lucky because of that."

"Oh I don't know," Molly replied a slight colouring appearing on her cheeks. "I can make butter and bake bread, and know how to cook all kinds of meat, I know how to serve at a table to the posh people, and I certainly know how to clean a house."

"Service is good training for any girl," Mr Atkins interrupted.

"So it seems," Chris agreed. "Do Mr Shawcroft entertain much?"

"Now and again," Molly replied smiling. "I like it when he entertains, if all go well, Mr Shawcroft will always give us an extra shilling at the end of the week."

"Yes he is a generous man I believe," Chris remarked. "I suppose his guests are nearby farmers etc, you are a long way off the main road for people to walk."

"Most come by horse and buggy," Molly replied completely relaxed. "But we do have a gentleman who comes by motorbike from Winchester."

"Really," Chris said, almost unable to conceal his excitement. "Would you know who that would be?"

"Of course I do," Molly replied with a smile. "I place their name cards where they should sit, you know lady next to a gentleman all around the table, if a odd gentleman is invited, then a lady would be invited to make the equal number, we have to do this when the gentleman from Winchester is invited."

"And who would be?" Chris asked.

"A Mr Adams," Molly replied.

Chapter Seventeen

lizabeth was at the door to greet him, she grabbed him and offered her lips, which Chris took willingly.

"I've been waiting for that," Elizabeth said a bit breathless but with a broad smile on her face. "I missed you last night darling," Elizabeth said. "It was cold in bed last night, and I was wishing that we were already married."

"I missed you as well, I have that same wish every night, cold or hot," Chris smiled as he patted Elizabeth's hand.

Elizabeth offered her lips again, which Chris took eagerly. "What was that for?" Chris asked as they pulled away from each other.

"A quick one," Elizabeth giggled.

The voice of Olive from the front room asking where they were, made them steady themselves.

"Are you alright darling?" Elizabeth asked.

"I think so," Chris replied taking a deep breath.

"I hope your passion will last longer than that when we are married," Elizabeth giggled grabbing Chris's arm.

"Please no teasing," Chris whispered as they took the few steps to enter the front room, where Olive was pouring out tea, and Ron was sitting in his usual chair with a newspaper resting on his lap.

"Chris kissed Olive on the cheek then looking at Ron who was smiling, alright Ron," he asked.

"Can't be better Chris, cold outside?" Ron asked.

"Brisk," Chris replied.

"Well drink this tea while it's hot," Olive said handing him a cup and saucer across the table where he had seated himself.

"Thank you Olive," Chris said with a smile.

Elizabeth who had seated herself at the table next to Chris, refused her mother's offer of tea. "I'm too excited to drink tea," she replied. "I want to see that house."

"Have a whisky then," Ron joked.

"That's enough of that Ron," Olive scolded. "I don't want my daughter encouraged to drink spirits."

"I was joking," Ron replied smiling at Chris. "You know Chris Elizabeth don't really know who she belongs to, it's all according to what happens, like my joke then she becomes my wife's daughter, should she do something that my wife disapproves of then she becomes my daughter, only at serious times I have to agree she becomes our daughter," Ron laughed.

"It's just a manner of speaking," Olive replied with a slight smile, sipping her tea.

"Stop it you two," Elizabeth said. "I belong to you both, and I would not have it any other way, no one could have better parents."

Olive smiled. "We both know that, you know we both love you very much."

"Well," Ron stood up. "When we are all ready we will go to the house."

"I'm ready," Elizabeth said standing.

Chris gulped down the remainder of his tea, he knew how excited Elizabeth was, and had a job to mask his own excitement.

Olive collected the cups and saucers, and putting them all on a tray took it into the kitchen, from where she returned immediately. "I'll wash up when we get back," she said. "Let's go."

The house was the last one of eight three bedroom bowed window houses that all had been built identical inside and out.

"It seems strange with no furniture," Elizabeth said as they all entered the empty house.

"Looks bigger to me," Ron added.

"Bit cold in here," Olive remarked. "Still get the fire going it will quickly warm the house through."

"It's in good condition Chris," Ron remarked as they went from room to room. "It seems to me that only your own style of decoration is needed, could be done before you are married."

"It's absolutely great Ron," Chris replied taking his hand and shaking it. "I really don't know what to say?"

"Just make our Elizabeth happy, which I know you will do," Olive smiled.

"You see Chris, Elizabeth belongs both to us now," Ron muttered.

"I heard that," Olive remarked.

"Oh Mum," Elizabeth said with tears in her eyes. "What a lovely present," she gave a little choke as she kissed her mother. "And you dad, it is all so wonderful and unexpected," she said kissing her father.

Ron looked at his daughter. "Your mother and I, we both want you to be happy, and who knows perhaps we shall eventually have a grandchild," he smiled.

"That's enough of that talk thank you Ron," Olive scolded.

456

Ron looked at Chris and shrugged. "You know Chris when you get married, the bride vows to obey you, but somehow after marriage, that vow gets twisted around, and the man ends up doing the obeying."

"I'm sure that both Olive and yourself have a very happy marriage," Chris replied. "I don't think for one minute that you could bare to be without each other, I have never seen such love between three people as I have seen with your family, and it makes me wonder what I have missed being an orphan."

"Oh Chris darling, what a lovely thing to say," Elizabeth said giving him a hug. "We are a family of four now darling, and I'll make up to you for what you have lost in life."

Chris felt the warmth of Elizabeth's kiss on his cheek. "You have already done that," he remarked.

"So what do you think about the decoration?" Ron asked.

"I shall want the house decorated," Elizabeth replied. "But it's a big house, just have the main rooms and one bedroom done now, the rest can be done when we live here."

"That's sensible," Chris remarked. "But it will be difficult for me with my job."

"We understand that Chris," Ron replied. "Olive and I will give a hand but we are not professionals, we could hire a handy man," he added.

"I agree," Elizabeth replied looking at Chris. "What do you think darling?"

"It makes sense," Chris agreed. "I know of none however, perhaps Alfie will know someone who wants a few hours work."

"I agree," Ron spoke up.

"You just want a pint," Olive scolded with a smile.

"But we only have a matter of weeks mum, we need someone quickly. Let dad and Chris go for a pint, and do the asking, we can discuss colours for a while, then tell them when they get home,." Elizabeth expressed her opinion.

"I suppose so," Olive agreed. "I have to put the beef in the oven soon, but I have all the vegetables ready for cooking, what do you say Chris, after all it's going to be your home as well, perhaps you would like to have a voice."

"I know very little about home decoration," Chris replied. "I am happy to let Elizabeth have her own way in the decor."

Chris and Ron entered the Rising Sun, it was half past twelve, and several customers were already in the pub, Chris looked to his right, the seat he normally sat was empty.

"Sit down Ron," he said. "I'll get the drinks, bitter I take it?"

"Thanks Chris," Ron said making his way to the seat.

Chris stood at the bar and watched Alfie as he finished serving a customer.

"Chris," Alfie smiled. "Glad to see you, your Sunday off I take it and the little lady allowed you out."

"Something like that Alfie," Chris replied. "I'll have two of your best bitter."

With a glass already under the pump, Alfie started to pull, Chris watched him with a smile. "It takes some pulling," Chris remarked.

"Gives your arm muscles," Alfie smiled as he started on the second pint.

"How's your good wife?" Chris asked as he put sixpence on the counter.

"So, so," Alfie replied taking the sixpence, and pulling out his cash till below the counter. "Marriage is a wonderful union," he said leaning on the counter. "In one way you can say a wife is a cheap servant, but if you love each other, the wife don't mind, and the man will do everything to make her happy, simply because he loves her and wants her to be happy. The wife who do all the looking after, the cooking, the cleaning and washing, we men do take for granted, the way we are brought up I suppose," Alfie smiled. "Because we saw our mothers doing it."

"So what is your advice for a happy married life?" Chris asked with a smile.

"Simple," replied Alfie. "Just let them do what they want, you get no nagging or slamming around the house, you see a man gets his chance of being boss when you are courting, the lady is all sweetness and obliging, do anything for you, but once that ring is on their finger, roles change, the man has to be all sweetness and obliging."

"You have it all worked out Alfie," Chris laughed loudly.

Alfie smiled. "I know, but I have to say, I wouldn't part with my Liz."

"When you got a moment Alfie," Chris said picking up the two pints. "Pop over will you, I like to ask you something?"

"Will do," replied Alfie answering another customer's call for a pint.

"Cheers Chris," Ron remarked lifting his glass and taking a drink.

"Cheers Ron," Chris replied. "At least all the wedding preparations are almost finished, according to what Elizabeth tells me."

"Pity really," Ron replied with a smile. "It's the only time Olive encouraged me to go and have a pint, strange really they keep on how bad drink is for your health, liver etc, but when they want you out of the way, go have a pint they tell you."

"Alfie has just told me the same sort of thing," Chris replied. "But it comes to the same end, Alfie would not part from his wife, no more than you would leave Olive."

"It's called one word Chris," Ron replied. "Love, that four letter word can forgive most things, and accept it allows you to change your ways, don't underestimate love though, it can really hurt."

"I understand what you mean when you say hurt, when I don't see Elizabeth for a few days, I miss her and it really hurts," Chris replied taking a gulp of his drink.

"You will find it hurts more if you have a row," Ron remarked.

"Never had one yet, touch wood," Chris replied knocking the table twice.

"In marriage you will have Chris," Ron answered knocking the table twice. "Love they say never runs smoothly, and no one who have been married for some time can honestly say they never had a row, for one thing it would not be natural, but as I have just said love can forgive and accept, on both sides."

Alfie came over all smiles as usual.

"Have a drink Alfie, I was so busy listening to your advice on marriage, I completely forgot to ask you," Chris said as Alfie seated himself.

"No, I'm alright, I have a glass under the counter already," Alfie replied.

"Why under?" Ron asked.

"It's not good for a woman to know everything," Alfie replied with a wink. "Anyway Chris how can I help?"

"I need a handy man to do some decoration in a house, painting mostly, I wondered if you knew anyone who wanted a few days work, he don't have to be skilled as long as he is capable," Chris replied.

"You got a house already?" Alfie asked.

"A present from the in-laws," Chris replied with a broad grin.

"You lucky devil," Alfie replied. "A top job, a beautiful wife to be, and now a house, I suppose some people are born under a lucky star, it was certainly asleep when I was born," Alfie laughed. "Where about the house?"

"Two doors up from Ron," Chris smiled.

"One of those, that is great, when will you need him?" Alfie asked.

"Well we want it decorated before the wedding, and you know we have only a few weeks left," Chris answered.

"How can I get in touch?" Alfie asked.

"Well Ron is in most of the time," Chris replied.

"That's right Alfie, he can call anytime on me," Ron agreed.

"Expect someone to call by Tuesday," Alfie answered. "I'll send the most capable chap up, he comes in here who will willingly do a couple days work."

"Thanks Alfie, you're a Godsend," Chris replied smiling. "Everything under control your end for the wedding?"

"You can be sure with no worries Chris, the wife has taken control of that," Alfie assured him. "Anyway expect a call by Tuesday, I have to go now a customer is waiting."

"A good chap that Alfie," Chris said to Ron as Alfie left. "He'll see us right I'm sure."

"I'm sure he will," Ron agreed. "We have time to have another before dinner," he said getting up.

Chapter Eighteen

Chris had a spring in his step as he entered the police station on the Monday morning, he had managed to see Elizabeth, but only for a moment.

"I can't stop long darling," she had said planting a kiss on his cheek. "I was so excited when I went to bed, thinking of what I will do with this and that room, that I could not sleep, then I must have dropped off in a deep sleep, if it had not been for mum, I would still be in bed."

"I was the same," Chris smiled holding her hand. "At least the wedding is all ready, thanks to you and Olive."

"I still have the two bridesmaids presents to get," Elizabeth remarked as she pulled up his collar. "They will keep the cold out," she smiled her eyes sparkling.

"You know, this wedding have proved to me that I am ignorant, I know very little on what you have to arrange, I did not know you had to give bridesmaids present," Chris said wondering.

"It's custom darling," Elizabeth smiled. "Don't worry I have already decided to give each one a small white bible, that they can keep all their life, you know darling," she went on as she planted another kiss on his cheek. "I am the happiest and luckiest girl in the world, will I be seeing you tonight?"

"I can't promise darling," Chris said looking down at her and wishing he did not have to leave her. "I have this murder on my hands, that I cannot seem to get into."

"I understand," Elizabeth said faking a sulk. "But I must go in now, I'll see you when I see you," she said, planting another kiss on his cheek. "Keep warm," she ordered as she entered the bank.

Chris had watched her enter the bank, before moving off.

"Cold outside?" George asked as Chris entered and took of his top coat and trilby.

"I did not notice," Chris replied. "I felt warm enough."

George smiled. "Well you look happy enough, better tell me before we settle down to business."

Chris sat at his desk a smile played on his face. "Well we saw the house, I tell you George it's a great present, there are three rooms downstairs and three bedrooms upstairs."

"Elizabeth has already told you what she intends to do with each room?" George interrupted with a smile.

"You know you are right, she told me lot of things what she wants with the decoration, did not include me," Chris laughed.

George smiled. "You have a lot to learn about women Chris, the home is the realm of the wife, your house will eventually represent her pride, and you will be proud."

"I guess you're right," Chris replied. "If she is like her mother, the house will be spotless, but she is so excited," Chris smiled to himself seeing her face in his mind.

"Anyway after we saw the house, Ron and I were allowed to go to the Rising Sun, while both Elizabeth and her mother decided on the colour of the decorations, we had only three pints, Olive had a roast beef ready for us, but by the time we had eaten it, Ron and I was ready for a cat nap, while the two girls cleared the dinner things and washed them up, Ron was fast asleep in his armchair."

"I can imagine," George muttered.

"I could not do that," Chris continued. "It would have been rude, but I felt like it, anyway most of the afternoon passed away with Elizabeth and her mother telling me what colours they thought would be best, to be honest I felt so much like a cat nap, that I can't remember what colours they told me about, I just agreed with what they were telling me, still I have no skill in that type of thing anyway, so I would not have been able to criticise," Chris swallowed. "After that of course I had to see the bridesmaids dresses, they looked pretty, must have taken Elizabeth and her mother some time making them, they did them themselves you know."

"Most women have some sort of dress making skill these days," George remarked. "It saves money."

"Then it was tea time," Chris went on smiling at his thoughts. "I still had my dinner blowing me out, but you can't say no to Olive, so I did manage to eat the trifle made of cake with jelly, custard and cream over it."

"You have a mother-in-law that treats you like a son Chris, if mine is like that when I get married, I shall be grateful, most mothers think the partner their son or daughter picks are not suitable, perhaps it's a bit of jealousy in the mothers who do not want to lose their child, but nevertheless many mothers are like it, Ron is OK as well isn't he, so think yourself lucky Chris," George said pleasantly.

"They do treat me like a son, I love them both to be honest, anyway," Chris felt himself blush a little. "Let's get down to our case, have you got anything?"

George got out his notebook, and opened a few pages. "I got here early this morning, my friend from the MET said he would phone me back about Mrs Shawcroft's Will, I got his phone call five minutes before you got here, anyway Mrs Shawcroft made a new Will out six months before she died, with Taylor and Taylor, Alresford solicitors," George paused while he turned a page. "She was a wealthy woman, she left fifty thousand pounds, twenty five thousand pounds to her husband and twenty five thousand pounds to be held in trust for any child that might be alive, until the age of twenty one."

"That's some Will George, she was indeed wealthy, no wonder Mr Shawcroft is now a gentleman farmer, he can afford it, I suppose having left no children the lot goes to Mr Shawcroft?" Chris replied.

"That's right," George concurred.

"She must have had good foresight," Chris remarked.

"How do you mean?" George asked.

"Well she was three months pregnant when she made the Will, at the time she had no children, she knew that the birth mortality rate was still a bit risky and prepared her Will in case, she may have thought that she might die," Chris remarked.

"I see what you mean Chris," George murmured. "Still it's a shame."

"Yes it is," Chris agreed. "I may be ignorant about preparing for a wedding, but since this case I have learnt a bit about what women have to go through in child birth," Chris replied.

"Poor women," George remarked. "It's a wonder how their bodies take it."

"Anyway the Will seems alright?" Chris asked.

"All in order as far as I'm concerned," George replied. "I did check a little on Mr Adams."

"You were busy on your day off," Chris remarked.

"I had nothing better to do, and I am very interested in this case," George replied.

"Good man," Chris answered. "What about him?"

"He came to Winchester about ten years ago as a junior, even at that time he was considered brilliant and very capable as a junior gynaecologist, however there do seem to be a cloud over him, perhaps it's nothing but there are rumours that he was once in debt, that was before he was promoted."

"Yes I think Bob Harvey said something about that, perhaps he gambles," Chris replied.

George shrugged. "Well he got in debt, it was all cleared up before he was promoted, it must have happened five or six years ago," George said.

"That's what getting at me George," Chris replied a little angrily. "We keep coming back to what may or may not have happened five or six years ago, and I wonder why?"

"Surely it's only background stuff," George answered noticing the disappointed expression on Chris's face. "After all the murders took place only last week."

"Of course you are right George," Chris replied a little calmer. "I keep wondering whether these murders are the result of what happened five years or so ago?"

"But what did happen back then?" George murmured. "Mr Adams have an affair with Mrs Wilson, and both were promoted."

"Don't forget that Mr Shawcroft lost his wife and his child, and Mrs Dummer had her child around that time," Chris replied.

"You have lost me now Chris," George answered.

"I've lost myself as well George," Chris replied with a smile. "Anyway I had two visits during Saturday, one from Mr Shawcroft's maid to make her statement and one from that midwife you missed seeing, a Mrs Steward, a fine figure of a woman if I remember rightly," Chris mocked. "You missed that one."

"Story of my life," George grinned.

"She was very informative, she did say that there was a rumour about a baby mix up, again here it comes, about five or six years ago, but that it passed over without much ado. Mrs Steward is a very unhappy person, she said that it should have been her promoted, she was senior at the time and had taken Mrs Wilson under her wing when she had been transferred from nursing to midwifery."

"I can understand that," George replied seriously.

"You can't guess what Molly the maid told me," Chris said to George a broad smile on his face.

"No idea," George replied honestly. "What did she tell you?"

"Well it seems during the year Mr Shawcroft hold a dinner party."

"He can afford," George interrupted.

"It seems one of his guest being Mr Adams," Chris ended.

"Another connection with the two murders," George replied. "Unbelievable but do it help us?"

"Early days yet," Chris replied. "But as you have just said, another connection of the both murders."

"What about Mr Dowling?" Chris asked.

"Haven't had time yet," George replied. "But I'll get on it today, although apart from being a loner and an odd job man, I have no idea what I shall turn up?"

"One never knows," Chris replied. "I was thinking about this chap with his cap pull over his ears, wearing glasses and wearing an overcoat with the collar pulled up who we know nothing about, Roger Webber and Mrs Hanks as far as we know the only two to have seen him."

"I put him down to be Mr Chalker, the missing clerk from the hospital," George answered.

"He might well be George, but we only have Mr Webber's word for it, we did not bother to check, we didn't consider him important, but we could check up on Mr Webber, even though we don't consider him a suspect."

"It can't do any harm," George replied with a grin. "This is going to take me time."

"You will manage George, you do have a certain charm," Chris praised him.

George smiled as he got up and took his overcoat.

"Flattery will get you anything," he smiled leaving the office.

Chapter Nineteen

George left the Police Station as the Guildhall clock struck the half past ten, he pulled up his collar, wondering to himself how he was going to get the information that Chris wanted, it wasn't going to be easy, there were no records he could look at, no authorities that could help him, it remains only for him to find the right people to speak to, but where would he find them.

Dodging the horse and carts and the cycles, George crossed the Broadway, and made his way towards the Three Tuns pub, he knew the pubs were now open, and what better place to start.

George entered the Three Tuns pub ten minutes later, there were two doors inside the entrance, one stated public bar where he and Chris had gone into last week, the other stated saloon bar which he chose.

The bar was empty, George pulled down his collar as he stood by the bar waiting for the landlord, he could hear voices coming from the public bar. He was undoing his overcoat buttons when the landlord arrived.

"I'll have a pint of your best bitter," George ordered a smile on his face.

The landlord pulled the pint, placing it on the counter in front of George. "You're a policeman aren't you?" the landlord asked taking the sixpence George had put on the counter. "You were here the other night with another bloke," he said giving three and a half pence back in change.

"You have a good memory considering you were very busy that night," George said having taken a drink.

"Coppers don't usually come in here," replied the landlord.

"I can't see why not," George flattered. "You serve a nice pint, and it's quite nice and warm in here."

The landlord did not replied or smiled.

"I need to ask you a few questions," George said.

"I can't talk about my customers to the police, I would lose them if I did, this is a bad side of the town for the police," the landlord continued. "Your beat bobbies this side usually walk in pairs."

"Nevertheless landlord, I am investigating two murders, I could ask you to come to the station to be questioned, but that would only give you bad publicity should the papers somehow get the story," George lifted his glass and took a drink, the landlord moved around the circular bar.

"Are you chaps alright?" George heard him ask whoever was in the public bar.

"We're alright Harry," George heard as the landlord reappeared.

"I got three in there playing darts," the landlord said unsmiling. "Now what do you want to ask?"

First of all landlord, George began. "Mr Dummer was a customer here, and you know by now that he was murdered, can you remember a tall chap wearing a pulled down cap and wearing an overcoat, wore glasses and kept his back to the counter last Friday week talking to Mr Dummer?"

The landlord thought for a while. "I do have a good memory," he admitted. "But to tell you the truth, I can't think of a person like that, he would have been a stranger, I would have remembered."

"Are you sure?" George asked disappointed.

"I am," the landlord replied. "I remember Rowland that night, the only one he spoke to was Mr Webber, I remember that because Mr Webber bought Rowland a drink."

"Is that so unusual?" George asked.

"It is for Mr Webber, because he brings in a lot of trade for me I give him his first pint free, and because he pays money to his workmen during the weekends in here, his glass is kept full with the half pints they give him, to be honest it's a rare occasion when Roger Webber pays."

"Is that so," George replied smiling.

"As far as your memory goes then" George smiled. "No such person was in here last Friday week?"

"No, as far as my memory goes," repeated the landlord.

"What can you tell me about Mr Webber and Mr Dowling?" George asked staring the landlord.

The landlord smiled for the first time. "Don't mix with them, both are very rough."

"I know Mr Dowling can be a handful, but I did not know Mr Webber was also," George remarked before taking a drink. "He seemed pleasant enough when we were speaking to him."

"Get on the wrong side of him, and you will find out," the landlord answered. "If he knew I was speaking to you about him, he would have my pub wrecked."

"I can assure you he will not find out through me," George replied. "He's as bad as that is he?"

"Very capable," replied the landlord, moving a few steps to take a look in the public bar. "I tolerate Roger Webber, because he fills my pub weekends, and men comes in during the week hoping to find him here wanting a work, but I'm frightened of him, he has a dark side to him."

"Can you be more specific?" George asked.

The landlord shook his head. "I hear a lot is said in the pub, bits and pieces you know, Mr Dowling is OK as long as people leave him alone, Roger Webber I feel is different, polite on the outside, but capable of anything."

"He is not known to the police," George replied.

"Who's going to report him," the landlord continued. "If someone did, I would hate to be in his shoes after, you would get no witness even if a dozen saw what had happened, you see in a way he is very powerful, the chaps rely on him to give them casual or full time work."

"Do you know where he lives, is he married?" George asked.

"He's single as far as I'm aware," replied the landlord. "I don't know where he lives, but I am told he lives in a bungalow on the outskirts."

"Mr Dowling," George continued. "Apart from his attitude what do you know about him?"

"As I have said, leave him alone, and he's alright, anyway he behaves himself in here, it's the only pub he's not been banned, I only let him here as a favour to Roger Webber."

"Is that so," George remarked finishing his pint.

"A refill?" asked the landlord.

"No thanks landlord, I'm on duty, thank you for your cooperation," George said buttoning his overcoat and walking to the door.

As George left, the landlord took the empty glass into the public bar, his mind wondering and worried.

George stood on the pavement outside the Three Tuns pub, looking up and down the North Walls he pulled up his

472

collar, there was a strong wind, he could put up with the rain, but he did not like wind. He had always thought that Mr Chalker's missing from the hospital was a mystery, but a gut feeling made him believe the landlord, he realised that Chris was right in his thoughts that such a man did not exist it must be someone we already know using a disguise.

With Mr Chalker in his mind, and knowing that today Monday he was due to pay his rent for his flat, George decided to take a walk to Andover Road and speak to his landlady again, he stuffed his hands in his overcoat pockets and walked towards the railway station. George cursed the wind as he turned in Andover Road, it was playing havoc with his mop of hair, which he tried to control by brushing it backwards with his fingers.

"I'll have to start wearing a trilby," he said to himself as he reached number 22, and stopped. A man in his forties, slender in build and about five foot, eight inches tall, wearing an overcoat and carrying a trilby was closing the front door of number 22.

George mounted the first step leading to the door, blocking his way. "Excuse me Sir," George said politely. "Would you be Mr Chalker who lives in the basement flat?"

The man hesitated before answering. "Who are you may I ask?"

"I am Detective Sergeant House of the Winchester CID," George replied.

"Why would the police be asking about me?" the man replied unsmiling.

"Because Sir," George replied. "You are reported missing."

"Well you see me now Sergeant, so I'm no longer missing, if you would please step aside."

473

"I am sorry Sir," George replied. "But I must ask you to come with me to the police station."

The man smiled. "Impossible Sergeant I have to catch a train within fifteen minutes."

"I'm sorry Sir, you will have to catch a later train," George replied sternly.

"Am I under arrest for something?" the man asked.

"No Sir, but we must ask you a few questions, you realise the whole force have been looking for you," George said.

"I have only been away for a while," the man replied. "I have no idea who could have reported me missing, however if I am not under arrest would you please move aside."

George looked at the man, he realised that he would have to arrest the man to get him to the police station. "In that case Sir, I am arresting you and taking you in for questioning about the disappearance of Mr Charles Chalker of this address."

"But I am Mr Chalker," replied the man. "This is madness."

"If you are Sir," George answered. "Once we are satisfied you will be free to go."

The man sighed and slapped his sides with his hands. "Mrs Walker will vouch for who I am," he argued.

"That will be to your benefit, but you must come to the station," George replied.

"Oh very well," replied the man angrily. "Let's get it over with, you could live to regret this bully action of yours arresting me without case."

George did not answer as he allowed the man to pass him and walk a step in front of him.

Chapter Twenty

*C*hris had just put his phone down, as the office door opened, and Mr Chalker walked in followed by George.

"Detective Inspector Hardie," George introduced closing the office door, and walking to his desk. "This is Mr Charles Chalker, our missing person."

Chris a little shocked, stood with a smile. "Thank you for coming in Mr Chalker," Chris said offering his hand. "Perhaps you would like a seat," Chris said indicating the interview chair.

Mr Chalker did not move and rejected the hand offered. "Do you always shake the hand of someone you arrest Inspector?" he asked.

A bit bewildered, Chris looked at George. "He would not come voluntarily," George explained.

Chris sat down and looked at Mr Chalker. "We have been looking for you Mr Chalker, police forces within twenty five miles have been looking for you."

"I had no idea that I have to tell the police I am going away, I always thought we were a free country, free born, not a communist state," Mr Chalker replied angrily.

Chris sat back in his chair and looked at Mr Chalker. "When one goes away someone is normally told, you didn't turn up for work, and left your flat, no one knew where you were, not even your sister, landlady, or your employer. You were reported missing to the police, then did it become a police matter, as a police matter you were wrong not to come in when asked, the matter of your arrest could have been avoided," Chris leaned forward to his desk.

"Now you can stand or sit, but I have questions that need answering before you leave this station," Chris spoke with the voice of authority.

Taken back a little with the outburst, Mr Chalker sat.

"Now Mr Chalker, would you tell me where have you been for the last ten days?"

"Staying with a friend at Bognor Regis," Mr Chalker replied.

"Why did you leave without telling anyone, do you realise the police spent a great deal of time searching for you?"

"It was a spur of the moment thing," Mr Chalker replied. "I had a lot on my mind, I just wanted to get away and think, a lot of trouble over nothing," he added.

"I agree with you Mr Chalker, you have caused a lot of trouble," Chris replied, a little anger in his voice. "Now you left your employment as a clerk in the Winchester hospital record office without a word to anyone, it was them that reported you missing."

"They had no right," Mr Chalker replied. "I resent being called a clerk also, I am the Hospital Registrar."

"Really," Chris replied looking at him his voice soften a little. "What exactly do that mean?" he asked.

"I sign all the death and birth certificates that happens in the hospital, only my signature on the birth or death certificates can be accepted as legal."

"Really," Chris was now interested. "Before signing these certificates, do you personally verify?"

476

Mr Chalker gave a faint smile. "No, I am given a notice form with all the details, birth or death on it and signed by a doctor, after my deputy writes the certificate up, I normally sign them within a week."

"Why the delay?" Chris asked with interest.

Mr Chalker shrugged. "Mistakes are sometimes made with the information, which comes to light within a week usually, I do not want to sign a false certificate."

"Quite," Chris replied deep in thought. "Do errors often happen?"

"Not really," Mr Chalker replied. "Very few actually, usually because of a junior."

"Do you have any problems regarding baby mix up?" Chris asked looking straight at Mr Chalker.

Mr Chalker averted the stare and looked down at his lap, twisting the trilby he held. "Can't remember any, at least not in the last few years, why do you ask?"

"No reason," Chris replied. "Now I am told that you and Mrs Wilson a senior midwife under Mr Adams are close friends?"

"Why do you ask about Margery?" Mr Chalker asked looking up.

"Don't you think you could have told her at least about you going away?" Chris asked.

"She did know," Mr Chalker replied. "That is why I'm amazed I was reported missing, I'm sure she would have spoke up, anyway I have only been back in Winchester an hour, I'll see her and get to the bottom of this mix up."

"I thought you had a train to catch?" George who had been listening remarked.

"I lied," Mr Chalker replied looking at George with a smirk.

"It do seem Mr Chalker that you were wrongly posted as a missing person, however as event took place, Mrs Wilson could not comment on your disappearance, I am sorry to tell you that Mrs Wilson died."

Chris hoped that he had not been too brutal in the way he told Mr Chalker of her death, he saw the blood drain from Mr Chalker's face, to a deathly white, his eyes became watery. "That can't be true, it just can't be," he half sobbed. "She did not have any ill health, she would have told me, what was the cause?" he asked in a whisper.

"I am afraid she was murdered, she was found at the field where she kept her horse on the Monday morning. Mr Bob Harvey, whom you would know attended and verified her being Margery Wilson," Chris replied gently.

"My God," Mr Chalker almost shouted as he covered his face with his hands, it was a few moments later when Mr Chalker took a hanky from his pocket and dabbed his eyes. "Have you found her killer?" he asked.

Chris shook his head. "Not yet Mr Chalker, but we are gathering information, perhaps you can understand now why we wanted to ask questions?"

Mr Chalker dabbed his eyes again and nodded. "I'm sorry I have no idea."

"Did you know a Mr Dummer?" George asked wanting to take part.

"I did not know him, but Margery had mentioned his name often."

"What about Mr Dowling, Mrs Wilson's step brother?" George continued.

"Again I have never met him, by all accounts he is not a pleasant man," Mr Chalker stated straightening up.

"What about a Mr Roger Webber?" George asked expecting the same reply.

"No I can't say that I have," Mr Chalker replied after some thought.

"He is foreman, runs gangs of labourers," George offered.

"Just a moment, yes, while I was walking with Mr Adams in the hospital grounds a few months ago, Mr Webber who had a gang working in hospital grounds, he was labouring in the hospital grounds when Mr Adams spoke to him, but that was about six months ago, Mr Adams asked who he was, and he told us his name and what he was doing, it seems that he was laying some sort of pipe work."

"Mr Chalker," Chris said. "I have been the bearer of dreadful news to you, I understand and feel for you, Mrs Wilson as far as we are able to make out was a competent and good person, if you can throw any light on why she might have been killed, now is the time, I have in mind that it is something to do with babies birth."

For a moment Mr Chalker looked at his lap, absently playing with his trilby rim, before looking up. "You could be right Inspector, however I have no proof of what I will tell you, most of it comes from Margery, it worried me so much, I had to get away and think."

"I can understand that Mr Chalker," Chris remarked in a gentle voice.

"Years ago, before Mr Adams became the head of his department, he and Margery had an affair, all went smoothly, until Mr Adams told Margery that he was in serious trouble regarding gambling debts, which amounted to thousands," Mr Chalker swallowed, before carrying on.

"During this time, a friend of Margery was admitted to the hospital having her baby, a Mrs Dummer, then a Mrs Shawcroft was admitted for the same reason, she was I believe a farmer's wife, at least that what Margery told me.

Margery as I understand it, got her friend in hospital because she was having it at home, and Margery feared that her baby was not quite as it should be, Margery told me she did not expect Mrs Dummer's baby to survive, don't ask me why, but Margery was keeping her fingers crossed."

Both Chris and George allowed Mr Chalker to continue without interruption, George was busy writing it all down.

"However with two women admitted in labour, with only Margery and Mr Adams were on duty, Margery looked after Mrs Dummer and Mr Adams looked after Mrs Shawcroft. According to Margery, Mrs Dummer was having difficulties in delivering, when Mr Adams came in and told her that one of her patients was in labour in Winchester and they wanted her straight away, and he told her he would look after Mrs Dummer and he would give her an injection to help her, according to Margery," Mr Chalker continued.

"She did not want to leave her friend, but also realised her duty, so she got on her bike, and went to her patient in Winchester, where a baby was delivered in good health. On her return to the hospital, she found her friend although asleep had a bonny baby boy, she also found out that Mrs Shawcroft and her baby had died. Margery had accepted this, it was all a part of having a baby, but a little later she was talking to a Mr Bob Harvey who carried out post-mortem, he told her that Mrs Shawcroft would have died giving birth, she had a tumour, a silent one, his only problem was why the baby died, baby should have lived, he told her."

Mr Chalker took a short pause before carrying on. "This must have put thoughts into Margery's head."

"Would you like a drink before going on Mr Chalker?" Chris asked.

"Glass of water perhaps," Mr Chalker replied, which prompted George into action, providing a glass of water. Mr Chalker drunk greedily, took a deep breath, and placed the glass on the desk in front of him.

"When we started courting, I believed in Margery was interested in me," Mr Chalker continued a faint smile on his face. "But I understood she was more interested in my record files than me."

"Why do you believe that Mr Chalker?" Chris asked.

"To find out if her thoughts were right I suppose," Mr Chalker replied. "You see what really cooled the relationship between Margery and Mr Adams was when a few weeks later he told Margery that his debts were cleared. He told her that he had sold shares that his father had left him."

"What was her thoughts at that time, did she tell you?" Chris asked.

"Much later she did," Mr Chalker replied. "She believed that Mr Adams took the living child from Mrs Shawcroft who had died, and swapped it with the dead child of her friend Mrs Dummer's child who at the time was asleep through the injection."

Chris and George stared at each other.

"Margery's opinion was that the dead baby Mr Harvey examined was Mrs Dummer's baby, she spent months going through medical books, and in the end came to the conclusion that although Mrs Shawcroft would have died in childbirth, she could have had a very healthy baby, in her mind she was sure that the babies were swapped, and although she was unable to prove it, it had to be Mr Adams who made the switch, he being the only one on duty that night," Mr Chalker took another drink. "What really made up her mind I think, was that Mr Adams got out of debt a few weeks later."

"Did she confront Mr Adams with her views?" Chris asked.

"I think she must have hinted, she broke up her relationship with him, and later that year when he became head of the department, he made her senior midwife, ahead of those who had longer service."

"Did she find anything in your record files?" George asked.

"I have records kept on all deaths and births since records began," Mr Chalker replied. "I don't think she would have found anything, however she was a very caring woman, and she was appalled at the number of unmarried girls who had to give up their child at birth, these details are all available in the records, she then got a bee in her bonnet, she wanted to open a special home where these girls keeping their babies, but that would take money, I know she got in touch with many of the fathers of these girls, hoping to start some sort of partnership in setting one up."

"Winchester men?" Chris asked.

"At the time," Mr Chalker replied, but during the years people move to other towns, so some would have left."

"Mr Chalker is there anything else?" Chris asked.

"I think that's all," Mr Chalker replied. "Can you tell me has Margery been buried?"

"Not yet, her brother Mr Dowling will be making all the arrangements, I can give you his address if you wish?"

"I know where it is," Mr Chalker replied. "I will have to think whether I should interfere or not, I doubt if he would have known that Margery and I were engaged to be married."

"Really Mr Chalker," Chris replied a little surprised. "I did not know."

"Is there anything else I can help you with?" Mr Chalker asked.

"Just one more thing Mr Chalker," Chris replied. "I can tell you now that Mr Dummer was murdered on the Sunday following Mrs Wilson's death."

"My God," Mr Chalker murmured clearly shocked. "I did not know him personally, but Margery always spoke well of him, I don't understand what's going on?"

"Nor do we at the moment Mr Chalker," Chris replied. "Would you know of any document that Mrs Wilson might have had that might concern Mr Dummer, you have given us a full picture of her thoughts, would she have had any document?"

Mr Chalker shook his head thinking.

"It could have been the blood samples, I know she had both Mrs Dummer's and her son's blood group, but whether or not she got Mr Dummer's blood group I have no idea," he replied.

Chris and George stood up, Chris offered his hand, which this time Mr Chalker took, Chris shook his hand warmly and thanked him for the information he had supplied.

George shook his hand, apologising for the way he had brought him to the police station.

"I now understand Sergeant, think no more of it," he said. "Will you keep me up to date?" Mr Chalker asked to Chris.

"Certainly Mr Chalker, you will be first to know," Chris promised.

Mr Chalker gave a faint smile and left the office.

Chapter Twenty-One

Chris looked at George and smiled. "Are you going to tell me, on what charge you arrested him George?" he asked interested.

"I asked him to come voluntarily but he declined, saying he had to catch a train, so I arrested him for questioning about a missing Mr Chalker."

"About himself," Chris smiled.

"Well I did not know Mr Chalker, anyone could tell me they were Mr Chalker, how would I know, so I told him when we were satisfied he would be allowed to go, I did not really charge him with anything."

Chris smiled. "That's first for me."

"For me as well," George smiled.

"Did you think his story was a bit pat, I mean no hesitation straight off his tongue," Chris asked.

"It verified your report on telephone calls you made of the people in Mrs Wilson's address book," George ventured.

"But they seemed hard press to give a straight answer," Chris reminded him. "You could also say it verifies Mrs Hanks remarks those men often come during the dark hours, left her house in the early morning, some told me that having missed their train to get back home, Mrs Wilson would allow them to sleep in the spare room."

"Are we going to dig into what Mr Chalker told us about baby swapping?" George asked.

"Not officially, it is not a part of our official investigation," Chris replied. "We have not had any report officially of this going on, but who knows, it might come to it with our investigation of these murders."

"Do you think it happens Chris?" George asked.

Chris smiled. "I keep an open mind on that, but at the moment, Mr Adams and Mr Shawcroft need another interview don't you think?"

George nodded. "Together?" he asked.

"It's now coming up to one, let's cut the time down and go separately," Chris smiled.

George smiled back. "I have a motorbike so I go to Mr Shawcroft," he grabbed his coat as he walked out of the office.

Chris having made enquiries at the reception, entered Mr Adams office, he found Mr Adams already standing with a welcome smile on his face.

"Pleased to see you Inspector," he said offering his hand. "Please take a seat, the weather don't seem to improve Inspector," Mr Adams continued coming from his side of the desk, and seating himself in another chair a few feet from Chris. "Would I be in order to ask how your case is progressing?" he asked.

Chris who was sat holding his trilby, looked at Mr Adams, he thought him handsome, and his smile seem to enhance that, he wondered why Mr Adams was not married.

"A case is like a jigsaw puzzle," Chris explained. "One hear bits and pieces some fits the puzzle, some don't, it takes time."

"I'm sure," Mr Adams replied. "Are you hoping that I can fit another piece?" he asked.

"I am always hoping that people I talk to will add a piece," Chris remarked. "However new names came into the inquiries, do you know a Mr Roger Webber, he runs gangs of men digging ditches?"

Mr Adams scratched his head in thought. "I'm sure I don't know Inspector he replied."

"That answer makes it awkward for me Mr Adams," Chris replied.

"Why Inspector?" Mr Adams asked. "Look Inspector say what you have on your mind, I can assure you I will not be offended."

Chrise paused for several seconds and went on."We have located Mr Chalker the hospital registrar who went missing, he tells us that while you were both walking in the hospital grounds a few months ago, you stopped and spoke to Mr Webber who had a gang working in hospital grounds."

"A few months ago you said Inspector?" Mr Adams asked.

"That's what we were told," Chris replied.

"Ah I remember, I was walking with Mr Chalker in the hospital grounds, now come to think of it we did see a gang working, but I am afraid you have it wrong way around Inspector, when we were passing this gang, Mr Chalker asked to be excused, and he went over to speak to a chap who was standing up by the edge of the trench, I don't know who it was, but I walked on, and Mr Chalker never did catch me up."

"Really," replied Chris annoyed not sure what to believe.

"Yes really Inspector," Mr Adams repeated.

"Do you remember what this chap looked like?" Chris asked.

"I wasn't interested Inspector that's honest," Mr Adams replied.

"How did you get on with Mr Chalker?" Chris asked.

"I never socialised with him, to be honest I never really liked him, I did hear that he had a filthy temper, I never experienced it, when we did meet and talk, he was always very pleasant, but way back when I was courting with Mrs Wilson, I sensed that he was, sweet on Mrs Wilson."

"Please forgive me Mr Adams, but it is my job to ask questions," Chris said intending to be blunt.

"I told you Inspector, I won't be offended," Mr Adams replied with a smile.

"During any investigation we always get a lot of background on the people who may be involved also on people who may not be involved," Chris remarked.

"So, what background information have you got on me?" Mr Adams interrupted. "Not all bad I hope?"

"Far from it Mr Adams," Chris replied thankful of the opening Mr Adams had just given him. "But we have heard that about the time you were having a relationship with Mrs Wilson, you were in debt, and we have heard talk of babies being swapped."

"You have been busy Inspector, but when I first knew you, I knew you were a man who would dig and dig, and learn things that had no bearing on the crime, I took a chance not telling you the full truth, it was personal and could not have helped your case," Mr Adams spoke.

"Perhaps you would care to tell me now," Chris replied. "It will go no further, if not irrelevant to the case."

Mr Adams clasped his hand together. "I did have a relationship with Mrs Wilson, but that more or less ended when I informed her that I was in debt, and should it get out, it could have affected a promotion that I was expecting to get," Mr Adams revealed.

"You see Inspector around that time, I started to gamble, it was a mistake, which I really regret, and then with the head of the department deciding to retire, which being his junior I was expecting to get promotion, I decided to stop, but before I was able to do that I had to clear the debt I was already in, and so stupid I gamble more hoping to clear the debt I already had," Mr Adams waved his hands. "Had I been sensible I would have known that that's not the way and would only make me more in debt, and it did."

"What was the amount?" Chris asked.

Mr Adams open his drawer, and took a slip from and handed it to Chris. "It was quite a large sum, I keep that slip to remind me, should I ever feel like being stupid again."

Chris looked at the slip, it was a paid in full slip of a bookie. "Yes, seven hundred, thirty two pounds and sixpence, quite a sum, but you managed to pay it," Chris replied.

"Yes I did, from an unexpected person, Mrs Wilson offered me the money."

"I see," Chris replied. "That is how Mrs Wilson came senior above those who should have had the position?"

"Don't get me wrong Inspector, Mrs Wilson was very competent and caring midwife, I never did regret making her so, she did save my bacon as we say, but that was not the reason I promoted her to senior, but I felt guilty about the other midwives who should have first chance, but I considered Mrs Wilson to be as competent as the others in her skill, but she was more caring, and more generous with time as far as her patients were concerned."

"I can understand your predicament Mr Adams, but where did Mrs Wilson get this kind of money?" Chris asked.

Mr Adams shrugged. "Never knew, I thought at first it was money left to her from her husband, but dismissed that after remembering that she had told me once that her husband had left her the house, but no money to run it."

"You had two women giving birth, a Mrs Dummer and a Mrs Shawcroft about five years ago," Chris said. "Was this money offered to you after these births or before?" Chris asked.

"I remember the births very well," Mr Adams replied. "I looked on Mr and Mrs Shawcroft as friends, when Mrs Shawcroft became pregnant I took care of her, I was not happy with her, in fact I advised her to have a termination, as she might be risking her life, but she would have none of it, and made me promise not to tell her husband I'm almost sure it was after."

"Is that so," Chris remarked remembering what Mr Chalker had told him Mrs Wilson had said.

"As it happened, I was right, when the coroner opened Mrs Shawcroft's body he found she was riddle with what we call cancer," Mr Adams said sadly.

"So you and Mr Shawcroft became friends?" Chris asked.

"Yes, I am usually invited to any party nights he has, and before you ask I do know about the murder at his farm, he has told me about it," Mr Adams said.

"What about Mr Dummer?" Chris asked knowing what Mr Adams had said to be true.

"Never knew him, Mrs Wilson wanted his wife to come to hospital, I understand that Mrs Wilson was not happy about her pregnancy, I saw no reason why not," came the reply.

Chris shifted in his chair. "Run me through the night Mrs Shawcroft and Mrs Dummer had their births."

"I was not at the births Inspector," Mr Adams replied. "I was called out earlier."

"Oh," Chris muttered. "I understood you were, you have also just told me that you took Mrs Shawcroft under your wing, because you feared for her life."

"Inspector," Mr Adams interrupted him. "Let me explain, I did look after Mrs Shawcroft, I gave her a bed here three days prior to the date she was due so that I could keep an eye on her, on the day Mrs Shawcroft gave birth I was called out to an urgent case, I checked Mrs Shawcroft before I left, I gave her a mild sedative just to keep her calm and allow her to rest, it would have been impossible for me to attend her for twenty four hours a day, I was also content in my mind that Mrs Wilson was on duty with me. However my call out took several hours, when I got back, I was told Mrs Shawcroft had died with her baby, and a Mrs Dummer had been admitted during my absence and given birth to a baby boy. I checked Mrs Dummer who was in a bad way, and gave her an injection to calm her and make her sleep for a while."

"You were not there when Mrs Dummer was admitted or her baby was delivered?" Chris asked.

"No," Mr Adams replied. "I had to sign a form, that I gave to Mr Chalker for the birth and deaths certificates as senior on duty, but the footnote on that form will tell you that Mrs Wilson senior midwife attended the deliveries."

"Well I think that's all I need to ask Mr Adams I thank you for your cooperation," Chris said beginning to rise.

"Just one more thing Inspector," Mr Adams said making Chris sit back in his chair. "You brought up about baby swapping, to me that is worrying, I have not heard of any such going on, had I, I would certainly look into it."

"It has been mentioned during our investigation," Chris replied. "However not officially, it is not a part of our official investigation."

"Going back to your case Inspector, I don't suppose it will do any harm now in telling you," Mr Adams spoke. "Few weeks or so ago, Mrs Wilson told me that she had applied for another position, she did not tell me where, but I took it was outside the county, she told me that should she get it, she would be handing in her notice at the end of the month, that would be around now."

"Really," Chris remarked his mind turning over. "I wonder why would she want to leave?"

Mr Adams shrugged his shoulders. "I wonder as well, she had a top position here, she wouldn't get a better one."

"Before I go Mr Adams, had you repaid Mrs Wilson the loan she gave you?"

Mr Adams looked uncomfortable. "We had an agreement Inspector, I repaid her fifty pounds a year, I still owe half of the loan, I wonder who I will have to pay now and will the reason for the loan be made public?"

"A written agreement?" Chris asked.

"No verbal," Mr Adams answered.

"Well I doubt if the reason will be made public," Chris replied. "Nothing down on paper, I should wait until everything is cleared up."

Chris returned to his office, his mind was mixed up, he believed Mr Adams version of events, Mr Chalker's version was second hand, only hearsay what Mrs Wilson had told him, and with Mrs Wilson dead it could not be verified, but Mr Adams could, he sighed as he sat behind his desk, he filled his pipe and lit it, and leaning back in his chair deep in thought blew out clouds of smoke.

George parked his motorbike a few feet from the front door of the farm house. He took off his goggles and attached them to the motorbike handle, then took off his gloves and stuffed them into his overcoat pocket before walking to the door.

The door opened almost as he touched it. "Morning Sir," Molly dressed in her maid's uniform welcomed as she opened the door for George to enter. "You were seen coming down the drive, the master is in the kitchen with the cook, he wants you to join him for tea."

George smiled as he step inside. "Thank you Molly, tea would be most welcome," he said rubbing his hands as he watched Molly close the front door.

"It's cold on a motorbike," George complained.

Molly smiled but did not reply as she led George to the kitchen, where she opened the kitchen door allowing George to enter before she departed.

"Come in Sergeant," Mr Shawcroft said with a smile. "Come and sit, you must be cold on that machine, I thought you were that other man, who was he, oh yes the police surgeon, did not recognised you at first."

George walked to the table and shook Mr Shawcroft's outstretched hand.

"Morning Sir," George said politely. "I hope I'm not here at a bad time," George said apologetically.

"No, no," Mr Shawcroft replied. "Sit yourself down, the cook will bring you a nice hot cup of tea, while you tell me how things are going, if that is why you are here?"

"Yes and No," George said as he unbuttoned his overcoat and sat, he smiled at Mrs Burton as she put a cup of tea and a slice of seed cake in front of him. "How are you Mrs Burton, you look well," he greeted her.

"Very well thank you Sergeant," Mrs Burton replied. "Very nice of you to ask."

"We will talk after you have finished your tea and cake," Mr Shawcroft remarked lifting his own cup. "I usually sit in the kitchen, much warmer than the rest of the place."

George did as he was requested, and enjoyed the tea and seed cake before he spoke.

"Mr Shawcroft you are aware that we found another body on the Monday morning following the death of Mr Dummer?" George asked.

"Yes I am Sergeant," Mr Shawcroft replied his face unsmiling. "My friend Mr Adams from the hospital filled me in, she was his senior midwife, a lovely woman."

"Do you know Mr Adams and Mrs Wilson?" George asked already aware that he did.

"Of course, Mr Adams looked after my wife, and Mrs Wilson attended my wife's labour on that fateful day."

"I see," George replied. "I did not know," he lied.

"No reason for you to know Sergeant, after all what could Mr Dummer's death and Mrs Wilson's death have in common?" Mr Shawcroft asked.

"Well they did know each other, and Mrs Wilson did deliver his son the same evening as your wife gave birth," George replied.

"I was very angry with Mr Adams, when the midwife told me that both my wife and my son had died, Mr Adams was supposed to have been in attendance," Mr Shawcroft remarked. "It was only later when Mr Adams explained he was on a call out, and the results of post-mortem examinations I understood that my wife was keeping her illness a secret from me, my wife was a very strong woman, did not surprise me."

"I'm sure she was," George remarked a little bewildered.

"Thank God, Mrs Dummer survived with her son, with the death of her husband she do at least have something to live for," Mr Shawcroft added. "Anyway Sergeant you said yes and no, how can I help you?"

"Progress on the case is slow," George told him. "There are couple questions I would like to ask, not important but might help, did you leave the house that morning before you went to Mr Dummer?" George asked looking straight at Mr Shawcroft.

Mr Shawcroft replied straight away. "Yes I did, I always check the chickens, I have a couple dozen laying hens at the back, I collect the eggs, and I always look for signs of a fox, we do get the odd fox prowling now and again."

"Can you see your wood from there?" George asked.

"Not the one Mr Dummer was in, I can see the other small part however."

"Well I am sure you would have told us if you had seen any movement Mr Shawcroft, but we have to be sure," George stated politely.

"I would have done Sergeant, had I seen any, but I did not," Mr Shawcroft answered. "It's a long way to come just to ask that question Sergeant, I could have told you on the phone."

"I was told to come by Inspector Hardie, who by the way sends his regards, he wanted me to put you in the picture, Inspector Hardie has a lot of compassion, he is very happy with the way you are helping Mrs Dummer," George replied quickly seeing that Mr Shawcroft had not taken his questions very well.

"I feel I have a duty you know," Mr Shawcroft answered this time with a faint smile on his face. "Mr Dummer and his father both worked on this farm, I feel there is a bond, also with Mrs Dummer giving birth the same time in the same ward as my poor wife."

"Do you see Mr Adams a lot?" George asked.

"Now and again, he comes over for the odd dinner party."

"Did you see Mrs Wilson after the death of your wife?"

"As far as I remember she came only once, you gave her tea and cake I remember cook," Mr Shawcroft said turning to the cook.

"That's right," Mrs Burton answered. "She was a lovely lady, she was over this way, she popped in wanting to know how Mr Shawcroft was bearing up, she seemed very concerned."

"I hear she did not have any immediate family?" Mr Shawcroft remarked.

"Her parents adopted a boy, so she has an adopted brother, who is her next of kin, he will get her house, and all her money, if the money belongs to her," George spoke.

"How do you mean?" Mr Shawcroft asked with a serious voice.

"We have heard that she and several others were donating money towards a special home where wayward young ladies could go and have their births, sparing them the taboo about unmarried mothers," George replied. "We believe that Mrs Wilson was keeping the donations until the required amount was reached, of course we shall dig into all her accounts to be sure."

"Would that be a part of your investigation Sergeant?" Mr Shawcroft seemingly interested. "After all, all you are only interested in is catching the murderer surely?"

George smiled. "Usually, but this case is a real puzzle, very little so far make any sense, we have to look at everything, who knows," George smiled. "There could be something hidden there?"

"Let's hope you are right," Mr Shawcroft muttered.

George considered this was a good time to make his exit, he stood up.

"I have taken too much of your time up," he said. "Thank you for the refreshments," he smiled at Mrs Burton who returned his smile, and shook hands with Mr Shawcroft. "I can see my own way out," he assured them.

Mr Shawcroft stood at the window and watched George ride off.

"Are you worried about anything?" Mrs Burton asked as he stared out.

Mr Shawcroft turned and walked towards the kitchen door. "Wondering, just wondering," he said leaving the kitchen without a glance at the cook.

George returned to the Police Station, and found Chris sucking his pipe. "You look a bit windswept George," Chris smiled.

"Riding a motorbike at twenty miles an hour creates that look," George replied sitting at his desk.

"How did it go?" Chris asked smiling at George who did not look happy.

"Mr Shawcroft was pleasant, we sat in the kitchen and the cook gave me tea and a slice of seed cake," George remarked.

"He told me straight away that Mr Adams often attend a dinner party at the farm, and Mrs Wilson made a courtesy call on him about two weeks after his wife and sons death. He did go outside before going to the body of Mr Dummer, as Molly said in her statement, it seems that he has chickens, he collects the eggs, to my question he said he could see one small part of wood from the rear of his house, but not the one Mr Dummer was in, he was a bit sarky when I asked if saw any movement in the wood, so I flattered him with kind regards from you."

"That was nice of you," Chris smiled. "So I take it we learnt no more than we already knew."

"That's about it," George replied. "Nothing I could put my finger on, although I am sure he is holding something back, you see he told me Mr Adams had told him about Mrs Wilson's murder. He asked if she had any dependence, I told him she had an adopted brother who would get her house and her money, should it be her money, I told him we would check up that. He asked me if that was a part of our responsibility, I thought that was a strange question."

"Strange indeed George, not a question one would expect, however let me tell you about my interview with Mr Adams," Chris said.

By the time Chris had finished, George was looking more interested. "So we have two statements one from Mr Chalker and one from Mr Adams, both on the same matter, both opposite to each other, who are we going to believe?" George asked.

"Well remember Mr Chalker's details of events were hearsay, and can't be checked with Mrs Wilson. Mr Adams's details can be checked, so I am incline to believe him."

"So we call Mr Chalker back again?" George asked.

"Won't do much good George, he will only say what Mrs Wilson told him, he already told us."

"If Mrs Wilson and Mr Chalker got engaged, as I remember Mrs Wilson only had a wedding ring on her finger, where is the engagement ring?" George argued.

"Perhaps he had not got round to buying one yet," Chris replied keeping an open mind. "It do happens."

"It don't make sense," George still argued. "Why would Mrs Wilson want to leave her safe job here after just getting engaged?"

Chris leaned back in his chair, to him the case was a puzzle, he had no idea which way it was going.

"You know George, perhaps we are investigating the case in a negative way, let me explain," Chris said leaning forward. "At the moment we are checking on negative issues like the baby swapping, we spent most of our time with this in our minds, and it all just assumptions, even this document we believe Mrs Wilson was going to give or gave to Mr Dummer is assumption, we don't know perhaps someone else was going to give him a document. I think we have to work with the positive information we have. It seems to me this baby swapping business have led us away from the real reason that Mr Dummer and Mrs Wilson's murder, although I am sure there is still a connection."

"You get no argument from me on that," George replied. "But what positive knowledge do we work on?"

"Well when Mr Adams told me that Mrs Wilson might be leaving I thought about her horse, she would certainly make some kind of arrangements for him, so I phone the big house while you were out, the owners are back from France, he told me that Mrs Wilson paid quarterly the field rent, and was not due until June. He told me that a man seem to be looking after the horse, I asked for his description, it had to be Mr Dowling when he told me that the chap was not handsome," Chris paused for a moment. "Mr Adams also said that Mrs Wilson was not sure yet whether she had got the position she had applied for, so I thought she might have been waiting for a letter, I have sent Constable Streeter to pick up any letter that may arrive since his last visit."

"Well that's positive," George remarked. "What is left, I can't see much headway being uncovered about the murders though?"

"Little by little George," Chris smiled. "Now I have decided for you to go on a little trip."

"Thank you," George replied with a smile.

"If the weather is right you should enjoy it, I want you to go to the addresses in her address book, confront the men in it, find out if they are telling the truth, I need to know," Chris remarked.

"Why do you have doubts?" George asked. "You spoke to them yourself, you seemed happy at the time."

"Yes slightly," Chris agreed. "But the way I see it, Mrs Wilson's savings are for a special home for the young pregnant women where they can keep their babies, if the money donated by these men, I would have thought they had saved more than enough to buy the home already."

George smiled. "When do I go, of course I go by motorbike," George remarked.

"Start in the morning George, you will have some ground to cover, your motorbike will allow you to travel without any train worry, Andover, Basingstoke, and several in Southampton, your motorbike will be handy, should you find you have to stay overnight, book in a hotel, I'll see all your expenses are paid," Chris assured him. "But at the moment we better complete our reports of our interviews before we forget."

Both looked towards the office door as a knock came and it opened, Constable Streeter poked his head inside.

"Come in Constable," Chris said a smile on his face. "Any luck?"

Constable Streeter entered the office and approached Chris. "Found two letters Sir," he said politely placing the letters in front of Chris.

"The place still the same?" Chris asked picking up the letters and studying them.

"In the same mess Sir," constable Streeter replied. "I did have a second look around, just in case, but no joy."

"Well thank you very much Constable, you have done well, are you off duty now?"

"Yes, on my way home now," constable Streeter replied.

"Are you married constable?" George asked knowing Chris wanted him in the Criminal Investigation Department (CID).

Constable Streeter smiled. "No, I live with my parents, when I do, I want the right one, today plenty of service girls throw themselves at you, they are willing to become a wife just to get out of service but I figure it's not for the right reason, you need a strong bond between to get married, not a reason."

"Very wise Constable," Chris said with a smile. "And thank you for these letters."

Chris looked at George when Constable Streeter had left. "Any idea?" he asked.

"The first few months will tell us," George replied. "I think he will fit in though."

"Well if we get him, he will be under your wing," Chris replied.

"Thanks very much," George replied with a smile. "Are these letters of any use?"

Chris opened the first letter that seemed important. "I was hoping for a letter from a hospital authority," Chris muttered as he took out the letter, and opened it up. "This one is from an estate agent," he remarked reading the letter.

Chris read and re-read the letter before passing it to George, then opened the smaller envelope, it was a letter from one of the names in Mrs Wilson's address book and contained a four pound postal order.

"That letter tells us that Mr Chalker was telling the truth regarding a home for young wayward women," Chris remarked. "According to this, she has plenty of money to buy it outright, I am getting the feeling that Mrs Wilson was not going to work in a hospital any more she was going to run the special home," Chris said.

"It looks like that," George replied.

"But why would she tell Mr Chalker, and not Mr Adams, Mr Adams believed that she was going to work in another hospital authority outside the county," Chris wondered.

"She is certainly going out of the county," George remarked. "Worthing is quite away, what's the other letter?"

Chris handed the letter to George. "This letter will save you the trip tomorrow, this letter confirms that these names donating money to Mrs Wilson, you see there is a four pound postal order with the letter."

"Do they help us?" George remarked.

"It clears up a worry," Chris answered. "These letters prove that Mrs Wilson was going to open a home, also she had men who were donating to it and according to this, she has plenty of money to buy it outright."

George shrugged. "I'm surprised she had this donation sent, you did phone the names last week."

"It could have been delivered before I phoned them, we haven't been to the house for several days," Chris replied.

"We are no nearer to finding the killer," George remarked. "What are you going to do with all this?" George asked handing the letters back to Chris.

"Let's wait a few days, but in the end, we will have to allow her solicitor to sort it out," Chris replied checking his watch. "But now I am off to meet Elizabeth, I'll see you tomorrow."

Chris was a half way to the bank, when he saw Elizabeth coming towards him, she saw him at the same time, a broad happy smile appeared on her face.

"Darling," she said her eyes shining as they met, giving him a kiss on the cheek. "It's a lovely night, but then we are in April," she smiled looking up into his face as she grabbed his arm.

Chris shook his head and smiled, he knew Elizabeth was alluding to the wedding month. "Really," he replied trying to keep a straight face. "Time goes so fast, I'm hardly aware of the day or month, why is April so special?"

"You are teasing darling," Elizabeth replied looking up at him and tightening her grip on his arm, which he felt.

"Of course I am," Chris said with a smile as he patted her hand. "You could cause poor blood flow to my arm."

"Serves you right teasing me," she replied relaxing her grip.

"Two weeks and two days to go," Chris remarked as they walked. "Time really do go fast."

Elizabeth giggled. "Then I shall have to obey you darling."

"You will find me a hard task master," Chris replied. "I am used to having my own way, and being obeyed."

Elizabeth giggled again. "Will you be so hard in the bedroom darling?" she asked.

Chris shook his head in despair. "You want a good scolding, you know us men cannot avoid showing desire, we are reaching your home, be good."

Elizabeth giggled, but did not answer as they came to the path leading to the front door.

"Up you go," Chris said releasing his arm from her grip and patting her backside as he let her go ahead of him. "No more bedroom talk remember."

Olive had the door open for them, she smiled to herself seeing the happiness on her daughter's face. "Dinner is on the table," she remarked.

With a kiss from both Elizabeth and Chris, she left them to hang up their top coats.

"The weather seems a bit brighter," Ron said having been kissed on the cheek by Elizabeth. "Perhaps we are in for some decent weather."

"Let's hope so," Chris replied. "It is April after all," he added taking a sneak look at Elizabeth who he found watching him.

"April is a spring month," Elizabeth interrupted as she helped Olive set the table. "I just know, it's going to be a warm month," she smiled looking teasingly at Chris.

"There is something that I should remember this month," Ron remarked his face serious. "Still I'm sure it will come to me."

"Dad," Elizabeth scolded.

"Stop your teasing Ron," Olive intervened. "Get out of the chair and get to the table."

Ron lifted himself from his armchair and sat at the table. "Orders, orders, orders," Ron muttered looking at Chris, a faint smile on his face. "You being the boss, so to speak, you are not used to taking orders are you Chris?"

"I suppose you can say that, but then I don't give many orders as well, George and I work as a team, I value his opinion," Chris answered.

"Which means you have a good working relationship," Ron replied.

"I suppose so," Chris replied picking up his knife and fork, the toad in the hole dinner in front of him made him realise how hungry he was.

"You will get used to taking orders when you get married," Ron teased as he started to eat.

Olive glared at Ron. "Eat your dinner and stop your teasing," she scolded. "You know how excited our daughter is."

"It's alright mum," Elizabeth said a smile on her face. "I know dad is just teasing."

"I don't hold with it," Olive replied. "Chris might take him serious, I know you will be a dutiful wife, you were brought up in the Christian way, Chris is the right man for you, I shall be proud to be his mother-in-law, otherwise I would not have given my daughter to him."

"Elizabeth have switched back to being her daughter now Chris," Ron said as he finished chewing and giving Chris a wink. "Elizabeth know we both love her," he said looking at his wife. "We are very happy with her choice for a husband, I'm sure that they will be very happy together, I hope we will all be friends, just like we are tonight," Ron dropped his knife and with his free hand touched Olive's hand and smiled. "Chris knows that I would not want to be without you."

Olive gave a faint smile. "Well then," she replied in a loving voice.

"I'm sure Elizabeth and I will be as happy as you and Ron," Chris said looking at Olive. "I for one will try my hardest to be so, and I know Elizabeth will do likewise."

"We won't have to try darling," Elizabeth said looking at Chris. "We are soul mates, it will come naturally."

With the dinner over, the rice pudding afters filled Chris up. Olive and Elizabeth cleared the table, and while they were washing up, Ron went into the kitchen returning with two bottles of Brown Ale and two glasses.

The evening passed happily, dominos were played during which time details of the wedding was discussed.

"We have had several response back to the wedding invitation," Olive said to Chris. "Have you by chance decided on your best man yet?"

"I can only think of George," Chris replied. "I have already sent a request to the Chief Inspector asking if it can be arranged for both of us to have the day off."

"Do you think he will Chris?" Ron asked.

"He's quite a decent chap," Chris replied.

The night passed quickly, they had a great time laughing and talking about anything and everything.

Olive stood up a smile on her face. "Ron and I will retire now, it's getting late," she said looking at Ron.

"Yes I have a busy day as well," Chris replied. "I have a lot of paper work to get through."

Goodnights were said all around.

Chapter Twenty-Two

Chris entered the Police Station, he had a few moment with Elizabeth on his way and had the feeling that it was great to be alive.

George was already at his desk when Chris entered.

"Someone is happy," George remarked.

"Actually I am George, it will take a lot to upset me today," Chris replied.

"Well there is a note in front of you, came in yesterday evening according to the desk sergeant."

Chris leaned forward and saw the note which he read. "I wonder what Mrs Dummer wants?" he remarked replacing the note on his desk. "Let me think, today is Tuesday isn't it?"

"All day," George smiled.

"I think she told me her husband's body is brought back today," Chris said. "I suppose I better get round there, want to come?" Chris asked.

"I'm waiting on a phone call from my mate of the MET," George explained.

"You wait then George, he may have interesting news, I'll pop round," Chris smiled as he got up. "At least the weather is improving," Chris remarked putting on his overcoat and taking his trilby. "I'll see you later then."

Mrs Dummer opened the door to the knock. "Inspector," she said giving a faint smile, I am so pleased you called."

"Are you well Mrs Dummer?" Chris asked as he stepped inside.

"Just upset and a bit nervous," she replied leading the way to the dining room.

"Make yourself at home," she said going into the scullery. "I have made a pot," she remarked returning, carrying a serving tray with two cups. "You know Row is brought home today," she continued, putting the cups on saucers and pouring out the tea. "Help yourself to milk and sugar," she offered.

"Thank you Mrs Dummer," Chris replied helping himself to milk and sugar. "Have you got any problems regarding your husband being brought home?"

"Oh no Inspector," Mrs Dummer replied after taking a sip of her tea. "I want him home, I have not said goodbye to him yet."

Chris took a drink of his tea. "Can I help you in any other way?" Chris asked.

"Can you tell me Inspector," Mrs Dummer asked. "Was there a connection between Margery Wilson's death and my husband's?"

Chris fiddled with the cup handle, wondering how to answer without causing her more upset. "I have not found any connection Mrs Dummer, but why do you ask?"

Mrs Dummer seemed to relax. "I'm so pleased, it's a thought, in fact Inspector I must tell, but believe me, what bearing it has I don't know," she said.

"I would be interested Mrs Dummer," Chris replied wondering what it was she could tell him.

"About three weeks before Margery was killed, she called and asked me if I would keep a couple letters for her, she showed me two letters which she put into a larger envelope, she told me they were important, and was afraid that they may be stolen."

"Really," Chris remarked getting interested.

"She then told me that she was buying a home for girls who get into trouble outside marriage," Mrs Dummer continued. "She told me several years ago she had taken a payment for doing something that was illegal, she did not say what, but told me she has never regretted it, as she felt was for the best. However, there was a man, this man found out, demanding sex in payment for his silence," Mrs Dummer paused and took a drink of her tea.

"She told me," Mrs Dummer continued putting her cup down. "She liked her job, and did not want to lose it, so she went along with this man, and gave him what he wanted. Then somehow this man found out about the home she intended to open, found out about the money donated and wanted a half of it," drawing a deep breath Mrs Dummer went on. "She told me that while she gave the man sex, she did not intend to give the money as well, she told me that she had enough money now to buy the home, and she intended to move away, give up being a midwife and run a home, she did not tell the address of the home nor the man's name."

"Have you got these letters now Mrs Dummer?" Chris asked getting excited.

"Yes I have Inspector," Mrs Dummer replied. "You see she told me that I was to post them should she suddenly gone, but she would get in touch with me."

"Can I see these letters Mrs Dummer?" Chris asked.

Mrs Dummer got up, went to the sideboard and took an envelope from a drawer.

"This is how she gave me the letters, I did not look at them, in fact I did not know at the time what to think, it was like a drama out of a novel."

Chris took the envelope but did not look inside. "I will have to take these with me Mrs Dummer," Chris said. "If they need posting I will do that for you."

"Thank you Inspector," Mrs Dummer replied. "You see I put the envelope on the shelf in the wardrobe, I only remembered about them yesterday, so I went to the wardrobe, and took them out and found one letter was open, I think Row must have found them and opened one letter by mistake, he never mentioned to me that he had done so, however, then my mind began to play tricks, I wondered if Margery and Row's death had anything in common."

"I'm very glad you told me of this Mrs Dummer, I wish you had told me earlier, but never mind, now you have not read the opened letter?"

"Oh no Inspector, that would have been very rude, Margery was a friend."

"But you are sure when given to you these letters were sealed, but one is now open, and you feel your husband must have opened it by mistake, no one else could have done?" Chris asked.

"Who would know the letters were there," Mrs Dummer replied. "Even Row did not know, but he is the only one who could have found them, I do not have people in my bedroom Inspector."

"I'm sure you don't Mrs Dummer," Chris replied. "It's the policeman in me, I always have to double check."

Mrs Dummer smiled. "Would you like another cup Inspector?"

"No, no, thank you, I do need to get back to the station, but first with your husband being brought home, do you want someone with you?" Chris asked.

"Thank you Inspector, but Mrs Ewing will be here when Row arrives."

"Thank you Mrs Dummer for what you have told me," Chris said as he led the way to the front door.

"I did the right thing in telling you Inspector?" Mrs Dummer asked as she opened the front door and Chris stepped outside.

"You may have helped me a lot Mrs Dummer," Chris said as he fitted his trilby to his head. "Please get in touch if you need anything, by the way would you mind if I send a constable along to collect your husband's bike, I will only need it for a day, I do need to check something."

"Of course not Inspector, it's standing outside at the back, you can take it now if you want?" Mrs Dummer offered.

Chris thought for a moment before answering. "Perhaps that might be wiser," he replied.

"Go through the back door," Mrs Dummer said as Chris re entered the hallway. "You can bring it straight through this way."

Chris smiled as he passed her to the back door.

Chris rode the bicycle back to the station, and took it inside the station with him.

"Good morning Sergeant Williams," he said to the desk sergeant. "Your turn on the desk then?"

"Afraid so Sir," sergeant Williams replied eyeing the bike.

"I want to keep this bike just for a while," Chris said. "I'll take it through to the office."

Sergeant Williams smiled without comment.

"I want to get hold of Constable Streeter," Chris said pushing his trilby to the back of his head. "Is there any chance of that today?" he asked.

"He usually calls in during the morning, I would say in one hour's time," sergeant Williams replied looking at his watch. "I'll let him know Sir."

Chris pushed the bike into his office, bringing a smile on George's face.

"Before you ask," Chris said parking the bike behind the hat stand and taking off his overcoat and trilby. "I need to check something later on, did you get your phone call from your mate of the MET?"

"Yes, a few moments ago," George replied. "Nothing on Mr Adams, nor Mr Webber, but the description I gave him of Mr Webber, do fit a man called Mr Webb."

"Really," Chris replied seating himself at his desk.

"It seems," George continued. "This Mr Webb disappeared from the East End of London some twenty years ago, he was a well known criminal, often arrested but the charges were always dropped, no conclusive evidence being found, but according to my mate, Mr Webb was a bad one capable of all major crimes."

Chris thought for a while. "Do you think this Mr Webb is our Mr Webber?" he asked.

George shrugged. "Could be, we will have to find out where he came to Winchester from."

"Thank your friend from me George, we may owe him a big one."

George smiled. "Anyway how did you get on?"

Chris took two letters from his jacket's inside pocket. "These George was held by Mrs Dummer for Mrs Wilson, the quick story is that she was leaving Winchester, but was also in fear that the letters would somehow be stolen, Mrs Dummer was asked to post them should she leave quickly."

"Why couldn't she post the letters herself?" George queried.

"A question I asked myself George," Chris replied. "I can only guess she wrote them, but was waiting for conformation of the home she intended to purchase before posting them, when she received no word regarding the home, perhaps she thought they would be safer hidden."

"I suppose," George replied not convinced. "You have read the letters?" George asked. "I see one is open."

"Mrs Dummer said she was given the letters unopened, she hid them in her wardrobe, the events of the last week took her mind off of them and has only just remembered them. She has no idea how one became open, she can only think that her husband found the letters and opened one by mistake, Mrs Dummer assured me she has not read the opened letter, and nor have I yet," Chris replied picking the opened letter up and taking out its contents. "It's addressed to the hospital," Chris said.

Chris read the letter before handing to George. "Well she first of all apologises for leaving without giving her notice, and forego any money due to her," Chris murmured. "That tells us she wanted to get away, where no one would know her," Chris added.

"She then goes on," George interrupted looking at the letter. "That some years ago she made an indiscretion, she had never regretted doing so, and in the same circumstances would do it again, however an unscrupulous person found out, and ever since have suffered blackmail, which she could no longer accept."

"That would be Mr Chalker," Chris replied.

"So you say," George replied. "You are accepting what Mr Adams told you over what Mr Chalker told us."

"I have still an open mind George," Chris replied. "But I think Mr Adams was telling the truth."

"The letter do not tell us much, I wonder why she didn't name her blackmailer?" George replied. "That letter proves nothing not even a name mentioned."

"She is not a revengeful person George," Chris answered.

"What is the other letter?" George asked. "It might tell us something?"

Chris picked up the other letter. "It's addressed to her solicitor," Chris said as he opened the letter taking out a single sheet of paper which he read.

"It don't tell us anything we don't already know George," Chris replied. "Just that any money she might leave first of all must shared out between those who have donated towards the home that she intended to set up, she has listed the names and addresses," Chris added handing the letter to George.

"Strange letter, you might be right, she did have a sense of fear," George remarked. "But she mentioned the repayments Mr Adams was making to her," George remarked. "Obviously Mr Adams did not know this, or he would have told you."

"It would be within her character," Chris replied. "If she got paid for her indiscretion she would not have kept the money for herself, anyway she was able to save Mr Adams reputation, and also brought happiness to the life of a woman and to a boy that is idolised by her."

"Perhaps the boy would have been idolised by his father," George remarked.

"If what we assume is right, the boy's father was about forty at the time, bringing up a boy without a wife for a man that age would not be all fun," Chris remarked. "Then we have to consider his wife's WILL."

Sergeant Williams put his head around the door. "Chief Inspector Fox is here Sir."

Chris looked at George and tossed his head. "Fingers crossed George," Chris said quietly. "Well let him in Sergeant," Chris replied.

Chief Inspector Fox entered the room. "Hardie," he said putting the briefcase he was carrying on Chris's desk. "I was in the darn neighbourhood, thought I would give you a look in," he turned to George before Chris could answer. "Relax George," he said unsmiling. "How are you fitting in, happy I hope?"

"I am happy and contented Sir," George replied.

"Good man, good man," he repeated turning back to Chris. "Murder darn well follow you Hardie, darn small city like this, London gets no more than you," he said seating himself in the interview chair. "You're making a darn name for yourself, soon be after my job I expect."

"I have no ambition there Sir," Chris replied politely. "I am quite happy as I am."

"Well at least you are bringing a darn good reputation to the force Hardie, what about these murders you are investigating now?" the Chief Inspector Fox asked.

"We are getting there Sir," Chris replied. "I'm hoping to clear it up soon."

"Good man," the Chief Inspector replied. "Now about this extra man you want, while I'm here might as well sort it out."

"We could do with one," Chris replied relaxing a bit.

"Darn it Hardie, you are two men in this office, should be enough for this darn place."

"As you pointed out Sir," Chris retaliated. "We are having our share of crime, major ones as well."

"Don't throw back at me my own words Hardie," the Chief Inspector scolded, then for the first time smiled. "It's been approved, you can have this constable, what's his name, Cam Streeter I believe, conformation will be on your desk by the end of this week, I have spoken to his Inspector, he is in agreement as long as he is replaced, I hope now you are darn satisfied."

"Extremely," Chris replied.

"Well that's that then, now what about this darn wedding of yours, how you ever find time to court a lady, I don't know," the Chief Inspector remarked with a smile. "You want someone to cover the office for the day?"

"I would like someone," Chris replied. "If granted I can have Sergeant House as my best man."

"Darn it Hardie, have you no other friends?" the Chief Inspector asked.

"Most of my friends are in the force Sir, I have little time to socialise," Chris replied smiling inwardly.

"Wouldn't this Constable Streeter be able to take over?" the Chief Inspector asked.

"He will be a novice to this office Sir," Chris remarked. "But with your permission I could leave him in charge."

"Well there you are then, you have my darn permission," the Chief Inspector said standing up and taking his cap. "I will see you next at your wedding, my wife sends her thanks for our invitation, darn it all Hardie," he said offering his hand with a smile. "My congratulations, I hear she is a very fine woman."

Chris shook his hand. "Thank you Sir, and yes she is a very fine woman."

The Chief Inspector Fox picked up his briefcase and made for the door which he opened. "If this darn Cam Streeter gets as good as you said, you will have a fine team here," he said closing the door behind him.

George smiled. "He has given you what you want?"

"Yes he did," Chris replied. "Now I can ask you, will you be my best man?"

"Honoured," George replied without hesitation.

"I could not ask you before, and Olive keeps on to me about who it will be, but I had to wait to see if I could get cover for that day, I did ask for an extra man, and cover for my wedding day in the same request letter, and of course his invitation went out about the same time," Chris remarked smiling.

"Crafty," George replied as a knock was heard on the office door and Constable Cam Streeter appeared.

"Come in Constable and sit for a while," Chris offered.

Constable Streeter crossed to the interview chair and sat. "Sergeant Williams said you wanted to see me Sir?"

"How friendly are you with Jessie Ford, that bicycle shop on the corner of Station approach in Chesil Street?" Chris asked.

"I have had a cuppa with him," the constable replied.

"Do you think he is knowledgeable regarding bikes?" Chris asked.

"There is not much he don't know about them," the constable replied. "He told me he was making bikes from scrap parts when he was a schoolboy."

"What I really want to know is, if I showed him a bike with a front wheel missing, and give him a selection of front wheels, could he pick out the wheel that belonged to the bike?"

"No idea Sir," constable Streeter shrugged. "I can ask him."

"Please do so Constable," Chris replied. "And let me know."

"Will do," constable Streeter started to rise.

"Sit back for a moment," Chris said with a smile. "Has Sergeant Bloom approached you regarding transferring to the CID branch?"

Constable Streeter hesitated. "Yes Sir, he did, I told him that I would like it very much, it's just that I wonder if I am capable detective work, I do not have much experience, I deal mainly with neighbours quarrels, but when I searched Mrs Wilson's house, I did try and kid myself I was a detective on a case, because of that I looked in every conceivable place, places that I would not usually think of, actually I was disappointed with myself when I found these documents in the toilet, simply because I had not thought of looking there."

"You are not the only one Constable," George spoke up. "We never thought of it."

Constable Streeter smiled. "If you are willing to take a chance with me Sir, I would love to work with you."

"Sergeant Bloom has faith in you and like myself, I am sure Sergeant House will welcome you," Chris rose and across his desk offered his hand, followed by the hand of George.

"Your conformation will be here by the end of this week, so you move in on Monday, I'll have a desk put in for you, you will be under Sergeant House wing, watch and listen to him, and don't be afraid to voice your own opinion," Chris advised.

"Well Cam while we are in the office discussing or just talking, we call each other by our Christian name, mine is Chris, and the Sergeant's is George, but outside rank must be respected."

"I understand Sir," the constable replied a broad smile on his face.

"At the moment however you are still uniform with an errand to do."

"I understand Sir," constable Streeter replied almost jumping up. "I'll get to it straight away Sir."

"By the way," George remarked as Cam was leaving. "On Monday get rid of that uniform."

"Thank you Sergeant, I certainly will," constable Streeter smiled as he left the office.

"I think he'll be alright George," Chris said. "He seems keen enough."

"I agree," George replied. "It will take time to settle in."

"Now George, I intend to call a meeting, let's see today is Tuesday, we have to make a breakthrough let's say Thursday, it will give me time to sort out a few bits."

"Who do we call?" George asked. "Only have a couple in the frame since we started, and no other names have appeared, and no conclusive evidence on any of them."

"Actually that's what makes this a close knit case," Chris replied. "It has to be one of those in the frame, I'll have Mr Chalker, Mr Webber, and Mr Dowling."

"Not Mr Adams, or Mr Shawcroft?" George asked.

"No," Chris replied. "Not unless I have to, can I leave that to you George, Thursday morning at eleven."

"Already done," George smiled as he left the room.

Constable Streeter entered the office as George left.

"Constable," Chris greeted him.

"I have spoken to Mr Ford, he said he is at your service whenever, he said he might not be able to tell what wheel a bike had when bought, he could tell however whether a bike had a wrong wheel on it."

"I see Constable," Chris said a little disappointed. "Would you ask him if he could call at the station around ten thirty on Thursday morning, he may be able to help?"

"Certainly Sir, I'll ask him straight away," Cam replied.

Chris smiled. "Do it tomorrow, you get off home now, and thank you."

George entered as the constable left. "Well that's done, they will be informed tonight by uniform with the threat of being arrested if not turn up, they would also be told that they could bring their representatives."

"Good," Chris replied. "Streeter has just told me that Mr Ford may only be able to tell whether the bike had a wrong wheel on it, however I have asked him to call on Thursday morning, you never know."

"What's all this about anyway?" George asked.

"When we saw Mr Webber in the Three Tuns pub, and I almost collided with his bike, I noticed he had a brand new front wheel, just being sure," Chris said with a smile.

Chapter Twenty-Three

Wednesday came and went, Chris went over his reports on interviews, he wanted no mistakes and made a list of all the vital points he wanted to bring up.

"I still can't see that we have evidences to accuse anyone of the murders?" George remarked finally having cleared his desk, which would be needed for the typist.

"I'm just hoping to get one of them to make a slip," Chris replied. "No doubt in my mind that one of them is responsible."

On the Thursday morning all was set, Chris felt a little nervous as he sat facing the three men, and a smile past his lips as he noticed no one had brought a solicitor, he looked at George who gave him a grin, and saw the woman typist sitting by him. Inspector Noal came to his mind. "Don't get distracted from what you are doing, keep on top, know what you intend to say, and keep on until one makes a slip," Inspector Noal would have said.

"Thank you for attending," Chris said opening the meeting.

"I don't know why you want me here?" Roger Webber burst out. "Calling me here, under the threat of arrest is a bit high handed, I do have responsibilities."

"I apologize for any inconvenience," Chris replied. "I need to get to the bottom of this case, I am sure all of you would welcome that."

"Of course we would," Mr Chalker spoke up. "But I was only in here a couple days ago."

"I know Mr Chalker, but please just bear with me, now if I might start with you Mr Chalker," Chris said selecting a single file from the many files on his desk.

"What you told me on Monday was all hearsay, it was what you had been told by Mrs Wilson."

"That's right," Mr Chalker replied. "How else would I have known?"

"Some information has come to us since, do not verify what you told us," Chris stated looking at him.

"I can only say what I was told," Mr Chalker replied.

"Fair enough Mr Chalker," Chris answered in a friendly tone. "One thing I would like to clear up, you told me you had become engaged to Mrs Wilson before her death, did you buy her a ring?"

Mr Chalker fidgeting uncomfortably in his chair. "Why do you ask that?" he said.

"Mrs Wilson was not wearing an engagement ring when she was found," Chris told him.

"Well I hadn't got around to it, I was going to," Mr Chalker responded.

"Did you buy it during your disappearance?" Chris asked.

Mr Chalker again fidgeting uneasily in his chair. "I don't know why it makes any difference to this case, I was away when Margery was killed remember."

"Yes I remember," Chris answered. "You had just got engaged, then you disappeared for a week without telling your fiancée, I take it you did not buy a ring while you were away?"

"No I did not buy a ring, I was upset in my mind," Mr Chalker replied angrily. "And Margery did know I was going to buy."

"Mr Chalker you did not turn up for work on Wednesday, four days before Mrs Wilson was murdered, in which time the entire hospital knew of your disappearance, they contacted us, don't you think Mrs Wilson would have told the authorities that you had gone away?"

Mr Chalker hesitated. "I asked her not to tell anyone," he replied meekly.

"Mr Chalker," Chris spoke his voice a little sterner as he picked up a letter from the file and held it in front of him. "The matter of whether or not you were engaged to Mrs Wilson have no bearing on this case, I just wanted to be sure of your truthfulness."

Chris saw the colour drain from Mr Chalker's face as he stared at the letter. "This letter has just come into our possession, it is quite damaging," Chris lied but remembering what Mrs Dummer had told him.

"Where did you get it?" Mr Chalker asked looking uneasy.

"This letter was given to a person to keep safe with another one, I believe Mrs Wilson sensed that it would be sought after by a certain person, and she wanted it safe."

"What is in it then?" Mr Chalker asked.

Chris ignored Mr Chalker's question. "I believe that this letter is the reason why Mrs Wilson and Mr Dummer was murdered," Chris enlightened the gathering.

"Well that let's me out," Mr Chalker remarked. "I was away."

"I'm afraid Mr Chalker, this letter implicates you," Chris lied hoping that Mr Chalker would slip up.

"How, what do it say, it is all lies," Mr Chalker started to rise. "I'm not sitting here and called a liar."

"Please sit Mr Chalker, I could arrest you on several charges."

"Go on then arrest me and tell me on what charge?" Mr Chalker shouted.

"Charges Mr Chalker, not charge," Chris replied sternly. "Suspicion of murder, blackmail, rape, signing knowingly false death and birth certificates comes to mind," Chris replied.

Mr Chalker laughed. "You do not know what you are talking about."

"Mr Chalker," Chris answered. "Murder is a hanging offence, with all the other offences taken into account, I would say you have no chance of escaping the noose."

"But I did not murder Mrs Wilson, nor Mr Dummer," Mr Chalker screamed. "I was away during that time."

"Mr Chalker, you were blackmailing Mrs Wilson, she wouldn't have got engaged to you, however if you did not murder her and Mr Dummer, perhaps you can start being honest," Chris saw both Mr Dowling and Mr Webber staring at him.

Mr Chalker slumped back in his chair, desperately wanting to know what was said in the letter. "What is it you want to know, you said the letter told you everything."

"Just to verify things Mr Chalker, you were blackmailing Mrs Wilson because you accused her of swapping babies, will you tell me how you thought this?"

Mr Chalker shrugged as he tried to keep calm. "I was not blackmailing Mrs Wilson, but the question of baby swapping did arise between us. I was walking in the hospital grounds one night several years ago, I passed under the window of the maternity waiting room, I heard voices, and heard what was being said about swapping of babies, the window must have been left open."

"Did you see who was talking?" Chris asked.

"No the window was too high for me to see inside," Mr Chalker replied.

"How was it then you came to blackmail Mrs Wilson then?" Chris asked.

"I'll repeat," Mr Chalker almost shouted. "I did not blackmail Mrs Wilson, however I was interested in who I might have heard speaking. The next day I checked who was on duty in maternity ward that night, only Mrs Wilson was on with Mr Adams, I checked who was admitted that night and assumed rightly what had taken place, Mrs Dummer and Mrs Shawcroft were admitted."

"How did you come to that decision?" Chris asked.

"Because Mrs Wilson did not deny it," Mr Chalker replied a faint smile on his face.

"Don't you realise Mr Chalker, true or false any accusation regarding the swapping of babies to a midwife would seal her career, she would never be employed by any authority as a midwife again, Mrs Wilson lived for her job," Chris paused for a while, he looked at George who was looking on with interest, and was glad that the typist was not too loud.

"Wait till I get you outside you bastard," Mr Dowling was shouting to Mr Chalker.

"But I did not kill her," Mr Chalker replied with a groan. "Why won't anyone believe me, I was away."

"So," Chris continued. "Mrs Wilson agreed to your terms for you keeping quiet, she could not afford to have the slightest suspicion against her, so you blackmailed her for sex," Chris said.

"No, she offered me sex to keep quiet," Mr Chalker shouted.

"According to her Mr Chalker, you were the one making demands, in that case every time you had sex with Mrs Wilson it was rape, against her will," Chris replied.

"That's not true," Mr Chalker responded.

"Come Mr Chalker, on suspicion you blackmailed Mrs Wilson, she would not want that type of suspicion against her, but are you not aware Mr Chalker, after you signed the death certificate and birth certificate for that night, you did not inform the authorities, it would have brought you down as well, you are the registrar," Chris added looking at Mr Dowling.

"Mr Dowling, I realise that this is distressing for you, but please be patient," Chris remarked.

"He deserves a damn good hiding," Mr Dowling replied angrily.

"Where did you carry out your demands on Mrs Wilson?" Chris asked to Mr Chalker.

"Her offer was carried out at her home," Mr Chalker replied not committing himself.

"That is where you became aware that she was collecting money to buy a home for the young ladies?" Chris asked.

"Not aware, was told," Mr Chalker replied.

"She also told you willingly how much she had towards the home then?" Chris asked.

"Showed me her post office book," Mr Chalker replied.

"Then you wanted some of it?" Chris stated.

"No, not at all," Mr Chalker replied angrily.

"According to Mrs Wilson," Chris informed him holding the letter up. "It was your greed, you wanted half of the money that had been donated for the home, but the money was for the young women's home, money was donated by other people, it wasn't her own money, greed Mr Chalker is your own downfall."

Mr Chalker shrugged his shoulders. "You must believe what you believe, none of it is true."

"We shall see Mr Chalker," Chris remarked turning to Mr Webber.

"Mr Webber, I have a couple of question for you."

"I was wondering why I had been asked here," Mr Webber replied. "I hope this meeting is not going to carry on long."

"When I met you in the Three Tuns pub last week," Chris continued. "You told me you knew Mr Dowling had a sister, but did not know her, even if you saw her."

"So," Mr Webber replied.

"It seems strange to me that shortly after that, you remarked to their deaths as first Margery, then Rowland, why I wonder with you not knowing Mrs Wilson would you call her Margery?"

"What is strange about that, I could have heard her name even though I did not know her," Mr Webber replied.

"What was also strange Mr Webb, you put their deaths in the right order," Chris replied. "One would have thought you would have said Rowland first, after all he was the one we were talking about."

"It just came out," Mr Webber stopped and looked at Chris with a open mouth. "You called me Mr Webb," he said annoyed.

"That is your birth name is it not?" Chris asked.

"You have been checking up on me," Mr Webber stormed. "What right do you have?"

"Every right Mr Webber," Chris replied. "But let's carry on, you might remember that I also told you that I had nearly hit your bicycle that stood by the wall outside the Three Tuns pub."

"So," Mr Webber murmured.

"I noticed that you had a new front wheel on it."

"I buckled the one I had, so I fitted a new one," Mr Webber explained. "No law against that is there?"

"Not at all," Chris replied. "You did cycle down this morning?"

"I did," replied Mr Webber.

"I have a bike expert examining your bike now Mr Webber," Chris said making Mr Webber jump up.

"You have no right," Mr Webber exploded. "What gives you the right?"

"Every right Mr Webber," Chris replied. "This is a murder case."

"So you think I took the wheel off of Mr Dummer's new bike do you?" Mr Webber stormed.

Chris inwardly smiled, that is the slip up waiting for. "Just two more questions Mr Webber," Chris continued. "How did you know that Mr Dummer bike's front wheel missing when we found?"

"I don't know," he replied nervously. "You or someone else must have told me."

"How did you know Mr Dummer had a new bike?" Chris continued.

"Perhaps I had seen him on it," Mr Webber replied now very nervous.

"That Sunday morning when he was murdered was the first time he had rode with it," Chris told him. "Still we can wait for the expert report."

"I don't know why you bother with all these things, according to your conversation with this man here," Mr Webber said pointing at Mr Chalker. "It's obvious he is the murderer."

"Inspector," Mr Chalker was on his feet.

"Yes Mr Chalker?" Chris replied.

"Perhaps I have done despicable things in my life, but being accused of murderer is the limit. I knew Mr Webb, well most of my life, we both came from the East End of London, however I never saw him after I left London until about six months ago, he was working in the hospital grounds," Mr Chalker paused and swallowed.

"You are right I was blackmailing Mrs Wilson, I fancied her, always wanted her, so when I heard this conversation outside the window, I took a chance, you may be right she did not dare to have these suspicions against her. The money she was being donated, I saw her post office book once when I was in her house, I also saw correspondence to estate agents. I suppose I got greedy, and told her I wanted a thousand pound, I remember we were in the hospital grounds, I never expected her reaction, she was very mad and angry, she told me I could do whatever I like about my suspicions, but she intended to leave, but before doing so she would inform the authority about me," Mr Chalker looked around him all listening intensely.

"She also told me that she would give Mr Dummer all the details of how I accused her of swapping his child. To be honest, I knew I had gone too far, and was afraid, blackmail is a serious offence, also with rape as you said, would certainly men prison, I was completely scared decided to get away for a bit, and left without telling anyone, hopping that Margery would change her mind. On the Wednesday night I went to railway station to catch a train, found I had an hour to wait, I popped into the Railway Inn for a drink, I saw Roger there."

"Shut up you damn fool," Mr Webber snarled at Mr Chalker. "You're putting a noose around our necks," he shouted angrily.

"You were quick saying that I must have been the killer," Mr Chalker snarled back. "So I'm telling the truth, I couldn't murder anyone, let alone Margery, whatever I have done, my feeling for her grew, I think I loved her."

"Mr Webber I must ask you to keep quiet, you won't do your case any good," Chris said watching him seat. "Now please Mr Chalker continue."

"As I said I did see Roger, over a pint I told him of my worries, he asked me how much it was worth if he managed to get hold of that letter you have, I told him I could raise two hundred, he told me not to worry, and I caught the train. That is all I know, the murders were quite a shock to me"

Chris looked at Mr Webber. "Well Mr Webber what have you to say?" Chris asked.

"It's all lies," he muttered.

"I don't think so Mr Webber, it all fits with what we already know, however I have never thought that you killed Mrs Wilson deliberately, Mr Dummer I'm not sure about."

The phone ringing halted what Chris was saying, he lifted the receiver after a few moment he smiled.

"Thank you Sergeant," Chris said. "Please thank Mr Ford, he could be called as an expert in cycles when the time comes," Chris replaced the receiver. "Now Mr Webber where was we?"

"That was your expert?" Mr Webber asked worriedly.

Chris nodded his head.

Mr Webber glared at Mr Chalker, realising taking the bicycle wheel had been a bad mistake. "You are right, I never meant to kill Mrs Wilson, I put my tie around her neck and tightened it wanting her to black out, I needed to search her, which I did right down to her underclothes, I thought she was alive when I left her."

"Did you mean to rape her?" Chris asked. "Her underclothing was around her knees."

"Of course not, there was no desire for that, but women keep things in unusual places," Mr Webber replied.

"So when you did not find it on Mrs Wilson, you thought about Mr Dummer, after you had left Mrs Wilson lying there, you went to the Three Tuns pub, and spoke to him, and found out where he would be that Sunday morning," Chris said to him.

Mr Webber paused for a moment then continued.

"I knew about the bridle path, so I rode my bike along Basingstoke road until I came to the lane, hide the bike as best I could, it was very dark, I wanted to get there before Mr Dummer. I walked up the bridle path and hid, I had no idea where he might come into the wood. Anyway, I hid until I heard him, as he passed I grabbed him around the neck, I was hoping that he would not see my face but he was stronger than I thought, he twisted himself around, and got me in a bear hug, his arms tightened squeezing my breath out of me, I could still use my hands, however I managed to get my knife out, and stabbed him in the back, he let go of the hug, but did not fall."

"I'll never forget the look he gave me, he turned and looked towards the edge of the field, I ran, coming out of the woods I saw his bike, it was brand new, so I used it to get back to where my motorbike was. I did need a front wheel for my bike, and like a fool I took his front wheel off, it only took a moment."

"Because Mr Dummer kept walking after you stabbed him, you were unable to search him," Chris questioned.

"That's right, I had calmed myself riding back to Winchester, then I decided to search Mrs Wilson's house, I knew where she lived," Mr Webber replied.

Chris looked at him, he knew that what he was saying was near the truth, and for a moment wondered how to continue.

"The man with his cap pull over his ears, wearing glasses and wearing an overcoat with the collar pulled up you described to me talking to Mr Dummer before his death, did not exist did he Mr Webber?" Chris asked.

"Afraid not," Mr Webber replied with a faint smile. "It's a disguise I use myself when I do not want to be recognised."

"So you searched Mrs Wilson's house, did you find what you were after?" Chris asked.

"You know I didn't, you have it on your desk," Mr Webber replied.

"How did you get in?" Chris asked.

Mr Webber was silent for a moment. "I found the key on Mrs Wilson."

"Mr Chalker," Chris said, for a moment ignoring Mr Webber. "When you saw Mr Webber before you caught your train, did you see anyone else in the bar?"

"I saw Mr Dowling, and a few other men I knew," Mr Chalker replied. "I often use the Railway Inn, it being near to my lodgings."

"Don't bring me into this," Mr Dowling almost shouted.

"Did Mr Dowling sit with you while you were telling Mr Webber of your woes?" Chris asked.

"How could I say anything in front of him, remember he was Margery's brother," Mr Chalker explained.

Mr Dowling stood up. "Well now that it is all sorted, perhaps I can go," he said.

"Please Mr Dowling what is your haste, please sit down," Chris said his tone demanding. "I have not finished yet," Chris held up a knife. "This is the knife that killed Mr Dummer, it is very sharp and pointed."

"The knife, I first saw it on your dining table, you told me and my Sergeant that you whittled a lot with bit of wood," Chris said. "When I saw it on your dining table, I thought I had seen it before, and took me some time to remember, it was similar to in Mr Dummer's back," Chris spoke with a confident voice.

"All knives look the same to me," Mr Dowling remarked. "Must be many of those about, can you prove that is my knife?" Mr Dowling argued. "Remember you saw my knife after Mr Dummer had been killed."

"You are right of course," Chris admitted.

"There you are then," Mr Dowling replied for a moment pleased with himself.

"These knives," Chris enlightened him still holding the knife in front of him. "Are made mainly for wood sculptress, made in pairs, owing to the different type of edge needed for this work, they are made and only sold in pairs, can you show me your two knives then Mr Dowling?" Chris asked.

Mr Dowling hesitated. "I lost one, I always carry one with me, when I am sitting in the park or somewhere, I often pick up a piece of wood and start shaping it, I must have left it somewhere."

Chris then showed the cigarette stubs found near the tree. "Someone had waited for Mr Dummer behind a tree," Chris continued. "While he waited, that someone smoked two cigarettes, these are the stubs, they were fresh, had they been there longer they would have been damp or soggy owing to the weather."

"Mr Webber have already told you he killed Mr Dummer, why are you doing this?" Mr Dowling snapped.

"Because Mr Dowling, this is your knife, and the cigarette stubs are tenners," Chris answered.

"Mr Webber smokes," Mr Dowling argued.

"Mr Webber smokes only Players cigarettes, you are a heavy smoker and smokes tenners."

"You can't say I killed Mr Dummer because you found tenners stubs, many people smoke tenners, it's a popular brand, anyway, Mr Webber have already admitted the killing," Mr Dowling still argued.

"You will have to produce your knife, if I am wrong Mr Dowling," "Chris paused for a moment before continuing. "Mr Webber has always been associated with criminals in the East End of London, they have a code, never grass their mates to the police, I can only think that Mr Webber is still following that code, when Mr Chalker had left, Mr Webber called you over, and asked you to help him. You had no love for your sister, nor any special relationship with Mr Dummer, and you agreed."

"So you are accusing me of having killed my sister as well," Mr Dowling shouted.

"When I first interviewed you Mr Dowling, you told me that your sister had been strangled, only the police knew that," Chris explained.

"Everyone was speculating as to how she died," Mr Dowling argued. "When I said she had been strangled, it was just a speculation."

"I disagree Mr Dowling, with Mr Dummer's murder, there was plenty of speculation from suicide to shooting, but your sister had only been found the morning I called upon you, no one knew of her death, then there was the matter of your sister's house key, it was not found on Mrs Wilson's body, we later found all her keys in her handbag, the only way Mr Webber could get hold of a key was with your help, you either had one, or knew where she had hidden one."

Chris looked at Mr Webber who was shaking his head, had let the argument carry on without interruption.

"Mr Webber and Mr Dowling you will be charged with the murders of Mrs Wilson and Mr Dummer," Chris looked at George, who was standing about to read them their rights before taken away by two uniform constables who had been waiting outside.

Chris then looked at Mr Chalker. "In my opinion Mr Chalker you should be locked away for a very long time, you are responsible for the death's of Mrs Wilson and Mr Dummer as well as the men already charged, their crime however have got you off the hook, I have no proof that you were blackmailing Mrs Wilson, but you know as well as me that you are guilty. However I am allowing you to be bailed for the moment, you did cause the deaths of these people by offering money to the guilty to retrieve a letter you wanted, but I want the best charge I can get against you, which will take discussion, Sergeant House will bail you at the desk before you leave."

George took Mr Chalker by the arm, and without any resistance march him out of the office.

Chapter Twenty-Four

With the office cleared, the typist having been asked to have a copy ready as soon as possible, Chris sat behind his desk, took out his pipe filled it and lit it blowing out clouds of smoke. He allowed his mind to relax and took some deep breaths, pleased with himself that he had solved the case.

George looked at him, he smiled. "If I can quote the Chief Inspector Fox," he remarked. "You are too darn Scots Hardie."

Chris feeling more relaxed, took his pipe from his mouth. "I know I went around the bush a little, but in the end I got there," he replied.

"You did well Chris," George spoke seriously. "I only hope I can do it as well, you went out of your way to cover the baby swapping though."

"I had my reasons George," Chris replied. "Although you and I know, there is no proof, even Mr Chalker can not swear that it took place, let alone the babies they were swapped, that part will never be brought up in court, that is why I had to bail Mr Chalker rather than charge him, he is nothing but a rogue."

"But that letter will be used as the motive for the defence," George argued. "How are you going to stop Mr Chalker when he is in the witness box?"

"All that letter tells us is that she was leaving, not being able to stand being blackmailed, no names," Chris replied.

"He might just say when cross examined that he was the blackmailer, and then bring up about the swapping," George still argued.

"But he did not see who was talking under the window of the maternity waiting room " Chris replied. "He was only guessing about babies swapped, he never mentioned Mr Shawcroft once, the Judge will not accept such evidence."

George pondered for a while. "Don't you think Mr Shawcroft broke the law then?"

"Of course he did," Chris replied. "Had Mrs Wilson been alive, it might have been different, but now we have no proof against him, anyway George would you like to be the one to tell Mrs Dummer that the son she has idolise for the last five years is not hers?"

George shook his head. "No I wouldn't, but I know you, you had a reason for letting him get away with it."

"I did phone the solicitor at Alresford," Chris started to explain. "I asked him if Mr Shawcroft had made a Will, I told him I was investigating a murder and any information he gave me would be strictly confidential," Chris puffed his pipe before continuing.

"I must be good at persuasion, he told me the gist of the Will, a boy name Thomas Dummer living at Union Street Winchester, will get the entire estates on Mr Shawcroft's death. If Mr Shawcoft is alive when the Thomas reached the age of twenty one, he will get a sum of ten thousand pounds, presented as an assurance policy and some arrangements had been made so that Mrs Dummer will receive one pound a week, now how can anyone go against that?" Chris asked.

"Do you think Mr Shawcroft regretted what he did?" George asked.

Chris shook his head. "I think he did what he thought was best for the boy, I'm sure he knew that Mrs Dummer would get the boy and was contented, he did know the family, I don't think he thought he could bring up the lad, he lost his wife at his birth, some men bear a grudge against such a child."

George nodded in agreement. "You were taking a chance regarding the letter."

"It was all I had to play with," Chris replied taking the pipe from his mouth. "I knew Mr Chalker did not know what it contained, so I played on it."

"And the knife?" George asked. "Are there sold in pairs?"

Chris smiled. "There I lied George, Mr Dowling had me in a corner, I just made it up on the spur of the moment."

"Naughty," George replied with a smile on his face. "It is strange how a lie can bring out the truth, Mr Webber surprised me, he was willing to take the blame," George remarked.

"It's the way of things in the criminal world George, no one will grass their mates to the police, in any case, when Mr Webber was telling his side, it became obvious to me that a man facing you in a bear hug, arms pinned to his side, could never have got out a knife from his pocket, even had he been able to, he could never have plunged the knife in so far up his opponent's back."

"Anyway, Mr Ford was a help to you?" George asked with a smile.

Chris put his pipe in the ashtray. "As a matter of fact, Mr Ford had no idea what wheel was fitted to Mr Dummer's bike when it was bought."

"Only because you gave the wrong impression when answering the phone," George said grinning.

Chris shrugged, picked up his pipe and sucked it.

Chapter Twenty-Five

It was April the19th, Chris scrambled out of bed at the sound of knocking on his bedroom door. "Come along son," he heard his landlady Mrs Dobson saying. "It's your wedding day, I'm getting your breakfast."

"Thank you Mrs Dobson," Chris replied sitting on the bed feeling groggy.

The night before he had gone on a stag party, apart from George his best man, he had taken a few of the constables who could not attend his wedding because of duty, he knew that with Sergeant Bloom, Constable Streeter would be able to cover the office. Chris had decided to go easy on the drinks, but found that his party had other ideas. As far as he remembered he had really enjoyed the night, but his mind did not yet focus on how he got home.

Chris shook his head, and rubbed his eyes, before standing, and almost fell back, he felt a little dizzy, after a few moments of deep breathing, Chris dressed himself the best he could, the room would not stop spinning. He managed to go downstairs to the scullery, where he found Mrs Dobson.

"You enjoyed yourself last night son?" she asked with a grin.

"It seems that way Mrs Dobson," Chris replied in a daze.

"Well you will soon be alright, wash your face in cold water, then come and have your breakfast, you'll soon be alright," she said motherly.

"Thank you Mrs Dobson," Chris replied. "I better have a shave first though."

"No leave that until you have had your breakfast, you will find your head will clear, I have put a couple of aspirins on the table, Tom will bring in the bathtub, I have plenty of hot water on the stove, we must have you bright and smart for your wedding," Mrs Dobson went on with an amused smile.

Chris did what he was told, he put his head under the tap, and for a while allowed the water to run over his head, he felt a little steadier as he wiped his hair in the towel. Chris went into the kitchen where a full English breakfast was waiting for him, he looked at it and for a moment felt a little sick.

"I know how you feel son," Mr Dobson said watching him. "The breakfast will do you good, take the aspirins after you have eaten," she smiled. "It's going to be a beautiful day son, God is making this marriage in heaven," she added as she left the room.

Chris smiled at her departure, and picked up his knife and fork, wondering if he could eat, but after a couple steady bites, he began to get the taste, and to his surprise cleared the plate.

Mrs Dobson returned and seeing the plate clean smiled. "That's better son," she remarked. "Do you feel better now?"

"I do actually," Chris replied. "I had too much last night, was I a nuisance?" Chris asked.

"No, of course not son," Mrs Dobson replied as she cleared the table. "Now take those aspirins then rest for a while, in an hour you can have your shave and bath, when your food has gone down."

"How long have I got?" Chris asked not knowing the time.

"It's eight thirty now son, your wedding is at eleven, you need time to get to the church, it's a long way to walk to St John Street," Mrs Dobson replied.

"What would I do without you Mrs Dobson, I shall miss you and Tom very much, you are the only family I have known," Chris said sincerely.

"Don't be silly son," Mrs Dobson replied putting on a brave face, knowing that she would miss him also. "You will have a beautiful wife to look after you, and a lovely house to move into, anyway," she sniffed. "We will visit each other."

Chris stood up, he put his arm around Mrs Dobson and hugged her close. "All my thanks anyway," Chris said trying to hide his emotions.

"Mrs Dobson pulled away, now take those aspirins, rest a while until Tom has got your bath ready, then we will leave you alone," Mrs Dobson said going to the scullery her eyes watering.

Chris shaved carefully, not wanting to cut himself, and took a bath, then went to his room to dress. George called, it was now ten, and it was his job to make sure that the groom got to the church on time. Chris already dressed in his grey, black striped trousers. "How do you feel George?" he asked.

"Getting over it," George replied.

"Got your speech, and of course the ring?" Chris asked.

"Don't worry Chris," George replied as he watched Chris put on a greyish waistcoat covered with designs over his white shirt and starched collar.

"What you think of this thing?" Chris asked referring to the waistcoat. "Bit of a show."

George grinned. "It's only once Chris, actually it looks alright."

Chris did not answer as he took his single breasted jacket from the wooden coat hanger and put it on, it was blue with tails. "Feel like a dog's dinner," he remarked moving his shoulders and allowing the jacket to stay open.

"I brought a carnation," George remarked, pinning the carnation to the lapel of Chris's jacket. "There," he said standing back a little. "Your bride will be proud of you Chris."

Chris smiled. "I suppose I'll have to wear this thing," Chris said picking up a grey top hat. "I will look daft in it."

"Carry it then Chris," George advised.

"Good thinking George," Chris replied with a grin. "Well Mr and Mrs Dobson will be waiting, we better make a move, it's a long walk."

Mr and Mrs Dobson followed by Chris and George who were walking behind, entered the iron railing gate surrounding the churchyard with fifteen minutes to spare.

A few people were standing outside their terraced houses in St John Street, mainly women on both sides of the street, they smiled at him as he passed and Chris heard several best wishes and good luck offered. A small gathering had already begun in the churchyard, and by the time he had spoken to them and shook hands, it was just five to eleven when he stood with George in front of the Altar waiting nervously.

He looked at the brides side of the isle that was beginning to fill up, men in their Sunday best, and women in dresses of all colours and designs, carrying their wide brim hats, again in all colours shapes and design.

"Women certainly like dressing up George," Chris whispered.

"If you didn't, you wouldn't be a woman," George replied with a grin.

Chris looked at his side mainly men he thought. Mrs Noal sat in the front row, he was sorry that the Inspector Noal was unable to get leave, Mr and Mrs Dobson sat beside her, they were chatting, Chris felt pleased, he smiled inwardly when he noticed Chief Inspector Fox and his wife, who was sitting by Sergeant Dawkins and his wife on one side, and the Police Inspector Mullard of the station on the other side. He smiled seeing Inspector Willett and his wife, and he caught sight of Inspector McNally and his wife who had help him so much in Scotland, he looked around, there were a few constables present, one from Easton, and one from Abbots Worthy, looking around, he realised that most of his invitation went to the police force, he felt satisfied.

Elizabeth had got up early, she was in such a state of excitement she couldn't sleep all night.

"You should have slept," her mother scolded her. "You want to look your best don't you?"

"Of course I do mother," Elizabeth almost snapped back feeling irritable. "I was far too excited to sleep."

"Well you know best," Olive replied putting toast in front of Elizabeth. "Are you sure that's all you want, you have a long day ahead of you."

"Your mother is only thinking of you love," Ron said to his daughter. "She don't want those beautiful eyes of yours looking red."

"I know dad," Elizabeth answered.

"You can still change your mind you know," Ron said teasing.

"Dad," Elizabeth scolded.

"OK, OK," Ron said a smile on his face. "This will be your day, you could say this is the first day of your new life."

"The good thing about beginning a new life is that, I'll have the people I love from the old still in it," Elizabeth said smiling at her father.

"And we will be glad to still be in it," Ron replied as Olive appeared.

"You have an hour before your hairdresser gets here Elizabeth, it's your bath time."

"Thank you mum," Elizabeth replied calmly. "Sorry I snapped earlier."

Olive turned to Ron. "Don't just sit there, get the tub in from the back, the water is in the kitchen, then clear off somewhere, my daughter needs privacy."

Ron smiled as he got up, he smiled at his wife. "Calm down love, you are looking full of nerves."

"Can you blame us women, we give ourselves to a man in marriage, trusting their every word that they will look after us and give us a happy life, what do we get, I tell you, we give ourselves into voluntary slavery," Olive replied.

"I agree," Ron replied with a wink at Elizabeth.

"Dad loves you mum," Elizabeth said drinking the last of her tea. "He adores you, and you adore him mum."

"Never let a man know that," Olive smiled.

"But dad do know it mum, when he is teasing he knows what to say to bring a smile to your cheeks, even though you smile without him seeing," Elizabeth said getting up.

"It's no good letting a man know everything," Olive replied taking up the breakfast things. "But if you are as happy in your marriage as I have been, I shall die a happy woman."

"Mum" Elizabeth said.

"Enough talk," Olive said cutting her off, wanting no emotion, she was hurting enough knowing that she would soon be loosing her daughter and she did not want to cry. "You go up get into your robe, then come and have your bath, your bridesmaids will be here within an hour."

Elizabeth had a nice long soak, then she began to worry because the time was going too fast. The hairdresser arrived, at the same time as the bridesmaids, and by the time the hairdresser had finished with her and the bridesmaids it was nine thirty.

"We will be late mum," Elizabeth said a worried look on her face. "We have to dress yet, and I haven't put on any make up."

"Don't worry so much," Olive replied. "You do your make up while the bridesmaids and I dress, then we will all help you, it won't take long."

"What time will the carriage be here mum?" Elizabeth asked.

"Another hour yet," Olive replied. "Now do your make up, and not too thick, your face is beautiful without it," she said leaving the room followed by the bridesmaids.

Elizabeth sat at her dressing table looking in the mirror.

"Chris, I hope you will be proud of me," she spoke to her reflection. She picked up her lipstick, it was bright scarlet, she rubbed a little on her lips, after which she pressed both her lips together, looking at them in the mirror, she felt satisfied. She pinched her cheeks, they looked pale, picking up her rouge, she faintly touched her cheeks, her mother had been right, not being able to sleep had left her eyes red, wiping the her eyelids with a cloth, she found that the redness was a bit lighter.

"It will have to do," she said to herself, my veil will cover them, by the time Chris sees them they might be back to normal. She leaned back in her chair, she touched the back of her newly styled hair, she had opted for a short neat bob cut, which showed the back of her hairline, with curls at both sides.

He mother came in followed by the bridesmaids, Olive's dress was a orange colour dress with wide shoulders flapovers, it was a loose dress, but suited her.

"We must get you dress now Elizabeth," she said. "Time is marching on."

"I better put on my shoes first mother," Elizabeth said, as she leaned forward and took the one strap buttoned white shoes with strong wide inch and a half heels, that lay by the side of the dressing table. Elizabeth was already dressed in her corset, and white stocking, covered by a long white satin slip.

"You need something blue," Joyce one of her bridesmaids said handing her a small box, that contained an inch wide blue garter.

"Thank you Joyce," Elizabeth said. "I have been in such a state, I have forgotten all about that custom."

Elizabeth stretched her shapely leg, and pulled the garter on above the knee.

"Thank you Joyce," Elizabeth repeated herself, as for a moment she admired the garter on her leg.

"I have bought you something new, it's brand new," spoke up Mavis the other bridesmaid.

"Elizabeth thanked her with a smile as she accepted the small lace hanky." "I'll keep it in my bloomers," Elizabeth giggled. "Thank you both very much."

"Well let's get that dress on you, time is getting on," Olive said as she went to the wardrobe and brought forth the wedding dress.

"That looks lovely," Joyce remarked.

"It certainly do" Mavis agreed. "You will look lovely in it."

"Hold your hair, while I slip the dress over your head Elizabeth," Olive said slipping the dress over her head. "It should fit perfectly," she added.

Both bridesmaids helped by easing the dress down her body, once Elizabeth's head was through the lace neck opening, Elizabeth looked straight into the mirror and a smile lit up her face. "It's beautiful mother," she laughed with joy. "Just wonderful."

The dress had been made in white satin and lace, long full sleeves with deep lace cuffs, a full skirt with borders of deep white lace just at ground level.

Olive stood back and looked at her. "You look beautiful darling," she said sincerely. "Chris is a very lucky man" she added.

"I hope he will think so," Elizabeth giggled.

"You already have something blue, something new, darling," Olive said standing in front of Elizabeth. "This necklace was given to me by your father's parents on my wedding day, I want you now to have it, it's something old."

Elizabeth fingered the necklace as her mother fixed it around her neck. "Thank you mother," she said feeling that a tear might come. "I love you."

"Don't start being sentimental now," Olive said choking back her tears. "It will spoil your make up, now for the veil and train," she added.

The wedding dress train, which was of Nottingham lace, was four yards long, it had been kept in a large box, folded, tissue paper had been placed between each fold, so it would not crease and the mark of the fold would not show.

"It's lovely," both bridesmaids remarked almost at the same time.

"I think it is lovely, but remember girls," Olive said looking at the bridesmaids. "There will be at least six feet trailing behind, so you must take extra care not to tread on it," Olive remarked.

Taking one end from the box, Olive covered Elizabeth's head with it. "The veil, down to your lips, do you think alright or prefer lower love?" she asked Elizabeth.

"Perhaps half way down the chin," Elizabeth replied.

Olive pulled a little then started to pin the lace to Elizabeth's hair, when she was satisfied she asked one of the bridesmaids to fetch her the head wreath that laid on the bed, Olive fitted it then stood back.

"How is that Elizabeth?" her mother asked.

Elizabeth giggled with excitement, she felt she would need to pee soon, she lifted the veil. "Chris will be able to kiss me?" Elizabeth giggled.

"Right, you will have to carry it gently, or you will pull it off," Olive said to the bridesmaids, as a knock came on the door.

"The carriage is here," Ron shouted with excitement from outside the door.

"You better come in and see our daughter first," Olive shouted.

Ron opened the door, his eyes fell on Elizabeth, he felt tears welling up in them.

"You look absolutely stunning," Ron choked with pride. "Now girls do you want to use the little room before we go, if so now is the time."

With a small laugh, the two bridesmaids decided to go, and left the room.

Elizabeth went up to her dad, she put an arm around his neck, and beckoned her mother over with the other. "Thank you both so very much," she said trying not to cry.

"No need," her father replied. "You are our daughter, we lived for you, your happiness will be ours."

"Go and have a pee," Olive said as she pulled away from the hug and giving a sniff. "We will all be crying if you don't."

The white four wheeled open top carriage drawn by two white horses, was pulled up at the bottom of the path, Ron turned to his wife. "You go first with the bridesmaids, sit with your back to the driver."

"I know," Olive said trying to keep her temper at Ron telling her what to do. "You mind you don't make my daughter slip."

Ron looked at his daughter and smiled. "Your mother wants to cry, she is so happy," he said.

"I know," Elizabeth smiled back as they started down the path, only for Elizabeth to stop.

"What's wrong love," Ron asked thinking the worse. "It's just nerves, they will pass."

"Not that dad, I forgotten my bouquet, it's on the front room table."

"I'll get it," Ron offered, glad that it was nothing more serious.

"I favoured this bouquet dad," Elizabeth said as her dad returned, she took the bunch of long stemmed flowers made up of orchids and lilies with trailing ribbons.

With the wedding dress train carefully resting over his arm, Ron steadied Elizabeth down the path to the carriage, the sound of clapping made her look, many of her neighbours that had been waiting for her appearance smiling and clapping. She waved back, before she carefully stepped into the carriage.

"What kept you?" Olive asked as she took the bouquet from Elizabeth.

"Nothing," Ron replied seeing Elizabeth seated. "Help me with the train," he asked.

Ron looked at the driver, who was looking at Ron for instructions. "Better go driver, it's now almost eleven."

Olive felt put out as the horses moved, she thought she should have sat facing the driver, the people paying their respects could only see her as she passed, she then looked at Elizabeth and forgot all about it, she patted Elizabeth's knee and smiled.

"We are going to be late," Elizabeth said as the clock is striking the hour.

"No you are not," Olive scolded her lightly. "You must not seem too anxious, it is customary for the bride to be a few minutes late."

The driver took the steeper route, by taking the cut through to Blue Ball Hill, the driver obviously knew his horses, and perhaps with half his brake on, the journey to the church took just four minutes.

Ron got out of the carriage, he helped his wife and the two bridesmaids out first, then with care helped his daughter. Elizabeth took hold of her father's arm, waiting a while, while the bridesmaids got behind her, both holding her train from the ground, they started walking.

"I'll go ahead," Olive said. "I must get our seats, now girls she said as she parted, mind the train, she looked at Elizabeth her eyes moist. "Love you," she mouthed.

The churchyard was empty of people who were all inside, only the usher who was waiting for them on the step.

As they reached the bottom step, the usher left and went inside, and then the piano started to play the wedding march, Ron felt as proud as he could be walking down the aisle with his beautiful daughter on his arm. Chris however catching sight of her, thought the blood would burst through his veins, he had never seen such a beautiful sight, he could not make out her face, her veil covered her head, and on her head she wore wreath of orange blossoms. Elizabeth could however see Chris, he looked so handsome, she saw his face as he stood to the right of the Reverend Wicks, he was just starring at her his face full of wonder.

Both Chris and Elizabeth had been a little nervous during the service, but they had found each others hand to steady themselves. With the service over and the register signed, they turned from the Altar to walk back down the isle as a married couple. With her long train sweeping the floor, Elizabeth full of happiness grasped her husband's arm as they unhurriedly walked towards the church door both smiling at their guests as they passed.

Elizabeth hoped that she could be a good wife to Chris, she worried a little, she knew nothing about sex, apart from what she did know was what other women had told her.

"Chris," Elizabeth whispered when they were about half way to the exit. "When mother wanted the19th of April, I checked my dates, I found that today gives me plenty of leeway darling."

Chris heard her slight giggle under her veil.

"My day has been marvellous, but tonight darling, there will be no barricade to prevent both our happiness."

THE END

Lightning Source UK Ltd.
Milton Keynes UK
UKOW03f2342240316

270846UK00001B/6/P